A FAMILY'S HEARTBREAK

When Jenny's mother abandons her and her younger siblings, Jenny is left at the mercy of her abusive father, Henry. And when Henry beats her so badly that she ends up in the hospital, it seems like there's nowhere left for them all to go. But carpenter Craig has fallen head over heels for Jenny, and he offers her a place to stay. Happy at last, Jenny begins a new life with him, but when tragedy strikes, she's left to pick up the pieces of both her broken home — and her broken heart. Desperately trying to make ends meet, Jenny is alone and working round the clock. Will she ever be able to give her siblings the happy home they deserve? Or is the worst yet to come . . . ?

KITTY NEALE

A FAMILY'S HEARTBREAK

Complete and Unabridged

MAGNA
Leicester

First published in Great Britain in 2019 by
Avon
a division of HarperCollins*Publishers*
London

First Ulverscroft Edition
published 2020
by arrangement with
HarperCollins*Publishers*
London

*A catalogue record for this book is available
from the British Library.*

ISBN 978–0–7505–4807–6

Published by
Ulverscroft Limited
Anstey, Leicestershire

Set by Words & Graphics Ltd.
Anstey, Leicestershire
Printed and bound in Great Britain by
T. J. International Ltd., Padstow, Cornwall

This book is printed on acid-free paper

For my dear friend, Elly Sayers.

This is dedicated to you and your lovely mum, Lynda Shaw, who is an avid reader of my books.

Elly — We've made such wonderful memories together and I'm looking forward to sharing many more special moments with you. You're an incredible woman, Smelly, and I love you loads!

1

London, Balham, 1961

Jenny Lombard chewed nervously on her
thumbnail as she listened to her parents arguing
again. They were in the living room with the
door ajar, while in the hall and out of sight,
Jenny hovered close by. Her mother Lizzie had
walked out on them, but still had a habit of
dropping in now and then. When she did, all hell
would inevitably break loose.

'What 'ave I told you about coming round
here if and when the mood takes you?' her father
yelled.

'They're my kids, Henry, and I've got every
right to see 'em!' her mother answered defiantly.

Jenny was a grown woman of twenty-two but
as she looked through the crack of the door she
felt like a child again. She could see her mother
sitting on the sofa cradling Peter, aged six, the
youngest of Jenny's four siblings. He had untidy
fair hair, and his blue eyes, wide with fear, made
his complexion look paler than normal. Jenny
wanted to run into the room to comfort him but,
scared of her father, she remained rooted to the
spot.

'You've no rights! You lost them when you took
off with your fancy man, and what's happened to
him, eh? I hear he's dropped you like a ton of
bricks 'cos he knows what an old tart you are.'

1

'I ain't listening to this, and neither should Peter,' she spat, and, kissing her son quickly on his forehead, put him to one side before abruptly rising to her feet.

With no time to react, it was too late to run out of sight, and as the door flew open Jenny found herself face to face with her mother.

'Earwigging again, Jenny? Well, I hope you heard every word that pig of a father of yours said to me. I'm sick to the back teeth of it, slagging me off when all I want to do is see you kids.'

Jenny's mouth opened and closed like a fish out of water, but no words came. She wanted to throw herself at her mother's feet and beg her not to leave again. She knew the moment the front door closed behind her mum, she, or one of her siblings, would bear the brunt of their father's anger.

'Get out of my way, girl,' her mother said, tutting as she brushed Jenny aside to head for the front door. 'I'm wasting my breath here.'

Jenny heard her father's heavy footsteps on the linoleum floor. He was coming her way! She pressed her bony back against the hallway wall and breathed in, trying to make herself as thin as possible. If she could have, she would have merged into it. She'd once stood in the way when her father was chasing her mother, only to be aggressively shoved to one side. She wouldn't make that mistake again. Wishing she was invisible, Jenny trembled, but thankfully her father dashed past her.

Just as her mother opened the street door, he

grabbed her by her long blonde hair and yanked her backwards. 'Lizzie, get back in here, you bitch, and see to your child,' her father ordered harshly.

It was only then that Jenny heard Peter wailing, and she rushed from the hallway to comfort her brother, leaving her parents fighting by the front door. Peter's face was screwed up as tears streamed down his cheeks. 'It's all right, love, I've got you,' Jenny said soothingly as she scooped him into her arms.

She could hear her parents still screeching obscenities at each other and had no doubt all the curtains in the street would be twitching, whilst some neighbours would be on their doorsteps. They were used to hearing them fighting — after all, it wasn't an unusual occurrence — but they were a nosy lot on her street.

'I want my mummy,' Peter cried.

Jenny sat on the sofa and pulled the boy closer to her, burying his head in her chest. 'I know you do, sweetheart,' she said, but couldn't find any words of condolence to offer. She wouldn't lie to him and tell him Mummy would be back soon, as the chances were she wouldn't. She couldn't tell him everything was going to be all right. It never was, not after their mother had visited. All she could do was protect the child from their father's fury, and offer herself up for a beating, a sacrifice for him to vent his frustrations on.

★　★　★

Henry slammed the front door with such force, it felt like the house shook. Lizzie had broken free from his grip and refused to come back in to see to Peter. He stormed into the lounge, furious with his estranged wife. He hated that two years ago she'd left him high and dry with five kids to look after. Worse still, the slag had showed him up in front of his mates by dumping him for another man. The humiliation of it! And yet Lizzie still had the audacity to return home on a whim and demand to see her children. Well, he wasn't going to stand for it again. As far as Henry was concerned, if she wasn't at home to look after her kids, then she could go take a running jump. Not that he would have taken her back. He loved Lizzie and probably always would, but she'd burned her bridges the moment she'd jumped into bed with Lesley Harrington. Of all the blokes she could have chosen, why Lesley bloody Harrington? He'd never get his head round that one. The man was a right ugly git, and a sly bugger.

Henry paced the floor, pulling at his hair as tortured thoughts of his wife raced through his mind. Images of Lizzie cavorting with Lesley teased him, keeping him awake at night and interrupting his day. He couldn't stand it — it was driving him to the brink of insanity, and whenever she came to the house, he'd feel his fury spill over.

Peter's gasping, juddering sobs shook him free of his thoughts and he snapped his head around to look at the boy. Jenny was holding him close, but he noticed Peter's eyes were red-rimmed

4

from crying, and his nose was snotty. This was Lizzie's fault, he thought, clenching his fists in anger. His wife's visits always upset the whole household.

'I want my mummy,' Peter cried again.

Henry's hackles rose further at the sound of his youngest son whingeing for his good-for-nothing mother. She didn't do anything for the boy, so why on earth would he cry for her? She'd coldly walked out on her children, yet they all hankered after her. It riled Henry that they couldn't see her for what she was, and in his temper he picked up an empty whiskey glass and launched it across the room. The glass shattered as it hit the wall above the sofa, showering Jenny and Peter with tiny fragments. Peter screamed, and Jenny flinched, inciting Henry even further. 'Get that fucking kid out of my sight,' he yelled, spittle flying as his mouth foamed like a rabid dog's.

Jenny scrambled to her feet, the boy clutching her, and scuttled towards the door. 'Where do you think you're going?' he demanded and reached out to grab his daughter's arm.

Jenny didn't fight back; she wasn't like her mother. As he felt her body go limp, he released her, and as she crumpled to the floor she pushed Peter towards the door, hissing urgently, 'Run, Peter, run.'

The boy didn't need telling twice and scampered from the room as Jenny, still on her knees, turned submissively towards him, her eyes lowered. Henry leaned forward until his face was just inches from the top of his daughter's head.

His stomach churned as he looked at her fine ginger hair, and he wondered again where she'd inherited it from. He was dark, the same as his other daughters, Gloria and Pamela. His wife had blonde hair, which was so light it looked almost white. His sons, Peter and Timmy, took after their mother, blonde and blue-eyed. But this one, Jenny, his eldest, with her bright orange hair and freckles splattering her face, she didn't look anything like a Lombard, and Henry wondered if he had a cuckoo in his nest.

★   ★   ★

Jenny kept her head down and avoided eye contact with her father. Experience had taught her that if she looked at him, he'd take it as defiance and beat her twice as badly. She held her breath in a futile bid to stop her body from shaking. He seemed to find her fear repulsive and would use it as another excuse to hit her harder. She felt she couldn't win.

'Look at me,' her father sneered.

Jenny slowly lifted her head to find herself staring into her father's dark eyes. Her heart sank. They were cold, hard, and his mouth was twisted in anger. When he was in this mood she knew that no amount of crying or pleading would touch him. It was as if he was a man possessed, and she silently cursed her mother for turning him demonic again.

'I suppose you want your mother too?'

Her father's voice was filled with hatred, and she tried not to recoil as his saliva splattered her face, smelling of stale alcohol. 'No,' Jenny answered in a whisper, almost paralysed with terror at what was coming.

'You're a liar — just like her!'

Jenny saw her father's arm pull back, and his clenched fist coming towards her. She closed her eyes as he punched her on the side of her head. Pain seared through her skull, and the force of the blow knocked her sideways. Instinctively, she curled into a foetal position and waited for her father to put the boot in. Her head throbbed, and though her eyes were shut tightly, she knew the room was spinning.

'Your mother's a whore! Nothing but a dirty scumbag whore!'

She felt the kick between her shoulder blades. It hurt, but it could have been worse. At least he didn't have his work boots on, but her relief was short-lived as the next couple of kicks jarred her body. She laid motionless and waited, praying he'd had his fill and would leave her alone. At least the kids are upstairs out of harm's way, she thought through a haze of pain. Then, to her relief, she heard her father walking away. She kept her eyes closed, aware of sounds, and realised he must have put his boots on when she heard his heels coming down hard on the hallway floor, followed by the sound of the front door slamming shut.

★ ★ ★

Gloria, who was sixteen, had been huddled on the bed that she shared with thirteen-year-old

Pamela. She hated top-and-tailing with her sister as Pamela would often wet the bed, especially after their dad had one of his rages. Gloria rolled her eyes, knowing she would wake up later tonight in the warmth of Pamela's urine.

Peter had thrown himself at Pamela when he'd come running upstairs, while Timmy, at nine the older of the two boys, ran to Gloria. When the front door slammed she peeled Timmy from her and put a finger to her lips to shush them. Then they all tiptoed to the top of the stairs.

Gloria whispered to the others to stay where they were as she began to creep downstairs. If he was still in the house, the last thing she wanted was to attract her father's attention, and she stepped over the fourth stair down, knowing it creaked. She threw a quick glance over her shoulder to see her brothers and sister waiting nervously at the top for her to give them the all-clear.

Almost halfway down, Gloria could see over the banisters and into the open living room door. She gasped, though she wasn't shocked to see Jenny looking dazed and picking herself up from the floor. Once again, her sister had taken a hiding from their dad. Thankfully, there was no sign of him now and though Gloria detested seeing her sister being hurt, she was relieved it wasn't her.

'He's gone,' Gloria called back to her siblings as she ran down the rest of the stairs and into the lounge. 'Oh, Jenny, are you OK?' she asked, concerned, as she scanned her sister for cuts and bruises.

'Yes, I think so,' Jenny answered, though she appeared wobbly on her feet.

'I hate him!' Gloria spat as she helped Jenny towards the sofa. Then she noticed the small slivers of broken glass and instead led her sister to the table and four chairs in the bay window. 'It ain't fair that he always takes it out on us.'

'I know, love, but try and be a little charitable. He's doing his best,' Jenny said and winced as she rubbed the side of her head.

'Charitable! He's just knocked you about again and you're suggesting I should be charitable! You're too blinkin' nice, you are. Ain't you angry about it?' Gloria asked, shocked at Jenny's response. She'd never understand her elder sister. Jenny was so quiet, and whenever she did say anything, it was never horrid. In fact, she couldn't remember a time when Jenny had lost her rag, or even raised her voice.

'Yes, Gloria, of course I'm angry, but I've got to control it. If I don't I'll be as bad as him. Where's Timmy and Peter? Are you all right, boys?'

Timmy spoke first. He was a confident lad, the joker of the family, and though it was probably a brave front, he never seemed to be too badly affected by his father's violent outbursts, except at night when the bad dreams would come. 'Yeah, I'm all right, Sis. Did our dad whack you again?'

Gloria answered for Jenny. 'Yes, he did, the 'orrible so and so. Pam, go and make Jenny a cup of tea. You two, your sister needs a bit of peace and quiet so get back up to your room, there's good boys.'

'Come on, Peter, I've got a new spider and I've made him a house. I'll show you,' Timmy said, before running from the room with his younger brother closely following.

Gloria pulled out a chair from the teak table and sat opposite Jenny. 'I think we should have a word with Mum, you know, tell her not to keep coming round here like she does. If she wants to see us, we can go to her.'

Jenny drew in a long breath before she spoke. 'The trouble is, you know what Mum's like. If you tell her not to do something, she'll be all the more determined to do it. And as for us going to see her, it's a nice idea, Gloria, but she's always on the move. I don't know where she is from one month to the next, or what sort of bloke she might be living with.'

'Well, the next time she shows her face, I'm going to say something to her. It ain't right that one of us, mainly you, gets it in the neck every flippin' time she comes around. I dread it. Don't get me wrong, she's our mum and I love her, but I'd rather not see her again than go through this each time.'

Pamela came into the room carrying a tray of tea. Both sisters looked at her as the china cups rattled in the saucers. Though she'd tried to hide it, they could see she'd been crying again.

'Don't upset yourself,' Jenny said softly, 'Mum ain't likely to show her face again for a few weeks and Dad will have calmed down by the time he gets home.'

'More like had a bloody skinful,' Gloria said as she shook her head.

Pamela placed the tray on the table and jumped when she heard a car door slam. 'I'll get the broom,' she said quietly, looking at the glass covering the sofa.

Gloria watched her sister scuttle off. Pamela was so thin and lived on her jangled nerves. Maybe she should be nicer to her and stop having a go about her bedwetting. It might make a difference, she thought. When Pamela returned, Gloria said, 'I was just saying to Jenny that it would be better if Mum didn't come here to see us.'

Pamela nodded, but didn't seem to be really listening. She was peering out of the window, obviously looking for their father, and by the way she was poised Gloria thought she was ready to sprint back upstairs if she saw him.

Gloria turned to Jenny. 'Do you know where Mum is now?'

'No, but she's not with what's-his-face. I heard Dad say that he'd dropped her like a ton of bricks. I'll pop in to see Gran later, see if she knows anything.'

Gloria tutted. 'Knowing Mum, she's probably got some other bloke on the go and is shacking up with him.'

Jenny's lips tightened, but she didn't answer. Gloria knew her sister didn't like it when she was derogatory about their mother, but for once she didn't chastise her.

'Can I come to see Gran with you?' Pamela asked Jenny in an unsteady voice.

'Yes, all right, love,' Jenny told her.

Gloria was barely listening as her thoughts

turned to her dad. She wished him dead and imagined sticking the bread knife in his chest whilst he slept. He'd turned Pamela into a bag of nerves, Peter was always crying, Timmy had nightmares and Jenny was covered in bruises. She couldn't blame her mother for their father's vehement mood swings. He'd always been like it for as far back as she could remember, only it was her mum that used to get slapped about, not them. Maybe if he'd been a better husband, she wouldn't have walked out on them. Gloria wished she could do the same, just walk away and leave the bloody lot of them to it.

2

Lizzie Lombard strode purposefully down Boundaries Road, thankful to put some distance between her and the three-bedroomed council house Henry lived in. It was her house too, her children lived there, and as far as she was concerned Henry had no bloody right to throw her out of it. But she was no match for his ferocious temper and knew that when Henry was in one of 'those moods', it was best to stay out of his way.

A car honked its horn as it passed her, which instantly put a smile back on Lizzie's face. She enjoyed the attention she commanded from men, and though she'd recently celebrated her forty-second birthday, she prided herself on her looks. She wasn't one of those old fuddy-duddy middle-aged women who dressed identically to their mothers. She liked the latest fashions and thought the new hemline, an inch above the knee, showed her shapely legs at their best. She'd heard women call her mutton dressed as lamb, but she put it down to their jealousy.

As she headed towards Balham High Road, her wavy blonde hair bounced up and down in time with her confident stride and sashaying slender hips. Earlier that morning, she'd put some lemon juice in her hair, and now, as the April sun shone on it, she hoped it would soon be a shade lighter. Roy liked her hair. He had complimented her on it many times. He said it was the blondest he'd ever seen and that it framed her heart-shaped face perfectly. She'd been seeing Roy Gumble for two weeks now, though she hadn't admitted to him that he was sixteen years her junior. In fact, he was only four years older than her Jenny.

Lizzie passed under the railway bridge into Chestnut Grove and stopped at the sweetshop to buy Roy's favourite, Barratt's Sherbet Fountain. It amused her that he liked the childish sweet, and that he liked to share it with her. She took pleasure in seductively teasing him. He would react to anything suggestive and watch with desire as she'd suck the sherbet from the liquorice stick. They'd met in the ABC Café where she'd been sipping a glass of Coca-Cola. She'd spotted Roy watching her from a table opposite, and as she had lifted her lips from the glass, she'd lasciviously licked them. Roy's jaw had dropped, and a few cheeky grins later he'd joined her. Soon afterwards he asked her out.

It was past noon, and the High Road was busy with shoppers milling around, though she guessed Roy would probably be just about waking up. They'd had a late night, and she smiled at the memory of their lovemaking when they'd returned home. Despite that, Lizzie had woken early, and if Roy questioned where she'd been it would be an easy lie to tell him she'd been up the market.

'It's me,' Lizzie called as she let herself into Roy's flat above the ironmonger's. All the curtains were drawn, blocking out the bright sunshine and leaving the place in darkness.

'Come and give me a cuddle,' Roy shouted from the bedroom.

Lizzie smiled wryly. She knew what he wanted. His appetite for her was insatiable, and she couldn't wait to climb between the sheets and feel his smooth, muscular body. He was like a finely tuned sports car, unlike the old jalopy she'd left a couple of years ago. Huh, she thought, Henry couldn't even raise a smile, let alone anything else.

★　★　★

Gloria had moaned about it but stayed home to look after Peter and Timmy whilst Jenny and Pamela headed off to see Edith, their elderly gran. Jenny had left specific instructions with Gloria. She'd said that if their dad came home and he wasn't drunk, she was to take the boys to Tooting Bec swings and not come home until teatime. The boys liked it there as they could wave to the trains as they passed. Gloria had agreed it was probably best to stay out of his way, though she'd said it was unlikely he'd come home sober. They all preferred it when their dad was drunk. He'd usually pass out.

When they arrived at their gran's, Jenny pushed open the shared street door and stepped into the communal hall. The house was divided in two, her gran's flat on the ground floor. Jenny had a key and let herself in and Pamela followed. The flat had one bedroom, a small lounge, a tiny kitchen and a toilet separate from the bathroom.

15

It had recently been updated with modern conveniences, but her gran said she preferred it as it had been. She'd lived there for the past twenty years, ten of them alone since her husband had died.

The smell of freshly baked bread greeted them, making Jenny's nostrils twitch. She breathed in the aroma and her mouth watered. Her gran's eyesight was failing, probably caused by cataracts, but she still managed to bake a loaf every Saturday and treat them all to jam tarts.

'Hello, love, you're early,' her gran said warmly when she saw Jenny in the lounge doorway.

'Hiya, Gran. I've got Pamela with me today. How are you?' Jenny asked as she bent to kiss her grandmother's wrinkled cheek. She visited her as often as possible, always on a Saturday, and during the week when she could. It wasn't easy, what with working full-time in Mullard's factory and her younger siblings at home.

'I'm all right, love,' the old lady answered, 'but I miss the Stewart family from upstairs. It used to be handy to bang me broomstick on the ceiling and Moira would pop down, but that new chap up there, he's as deaf as a bleedin' post. Don't get me wrong, he's a lovely young man and nice enough, but it ain't no good to me if he can't hear me when I need something.'

'What do you need, Gran?' Jenny asked. She missed the Stewarts too. It had given her peace of mind to know they were keeping an eye on her gran, but they'd moved back to Scotland.

'Nothing, but I had the fright of my life the other evening. I was sat here, minding my own

16

business, and I'm sure a mickey ran over my feet.' Edith shuddered at the memory. 'I can't stand the little blighters, ergh! Trouble is, my eyes ain't what they used to be, and I can't see 'em. Moira would have come down and checked the room for me.'

'We'll have to do something about them, Gran.'

'Yeah, I know. Pamela, take some coins out of my purse, it's in my bag on the sideboard. Be a good girl and pop to the shops for a few of them mice trap things. I hate the snapping noise they make, but I'd prefer 'em with broken necks rather than running riot in my flat.'

Pamela fished out a few coins, quietly left and Edith frowned. 'Is she all right? She ain't said two words since she's been here. Has your father been kicking off again?'

Jenny sighed. She didn't like telling her gran about the unbearable situation at home, but Edith had always been her confidante and she'd found solace in her gran's small but homely flat. 'Yes, he went berserk this morning after Mum called in to see the boys.'

'Oh, Jenny, who got it this time?'

'Me . . . again. The rest of them were hiding upstairs, and Gloria told me that Pam had her hands over her ears from the minute Mum and Dad started arguing.'

'Oh dear, you poor loves. I wish I had the strength to go round there and give him a piece of my mind! Did he hurt you?'

Before they'd left the house, Jenny had run a brush through her hair and found a sore place on

17

her head where her dad had punched her. 'No, not really,' she fibbed, 'sometimes his bark is worse than his bite. It puts us all on edge though, Pam especially. She's always been a bit more sensitive than the rest of us.'

'Yes, she has, bless her. Is she still wetting the bed?'

'Occasionally, but don't mention it in front of her 'cos she gets ever so embarrassed about it. I've tried putting plastic bags under the sheets, but Gloria moans that they make a crinkling racket when she turns over. I don't know what to do for the best, Gran. They need a new mattress, but I can't afford one and I daren't ask me dad.'

'Have you tried getting her up in the night and making her use the loo?'

'Yes, but all that achieved was wearing myself out for work the next day. I'm hoping she'll grow out of it soon.'

'You said your mother called in earlier. How is she? I know she's me daughter, but you wouldn't think so! She ain't been in to see me for weeks now.'

'It's the same for us. She doesn't come to see us regularly, and sometimes it's months before she turns up again. I didn't get a chance to speak to her this time, but I think she's split up with Lesley,' Jenny said, glad about that. She'd only met him once but had taken an instant dislike to the man.

'I can't say I'm surprised. They never seem to last long with your mother. Anyway, I'm parched, so make us a cup of tea, love. You'll find jam tarts in the usual place. I've made enough to sink a battleship, but I don't suppose they'll last two minutes with the boys.' Edith chuckled. 'You should've brought them to see me too.'

'I will next time,' Jenny told her.

She went into the kitchen and filled the kettle. The walls were painted bright orange, and the four cupboards chocolate brown. As she waited for the water to boil, she took a biscuit tin from the larder cupboard. It was filled to the brim with the home-baked jam tarts. Her gran was right, Peter and Timmy would gorge on them later and make themselves sick if she didn't ration them.

A few minutes later, with a pot of tea beside them, she sat on an armchair next to her gran. She studied the woman's face. Her eyes looked cloudy but, despite her poor sight, her grey hair was neatly pinned up in a bun, and her clothes were freshly laundered and ironed. Jenny was pleased to see her gran was still managing to take good care of herself. 'How's your hip, Gran?'

Her gran rubbed her left side. She was a wide woman, small-busted but with thick thighs. 'Not too bad, love. It's a lot better now the weather is warming up. What about you, have you found yourself a nice young man yet?'

'Oh, Gran . . . no. I've told you, I'm not interested in meeting blokes. I've got enough on my plate as it is.' Jenny could feel her cheeks had flushed at the mere mention of a man.

'You're a pretty little thing and I'd hate to see you become a washed-up old spinster. You should go out more. There's always a fancy dance going on at the ballroom above the ABC.'

Jenny sat back in her chair and heaved a sigh. Just the thought of walking into the ballroom made her heart race. A few of the girls at work went regularly and had encouraged her to join them, but she couldn't pluck up the courage to go. 'No, Gran, I prefer being here with you, or at home looking after the boys.'

'Oh, get orf with you! You're a young woman in your prime. You shouldn't be sat with an old woman or babysitting your brothers. Gloria and Pamela are old enough to do that, and anyway, they're your dad's responsibility, not yours. You should be out enjoying yourself. So next Saturday, just to please me, I want you to get spruced up and go to the dance.'

Jenny would do anything to please her gran, but she could feel her face burning again. She reckoned her cheeks were probably as red as her hair and was grateful when she heard a knock on the door. 'That must be Pam back with your mousetraps,' she said as she got up, avoiding answering her gran's request.

'That was quick,' Jenny said as she opened the door, but was surprised to find a man on the doorstep. He looked young, possibly about the same age as her or maybe a few years older. He had light brown eyes and longish sandy-coloured hair. Flushing, she lowered her eyes, and was surprised to see that he was wearing slippers.

'Hello, I'm Craig from upstairs,' he said.

That explains the slippers, Jenny thought, too shy to look up at him again. 'Oh . . . erm . . . hi,' she managed to stutter.

'Is that Craig?' Edith shouted.

20

Jenny spun around towards the lounge. 'Yes, Gran.'

'Bring him in . . . tell him you've just made a pot of tea.'

Jenny slowly turned back to face Craig and looked at him through the hood of her amber lashes. 'You'd, er, best come in.'

Craig followed Jenny through to the lounge. She could feel his eyes on her back and felt very self-conscious.

'Hello, sit yourself down, and Jenny, fetch another cup,' her gran instructed in her usual friendly manner.

Jenny was pleased to be away from the lounge and out of Craig's sight. She found his long gaze intimidating, and as usual didn't know what to say. Unfortunately, with no excuse to dawdle, she was soon back in the lounge and pouring Craig a cup of tea.

'So you're Jenny,' Craig said, smiling warmly. 'You're Edith's eldest granddaughter. I've heard lots about you.'

'Don't worry, girl. I've only said nice things,' her gran said, chuckling.

'Yes, that's right,' Craig agreed. 'She told me you work at that electrical component place. A fiddly job that. I'm quite handy with my hands too — I make small items of furniture.'

It was obvious he was trying to make conversation, and, much as Jenny would have liked to participate, she was finding it very difficult. It didn't help that her gran seemed to be scrutinising her, though Jenny doubted the old woman could see very much. 'Would

'. . . would you . . . like a jam tart?' Jenny offered quietly.

'I'm sorry, can you repeat that please?' Craig asked.

Edith interrupted. 'I've already told you he's deaf, Jen. You have to make sure he can see your face when you talk to him, and then he can read your lips.'

'Oh! Sorry,' Jenny said to Craig, more embarrassed than ever, and slowly repeated her question.

'Yes, please. I love your gran's cooking,' Craig replied with gusto.

Jenny went through to the kitchen and fumbled in the biscuit tin. Pull yourself together, she thought. Not only was she incredibly shy, she'd never met a deaf person before, though if her gran hadn't told her she'd never have guessed that Craig was hard of hearing.

There were only two armchairs in the lounge, bottle-green fabric with wooden armrests. Craig was sitting in one and her gran in the other, but when Jenny came back into the lounge, he was quick to offer her his seat. She politely declined, and instead sat at a small table tucked up against the wall.

'These are delicious, Edith, melt in your mouth,' Craig said as he swallowed the last of his tart.

'My granddaughter's a good cook too, ain't that right, Jen?'

Jenny's heart sank as she realised her gran was playing Cupid. If that was her game, she could think again and re-aim her crooked arrow, Jenny

22

thought. She wondered if Craig had cottoned on.

'Well, she's had the best teacher.'

' 'Ere, I've just had a thought,' Edith said, and moved to the edge of her chair. 'Why don't you take Jenny to the dance in the ballroom next Saturday?'

Jenny could feel herself squirming and wanted to tell her gran to shut up. She lowered her head, not daring to look at Craig, wondering if he felt just as embarrassed.

'I'd love to, Edith, but I'm not a good dancer. I can't hear the music and I've got two left feet. But there's a St Trinian's film playing at the cinema. It stars George Cole, he's a right funny one. Do you fancy coming with me to watch it, Jenny?'

Jenny looked up but couldn't find her voice. Craig was good-looking, and she liked him, but he was probably only asking her out because her gran had put him on the spot.

'Yes, she'd like that, wouldn't you, Jen?' her gran said, answering for her.

'Er . . . yes . . . I suppose,' Jenny eventually stuttered.

'Great,' Craig said, smiling.

To her relief, Jenny heard another knock on the door and jumped up. 'I'll get it. It'll be Pamela,' she said, relieved to escape for a moment to gather her thoughts. Craig had a relaxed, easy-going air about him, but she'd never been on a date before and the thought terrified her. Maybe she could say that she'd just realised that she was busy and couldn't go.

'You look at bit pale. What's wrong?' Pamela

23

asked worriedly as she stepped into the flat.

'Nothing,' Jenny whispered in reply. 'Gran has a visitor.'

'Oh, who?'

'The bloke from upstairs, Craig. He's deaf but he can tell what you're saying by reading your lips.'

'Deaf? What, he can't hear anything?'

'Not a word, so when you talk make sure you're facing him.'

'Blimey, I've never spoken to a deaf person before. I wouldn't know what to say.'

'Don't worry, other than his hearing he's just like anyone else. Just be yourself,' Jenny answered, thinking it ironic that she was giving advice to her younger sister, yet she herself was struggling to communicate without blushing.

'This is Pamela, another of my granddaughters,' Edith told Craig as they walked into the lounge.

'Hello, Pamela,' said Craig, smiling warmly.

Pamela managed to stammer hello, and then Craig rose to his feet. 'I'd best be off, but before I go, is it all right if I pick you up next Saturday, Jenny, or I could meet you here?'

'You can meet her here,' Edith said quickly.

'Right, see you next week. Nice meeting you, Pamela, and see you soon, Edith. Don't worry, I'll see myself out.'

Pamela waved in slow motion, seemingly fascinated and in awe at meeting a deaf man. As the front door closed, she asked, 'What did he mean about next week?'

Jenny let out a long-held breath, and slumped

onto a chair, and her gran chipped in before she could answer. 'Your sister's got a date.'

'With Craig? But . . . he . . . he's . . . '

'Deaf, Pamela, yes,' Jenny told her. 'Craig can't hear, but as you just saw for yourself, it doesn't hold him back.'

'Where's he taking you?'

'To the cinema,' Jenny replied coyly.

'That's nice. What are you going to see? What will you wear? Do you want me to help you with your hair?'

'Whoa, slow down, Pamela,' Edith urged. 'Give your sister a chance to breathe! But you're right about her needing some help with her hair.'

Jenny patted her frizzy ginger curls. Her hair was unruly and could do with some taming, but the hot blower or curling tongs could do nothing to style it. Instead they made it look even wilder than normal, so now Jenny normally tied it back. She doubted her thirteen-year-old sister could do anything with it either, but it was nice to see her looking animated and, for now, not looking nervous.

'I don't know where you get that red hair from,' Edith mused. 'Must be from your father's side.'

On many occasions, Jenny had heard her dad ask her mother the same question. She'd overheard his accusations and wondered if that was the reason he always seemed to beat her so severely. He didn't believe he was really her father. And on days like today, when her head still pounded from the force of his fists, she wished he wasn't.

25

3

The following week, Craig looked out of the window and caught a glimpse of Jenny arriving at her gran's. He thought she looked stunning and quickly checked his own reflection. 'Who are you trying to kid?' he asked himself. 'A woman like her would never be interested in a bloke like you.'

Though Craig thought Jenny was accompanying him to the cinema out of sympathy, he still intended to make the most of the evening. It was only the second occasion he'd taken a woman out and he cringed at the memory of the first time. It had ended in disaster when he'd misread her words so when she'd said she played the guitar, he'd thought she said she peed in a jar. When he'd realised his mistake, he had roared with laughter, but unfortunately his date didn't seem to have a sense of humour or the patience to understand the limitations of lip-reading.

Craig hoped this evening would go more smoothly. He'd been looking forward to this all week, but once again he reminded himself not to get his hopes up. Jenny could have the pick of blokes in Balham so was unlikely to choose him. He'd discovered that once women found out about his inability to hear, they normally did a runner. Granted, Jenny already knew he was deaf and had still agreed to go out with him, but he had to admit to himself that she hadn't seemed very enthusiastic and he guessed she'd only said yes because she felt sorry for him. Still, it was nice to have someone to go to the cinema with for a change. At least he wouldn't be sitting there alone, surrounded by couples. In fact, he'd have the best-looking girl on his arm, and even if they just became friends, it was better than being lonely.

★   ★   ★

'Oh, Jen, you look a picture,' Edith said when Jenny walked in.

'Pamela helped with my hair. I'm amazed at how she's styled it. Perhaps she could get a job as an apprentice hairdresser when she leaves school.'

'You scrub up smashing. It's nice to see you dolled up for a change. Are you looking forward to tonight?'

'To be honest, Gran, I've been having second thoughts,' Jenny answered, omitting that her stomach was in knots with nerves and she'd hardly slept because of worrying about it.

'Why? Craig's ever so nice. Yes, he's deaf but you could do a lot worse, you know!'

'It's not him. I'm sure he's great.'

'So, what is it then? First date nerves?'

'I suppose so. I'm not very good at talking to men.'

'Don't worry, sweetheart, everyone gets butterflies at first. You'll soon relax, and then I'm sure you'll have a lovely time. I reckon Craig will

27

be feeling just as nervous.'

'Do you think so? I wasn't even sure he really wanted to take me out.'

'Oh, he's keen on you, I could tell. He couldn't take his eyes off you and when I suggested the dance, he was quick to invite you to the cinema instead. Now stop worrying and just enjoy yourself.'

Jenny heard a light tap on the front door and her stomach flipped.

'Go and answer it then,' her gran urged.

She took a deep breath to compose herself but could feel her cheeks burning. Her pale skin made blushes really stand out, and she guessed her neck and chest would be red too. She opened the door but could hardly bring herself to look at Craig.

His voice upbeat, he said, 'Hiya, Jenny. You look fantastic. Are you going somewhere nice?'

Jenny panicked. Had he forgotten about their date? She looked at him now, her eyes wide.

'Only kidding,' he said, grinning. 'You do look fantastic though.'

'Thanks,' she muttered. 'Come in.'

Craig followed her through to the lounge and stood by her side as he said hello to Edith.

'Well, I say,' her gran said proudly as she eyed them, 'don't you make a handsome couple.'

Jenny's cheeks were already flushed and the last thing she needed was her gran making remarks like that. 'We'd better go. We don't want to be late,' she said, trying to get them out of the door before her gran said anything else to embarrass her.

'Righto. See you later, Edith. Don't worry, I'll take good care of Jenny and make sure she's home at a sensible time.'

'I'm sure you will, young man,' Edith called, though Jenny knew Craig couldn't have heard her.

★   ★   ★

Lizzie shoved her arm through Roy's and reached up to kiss him on the cheek.

'What was that for?' Roy asked.

'Do you really want to see this poxy film? I could think of better things to do than queuing up outside the Ritz.'

'Oh yeah, like what?'

Lizzie stood on tiptoes and whispered in his ear, 'Let's go back home and I'll show you. We can have an early night.'

'You saucy little minx,' Roy said, beaming. 'Come on then.'

Lizzie knew how to twist Roy around her little finger, and the suggestion of going to bed always worked when she wanted to get her own way. She wasn't interested in seeing a film about a girls' school. It sounded daft to her, so with an arm still hooked through Roy's, they left the queue. To Lizzie's horror, she spotted a familiar face in the line of people, and her eldest daughter had seen her too.

'Mum, hello. I . . . I didn't expect to see you here.'

Lizzie flashed a quick look at Roy. The man looked confused, but it wasn't any wonder considering she still hadn't mentioned any of her five children.

'We're not stopping. Gotta dash, see ya. Hope you enjoy the film,' Lizzie said quickly and pulled on Roy's arm, dragging him down the street and away from the awkward situation.

'Did she just call you Mum?' he asked, clearly perplexed.

'Yes, but it's not what you think,' Lizzie answered, trying to buy some time to think of a good get-out.

'So, she's not your daughter?'

'Well . . . she is . . . but — ' she stammered, unusually lost for words.

Roy tugged himself away from her grip, then angrily said, 'For Christ's sake, Liz, why didn't you tell me?'

'Don't be like that, Roy. It's not like I lied to you or anything. I just haven't got around to mentioning it to you.'

'You've got a grown-up daughter who doesn't look that much younger than me and you didn't think to say something? As for not lying to me, how old are you really?'

'For goodness sake, a lot of women tell fibs about their age, and anyway, what does it matter?'

'It matters to me. I don't want to be lumbered with some washed-up old tart! What are you, thirty-five . . . forty?'

Lizzie bristled, her temper rising, 'I'm forty-two, as it happens,' she snapped, 'and I've got five kids who live with their father. You've just met my eldest, Jenny. She's twenty-two, and yes, that's right, just a few years younger than you.'

Roy fell silent, but Lizzie could see he was shocked by her revelations. She didn't want to lose him and kicked herself for losing her rag. 'Look, it's not the end of the world. All right, I've got kids, but it doesn't mean anything has to change between us. Come on, let's go home and have that early night,' she suggested, licking her lips suggestively.

'You deceitful bitch!' he growled, his eyes cold and hard. 'What makes you think I want to be with a grandmother, eh?'

'Leave it out. I ain't a grandmother!'

'Maybe not, but you soon could be. Blimey, it won't be long before you're tucking your tits into your knickers and walking with a stick! Nah, Liz, this ain't on. You duped me into sleeping with you, but now you can get your stuff out of my flat and sling your fucking hook.'

Roy stomped on ahead, leaving Lizzie reeling. She hadn't expected him to take it so badly and quickened her pace to catch up with him. 'Roy . . . wait . . . Roy,' she called, but he carried on marching ahead of her.

Finally, as he opened his front door, she caught up with him. 'Please, Roy, let's not be hasty. Come on, let's go to bed,' she purred, confident that she'd be able to seduce him, and he'd forget about her age. 'We can talk about this again later.'

'Ugh, no thanks. The thought of sleeping with you turns my stomach now. Bloody hell, Liz, it'd be like sleeping with my mother! You're a looker, but I need a girl of my own age. Sorry, but we're finished.'

Lizzie's heart sank as she realised she wouldn't be able to persuade him to change his mind. Worse still, she'd be homeless again. 'Please, Roy. I understand but give me a chance to get myself sorted. I can't go tonight. I haven't got anywhere to go.'

Roy looked her up and down with disgust, then spat, 'Tough. That ain't my problem. Go back to your old man and look after your children — like a proper mother!'

He opened his door, walked in and then slammed it shut behind him, leaving Lizzie dumbfounded on the doorstep. She slowly lowered herself and sat on the cold concrete step as Roy's words spun in her head. She couldn't go back to Henry. Roy didn't understand what her husband was like. Of course, she would have liked to take her children with her when she left, but where could she have gone with five kids in tow? Lesley hadn't wanted them. Anyway, she reasoned, they were better off in their own home, and whatever Henry was or wasn't, he was at least a good provider. But that didn't mean she'd put up with his punches again. No, she would never go back to him, never. Though she might try and cadge a few quid out of him now.

* * *

Gloria had tucked the boys into bed, and when her dad had come home from the pub she'd warmed his dinner through. He hadn't eaten it, but she was thankful that he was in a mellow mood. He'd stumbled up the stairs to his room, and now Pamela had taken herself off to bed too.

Gloria sat alone in the front room, listening to the radio whilst waiting for Jenny to come home. She couldn't wait to hear all the details of how her older sister's date had gone. Before long, she heard the front door quietly close and Jenny breezed into the room. From the look on her face, Gloria could tell it had gone well. 'Someone looks happy! Tell me all about it, I've been dying to know.'

'Oh, Gloria, it was amazing! We held hands watching the film. I was a bit worried because I thought my palm might have been all sweaty, but he didn't let it go. Then after the film he took me to the coffee bar and we talked and talked and talked some more. He insisted on walking me home, then out there, in the street, he kissed me! Just a little peck but it was on the lips. Honestly, it feels like I've known him forever! And you'll never guess who we bumped into?'

'No, go on, tell me.'

'Mum. She was there with a bloke who looked young enough to be her son. You know her though, she hardly said two words to me and didn't hang about.'

'Nothing that woman does surprises me any more. Enough about her, you'll be seeing Craig again then?'

'Yes, and I can't wait. I said I'd call in to see Gran on Tuesday after work, so he said he'll take me out for something to eat. Do you mind cooking dinner for you all that night and keeping an eye on the boys?'

'I suppose so, but don't make it too often, they ain't my responsibility.'

'How have the boys and Pamela been?'

'Don't worry about them, they're fine. Timmy had a bit of a bellyache, but I reckon he was swinging the lead 'cos he wanted to wait up for you to come home. Dad's upstairs, probably passed out by now. Anyway, what did it feel like to be kissed?'

Jenny threw herself back on the sofa and sighed deeply before answering, 'Dreamy.'

'Blimey, 'ark at you, you're swooning,' Gloria chuckled. She would never admit it, but there was a part of her that was jealous. Yes, she was happy for Jenny, but she wished it was she who had a boyfriend. Someone, anyone, who could take her away from the hell of living with their father. She had someone in mind, but so far she hadn't attracted his attention.

4

Craig awoke to his silent world, but he felt as if a rapturous riot was occurring in his head. He'd fallen asleep with a smile on his face and now, as his eyes opened, his first thought was of Jenny and he smiled again.

Their date couldn't have gone any better; it had been the best night of his life. Once Jenny had overcome her shyness, they'd chatted like old friends, and the more he got to know her, the more he found he liked her. They'd arranged to see each other again on Tuesday, but today was Sunday and their next date felt a lifetime away. He wished now that he'd invited her to lunch today, but he hadn't wanted his keenness to frighten her off.

Craig almost skipped out of bed, then put the kettle on. As he stood waiting for the water to come to the boil, his mind filled with images and thoughts of Jenny. He found it sweet when she'd tap her fingers on her cheek when thinking, and tuck imaginary strands of hair behind her ear when being serious. He liked how her nose would wrinkle, like a mouse's, when she sniffed, and he adored the dimples that showed when she smiled.

'Get a grip of yourself, man,' Craig said out loud as he poured hot water onto tea leaves. 'You're acting like a schoolboy with a crush!' He tried to contain himself, but found he was overwhelmed with feelings for Jenny. He'd never felt like this before about anyone, and hoped she felt the same.

⋆ ⋆ ⋆

A short while later, Craig decided to head for his workshop. There wasn't much else to do alone on a Sunday, other than take a walk or go to church. As he trotted downstairs, Edith's door opened and the woman stepped out with her arms folded across her chest and a mischievous grin on her face.

'Well then, how was your date?' she asked.

'Morning, Edith. Have you been standing behind your door waiting to accost me?'

'You cheeky bugger, but yes, as it happens, I have.'

'I'm surprised you weren't waiting up for me to come home last night.'

'I was, but I must have nodded off. Well?'

'Well what?' Craig asked, enjoying teasing the old woman.

'Don't make me drag it out of you,' Edith warned and wagged her finger.

'It was very . . . pleasant.'

'Pleasant, is that it, pleasant?'

'Actually, it was better than pleasant.'

'The kettle's just boiled, do you want to come in and tell me all about it?'

Yes, Craig wanted to. He couldn't stop thinking about Jenny and would like nothing better than to talk about her too. As he followed Edith into her cosy home, he announced, 'Do you know what, I'm absolutely smitten.'

Edith turned and smiled warmly. 'Good. You've made an old woman very happy. Jenny deserves a bit of happiness and it's about time she met a nice, decent man.'

Craig sat down and made no secret of his feelings. His cheeks ached from grinning so much, but he couldn't help himself. 'She's lovely, Edith, really lovely.'

'I know, she's a good girl, you won't find kinder.'

'I won't be looking! Honestly, Edith, call me soft if you want, but she's bowled me over. I hope she likes me too.'

'Tell me to mind me own business, but did you give her a kiss goodnight?'

'Edith! You can't ask me something like that,' Craig answered, pretending to be shocked.

'Don't be bleedin' daft. Did you or didn't you?'

'Yes, I did, but don't you go giving me an ear-bashing. I swear, I was every ounce the gentleman.'

'I'm sure you was and I'd expect nothing less, but my point is, if Jenny allowed you to give her a kiss, then I guarantee she likes you too. I know my Jen. Trust me, the feelings are mutual.'

'Thanks, Edith, it's nice to hear. I feel a bit stupid, and to be honest, I don't know what's come over me.'

'It's called love, Craig. Me and my husband were just the same when we first met. When you meet the one, you know it.'

Craig sat back in the armchair and sighed.

37

He'd known immediately that Jenny was 'the one', but had told himself it was too soon. Of course, he wouldn't reveal his feelings to Jenny just yet, but now that Edith confirmed it, he knew he was falling head over heels.

★　★　★

Henry turned over in bed, opened his eyes and blinked against the bright sunlight beaming through the window. It took him a minute or two to get his bearings but then he realised he must have fallen asleep without drawing the curtains and was still wearing all his clothes. He hardly remembered coming home last night but had recollections of lumping Jerry King. The man had been having a laugh at his expense about Lizzie with some toy boy. A bloody nose had soon shut Jerry up, but he couldn't recall if he'd been barred from the pub or not. If he was, he wasn't bothered — he'd spend his hard-earned cash in the Grove Tavern instead.

With his mouth feeling like the bottom of a parrot's cage, Henry grimaced as he glanced at his bedside alarm clock. Bloody hell, it was nearly eleven. He must have been well plastered to sleep in this late. He could hear Timmy and Peter playing in the hallway downstairs. Blinkin' kids, he thought; with his thumping head the last thing he needed was them lot mucking about. He threw his legs over the side of the bed, then sat with his head lowered. At least it was Sunday, so he didn't have to go to work.

He was a dustman. It was a stinking job, but he liked working in the outdoors and the lads on the dustcart were a good bunch of blokes. There were perks to the job too, often half-decent bits and pieces put out that they could flog, splitting the cash between them.

Henry's stomach grumbled loudly. He had no idea when he'd last eaten. He straightened his back, stretched his arms and slowly stood up to go downstairs. Late up or not, one of the girls could cook him breakfast. There wasn't much good he could say about his wife, but she had taught them how to cook and a big fry-up was exactly what he needed right now.

★　★　★

Jenny was in the kitchen, peeling potatoes in preparation for their Sunday dinner. She was still feeling elated from her date with Craig but tensed when she heard her father's footsteps overhead. He'd be coming downstairs soon and was sure to have a hangover which meant he'd be like a bear with a sore head. She spun around and said quickly to Pamela, 'Get the boys and take them to the back yard. Hurry.'

Pamela jumped from the kitchen table, rushed into the hallway and soon returned with Peter holding one hand and Timmy the other. 'Let's have a game of football,' she urged as she dragged them through the kitchen.

Just in time, Jenny thought as her father walked in. 'Morning, Dad. There's tea in the pot,' she said, not expecting to receive anything more than a grunt in response.

'Pour me a cup, and I'll have some bacon and eggs with it,' he answered before sauntering off to the front room.

Jenny wrinkled her nose at the foul smell of his body odour and the stench of stale beer. It was bad enough that he came home every night with the pong of rubbish on him, but she couldn't abide the stink of tobacco and alcohol that lingered on his clothes from when he'd been in the pub.

Though it was closer to lunchtime, she set to cooking his breakfast. Gloria walked into the room, done up to the nines. 'Where are you going dressed like that?' Jenny asked.

'Nowhere,' Gloria answered offhandedly.

'So, what's with all the fancy clobber?'

'I just like to look nice.'

'So you're not going out, and just dressed up like that for no reason,' Jenny challenged.

'I might go for a walk.'

'Where to? The shops will be closed today.'

'I dunno, down to Chestnut Grove maybe.'

Jenny narrowed her eyes suspiciously. 'Isn't that where Dennis Henderson lives, above Queenie's fag shop?'

'Might be,' Gloria said and strutted across the kitchen to pour herself a glass of tap water.

'I knew it! You're hoping to bump into him, aren't you?'

'Well, he is rather dishy.'

'Yes, he's a nice-looking lad, but from what I've heard he's a bit of a so-and-so. You could do so much better.'

'But I like him, Jen. I just wish he'd notice me.'

Jenny hoped he wouldn't. She worked in the same factory as his mother and had heard the woman complaining about her son, saying he couldn't hold down a job because she could never get him out of bed. 'If he sees you dressed like that he'll notice you all right, though I think you'd be better off giving him a wide berth and setting your sights higher.'

'Don't nag, Jen. I ain't trying to marry him. I just want a bit of fun for a change and hope he'll ask me out on a date.'

With their often bleak lives, Jenny couldn't blame Gloria for wanting a bit of fun, but she worried that her sister was really looking for love. 'Fine, it's your life, but if you're determined to see him I suggest you leave now, quickly, before Dad sees how short your skirt is.'

'Yes, you're right. He wouldn't let me out the house like this. Wish me luck and I'll see you later.'

Jenny just smiled. She couldn't bring herself to wish Gloria luck in wanting to date the boy, but she couldn't stop her. Gloria was headstrong and though Jenny tried her best to guide her, Gloria would often retaliate with anger and do her own thing regardless.

She heard the front door close, and for a while all was quiet, but then she heard heels tapping along the hallway before the kitchen door opened again. She was about to ask Gloria what she'd forgotten, but her heart sank when she heard her mother's voice.

'Morning, Jen, where's your father?'

'He's in the front room, but don't go upsetting him. He had a few beers last night, so he might have a hangover.'

'Upsetting him! It's me who's bloody well upset!'

Her tone was shrill, but before Jenny could say anything her dad came bounding from the front room.

'I thought I heard your fucking voice. If you're hoping to see the kids, you can think again.'

'No, actually, Henry,' she said, smiling softly as she looked up at him, 'it's you I want to see.'

It appalled Jenny when her mum would try and use her feminine charms to soften her dad. It was obvious she was after something.

'Oh yeah, what do you want to see me about?' Henry asked.

'Let's go into the front room and have a chat,' Lizzie suggested.

'Yeah, all right.'

Jenny watched as her mother followed her father, throwing a smug grin over her shoulder as she left the kitchen. I hope she gets what she's come for, Jenny thought, and doesn't rile him. She finished cooking his breakfast, and once it was plated up, Jenny wondered whether she should take it through to him or keep it warm in the oven. Trouble was, the fried eggs would go hard, which would give her father another reason to kick off. She hadn't yet heard any raised voices so decided to serve it up. She placed the plate on a tray then tapped gently on the front room door.

Her father was quick to shout, 'What?'

As Jenny walked nervously into the room, balancing the tray, her father looked at her and said scathingly, 'Your mother's got some fucking nerve.'

'Well, if it wasn't for gobby there, I wouldn't be in the situation I am now,' Lizzie said, and raised her eyebrows at Jenny.

Jenny didn't know what to say and wanted to flee from the room.

'What's Jenny got to do with anything?' her father asked.

'Last night she went and opened her big gob. She called me Mum, and that put me in this very difficult position. I hadn't yet told my fella that I had kids and he chucked me out. Yeah, and come to that, Jenny, who was that bloke you were with?'

Jenny could feel her parents' eyes boring into her, but her throat felt frozen with fear and she was unable to answer. Instead, she walked cautiously over to her dad to offer him the tray. To her utter shock, instead of taking it from her, he whacked the tray from underneath and sent it flying across the room. Greasy bacon and runny egg yolk slid down the faded wallpaper as the plate and tray crashed to the floor.

'You're taking the fucking piss out of me, Lizzie,' he yelled. 'This bloke chucked you out, you're blaming Jenny for it, and now you've come here trying to tap me for money. Get out of my house, you money-grabbing whore!'

Her mother flinched but, as though she didn't want to show any fear, she flicked her hair back defiantly then marched from the room. In a haughty voice, she called over her shoulder, 'Fine. You can poke your rotten money where the sun don't shine, Henry Lombard.'

As the front door slammed, Jenny stared at her father, petrified at what was coming.

'That bitch left me with you five to look after and then has the front to come round here with her hand out asking for money. And what the fuck was she on about? Was you out with a man last night?'

Jenny nodded.

'And you saw your mother?'

Again, she nodded.

'Was the fancy bloke she was with a young 'un?'

Jenny went to nod yet again, but her father moved fast and placed his large calloused hand around her neck. She would have stumbled backwards but he had a tight grip of her. She could feel the blood rushing to her head.

'Did you have a nice time, the four of you? Cosy, was it?' he asked menacingly.

Jenny wanted to tell him that it wasn't like that, but her father's tightening hold was nearly choking her. She didn't see it coming, but suddenly felt a searing hot pain across her face. He'd viciously slapped her, but he'd let go of her throat and she crumpled to the floor. She didn't have time to curl into a foetal position before he began raining blows down on her. Her ribs, her arms, her head, her whole body felt under assault from his punishing punches and kicks.

'You're a fucking tart just like your mother,' he screamed.

Jenny closed her eyes, but she couldn't blot out the pain as blow after blow smashed into her already bruised body.

Finally spent, and gasping for breath, her father walked away, leaving her close to passing out and bleeding on the worn floorboards. Jenny felt as though she was drifting away, and the last thing she heard was the front door slamming before she sank into unconsciousness.

★ ★ ★

Gloria had passed her mother as she left the house. Lizzie had eyed her short skirt with disapproval, and Gloria had scuttled past, saying she was in a hurry. She carried on walking, but her conscience kept nagging at her to go back home. It was obvious that her mother was heading there, and wherever she went, so did trouble. If her mother infuriated her dad, she knew Jenny would end up being used as his punchbag.

Gloria was about to turn back, but then decided she was better off out of it, and safe from her father's temper. She'd rather Jenny be getting it in the neck than her. Nearly twenty minutes later and close to Chestnut Grove, some impulse made her suddenly spin on her heels again and head home. If everything was all right, she could always go out for another walk, and anyway, she consoled herself, it was still a bit early and Dennis might not be about yet.

As Gloria hurried round a corner, she came face to face with her mother. She'd promised Jenny she wouldn't say anything, but, worried about the chaos her mother had probably left behind, she couldn't help herself and blurted, 'Have you been to see me dad?'

'Yeah, but it was a waste of time. The tight git.'

'Can't you just stay away, Mum? Every time you visit, you upset Dad, and when you leave one of us always gets a hiding. Do you even care that he beats Jenny because of you?'

'Don't be such a drama queen, Gloria. If he hits any of you, I've no doubt you deserved it. My father used to take the strap to me, it's what dads do. It's called discipline and it won't do you any harm.'

'It's got nothing to do with telling us off! It's Jenny that mostly gets the brunt of his temper and she doesn't do anything to deserve it. Please, for her sake, for all our sakes, don't visit us again.'

Gloria was stunned when her mother just glared at her and pushed past her without saying another word. It was obvious she didn't care about them. Gloria picked up her pace and, just as she reached home, her father came steaming from the house. His face was contorted with rage and his eyes black. He didn't so much as look at her as he passed, and Gloria instinctively knew he'd beaten Jenny again. She dashed up the short path to the front door, dropping her key in her haste. Once inside, she flew straight to the front room and looked down in horror at Jenny lying unconscious on the floor.

'Pamela,' she yelled. 'Pamela, run up to the phone box and ring for an ambulance.'

Gloria dropped to her knees beside her sister and gently brushed Jenny's hair from her bloodied face. 'It's all right,' she soothed, 'help will be here soon.'

Jenny groaned in pain and a knot formed in Gloria's stomach. Her father had done this, inflicted these terrible injuries, and she hated him, detested him. Her mother might not have landed the punches, but she'd played a part in this, and she hated her too.

Once again Jenny cried out, and Gloria's eyes filled with tears. This was the worst she'd ever seen it. Her sister looked in a bad way — a very bad way, and she feared that this time Jenny wouldn't pull through.

5

Thankfully, Gloria's fears were unfounded, but even now Jenny winced as she rolled over in her bed. It had been two weeks since her father had attacked her, but she still felt bruised and sore. She'd told the hospital staff she'd fallen down the stairs. If they'd known the truth, she worried that, hearing what her father was capable of, they'd take the boys away. Jenny wondered if they'd be better off in a children's home — at least they would be safe — but she couldn't bring herself to break up the family. She'd always done her best to protect them, but it seemed her father's violence was escalating. With that in mind, she forced herself to climb out of bed. Every bone in her body ached and she felt weak, but she couldn't risk staying in her room any longer.

There was a light tap on her bedroom door, then Gloria popped her head in. 'I thought I heard you up and about,' she said, then rushed over to offer Jenny an arm to lean on.

Jenny was touched by her sister's solicitude. Gloria could sometimes be selfish, but she'd been marvellous since she'd come home from the hospital, Pamela too. 'I can't stay in bed forever. Dad will be home from work soon and I'm worried he'll start on the boys. Anyway, why aren't you at work?'

'Don't worry about Timmy and Peter.

Between us, Pamela and me have got it all in hand. Can you hear anything?'

'No,' Jenny replied, thinking that the house was strangely quiet.

'That's because Pam has taken them to Tooting Lido. They won't be home for ages yet, so get yourself back into bed.'

'No, it's about time I was up and about. You still haven't said why you're not at work.'

'I'll tell you later. Do you want me to make you a cuppa?'

'Thanks, that would be nice,' Jenny answered, but got the feeling that Gloria was trying to fob her off about her job. 'Give me a few minutes. I'll get myself dressed and then I'll be down.'

Gloria closed the bedroom door behind her, leaving Jenny to struggle to put her clothes on. Her wrist was badly sprained and at least one of her ribs was fractured. She managed to pull on a dress that buttoned down the front, but brushing her unruly ginger locks proved more of an effort. It hurt to lift her arm above her head. She looked in the mirror, and gently fingered her eye. The swelling had gone down, but the bruise was now yellow, and her split lip still hadn't healed. She'd rarely smiled lately, but each time she attempted to, the cut on her lip would sting and open again.

By the time Jenny came downstairs, Gloria had brewed a fresh pot of tea and had poured two cups. Jenny eased herself slowly onto a chair and quizzed her sister again.

'The truth is, Jen, I got the sack.'

'Oh no, that's all we need. I'm not going to have any pay coming in again this week and now you've gone and lost your job! What did you do?'

'Nothing! Old Fletcher said I couldn't have any time off to look after you, so I told him what he could do with his poxy job.'

Jenny couldn't be angry with Gloria, but she was concerned about money. Their dad provided for the rent and bills and contributed towards the groceries, but between them Jenny and Gloria topped up the housekeeping. Without the extra money, they'd be back on a very basic diet and there wouldn't be any treats for the boys. Then a thought crossed Jenny's mind. 'How has Pamela managed to pay for the boys to go swimming?'

'It's all right, Pamela's best friend's brother is a lifeguard. He'll get them in for free.'

'That's good. We can't afford to waste any money for a while. Did you take that letter to the factory for me?'

'Yes, and Miss Aston was fine about you being off sick. She said you're not to go back until you're one hundred per cent better. She seems like a nice lady. I wish I worked at your factory.'

'Did you ask her if she had any positions available?'

'Nah, I still need to be here, so I thought I'd wait 'til you're back at work and you can ask for me,' Gloria said with a cheeky grin.

'Does Dad know you've lost your job?'

'Yeah, and he did his nut. He said that now I'm sixteen I ain't his responsibility and he won't be paying for my keep. I've got two weeks to find another job and if I don't, he'll chuck me out.'

'Blimey, Gloria, you'd better go and see Miss

Aston tomorrow. Oh, no, you can't, it'll be Saturday and the factory is closed, but you can try first thing on Monday. Dad doesn't make idle threats, you known what he's like.'

'Yeah, I suppose. He also said that the apple doesn't fall far from the tree and I'm just like my mother, selfish and lazy. Do you know what . . . the more I think about it, the more I understand why she left him!'

There were times when Jenny agreed with what her dad had told Gloria. Her sister could be self-centred and was prone to idleness. 'What about Gran? Have you been to see her?' she asked.

'Not yet, I haven't had a chance.'

'Oh, Gloria, she'll be worried sick that she hasn't heard from us. You should have called in on her.'

'The silly old bat is getting so forgetful I doubt she noticed.'

Coming downstairs had taken its toll on Jenny. She was tired and didn't have the energy to argue with Gloria but knew her gran would be beside herself with worry. It was painful just to stand up, so Jenny knew she wouldn't be able to walk there. It was pointless asking Gloria to go, but she'd send Pamela to see her tomorrow.

Gloria sipped her tea then studied her painted fingernails while Jenny watched, thinking that her father was right. Gloria was very much like their mother. Both were vain and self-centred, though she hoped that, without their mother around to influence her, Gloria would lose some of her selfish streak. Once again Jenny had to

51

admit that Gloria had stepped up since she came home from hospital, and for that she was grateful, but to leave their gran to fret showed there was still some way to go.

★ ★ ★

At six o'clock, Craig packed up his tools and prepared to go home, though he wasn't looking forward to spending yet another weekend alone. As he padlocked the door to his furniture workshop, he thought again how lucky he was to have found the place. Mr Rendall owned the small building and had worked in it for years, but since his retirement he'd been happy to rent it to Craig.

When he arrived home and walked into the house, Craig paused briefly outside Edith's door. He hadn't seen her for a while, or Jenny. They'd arranged another date, and he'd been more than disappointed when Jenny stood him up. He shouldn't have been surprised. After all, he didn't think any pretty young woman in their right mind would want to be lumbered with a deaf boyfriend.

He'd avoided Edith since then, but as he was about to walk upstairs, on impulse he turned back and knocked on her door. It wasn't the old woman's fault that Jenny wasn't interested in him, he thought as he knocked again, harder this time. He waited a minute or two, but when Edith didn't come to the door, worry began to niggle at him. Edith was almost always at home and he had a feeling that something wasn't right. He hammered the door now and called out her name. The door had a lock but no letterbox, so when there was still no response he dashed outside and peered through her front room window. It wasn't easy to see much through Edith's net curtains, but panic rose when he spotted her legs. She looked as if she was lying in the doorway, but her top half was obscured.

'It's all right, Edith,' Craig shouted, 'I'm coming.'

He ran back inside and threw his shoulder at her door, but it didn't budge. Then, as his mind raced, he darted upstairs and a few moments later came back down with a crowbar. 'Don't worry, I'm going to get this door open,' he shouted.

Thankfully, with leverage, it gave way and Craig ran up the small hallway and almost slid to his knees beside Edith. She was flat on her back and he couldn't see her chest moving. If she was breathing, it was very shallowly.

'Edith,' he said, gently shaking the old woman and silently praying that she was alive, 'Edith, it's me, Craig. Can you move?'

To his relief, she groaned and slowly opened her eyes. 'Oh . . . Craig . . . I've had a bit of a fall,' she croaked weakly, and grasped his hand.

He couldn't see any signs of obvious injury. 'I can see that. Do you think you've broken anything?' he asked.

'No, I . . . I think I'm all right.'

'Shall we see if I can help you up?'

'Yes,' she agreed.

'Good, come on then, gently does it,' Craig said as he eased Edith to a sitting position. 'Right, good, stay there a moment and I'll get you a glass of water.'

Craig left Edith and rushed to her kitchen then returned with the refreshment. 'Here you go, sip slowly on this,' he said, offering her the glass.

Edith gulped a few mouthfuls, then said, 'I've been lying here since yesterday. I was banging and shouting as loud as I could, but of course you couldn't have heard me. Silly old sod, aren't I?'

'No, and I'm so sorry. Do you think you can stand up or should I call the doctor, or an ambulance?'

'I don't need an ambulance, or the doctor. I just feel a bit dizzy, that's all. Perhaps you could pop around to Jenny's for me? Ask her if she, or one of the other girls, can come here to look after me tonight.'

'Yes, of course, but if you're feeling dizzy perhaps you really should see the doctor.'

'No, Craig, there's no need to make a fuss. I just tripped over, nothing to worry about. Now, take this glass and give me a hand up.'

The woman looked frail, but Craig liked her spirit. She was made of strong stuff and wasn't prepared to let a little fall faze her. 'What's Jenny's address?' he asked. 'I'll make you a cup of tea then go straight there. I'm not sure she'll be too pleased to see me, though. We were supposed to be going out again the week before last, but she didn't turn up.'

54

'Didn't she? That's not like her. In fact, I haven't seen her since you two went off to see a film. I've been worried sick that she hasn't been in to see me. The other kids don't call in that often, but Jenny always comes at least once a week. I hope everything's all right.'

Craig managed to get Edith into her armchair. 'I'm sure it is. Jenny probably stayed away to avoid me.'

'No, my Jenny isn't like that. I hope her bleedin' father hasn't given her another good hiding. Pass me that pen and paper on the table please. I'll write down the address while you make me that cuppa.'

Craig couldn't hear the urgency in Edith's voice, but he noticed how worried she looked.

'Sorry, Edith, did you say that her father hits her?'

'Yes, he's not been right since their mother walked out. But don't say anything. She doesn't like people to know.'

Craig tried to get his head around what Edith had said. It was outrageous! He'd never understand how any man could hit a woman, let alone his own daughter. Jenny hadn't told him about it, but he recalled how she'd tensed when he'd mentioned her father, then she'd quickly changed the subject. He hadn't thought much about it at the time, but now it made sense. As he waited for the water to boil, he could feel his heart pounding faster at the thought of seeing Jenny again. He liked her. He liked her a lot and couldn't stand the thought of her being hurt. Something had to be done. He

55

didn't know what, but there would be no way he'd stand by and allow anyone to ever lay a hand on her again.

★   ★   ★

Jenny checked the clock. Their dad wasn't home yet so she assumed he was in the pub. Pamela had come back with two very hungry and tired boys. Gloria had fed them and they were now tucked up in bed. Jenny sat back on the sofa with thoughts of Craig. She felt awful about not meeting him for their date but it'd been impossible to get word to him.

Gloria broke into her thoughts, saying, 'That'll be another dinner wasted then.'

'Keep it warm, he might eat it when he gets home,' Jenny answered, though she doubted he would, he rarely did.

'I think I'll go up and read my book. Night, night,' Pamela said quietly, and slipped from the room.

'She's been pissing the bed every blinkin' night since Dad bashed you up, and I can't stand it,' Gloria hissed.

'Pamela can't help it. Maybe she should have my room until she stops, and I'll share with you.'

'Why can't I have your room and you share with Pam?'

'No, Gloria, the idea is that if Pam has her own bed, she won't bother anyone when she has her accidents.'

'But it isn't only Pam. I hate sleeping in a room with the boys. Peter's always crying for

56

Mum and Timmy has nightmares, waking us all up.'

'Well, I'm sorry, but there are only three bedrooms and my room isn't big enough to swing a cat. You'll have to put up with it and as soon as my ribs feel better, I'll swap with Pam,' she said. Any further protests from Gloria were halted by a knock on the door.

'I'll get it. It'll probably be Joan next door on the cadge for some tea or milk again.'

While Gloria went to answer the door, Jenny strained to hear what was said. She hoped her sister would be polite to Joan, who was really struggling since her husband had been laid off. She could hardly believe her ears when she recognised Craig's voice. Her stomach flipped.

'Hello, I'm Craig. Is Jenny at home, please?'

'Yes, just a minute.'

Gloria came back into the room all wide-eyed and smiley. 'There's a good-looking bloke at the door for you,' she said teasingly.

'I know! I heard! It's Craig! What's he doing here?'

'I don't know, shall I invite him in?'

'No, I'll come out. I don't want Dad to come home and find him in here. Oh gawd, look at the state of me,' she exclaimed as she stood up and tried to straighten her old dress before walking tentatively down the hallway, eager to see Craig, yet also dreading it. She was also conscious that her cheeks would be glowing bright red.

'Jenny, hello.' Craig smiled.

Jenny thought her heart had missed a beat at

the sight of him. 'Hello,' she answered shyly. She heard a muffled giggle and guessed that Gloria was probably standing behind the door, trying unsuccessfully to suppress her mirth as she eavesdropped on them.

'I hope you don't mind me calling like this, but your gran has had a bit of a fall and asked me to come round. Oh, blimey, are you all right? You look like you've been in the wars too.'

'I . . . I'm nearly better now, but what about my gran? Is she all right?'

'She hasn't broken any bones, but it's left her a bit weak and dizzy. She's hoping you, or one of your sisters, would stay the night with her.'

'Oh, no! Poor Gran! Are you sure she hasn't broken anything?'

'She seems fine, just but a bit shaky. She tripped over and couldn't get herself back up. She's a bit unsteady on her feet at the moment though and that's why she'd like someone with her.'

'Yes, of course. I won't bother to ask my sister Gloria, she'll only make some excuse not to go, but I'll send Pamela straight over. In fact, as it's dark now, would you mind if she walked back with you?'

'Of course not.'

'Gloria, I know you're there, so go and tell Pam to pack an overnight bag. Tell her to hurry up.'

Gloria emerged sheepishly from behind the door and flashed Craig a smile before running upstairs.

'How have you been?' Craig asked.

'Not bad, thanks. Look, I'm sorry about the other week.'

'It's all right, I understand,' Craig answered.

'No, I don't think you do. I did want to go out with you, but after the accident I was kept in hospital for a few days.'

'An accident? What happened?'

'I fell down the stairs. Silly really, just missed my footing,' Jenny said. She didn't like telling him lies but couldn't bring herself to reveal the awful truth. 'I fractured a couple of ribs and I've been in bed since I was sent home. I'm a lot better now though and this is my first day up.'

'That sounds painful, Jenny, but I'm glad to hear you're feeling better. Your gran will be pleased to know that it wasn't your father again.'

'What?'

'Shit, sorry, I wasn't meant to say anything. Edith was worried, she told me about your dad.'

'Oh, I see. Well, she shouldn't have, and as it happens, the accident had nothing to do with my father,' Jenny replied, and lowered her eyes. She was embarrassed and didn't want Craig to see that she'd been untruthful.

'She didn't mean any harm, but Jenny, does this mean that when you've fully recovered I can take you out again?'

Jenny wanted to shout *yes please!* — there was nothing she would like more. Instead she shyly nodded her head.

'Great, well, when you're ready, I'll take you out to dinner.'

When Pamela came downstairs, Jenny turned

to her and said, 'Give Gran my love and tell her I'll call in to see her as soon as I can.'

'Yeah, all right,' Pam agreed.

'See you soon, Jenny,' Craig husked, smiling softly.

She felt her cheeks flush, and before closing the door, stammered, 'Y-yes, see you.'

As they walked back along the hall, Gloria smiled and said, 'He really fancies you.'

'Stop it, we're just friends.'

'Pull the other leg, it's got bells on it. I only got the tail end of what was said when I came downstairs with Pam, but from what I heard it sounds like you've arranged another date?'

'Yes, we have, but I'm not sure it's a good idea.'

'Why on earth not?'

'If Dad does this to me again, I'm not sure how Craig would react. It's not fair to involve him in my problems.'

'Your problem is that you think too much. Just go out with the man and enjoy yourself.'

'Maybe, but I can't think about it now. I'm tired, Gloria, and I'm going to bed.'

'Righto, nighty night.'

Jenny wearily climbed the stairs to her room. She wished Gloria had called in to see their gran when she'd been asked to, but at least Pamela would be with her now. She undid the buttons on her dress and allowed it to fall to the floor then stepped into her winceyette nightclothes. It was easier to pull the nightdress up than put it over her head.

She slowly climbed into bed, with thoughts of

Craig flying around her mind. It had thrilled her to see him again, and though it was against her better judgement, she liked the idea of going to dinner with him. Maybe she should take Gloria's advice to just go out with the man and enjoy it. As long as she kept Craig and her father apart, surely it would be all right?

★ ★ ★

Even though it was almost dark, Pamela would have preferred to walk alone to her gran's flat. She felt awkward with Craig and hoped he wouldn't talk to her. Jenny had already told her to make sure he could see her lips, so he'd be able to understand what she was saying, but she still didn't feel comfortable.

'How old are you, Pamela?' Craig asked.

Oh no, she thought, he'd gone and asked her a question. She turned her face to look at him, then answered, 'Thirteen.'

'Thirteen, a ripe old age. Do you know what you want to do when you leave school?'

'I dunno. Work in a factory, I suppose, like my sister.'

'A factory, eh? Have you ever thought about doing anything else?'

This wasn't as bad as Pamela had thought it was going to be. Craig understood everything she said. 'I did think about hairdressing, but I really want to be a fashion designer, like Mary Quant. Fat chance though. Things like that don't happen to girls like me.'

'Don't say that, you never know what the

future holds. Who's Mary Quant? I've never heard of her.'

'It doesn't matter,' Pamela said, smiling.

She found herself warming to Craig and decided she quite liked him. They were soon at her gran's, and she was pleased to see the old woman was mostly unharmed from her ordeal. 'Can I get you anything, Gran?'

'Yes, love, a cup of hot milk and a couple of aspirins. It might help me to sleep.'

Pamela scuttled off to the kitchen, but she could still hear what was being said in the living room.

'How was Jenny?' her gran asked.

'She's as bad as you, Edith. She's taken a tumble down the stairs and that's why she hasn't been to see you for a while.'

'Stairs, my arse! Is that what she told you?'

'Yes, why, don't you believe her?'

'No, I bloody don't! You can bet your last farthing that her old man has given her what for. I'm telling you, Craig, if I was younger and fitter I'd skin that man alive.'

As soon as Pamela returned to the lounge, her gran asked pointedly, 'Did Jenny hurt herself badly when she 'fell down the stairs'?'

Pamela hated having to fib, but she'd promised her sister she wouldn't tell anyone what really happened, though from what she'd just overheard they'd worked it out for themselves. 'Yes, it was pretty bad. We had to get an ambulance for her. She wasn't awake for a while . . . and . . . and it was really scary.'

'Oh, sweetheart, it must have been terrifying

for you all, especially Jenny. Was your dad at home? Did he call the ambulance?'

Pamela suddenly felt she was being interrogated and hoped she wouldn't crack under pressure. 'Yes, er, no . . . he . . . er . . . he was out,' she stuttered nervously.

Her gran seemed to be scrutinising her, then asked, 'Did he go out before or after Jenny fell down the stairs?'

'I . . . I think it was before.'

'Are you trying to hide something from me, young lady? I don't know who you think you're protecting, but I know when you're fibbing to me.'

Her gran's voice was unusually stern, and Pamela could feel herself beginning to crumple. 'Oh, Gran,' she blurted and felt a sob catch in her throat. It was as if all the fear and sadness she'd bottled up for weeks were suddenly unleashed. 'I thought he was going to kill her . . . I thought he was going to kill us all!'

Pamela ran to Edith, dropped to her knees and then cried into her gran's lap.

Edith softly stroked her hair, and soothed, 'It's all right, love, you're safe here.'

Pamela wished she could stay in her gran's flat forever, away from her father's aggression and the pain he caused. It wasn't possible, though: there was no room, and anyway, they all needed to escape, not just her.

With her head still in the old woman's lap, Pamela didn't see her gran look up at Craig and silently mouth, 'I'd like to kill the bastard.'

6

Jenny hadn't slept well. It wasn't just the discomfort of her ribs that had kept her awake; she hadn't been able to shift thoughts of Craig from her head. She managed to get out of bed and dressed and was about to creep downstairs when she heard a small voice.

'Morning, Jen,' chirped Timmy as he emerged from his bedroom, rubbing his eyes.

'Good morning,' Jenny answered quietly. 'Is your brother still asleep?'

'No, I'm awake,' Peter announced as he followed his older brother.

'Yeah, me and all, thanks to you two little brats,' Gloria called from the bedroom.

Jenny grinned at the boys, and asked, 'Did you jump on her again?'

'No,' Timmy answered, 'we drew on her face.'

'You didn't! She'll have your guts for garters. Come on, get yourselves downstairs and let her have a lie-in.'

The truth was, Jenny didn't want the boys' jovialities to disturb their dad. Luckily, he was a heavy sleeper, especially after he'd had a good drink.

In the kitchen, Jenny gave the boys a glass of milk and made them some bread and jam, along with a pot of tea for herself. It hurt to lift the kettle, but she hid the discomfort from her brothers.

'Where's Pamela?' Timmy asked.

'She went to stay with Gran last night.'

'Can we go to see her today? Gran might have made some cakes!'

'Not today, but we'll go next Saturday,' Jenny answered. Craig had said that Gran was fine, just shaky, but she wasn't sure the old woman would be up to seeing the boys.

'Can we go to the common then?'

'Well, if you stop being mean to Gloria, she might take you. You can take the old bread and feed the ducks.'

'Cor yes,' Timmy said excitedly. 'I like the ducks, but the geese are a bit frightening.'

'I don't want to go to the common,' Peter said sullenly.

'Why not?' Jenny asked.

'I just don't want to. I want to stay at home today.'

'But it's going to be a lovely sunny day and you'll have lots of fun.'

'I don't care. I'm not going!' Peter said firmly, then sat with his arms folded.

'Don't be daft, Peter. You're coming with us,' Timmy told him.

'No, and you can't make me!'

Jenny pulled out a chair and sat opposite Peter. 'No one is going to make you do anything you don't want to, but can you tell me why you want to stay at home today?'

Peter's bottom lip began to quiver, and his big blue eyes glistened. 'Mummy might come to see us today,' he cried, 'and I want to ask her if I can live with her.'

Jenny's heart broke for the boy. 'I don't think she's coming today and I'm sorry, Peter, but I doubt she's got room for you. Anyway, I don't want you to leave us. We'd all miss you too much.'

'If Peter goes to live with Mum, can I go too?' Timmy asked.

'No, I'm afraid the two of you aren't going anywhere.'

'But you said I don't have to do anything I don't want to . . . and I don't want to live here!' Peter cried, his cheeks now wet with tears and his nose beginning to run.

'I know that's what I said, but that was about going to the common.' Jenny turned her head and said, 'Do me a favour, Timmy, go and get your brother a hanky to wipe his nose.'

As the boy ran off, Jenny pushed her chair back and went over to Peter. She crouched beside him, placing her arm across his shoulders. 'Come on, darling, stop crying now. Why don't you want to live with us?' As soon as she'd asked the question, Jenny regretted it and knew what his answer would be.

'I do . . . but . . . but . . . '

'It's all right, I know,' Jenny interrupted. 'Dad frightens you.'

Peter nodded his head and asked, 'Does he scare you too?'

'Sometimes, but when he's in a bad mood it doesn't last long. He soon gets over it and goes out to the pub.'

'But he hits you . . . and I think he's going to hit me too.'

'No, he won't. I won't allow him to. Dad will never lay a hand on you, not while I have breath in my body. I promise.'

'Really? Cross your heart and hope to die? Stick a needle in your eye?'

'Yes, I really, really, promise.'

'But last time he hit you, an ambulance took you away,' Peter said and began crying again.

'But I'm fine now, so you've nothing to worry about.'

Timmy appeared with a hanky, scowling as he said, 'When I grow up, if I see Dad bashing you I'm going to kick his head in!'

'Timmy, you mustn't say things like that. Violence doesn't solve anything. When Mum walked out on us, Dad could've sent you to live in a children's home, but he didn't. He does his best, and all right, he loses his temper now and then, but as I said before, he soon gets over it.'

Peter sniffed, took the hanky and wiped his nose while Timmy said, 'It might be nice in a children's home.'

'No, love, it wouldn't be nice at all. Now come on, Peter, no more tears, and no more talk of kicking Dad's head in, Timmy,' she said sternly, then, trying to lift their spirits, she forced a smile and said, 'Now, who would like a biscuit, a nice custard cream?'

There were only three biscuits left and now that Gloria was out of work, and Jenny on unpaid sick leave, she doubted they'd be having any more biscuits in the house for a while. For now, though, two enthusiastic hands shot in the air, and both boys piped up, 'Me, I'd like one please.'

Jenny handed her brothers the treat and saved the last one for Gloria. The girl had a terrible sweet tooth. With all the sugary snacks Gloria ate she should have been the size of a bus, yet somehow she managed to keep her trim figure. 'Now that's sorted I'll ask Gloria if she'll take the pair of you to the common later.'

'Did I hear my name mentioned?' Gloria asked, as though on cue as she walked into the kitchen. 'Oh, biscuits, lovely. Where's mine?'

'In the tin. I saved you the last one, but surely you'll want your breakfast first.'

'One biscuit won't spoil it,' Gloria said, and raided the tin.

'I said you'd take the boys to the common later.'

'No, not today,' Gloria answered.

'Please, Gloria, please take us . . . ' Timmy begged.

'Nope, I've got far better things to do. You'll have to wait for Pamela to get back from Gran's.'

'What better things?' Jenny asked.

'I've got my hair to set, my nails to paint, my skirt to take up and then I might see if Dennis is hanging around the ABC Café this afternoon.'

'I see, and that's clearly far more important than taking your brothers out today.'

'Well, yes,' Gloria said, 'of course it is.'

'But we want to go to the common,' Peter cried.

'I'll have to take you, but I can only walk slowly so no running off,' Jenny told them and as they ran around whooping with glee, she said to Gloria, 'It's a fair way to the common and I hope I can manage.'

'I'm sure you'll be fine, and a bit of fresh air will do you good.'

Jenny wasn't surprised by her sister's selfishness. What Gloria wanted always came first, but at least she'd taken up the reins while Jenny had been out of action. However, now that she was out of bed, it was obvious that Gloria considered her well enough to take over again.

★   ★   ★

Craig couldn't get Jenny off his mind, but now it was because he was so worried about her. From what Pamela had said last night, things were beyond bad with their father. He sounded like a nasty piece of work, and not a man that Craig would like to go up against, but he couldn't stand by and do nothing. Craig wasn't a fighter, and he'd thought long and hard about what he could do, before he finally came up with what he hoped was a solution. He wasn't sure Jenny would go for it, but he had to try. It wasn't ideal, but at least she'd be safe and anything had to be better than living in fear for her life.

Feeling determined, he jumped out of bed and quickly washed and dressed. There was no time for breakfast; he had to act fast. Living under her father's roof left Jenny in imminent danger. Henry had hospitalised his daughter. What if he went for her again?

69

As Craig marched to her house, he planned what he was going to say. By the time he arrived, he thought it was clear in his mind and knew it was the right thing to do. He'd never forgive himself if Jenny was hurt again and he hadn't tried to protect her. He knocked and Gloria answered the door. She looked different without all her make-up on. Younger, more like a child than a woman.

'You again,' she said, grinning. 'It seems you can't stay away. I suppose you'd like to see Jenny?'

'Yes, please.'

'I'll tell her you're here. After all, who am I to stand in the way of true love?'

Though a younger sister, she seemed to Craig much bolder than Jenny, especially when she called over her shoulder, 'Jenny, your handsome lover-boy is at the door . . . again.'

Craig's brows rose as two lively boys charged out. 'Who are you?' the taller of them asked.

Jenny had spoken of her brothers with deep affection, but this was the first time he'd seen them. 'I'm Craig, I live upstairs from your gran. What's your name?'

'Peter.'

'Hello, Peter.'

The other boy said something, but as he was running up and down the short front path, Craig couldn't quite get what he said.

'Sorry, I'm deaf so I have to see your lips to know what you're saying. Can you stand still and repeat it, please?'

'You're deaf?' Timmy asked, looking astounded.

'Yes, that's right, but I can understand what you are saying by the way your lips move.'

'I said, my name is Timmy.'

'Pleased to meet you, Timmy,' Craig said, smiling down at the lad.

'So, you can't hear nothing?' Timmy asked then turned his back for a few moments before spinning round again. 'Did you hear what I said then?'

'Nope, afraid not.'

'Blimey, Peter, he really *is* deaf!' Then Timmy looked at Craig again, and asked, 'But you know what I'm saying now.'

'Yes, I do.'

'Wow, can you teach me how to lip-read? I'd know what Terry and Bruce are saying when they're whispering to each other.'

'Who are they?'

'A couple of boys in my class. Will you teach me? Will you?'

Before Craig could answer, Jenny appeared and said, 'That's enough, boys, go inside.'

'But I want to talk to Craig,' Timmy whined.

'I said go inside. You can talk to Craig another time. Now do as you're told or there'll be no trip to the common.'

'Hi, Jenny. Did you just say you're off to the common today?' Craig asked.

'Hello and yes.'

'I know you wasn't expecting to see me today but I have to talk to you. May I join you?'

'Go on, Jen, say yes!' Peter and Timmy urged.

'If you want — looks like I'm outnumbered anyway,' Jenny answered, smiling at Craig. 'Peter, ask Gloria to start making us some sandwiches.'

The boys skipped inside, and looking at Jenny, Craig saw she was blushing again. He found it so endearing.

'Is everything all right? Is my gran OK?' she whispered.

'Yes, as far as I know. That's not what I want to see you about.'

'Oh, what is it then?'

'We'll talk at the common,' Craig answered. He was eager to pitch his idea to her, but on the doorstep wasn't the best place.

Jenny frowned worriedly, then said, 'I'd invite you in, but my dad's still in bed and I don't want to disturb him. If you don't mind waiting out here, I'll get myself and the boys ready now.'

'Of course I don't mind,' Craig told her, thinking it was probably just as well that they didn't disturb her father. He wasn't sure how he'd react to the man and though he wasn't one for violence, he wouldn't stand for him laying into Jenny again.

Jenny quietly closed the door and Craig meandered up the street. He tried to keep his mind focused on his proposition, but seeing her again had flustered him. She did something to him, something he couldn't explain, but he had to admit, he liked it. Whatever it took, Craig was determined he'd protect her from her father's brutality and now could only hope she'd allow him to.

★ ★ ★

Though still in pain, Jenny did her best to hurry up the boys. She stuffed sandwiches into a shopping bag along with some stale bread and a bottle of lemonade.

'Calm down, Jen, it's only a stroll on the common,' Gloria said.

'I know but look at the state of me, I'm a complete mess.'

'You look fine.'

'Where are my shoes?' she asked frantically, her eyes darting around.

'In your bedroom I should think.'

Jenny couldn't run upstairs, but walked as quickly as she could, to find her father emerging from his room.

'What's all the fucking commotion about?' he growled.

'Sorry, Dad. The boys are a bit excited because I'm taking them to the common, that's all.'

'Good. Get a move on and get them out from under my feet then. Where's your sister? I want some breakfast.'

'Gloria's downstairs, Pamela has gone to stay with Gran 'cos she had a fall.'

'Huh, your mother should be looking after the old girl. Is your gran all right?'

'Yes, just a bit shaky, I think.'

'Right. I ain't got time for your mother, but Edith's a good woman. 'Ere, take this and get her some flowers or something . . . make sure you say it's from you kids though. I don't want her thinking I've gone soft in the head.'

Jenny tried not to show her astonishment as

her dad fished in his trouser pocket and handed her five bob. She muttered, 'Er, right, thanks.'

He barged past her and she stood bewildered as he stomped downstairs. This was turning into a day of surprises. Once in her room, Jenny shoved the money into her purse, put her shoes on, ran a brush through her tangled hair and grabbed a light coat. Although she was still sore, the thought of meeting Craig muffled her pain. She took a last quick glance in the mirror and decided there wasn't any need to pinch her cheeks: they were red enough already. Too red, in fact, but there was nothing she could do about her persistent blushing.

She drew a long, deep breath, which was a mistake and she gasped at the pain in her ribs. Shallow breathing was all right, and they'd have to walk slowly, but she was thrilled that Craig was joining them. Slowly she walked downstairs, to see Timmy and Peter hovering at the street door. 'Come on then, boys, let's go,' she said, and called, 'See ya later.'

Craig was casually standing close by, and as she walked up to him, once again her stomach somersaulted. She tried to act cool, though felt sure her glowing neck and cheeks gave her away. 'Hello again.'

'That was quick,' Craig said cheerfully.

'We was ready before Jenny,' Timmy piped up.

'And we've got a picnic,' Peter added, then they ran on ahead.

Craig took the shopping bag from her and frowned. 'You look a bit uncomfortable. Is this walk going to be too much for you?'

'As long as we take it slowly I'll be fine.'

The boys were in a rush, and Jenny had to call them back a few times as they ran on ahead, but eventually they reached the common and stood by the pond.

'Can we have some bread for the ducks now?' Peter asked.

'Yes, here you go,' Jenny answered. She took the bag from Craig, fished out the stale bread and broke it in two. The boys merrily skipped off and Jenny smiled. It was nice to see them so happy and carefree, especially after how upset Peter had been earlier.

Craig removed his jacket and laid it out on the grass bank. He offered Jenny his hand and helped her to sit down. 'Penny for them,' he said.

'I was just thinking how lovely it is to see the boys relaxed and having fun.'

'I know it's none of my business, but I can't imagine it's easy for any of you with your dad being the way he is.'

He sounded so sincere and sympathetic that Jenny found herself opening up to him. 'No, it's not easy. The boys are too young to understand why my dad behaves the way he does. When he loses his temper, it frightens them, and while my sister Pam lives on her nerves, my other sister Gloria is filled with hate. I just wish there was more I could do to protect them.'

'Well, maybe there is.'

'I don't see how,' Jenny answered. She'd thought long and hard but hadn't come up with a solution. She couldn't afford to rent somewhere for them all and even if she tried to

75

squeeze them all in to her gran's flat, she knew that would be the first place her dad would look.

'That's what I wanted to talk to you about. I think you should all move in with me.'

Jenny gasped. Craig's suggestion had taken her by surprise and the idea seemed ludicrous. 'But . . . but we can't — '

'Wait, hear me out. I realise space would be tight, but me and the boys could sleep in the lounge and you girls could have the bedroom. It would only have to be temporary. With my earnings, plus yours and Gloria's wages, we could look for somewhere bigger.'

She gawped at Craig and spluttered, 'No . . . no . . . we . . . we can't move in with you. What would people say? I . . . I'd be labelled a slut.'

'We can put them straight, tell them we aren't a couple, and anyway, who cares what people think? This is about getting you all out of harm's way. I can't stand the thought of your dad hurting you again and though I know it isn't ideal, you'd be safe. What do you think?'

Jenny didn't know what to think. 'It's mad, bonkers and . . . and why would you do that for us?'

Craig rolled his eyes, then took Jenny's hand. 'Isn't it obvious? I know we've only just met, but I like you, Jenny. I want to protect you, the boys and your sisters.'

Jenny gazed into Craig's eyes and felt his offer was genuine. There was no ulterior motive, just an honest offer of help. She was worried about her dad's increasing violence, and longed to take her siblings to safety, so Craig's suggestion made sense. It could work, but her reputation would be in shreds. Could she stand the pointing fingers and the gossip? 'I . . . I don't know, Craig. Thank you so much for your offer, but I . . . I need to think about it.'

'What's there to think about? I don't want to sound like I'm rushing you, but if your father kicks off again and hurts you, I'd never forgive myself for not putting pressure on you to agree.'

'I know, but, it just doesn't seem right. Are you sure you've thought this through? You'd be giving up a lot by having my family living with you.'

'Jenny, I've been thinking about it all night. Like I said, it wouldn't be for long and then we'd find somewhere bigger, more suitable, but for now, I'd know that your father couldn't get to you and I'd sacrifice anything for that sort of peace of mind.'

Jenny was touched by Craig's concern and had to hold back from crying. The idea was appealing, but she couldn't shake the worry about what people would think.

Craig squeezed her hand. 'I didn't have any breakfast, so what have you put in those sandwiches? Let's eat, it'll give you a moment to think.'

Jenny pulled one out, 'I'm afraid it's only fish paste.'

'That'll do me,' he said, biting into it with relish.

With her mind all over the place, Jenny watched the boys playing. She thought about

Peter's behaviour earlier, how he didn't want to live with their father, and of Pamela who was so afraid of him that she constantly wet the bed. What would their father's reaction be if they all left? He wouldn't know they were just upstairs from Edith. Yet why was she thinking about that? It was impossible, they couldn't all move in with Craig! Could they?

7

'I sure do love you, Lizzie, you're one hell of a gal!'

Lizzie was straddled across Dwight's naked body. She ran her finger down his bare chest. 'Yes, I am, and don't you forget it,' she said before climbing off him and pulling her blouse around her chest. She walked over to the desk in his bedroom and took a cigarette from a packet. As she lit it, the smoke curled up and made hazy circles in the sunlight beaming through the window.

'They don't make gals like you in the US of A, not in Alabama where my momma and papa live.'

'Yeah, I'm unique. You won't find many like me in Balham either,' she said, then sat on his desk with her legs slightly parted.

'You're such a tease. It's only ten in the morning and you've already had me up twice. A man needs a bit of time to recover.'

'If you need to keep your strength up, Dwight, how about you make us some of those delicious pancakes?'

'I can do that . . . anything for my pretty gal.'

Dwight stood up and pulled on his under-pants. He winked at Lizzie then sloped off to the kitchen. Lizzie threw herself down on his bed and pulled hard on her cigarette as she stared up at the ceiling. She liked being with Dwight in his small flat. She thought his strange accent made him sound a bit thick, but he treated her like a queen. From what he'd told her, she'd learned he was an American GI who'd been posted to London during the war. He'd got a British woman in the family way and had felt obliged to marry her. Lizzie thought that was typical of him, he was so polite. As it turned out, the woman wasn't pregnant and passed away a few years later. He'd never been back to Alabama, though he said he would one day, and when he did, he'd take Lizzie with him.

She was so wrapped up in Dwight that she hadn't given a thought to her kids in a while, but Lizzie wasn't worried about them. They were housed and fed, which was more than she'd been at times. The smell of the sweet pancakes wafted through to the bedroom and she could hear Dwight whistling a tune she didn't recognise. She wondered if it was one he'd written himself. He played guitar in a band. That's how she'd met him. She'd been swaying to the jazz and had caught his eye. It had only been a week ago, but she already had her feet firmly rooted under his table.

She heard Dwight call, 'Hey, pretty lady, your breakfast is ready.'

'I'll take it in bed, thanks,' she called back, and puffed up the pillow behind her.

Dwight came in carrying a tray and asked, 'Is there anything else you'd like?'

Lizzie eyed him up and down, from his broad, toned chest, to his long, muscular legs. 'Yes, there is,' she purred, 'But after breakfast.'

★ ★ ★

After some gentle coaxing, Craig had finally persuaded Jenny that moving in with him would be for the best. She'd eventually agreed but he smiled as he recalled her firm stipulation that there was to be no funny business between them. He'd assured her that he would never take advantage of her, though how she thought that could happen with six of them crammed into his small flat was beyond him. He was just relieved that she'd no longer be subjected to her father's sickening temper.

Since then he'd had a week of frantic activity, arranging extra beds and bedding to accommodate the impending arrival of the Lombard siblings later today. With the beds sorted, he went downstairs to give Edith an update.

'So, they're all moving in today? Doing a runner whilst Henry's at work?'

'Yes, that's right. I reckon they'll be here in about an hour.'

He was pacing the room and repeatedly looking out of the front window.

'Craig, will you please sit down! It's making me dizzy just looking at you.'

'Sorry. I know Jenny said to wait here for them, but I really think I should go and help. What if Henry comes home and catches them? And there's all their stuff to lug here,' Craig said, and after only just sitting down he jumped up again, 'Yes, I'll go and help, just in case.'

'Craig!' Edith shouted, 'I don't know why I'm raising me voice 'cos you can't hear me. If Jenny

81

needed you, she would have said so, wouldn't she?'

'Yes, I suppose so.'

'Right, go and make yourself useful and make us both a drink.'

Craig smiled warmly at the old woman, then said, 'Don't tell Jenny I got myself all worked up, will you?'

'No, I shan't say a word. Go on, bugger off, you silly sod. That kettle won't boil itself.'

Craig normally felt relaxed and at home in Edith's flat, but today he was fretting. He'd done everything he could to make his place comfortable for his new lodgers and hoped Jenny would like it. He made the tea and handed Edith a cup.

'I know what you're thinking, but stop worrying, young man. Jenny will be happy up there with you. You've assured me that there won't be any funny business going on over my head, yet no doubt there'll still be gossip. If I hear anything said I'll put them in their place, but all that matters to me is that Jenny will be away from her father.'

Craig hoped he could keep them all safe but worried that once Henry found out where they were, he'd come storming round to drag them all back. The man could try, and though Craig had no doubt that Henry could flatten him, he'd still fight if he had to. He shook his head as if trying to shake some sense into himself, but it was no use. He knew, if it came to it, he'd put his life on the line for Jenny.

★　★　★

Jenny still had misgivings about moving in with Craig. She knew there'd be gossip, or even women spitting at her in the street. She'd probably be ostracised too, but the thought of being beaten like a dog by her father again was far worse. They'd all be safe at Craig's, so not just for her own sake, but for the others' too, she'd agreed.

They were moving out that day, but Gloria leaned against the kitchen table with her arms folded and lips pouting. 'I ain't happy about us all being crammed into Craig's flat. I don't see why I have to go with you . . . why can't I stay here?'

Jenny looked at her sister in disbelief. The girl hated her father, so she couldn't understand why she'd want to remain living with him.

'Don't look at me like that,' Gloria snapped. 'Once you're gone, I'll have my own room at last and maybe when you ain't here he won't be as bad.'

'And maybe he'll beat you up instead of me. Have you thought about that?'

'Yeah, well, maybe he won't!'

'Gloria, listen to yourself. You sound really childish. Anyway, I'm not prepared to leave without you, so either we all stay, or we all go.'

'That's blackmail!'

'I don't care what it is. I'm only concerned for your safety. So, what will it be?'

Gloria stamped her foot and threw her arms around as she trudged out of the kitchen, shouting, 'All right, you win . . . we all go.'

Jenny momentarily closed her eyes and sighed with relief. Gloria digging her heels in was the last thing she'd expected.

'What's Gloria on about?' Timmy asked as he ran into the room with his brother.

'Yeah, where are we all going?' from Peter.

Jenny hadn't told her brothers they were going to live with Craig for fear of one them accidently saying something in front of their father. She'd warned her sisters to say nothing too, but now Gloria had let the cat out of the bag. 'Right, sit down, I've got something to tell you.'

The brothers exchanged a glance, then quickly sat at the table.

'Do you remember Craig?'

'Course we do. He's the deaf bloke,' answered Timmy.

'He lives in a flat above Gran, and we're all moving in with him. Not Dad though, he'll be staying here.'

'What, forever? Not just for three days or seven years? We're going to live with Craig forever? Timmy asked.

'Yes,' she said, watching Peter's face light up. 'Eventually we'll have to find a bigger place, but we won't be coming back here. Craig's flat is a bit small, and you two will have to share the front room with him while we girls have the bedroom. Hopefully it won't be for long. I'm back at work on Monday, and I'm sure Gloria will find a job soon, so we'll be able to find a larger flat or even a little house to rent.'

Gloria stamped back into the kitchen. 'Are you still going on about me finding a job? I told you, Queenie said I can work part-time in her fag shop, starting next week.'

'Yes, but I'm not happy about that. You need to be bringing in full-time wages, and that Dennis upstairs will be too much of a distraction for you.'

'Stop telling me what I can and can't do! It's bad enough that you try to dictate where I work and who I see, but now you're telling me where I've got to live too. You're not my mother!' Gloria glowered at her sister.

'No and thank goodness for that! I'd be ashamed to have such a brat as a daughter!' Jenny snapped. She hadn't meant to be so harsh, but now it was said she couldn't retract it. Her sister really was trying her patience.

Gloria threw her a vile look, but Jenny could see it was masking her hurt, then she spun on her heels and walked out.

'Gloria . . . wait . . . I'm sorry,' Jenny called.

Pamela then slipped into the room and asked, 'What's the matter with Gloria? What's going on?'

'I said something I shouldn't and now she's got a strop on,' Jenny replied, rubbing her forehead in despair. She'd hoped this would be a happy day, but it didn't appear to be for Gloria. 'I'll just have to grovel a bit and maybe she'll come round.'

'We're all moving into Craig's flat and Daddy isn't coming,' Peter said with gusto.

At least the boys were pleased, and though Pamela didn't show her feelings, Jenny knew she was too. 'Will you take your brothers upstairs and help them to pack their things?' she asked her sister. 'Remember, only take what they really need. There won't be room for everything.'

The boys ran upstairs with Pamela following. Jenny relished the silence as she pulled a notepad and pencil from her pocket. She sat at the table and began to write.

Dad,

I've taken the boys and my sisters to live somewhere else.

I'm sure this won't come as too much of a shock to you, and I don't suppose you'll be sad about it.

I know you did your best, but it wasn't good enough.

Take care,

Jenny

The note was short, simple and to the point. She couldn't bring herself to sign off 'with love' or to add any kisses. She didn't feel the need to spell out their reasons for leaving as she figured he must be aware of the pain he'd caused her, and how much he'd scared his own children. She pushed the note to the middle of the table and took one last look around the kitchen. It was the only home she'd ever known. She and her siblings had all been born in this house, but she wasn't sad to say goodbye to it. Any happy memories she'd once had were tarnished now by her father's viciousness.

Their home had been ruined the day their mother had left it.

★ ★ ★

Later that evening, Henry was fuming as he marched out of the pub and stomped home. He hadn't liked hearing that Lizzie was now hooked up with an American musician, and she'd already been throwing rumours around about marrying the bloke. One week! She'd been shacked up with the wanker for one week and she was talking wedding bells.

'Over my dead body,' Henry muttered through gritted teeth. She couldn't marry the idiot if she wasn't divorced, and there wasn't a hope in hell of him agreeing to one.

When he arrived home, Henry was too wrapped up in spiteful thoughts about Lizzie to realise that his kids weren't around. He marched through to the kitchen, expecting his dinner would be in the oven, but he couldn't eat. Instead, he reached to the top of the larder for his bottle of whiskey. He dragged out a wooden chair and slumped down, then unscrewed the bottle to take several large glugs of the alcohol before shouting, 'Where the fuck is everyone? Jenny!'

As Henry was about to take another swig from the bottle, he noticed the note on the table. He reached out, grabbed it and read it through bleary eyes. 'Huh, so you've all fucked off . . . just like your mother, the fucking lot of you! See if I care. See how you manage without my pay packet.'

He read the note again, but it didn't occur to him that he could be the reason they'd left. He didn't look at himself and question why. He screwed the note up and threw it to the floor before drinking from the bottle again. Sod the lot of them. His house and his life would be quiet from now on and that suited him fine. He'd have more money in his pocket, and with the kids gone there'd be no excuse for Lizzie to turn up. He might miss the boys a bit, but he didn't want to set eyes on any of the bitches again; no, he didn't want to see his wife or his daughters.

8

It was mid-June and Jenny had been living at Craig's for a month now. She'd felt awkward at first, especially about Craig seeing her first thing in the morning with her wild red hair. Now, though, she was more relaxed and they'd all settled into a routine. All except for Gloria. Jenny had expected her sister to show Craig a bit more gratitude but instead she was often nasty to him and made it quite clear that she didn't enjoy living there. Jenny took some solace in knowing they'd all be moving to a larger home, just as soon as she and Craig had saved enough money. She hoped Gloria would then be happier and a bit more charitable towards her brothers and sister too.

Jenny heard a tap on the front door and felt herself tense. She still feared her father would find them, though as far as she knew he hadn't been to their gran's to look for them. She glanced across at Pamela. The girl was sitting on the sofa eating her breakfast but had turned deathly white.

'What's wrong?' Craig asked.

'There's someone knocking on the door,' Jenny answered.

'What, up here?'

'Yes . . . w-w-what if . . . '

'Don't worry, I'll answer it,' Craig said reassuringly.

Moments later, Jenny heard muffled laughter and once again relaxed. Then Craig returned to the front room carrying a large box wrapped in brown paper. He looked to be struggling so Jenny suspected the package was heavy.

'It was a delivery I've been expecting. Edith had let him in downstairs.'

'What's in the box?' Timmy asked as he and Peter ran in from the bathroom.

'A surprise,' Craig answered and placed it in the middle of the floor.

'Is it a surprise for us?' Peter asked.

'It's for all of us.'

Timmy ran forward and sat next to the box. 'Can we open it?'

'Wait for Gloria, then we can all open it together.'

'I wouldn't worry about her, she'll be ages in the bedroom doing her face,' Jenny said. As much as she loved her sister, she didn't want Gloria's mood or scathing comments spoiling the moment when the mystery in the box was unveiled.

'All right then. Go on, boys, you can open it.'

Jenny watched with delight as her brothers tore at the brown paper, then Craig helped them. She heard Peter squeal, and Timmy jumped up and down excitedly. 'What is it?' she asked, intrigued.

Peter spun around to look at her and said, 'It's a television set! I can watch *Andy Pandy*!'

Jenny gasped. Many homes now had televisions, but they'd never had one. Part of her wanted to be annoyed at Craig for being so extravagant when they were supposed to be

90

saving for a home, but seeing the thrilled faces of her brothers melted away her annoyance. 'Wow, that must have cost a packet,' she commented, but with a smile.

'Actually, it didn't. My uncle sent it for us. He said he hardly uses it and thought we'd appreciate it.'

'How kind of him. Yes, the boys will definitely appreciate it, I should think even Gloria will like it too.'

'What will I like?' Gloria asked as she sauntered into the room.

Jenny thought her sister looked very pretty and glamorous but it was a shame about her miserable face. Perhaps the surprise would cheer her up? 'Craig's uncle has sent us a television set and I said you'd like it.'

'Yeah, right, as if I'd ever get a chance to watch anything that I'd like to see.'

Jenny pursed her lips but didn't respond. Nothing seemed to be good enough for Gloria lately and her negative attitude was beginning to get on Jenny's nerves.

'Can we watch something now?' Timmy asked.

'No, not at the moment. I've got to set it up and you've got to go to school, but when you get home this evening, you can watch the television then.'

'Please, just for a little while?'

'There's no time. Come on, boys, we'll be late for school,' Pamela said, and ushered them from the room.

'I'm off too, see ya,' Gloria said and followed her siblings.

'Aren't you going to be late?' Craig asked Jenny.

'Actually, I've got the day off. The dock strike has affected the factory getting parts in time so Miss Aston offered us a day off, unpaid mind.'

'Well, seeing as I'm my own boss, how about I skive off today and we can spend it together, unless you've already got plans?'

'No, nothing planned, that would be great.'

'In that case, let's jump on the underground up to Trafalgar Square and we can have a look in the National Gallery.'

'At art?'

'Yes, why? Not your cup of tea?'

'No, not really. It's such a nice day, couldn't we just walk around London and look at the sights?'

'If that's what you want. I couldn't care less what we do, as long as I'm with you.'

Jenny could feel herself blushing again, but she felt the same. In fact, she missed Craig when she was at work and was always eager to get home to be with him. Still embarrassed by his comment, she said, 'And we could pick up some fish and chips for supper tonight.'

'Smashing,' he replied, 'I'll get this set up and then we can go.'

He lightly brushed his lips on hers before turning his attention to the television. Jenny was left feeling like an electric current was buzzing through her. Even the slightest of touches from Craig excited her and there were times when she dreamed about creeping to be beside him on the sofa at night. Of course, she wouldn't dare and

Craig had kept his promise about no funny business, so they hadn't done anything more than kiss. She would have liked to go further and she thought Craig would too, but it wasn't possible, not unless they were married.

It was odd, living together but separately, but she was so glad Craig had talked her into it. He'd rescued her, saved her life, and she'd never been happier. If only Gloria could be happy too, then everything would be perfect.

★   ★   ★

Henry woke up. Though his children had left home over a month ago, he hadn't adjusted to the silence. The house felt empty without them. He'd thought about finding them to bring them back but Jenny and Gloria were old enough to leave home and would probably refuse. That meant there'd only be Pamela to do the cooking and cleaning, along with looking after the boys, and he doubted the jumpy cow was up to it.

So far he hadn't seen Lizzie, but like a bad penny he knew she'd eventually turn up. When she did, he'd take great pleasure in telling her that all the kids had buggered off and there was no need to show her face at his door again.

Henry put the kettle on the gas to boil and decided that once and for all, he was better off without the lot of them. He had more money in his pockets, and though the house might feel empty, it was nice and quiet. He looked at his watch. He'd have to get a move on or he'd be late for work, but his stomach growled. As he removed the lid from the bread bin, Henry recoiled in disgust at the green, mouldy loaf. The milk was no better — it had curdled — and he doubted the last remaining egg would be fresh enough to eat.

Frustrated, he slumped on a chair, then kicked the one in front of him. His eyes roamed the room and he realised how much he'd let the place go. It was filthy. Plates and cups filled the sink, and flies were buzzing around. He couldn't stand it, but he had no intention of cleaning it. That was women's work, and with no daughters at home and a tart for a wife, he decided he'd have to find himself a new one. This time, though, he'd make sure she was barren and wouldn't be the sort to answer back.

9

Jenny walked towards the factory gates still on a high from the day before. They'd had a lovely day, she and Craig, but the time had flown by so quickly. He'd taken her down Carnaby Street, which had been amazing. A new restaurant had just opened that Craig told her was vegetarian. She thought that was very peculiar and couldn't imagine a dinner with just spuds and veg.

She wished they could have more days like yesterday. She'd been so carefree with Craig and all her worries had felt far behind her. She'd laughed when he'd splashed her with water from the fountain at Piccadilly Circus, and she'd giggled when he'd chased her up and down the steps of Nelson's Column, threatening to squidge an ice-cream cone in her face. Today, though, it was back to reality and Jenny prepared herself for another tedious day on the factory line.

She didn't mind the work; it was easy enough, and the factory were fair employers. The women she worked alongside were nice enough, though Jenny often found them brash and loud. They enjoyed a good gossip, but she rarely joined in. Now she hoped they wouldn't discover that she was living with Craig as she would surely become a topic of their conversation.

As Jenny approached the gates, she heard the sound of a large vehicle trundling down the road and glanced over her shoulder. She was suddenly struck with fear when, to her horror, she realised it was a dustcart. She had no idea if her father was on the truck and panicked. Instead of darting for cover, she stood transfixed, staring at the cart as it drew closer. Her breaths became fast and shallow and the world began to spin. Run, Jenny, run, she told herself, but her trembling legs wouldn't budge.

As the truck slowly passed, Jenny turned her head and followed it with her eyes. Her father wasn't riding on the back and Jenny's body slumped with relief. She took a few deep breaths and tried to calm herself. That had been close, far closer than she felt comfortable with. She had no idea how her father would have reacted if he'd seen her, but it was something she'd rather not discover.

Jenny resumed walking but picked up her pace. She was safe in the factory, out of harm's way. She was safe at home too, thanks to Craig, and wished she was back there now, secure in his reassuring arms. He knew what she'd been through and had sworn he'd always look after her. She believed he would, but he couldn't be with her every minute of every day, and moments like just now made her realise how much she still lived in terror of her father.

★　★　★

Gloria detested every minute of living in Craig's flat. Being in such close proximity to everyone drove her mad and she began to dislike them all.

96

Jenny was a goody-two-shoes, Pamela was a wimp, the boys were irritating and Craig, well, Craig was deaf and as far as she was concerned that was a good enough reason not to like him. At least she could make scathing remarks about him behind his back and he couldn't hear her. It was something she did regularly to amuse herself, much to Jenny's disgust.

Gloria grimaced. Then there was her gran living downstairs and too close. She was always spoiling the boys and singing Jenny's praises. Gloria couldn't stand listening to her, so she'd stopped popping in to see the old woman. She didn't miss her.

She'd also defied Jenny and was now working part-time in Queenie's. She refused to hand over any of her wages, using the excuse that she didn't eat at Craig's so why should she contribute? Craig didn't have to pay extra rent because they were living there. And what Jenny gave him would cover any larger bills. The sooner she got out of there, Gloria thought, the better.

That morning, she stood behind the shop counter and smiled wryly when she heard Dennis's footsteps above. He was out of his bed at last, and Gloria knew he'd be down to see her soon. She quickly grabbed her handbag to pull out a compact and her red lipstick, making the effort as always to look nice for her man. They'd been seeing each other for three weeks now, since the morning when he'd called into the shop and she'd caught his eye. Gloria would often slip up to his room after work. It made working in Queenie's far more enjoyable.

'Hello, gorgeous, how's my favourite girl this morning?' Dennis drawled as he sauntered into the shop.

'I'm not just your favourite girl, I'm your only girl,' Gloria said, and slipped him a packet of cigarettes. She had no intention of putting the money for them in the till. She would often pinch a bob or two as well. She reasoned it was no more than she deserved, since Queenie paid such crap wages.

'Are you coming up to mine later when you've finished?'

'Yeah, but can't you stay down here for a bit and keep me company? It's quiet today and I'm bored,' Gloria asked, fluttering her eyelashes.

'Queenie doesn't like me hanging about in the shop.'

'Well, Queenie isn't here, is she?'

'All right, but only for half an hour.'

'Thanks, Dennis. That's cheered me up.'

'Why, what are you unhappy about?'

'Everything! You're the only good thing in my life. I hate living at Craig's. Can you imagine what it's like? Six of us all crammed into a one-bedroom flat. Every time I go in the bathroom, someone starts hammering on the door for me to hurry up. There's no privacy or anything. Gawd, I could go on, but I don't want to bore you.'

Dennis put his hand under her chin and tilted her face up, his own just inches from hers. 'Move in with me then?'

They were the words Gloria had been

desperate to hear. 'But what about your mum? Won't she mind?'

'Bugger my mother. You'll be in my room with me. It's my home too so I can have whoever I want to stay with me.'

'Oh, Dennis,' Gloria squealed, and threw her arms around his neck. 'You're the best!'

★   ★   ★

As soon as she'd done her hours in the shop, Gloria rushed to Craig's flat, eager to collect her things and move in with Dennis. This was a dream come true for her. She'd be living with the man she loved instead of a family who got on her nerves.

When she arrived, the flat was empty. Pamela and the boys were at school, and Jenny and Craig were at work. Before grabbing a bag, she glanced at the television set in the corner of the lounge. How stupid, she thought, there was barely enough room in the place already, without adding that monstrosity.

She quickly shoved some clothes into the bag, then dashed to the bathroom to pick up her toothbrush and bubble bath. The bottle was half-empty, so she guessed her brothers had been using it again. It was just another thing that annoyed her and reinforced her decision to leave.

Gloria was about to leave, but then as an afterthought decided she'd better write them a note. If she just went missing, Jenny would turn up at the shop looking for her and no doubt there'd be an argument. After rummaging in the kitchen drawers she found an old envelope and a pen, then quickly scribbled a few lines about where she was. To appease Jenny, she said she'd pop in to see them soon. That should do, she thought, keen to get back to Dennis, and she left the note on the shelf above the fireplace.

When she flew back downstairs and outside, Gloria paused for a moment, lifting her face to the sun's warmth. She felt invigorated and free, no longer constrained by her family and their problems. There'd be nobody to tell her what to do or when to do it. No responsibility of young children. Her life was finally her own, and she intended to enjoy it.

★ ★ ★

Craig arrived home before Jenny to be greeted by Pamela looking more anxious than usual. 'What's troubling you?' he asked as he took off his work boots.

Pamela didn't say anything but handed him a note. The writing was scribbled, probably rushed, and difficult to decipher, but once he read it Craig's heart sank. This was sure to upset Jenny. 'Oh, blimey,' he said.

Peter and Timmy were playing with their toy cars, but Peter looked up and asked, 'What's going on?'

'It's all right, mate. Nothing to worry about.'

Jenny arrived home minutes later, breezing through the door looking happy. 'Hello, you lot,' she said. 'It's a scorcher out there today.'

Craig didn't want to break the bad news to

her, but knew he had no choice. He stood in front of her, and the second Jenny saw his face, her own dropped.

'What is it?' she asked. 'It's not my father, is it? I saw a dustcart earlier but I don't think he was on it. Has he been round here on the warpath?'

'No, love, but come and sit down. Pam, take your brothers to your room or down to see your gran,' Craig said.

Once the room was clear, Jenny looked at him, searching for answers. 'You're worrying me,' she whispered.

'It's not that bad but read this.'

Jenny took the note and gasped. 'She can't do this. They can't live together, they're not married! I'm going straight round there, and if I have to I'll drag her back screaming and shouting.'

'Do you think that's wise? I mean, you know how strong-willed she is.'

'Gloria is hardly more than a child and that Dennis is no good for her. Oh, the silly, silly girl. I can't just leave her there.'

'Right then, I'll come with you.'

★ ★ ★

After ensuring that Pamela and the boys were all right with their gran, Jenny walked beside Craig in silence. Her mind was in turmoil thinking about how she would deal with her sister. Craig was right, Gloria was strong-willed, and Jenny doubted she'd be able to talk any sense into her. If Gloria refused to come home, it was unlikely she'd be able to drag her back.

A narrow door next to Queenie's shop opened onto stairs that led up to Dennis's flat. At the top, Jenny rang the doorbell. Thelma, his mother, answered it. She was a skinny woman with a deeply lined and drawn face. Jenny had never seen her without a cigarette hanging from the side of her mouth, and her black hair was always in curlers, covered with a scarf. She seldom cracked a smile, and when she spoke her voice was hard.

'I guessed you'd turn up when you heard.'

'Gloria left a note saying she was here. Is she in?'

'Yeah. She's just like your mother, that one, as bold as bleedin' brass. I told her I don't want her here but the pair of them are in Dennis's room and taking not a blind bit of notice of me. Come in. You can try talking to her. I hope she'll listen to you, but I somehow doubt it.'

As Jenny stepped inside, Craig behind her, Thelma asked, 'Who's this then? Your boyfriend? I've heard talk that you're living together.'

'Er, yes, but it's not like that. We share a flat but sleep in separate rooms.'

'It doesn't matter to me what you do. It ain't none of my business and all I care about is getting that sister of yours out of my house. Go on through there, second on your left.'

Jenny and Craig stood in the hallway outside Dennis's door as Thelma disappeared into another room. Jenny tapped nervously, then waited.

'Go away,' Dennis shouted.

'It's Jenny . . . I'd like to talk to Gloria.'

'Tough. She doesn't want to talk to you.'

Jenny looked at Craig, but he couldn't hear what was being said through the door.

'Gloria . . . please open the door. We need to talk.'

She heard some muffled giggles and frantic whispers, then the door eventually opened. Gloria stood there, her chest pushed out defiantly as she said, 'I'm not coming back with you, so if that's all you've come to say, forget it.'

She went to close the door again, but Jenny pushed against it and pleaded, 'Wait. At least listen to what I've got to say.'

There was a pause, then Gloria prompted, 'Go on then, spit it out.'

'I know it's not easy, the six of us in a small flat, but we're working hard to change that. We think we'll have enough money saved for a deposit on a bigger place soon, maybe even a house. Please, Gloria, come home.'

'No way. I'm happy where I am.'

'But you can't live here. You're not married.'

'That's rich, coming from you,' Gloria sneered. 'You and Craig are living together too.'

'That's different and you know it. Craig and I don't share a bed.'

'No, you're too bloody prudish for anything like that!'

Jenny heard Dennis snigger. 'You can't stay,' Jenny insisted, 'Anyway, Thelma doesn't want you living here.'

'Well I do, so tough,' Dennis said as he came to stand next to Gloria.

Jenny ignored him. 'Please, Gloria, come home. You can help me to find a nice house and Dennis can start courting you properly.'

Gloria laughed. 'Listen to yourself. Courting! Next you'll expect to be our chaperone.'

'Don't be silly. It's a bit late for that.'

'Yeah, it is, and I'm staying put, so see ya!' Gloria snapped as she slammed the door in their faces.

Jenny banged on it again and again, but Dennis just shouted for them to bugger off. She felt Craig's hand on her arm and then he said, 'Come on, love. She's not going to come back with us, so we might as well go home.'

As Craig led her along the hallway, Thelma appeared, leaning against a doorway. 'Waste of time then?' she asked.

'Yes, but I had to try. I'll see you at work tomorrow, Thelma.'

'Yeah, whatever.'

Once they were back outside, Jenny found herself having to fight back tears. She felt she'd failed her sister and worried about the girl's future. Her own reputation was probably ruined, and now Gloria's would be too. She had to do something. 'Gloria won't listen to me, but maybe she'll take notice of my mum,' she said.

Craig looked surprised, then asked, 'Do you know where she is?'

'No, but if she went round my dad's to see the boys, he'd have told her we've all left home. You'd have thought she'd look for us, maybe wait for me outside the factory to find out where we're living.'

'Perhaps she hasn't been round to your dad's.'

'It's possible. When she gets a new boyfriend my mother becomes too wrapped up in him to bother about us. She's probably shacking up with one now, but I'll find her,' Jenny told him, determined to do just that and keep her family together.

10

Timmy came running from the bedroom with one of Jenny's stockings over his head and a bag over his shoulder. He began creeping around the front room and putting ornaments in the bag. Jenny watched, wondering what her brother was up to. Next came Peter, running in from the kitchen, and she saw with amusement that he had a saucepan on his head, and his hand clutched a rolling pin.

'Stop, you're under arrest,' Peter shouted, trying to make his voice sound very deep.

Timmy giggled, and dashed to hide behind the curtains.

'We're playing cops and robbers,' Peter announced, smiling at Jenny with a big toothless grin.

'Yes, I can see that,' she said, stifling a chortle. Timmy's face looked funny with a stocking over it, his nose flattened, and Peter looked more like something from outer space than a policeman. But they were enjoying themselves, and as far as Jenny was concerned, that was all that mattered. The boys didn't seem to mind the cramped living conditions, she mused. In fact, they were thriving. Timmy's nightmares had stopped, and Peter no longer cried for their mum. Even Pamela hadn't had one of her nightly accidents for two weeks and was beginning to come out of her shell. Everyone was happy . . . except Gloria.

'Listen up, boys. Pam is downstairs cooking dinner with your gran. You'll be eating down there today, but I want you to promise me you'll be very good. Your gran has a sore knee, so no getting her running around after you, OK?'

'OK,' Peter agreed.

'Is you and Craig eating downstairs too?' Timmy asked.

'*Are* you and Craig,' Jenny corrected him. 'No, love, we've got some things to do today. We'll be back before your bedtime and Craig will finish that story he's been reading to you.'

Jenny daren't mention that she was going on a mission in search of their mother. And even if she found her, she'd already decided not to divulge where they were living. Pamela and the boys were settled, and she didn't want them to be upset by their mother's inconsistency and empty promises.

'Craig, can I come to work with you soon?' Timmy asked.

'Yes, mate. When you break up from school for the summer holidays, you can both come to my workshop.'

'What do you do again?' Peter asked.

'I make furniture, then sell it to a posh shop in Chelsea.'

'What, like this cupboard?' Timmy questioned, pointing to an elaborately carved oak sideboard.

'Yep, exactly like that. Actually, I made that one several years ago.'

'Cor, that's amazing,' Peter said, 'I never knew that! Can we make furniture when we come to work with you?'

'Absolutely. It's about time you two earned your keep,' Craig said, tongue in cheek.

Jenny noticed it was nearly midday. On Sundays the pubs only opened for a couple of hours, which didn't give them much time. 'Craig, we should go, and you boys can carry on your game downstairs.'

Craig stood up and grabbed the flat keys from the sideboard. 'Right, come on then.'

As the boys raced on ahead Jenny said, 'Honestly, I don't know where they get their energy from. They do everything at double speed.'

'They're just kids, Jen. I bet you were the same at their age,' Craig said as Pamela opened the door and the boys ran into their gran's flat.

Jenny waved at her, called out that they'd be back as soon as they could, and as the door closed again she said to Craig, 'I don't remember being so boisterous, and neither was Pamela. Gloria was a little character though. We used to call her a wild cat, but she never used to charge around like those two. I suppose it must be a boy thing. Were you like them?'

'Not that I recall, but I didn't have much opportunity to run around. My parents were very protective of me. I think they mistakenly thought that being deaf made me fragile.'

'They were probably like that because they loved you.'

'Yes, I know. I was lucky to have such wonderful parents. It could have been worse . . . '

'Like my mum and dad,' Jenny said as they walked along the road. 'Talking of which, fingers crossed that my mother's out for a drink this afternoon, or, if she isn't, that we can find someone who knows her and where she is.'

* * *

'No, Dwight, I don't want to go to the Bedford. Henry will probably be in there with all his rotten dustcart mates. How about the Duke of Devonshire?' Lizzie suggested.

'Sure, honey, I don't mind where we go, just as long as I've got my gal on my arm to show off.'

Lizzie retouched her lipstick and added a pair of ruby and diamond earrings. 'I love these, Dwight,' she said, and lifted her hair to show the earrings to their best effect.

'They look mighty pretty on you. And you never know, you might be getting a matching necklace soon. When I saw them in the shop, I thought to myself, them rubies need to be worn with my lady's luscious red lips. Now how about that, you look perfect.'

Lizzie had grown fond of Dwight's Southern drawl, but she liked it even better that he had money and wanted to spend it on her. He worked a few evenings a week playing with the band at the ABC dancehall and did two afternoons teaching music to a small group. She knew he wouldn't earn much from that, but he'd told her he received annual payouts from a legacy left him by his grandfather. Apparently, the man had discovered oil on his ranch and the whole family had benefited from the new-found wealth it generated. She'd questioned why he lived in a housing association flat, and he'd said it suited his needs. Why buy a house when he'd rather lavish his money on her? he'd drawled. That suited Lizzie, and she intended to ensure she got as much out of him as she could. One thing Lizzie had learned was that nothing lasts forever. If Dwight dumped her, at least she'd have his expensive gifts to sell or pawn.

The pub was quite a walk up the High Road, and by the time they arrived Lizzie was beginning to perspire. She was looking forward to a long, iced gin and tonic. Dwight held the door open for her, but as she was about to enter, to her dismay she heard her daughter Jenny's voice calling. She clenched her jaw and spun around. The girl always seemed to show up lately at the most inopportune times.

'Mum, thank goodness I've found you.'

'Why? What do you want?' Lizzie asked, not attempting to conceal her irritation.

'I need to speak to you about Gloria.'

Dwight stepped towards Lizzie and placed his arm around her waist. 'Are you going to introduce us?' he asked.

'If I must. Dwight, this is Jenny, my eldest daughter.'

'Jenny, such a pretty name. My second cousin is called Jenny and she's got beautiful red hair, just like yours.'

'Thanks, and this is Craig, my boyfriend.'

'Pleasure to make your acquaintance, young man,' Dwight said, and held out his hand to Craig.

'I'm sorry, I didn't catch what you said. Could

you repeat it please?' Craig asked as he shook Dwight's hand.

Jenny quickly stepped in and explained, 'Craig's deaf. He lip-reads, but he struggles with accents.'

Dwight raised his voice so that he was almost shouting, and very slowly repeated what he'd said. '*I — am — pleased — to — make — your — acquaintance.*'

'It doesn't matter how loud you yell, he still won't hear you,' Jenny snapped.

'I'll thank you not to take that tone with Dwight.'

'I'm sorry, Mum, it's just that I'm worried sick about Gloria.'

'Why? Don't tell me she's got herself up the duff?'

'No — but she's moved in with her boyfriend, so it could happen. I've asked her to come home, but she won't listen to me. I thought you could have a word with her, see if you can change her mind.'

'What's it got to do with you, or me, who she chooses to live with? It's up to her and if she's happy, leave her be.'

'But, Mum, it isn't right, she's only sixteen.'

Lizzie took a cigarette from her small clutch bag. Dwight was quick to pull a lighter from his trouser pocket and light it for her. She dragged deeply on it in an effort to calm her annoyance, then spoke. 'I don't need you to tell me how old my daughter is and at sixteen she's of an age to make up her own mind. Christ, I was barely a year older than her when I met your father.'

'So that's it? You're washing your hands of any responsibility?'

'What responsibility? She doesn't live with me, so your dad should sort her out.'

'Well, thanks, Mum, thanks a lot! She's ruining her reputation, but you don't give a damn,' Jenny said, then turned to Craig. 'Come on, I should have known this would be a waste of time.'

As Jenny marched off, Dwight said, 'Wow, Lizzie, you're nothing like my momma. She would have banged on that man's door and given my little sister a slap across her face before pinching her ear and pulling her all the way home.'

'You make your sister sound like a child, but surely Gloria is old enough to make her own decisions?'

'It's not for me to say.'

'But you think I should make her go home?'

Dwight sighed, sounding impatient as he said, 'It's your decision. Now come on, forget it for now and let's have that drink.'

★   ★   ★

'I should have known better so I don't know why I'm disappointed at my mother's reaction,' Jenny moaned as she stomped along the High Road.

'At least you tried. You've done your best, Jenny, don't give yourself such a hard time. Your family are lucky to have you looking out for them,' Craig replied.

'I suppose, but maybe my best isn't good enough.'

'Gloria's young, yes, but she's old enough to make her own choices in life. You've tried to show her right from wrong but it's down to her now. There's nothing more you can do, so let's make the most of having a few hours alone.'

Jenny felt her mood lift and finally smiled. It was rare for her and Craig to have time without her brothers around, and yes, she wasn't going to allow Gloria or her mother to spoil it. 'What have you got in mind?' she asked.

'Fancy a stroll on Wandsworth Common?'

'Yes, the sun is out, that would be nice,' Jenny answered and felt Craig's hand slip into hers.

They were soon on the edge of the common, but rather than take the well-trodden path, Craig pulled her towards a large oak tree that stood all alone.

'I've always loved this tree,' he said as they stood underneath its gnarled branches. 'When my parents died, I often used to come and sit here. I know it sounds silly, but this big old oak used to comfort me.'

'That doesn't sound silly, but how does a tree comfort you?'

'I don't know. Maybe because it's been here for hundreds of years. It's strong and wise. I always felt safe sitting with it. Look . . . '

Craig pointed down to about a foot from the base of the tree. Jenny leaned closer and saw the bark had markings.

'That's your name,' Jenny said, 'and the date . . . is that 1954?'

'Yes.'

'And here, it says 1955 ... and 1956 ... 1957 ... '

'Yep, I leave an engraving every year. Come, look,' Craig said and led Jenny around to the other side of the tree. 'Here.'

Directly in front of Jenny, at eye height, she saw a large love heart etched into the wood. Craig's initials were on one side of the heart and hers on the other. In the middle, Craig had carved the names of Peter, Timmy, Pamela and Gloria.

'Oh, my goodness, Craig, that's ... beautiful,' Jenny whispered, almost at a loss for words.

Craig came to stand closely behind her and wrapped his arms around her waist. Then she felt his warm breath on her neck and he husked into her ear, 'We'll always be together, Jenny, forever etched into this tree.'

She felt a tear escape her eye. It was so romantic and he understood how much her family meant to her. She turned around so he could see her lips and said simply, 'Thank you.'

At that moment, as a warm, gentle breeze rustled the leaves of the old oak, Jenny knew she loved Craig and just like their names in the wood, she knew she'd love him forever.

11

It had been nearly a week since Dwight had met Lizzie's eldest daughter. He'd asked about her other children, and the offhand way she spoke about them shocked him. He thought Lizzie had many good qualities, but she certainly wasn't maternal. Still, he didn't want to have babies with her, so it didn't bother him. The woman was insatiable in bed and that's why he liked her.

It was now Saturday morning and as he walked along the street Dwight felt on top of the world. The morning had started off well. He'd had a long soak in the bath and Lizzie had come into the bathroom to pleasure him with her mouth. She'd then brought him coffee and washed his back. What more could a man want? Lizzie could be the sweetest angel and she looked as pretty as one too.

They'd run out of cigarettes, so he'd left her eating ice-cream whilst he popped out to buy some, and wow, she even managed to make that look sexy. The first shop he went to didn't have his preferred brand, so as it was such a glorious morning, he decided to take a stroll to find another tobacconist.

It was some time later when Dwight came across Queenie's. He walked into the shop, brow lifting when he saw the young woman behind the counter. She was a stunner and he thought he recognised her from somewhere.

'Good morning, what can I get you?' she asked.

'I'd like a packet of Players, please. I say, Miss, I don't mean to sound fresh, but you look mighty familiar. Have we met?

'No, I don't think so. I'd remember that American accent.'

'Maybe I've seen you at the ABC dancehall? I'm in the band.'

'I've never been in there.'

'If you'd like to, I can get you free tickets.'

'No, thanks. My boyfriend wouldn't like it,' she said, placing the pack of cigarettes on the counter.

'You've got a boyfriend? Well, of course you have, a pretty young thing like you. I hope he treats you right?' Dwight said as he paid for the Players before pocketing them.

'Yes, he does, though he'd be right moody if he heard you flirting with me.'

'I apologise, I wasn't trying to flirt. This is just my ridiculous attempt at getting better acquainted with you. I love talking to beautiful ladies. I can't help myself, it's an illness,' he said, grinning.

'Illness,' Gloria mused, but with a smile. 'I somehow doubt that.'

'Let me be correct and introduce myself. My name's Dwight. Can I ask what yours is?'

'Gloria . . . Gloria Lombard. I really like how you talk, it's so different.'

So that's it, Dwight thought. The girl looked familiar because she was Lizzie's daughter, the one who'd left home. He should have known.

She had the same light blonde hair, and a naughty twinkle in her blue eyes. 'Why, thank you, Gloria. I'm from Alabama and we all talk like this in the South.'

Gloria leaned forward and rested her elbows on the counter. Dwight's eyes were drawn to her firm breasts, and he noticed that she didn't seem to mind him ogling them. It appeared she was very much like her mother, only younger and prettier. At that moment a thought occurred to him.

'Well, Miss Gloria, it's been delightful meeting you, and I hope to see you again sometime. If you change your mind about those free tickets, you call in any Saturday night and ask for me.'

'Yeah, sure, thanks,' Gloria answered.

Dwight turned to leave with a wicked smile on his face. A plan was beginning to form in his head, and he turned it over in his mind as he walked home. By the time he arrived, Dwight had worked out how to bring his plan to fruition. Lizzie was partial to a gin or two, so he'd ply her with a few drinks, turn on the charm, and his powers of persuasion should work on her.

As he stepped into his flat, Dwight was happily anticipating the future. He'd convince Lizzie that Gloria would be better off living with them, sure that he'd soon have the daughter in his bed — and then he'd get rid of the mother.

★　★　★

Jenny snuggled up to Craig on the sofa, then looked up at him to say, 'It's so peaceful and quiet.'

117

'I hoped it would be.'

'Ah, so that's why you gave Pamela the money to take the boys to Saturday morning pictures!'

'Yep, I wanted to spend some time alone with you,' Craig said, and pulled Jenny closer.

'Is having us here getting on your nerves?'

'No, not at all. I've got used to sleeping on that lumpy sofa, and the place wouldn't be the same without tripping over wooden cars and stepping on Meccano. The bathroom would have something missing if there weren't nylons hanging up, and the kitchen looks great with sticky fingermarks over the doors.'

Jenny could see Craig was joking but pulled away from him and pretended to look hurt.

'Come here, you silly sausage,' Craig said, pulling her into his arms again. 'I love having you all here and I love you.'

With a sharp intake of breath, Jenny looked into Craig's face. He'd said the three words she'd been longing to hear.

'I said it, didn't I? I told you that I love you . . . '

Jenny was so overwhelmed that she was unable to speak and just nodded her head.

'Oh dear, is it too soon? I shouldn't have told you yet. I should have waited.'

She looked up into his brown eyes and found her voice. 'No. I feel the same. I love you too, Craig.'

'Thank goodness,' he said, hugging her. 'I thought I'd blown it.'

The precious moment was sealed with a long and passionate kiss. Jenny could feel sensations stirring in her body that she always experienced when Craig held her. He gently eased her backwards on the sofa, still exploring her mouth with his tongue, then she felt the weight of his body on hers. Everything was tingling, and she didn't want it to stop, but she forced herself not to open her legs. She clasped his face in her hands and whispered, 'Craig, no . . . not yet.'

He immediately lifted himself off her and said, 'I'm sorry, Jen, I was getting a bit carried away.'

'I know, me too, but I can't, not until, well, not until — '

'We're married,' Craig interrupted, finishing her sentence. 'Fair enough, but once we are I'm going to ravish that sexy body of yours. I'm really looking forward to our wedding night,' he said, then gently kissed her cheek and playfully pinched her nose.

Jenny frowned, feeling bewildered. Craig was talking as if they'd already planned to get married. Had she missed something somewhere? In a bold move for Jenny, she summoned up the courage to ask, 'Was that some sort of strange proposal?'

'Yes, I suppose it was! I've always known you're the one for me and I just assumed we'd get married. They say you don't truly know someone until you live with them. Well, we've been living together for over a month now and that must surely be the equivalent to years of dating. It seems sudden, but if you think about it, it's not really. So, Jenny Lombard, will you do me the honour of becoming my wife?'

Jenny felt tears begin to stream down her

cheeks, and Craig's eyes were glistening too.

'Oh, bugger, I didn't get down on one knee,' he added.

'It doesn't matter,' Jenny said. 'My answer will still be the same. YES!'

12

'So where do you suggest she sleeps? There's only the sofa,' Lizzie said.

Dwight had been working on Lizzie for over a week and on Sunday it sounded like she was finally considering the idea of bringing Gloria to live with them.

'The sofa's mighty comfortable, or I can buy her one of those Z-bed things. She's young, Lizzie, and needs her momma's guidance.'

'All right, if you say so, but it's going to change things for us. For one, there won't be any more late-afternoon hanky-panky on the sofa, or early-morning canoodles in the bathroom. We'll be confined to the bedroom, and we'll have to keep the noise down.'

'I realise that, but don't you think it's a small sacrifice to pay for knowing your daughter is safe and sound?'

'I suppose so,' Lizzie mumbled.

Dwight didn't think she sounded sincere or happy about it. She had her back to him, scrambling eggs on the stove, and he walked over to wrap his arms around her waist, nuzzling her neck.

'That is so nice,' she husked, reaching round to cup his engorged manhood. 'And someone's a big boy! You must really, really, really like my scrambled eggs.'

'Oh yeah, Lizzie, I sure do,' Dwight answered,

but in truth it was the thought of Gloria's young body that had aroused him.

* * *

On that same Sunday morning, Jenny had gathered Pamela and the boys in her gran's flat. Her gran was in one chair, Pamela in the other, and the boys sat cross-legged in front of them. Craig stood by her side.

'What's this all about?' her gran asked.

Jenny could feel herself reddening as all eyes were on her. 'We . . . Craig and me . . . we've got something to tell you . . .'

She felt Craig's hand in hers and quickly glanced nervously at him. Fortunately, he continued with the big announcement. 'I asked Jenny to marry me last week, and she said yes!'

The boys exchanged a wide-mouthed glance and cheered but it was her gran who spoke first. 'Oh, Jenny, that's wonderful news. Congratulations to you both, I'm chuffed to bits, I really am, but why wait a week to tell us?'

'We just wanted to keep it to ourselves for a while, that's all.'

'You soppy pair of lovebirds,' her gran said, but she was smiling happily.

Jenny looked at Pamela and saw that she didn't look happy. 'What's wrong?' she asked.

'Nothing,' Pamela answered.

'Aren't you happy for me and Craig?'

'Of course, I am . . . but . . . but . . . what's gonna happen to us?'

'Oh, Pam, nothing much will change. We'll all

still live together but hopefully in a bigger house soon. Don't worry, I'll always look after you and the boys.'

At last Jenny saw her sister smile. She'd hoped they'd all be thrilled about the wedding and now it seemed they were, though she doubted Gloria would be as pleased when she told her later that day.

★   ★   ★

Henry arrived home from the pub and when he opened his front door he immediately noticed that the house smelled fresher. As he walked into the kitchen, his nostrils again twitched at the aroma of a Sunday roast dinner. He'd met Audrey the week before and already the woman had moved in. It suited him that he now had a full-time cook and cleaner on hand. He couldn't say he was overly attracted to her, but she'd do for when the mood took him, which was normally only after he'd had a few beers.

He went through to the kitchen to find her sitting at the table, nervously biting her nails. She looked up at him with her brown, wonky eyes. When they'd first met he'd joked and asked if one of her eyes was going to get the fish whilst the other got the chips. She'd smiled weakly at the time, and he'd felt a bit mean and quickly bought her a drink.

Looking at her face now he could see she was worried. 'What's wrong?'

Audrey pulled her hand away from her mouth

123

and spoke in almost a whisper. 'I . . . I've over-cooked your chicken a bit.'

'Not to worry, love, I like it well done,' Henry answered, then pulled out a chair opposite her. 'Pour me a whiskey, will ya? It's on top of the larder.'

Audrey jumped up and scurried across the kitchen. He eyed her up and down as she strained to reach the bottle. She was a tiny thing, less than five foot tall, with short, light brown hair. She didn't have much of a figure and wasn't good-looking, but at least she wasn't mouthy like Lizzie. She was grateful too, grateful for any small kindness, and for the rare occasions when he used her body.

She placed a glass of whiskey in front of him, then asked, 'Would you like me to dish up your dinner, Henry?'

'No,' he said, grimacing, 'my shoulders are still aching from the overtime yesterday, so give them a massage first.'

'All right,' Audrey agreed quietly as she moved to stand behind him.

Henry knew that lifting the heavy dustbins was beginning to take its toll, but no doubt he'd be doing the job until he died, and then they could carry his body out in a bin rather than a coffin. He took a large mouthful of whiskey, hoping that along with a massage it would ease the pain. Only minutes later his temper flared. There was no relief. The woman wasn't strong enough to punch her way out of a paper bag, let alone undo the knots in his muscles. 'Gerrof,' he snapped. 'You ain't helping.'

Audrey quickly stepped back, saying nervously, 'I'm sorry, Henry.'

She was so skittish that he guessed she'd had a few backhanders in the past, but it had made her more pliable and that suited him. He ignored her apology and snapped, 'Go and run me a bath. The hot water might help.'

'But your dinner?'

'Sod me dinner. I'll eat it later.'

'All right,' she said, then hurriedly left the kitchen.

He finished his whiskey, and then Audrey was back, telling him his bath was ready. He went upstairs, and seeing the bubbles on the surface of the water, he wasn't sure whether to laugh or feel irritated. 'The silly cow,' he mumbled, shaking his head as he stripped off his clothes.

It wasn't like Henry to bathe at this time of day. He usually had a bath on Sunday evenings, but on this occasion he hoped having it earlier would ease the pain. 'Audrey,' he yelled. 'Audrey!'

Within minutes she appeared and stood in the doorway biting her thumb.

'Give my back a wash,' he ordered.

'Yes, Henry,' she agreed.

He smiled. Audrey had only been there a week, and already he was enjoying the pleasures of being pampered, waited on hand and foot. She would never excite him like Lizzie had, and she wasn't as passionate as his wife either. Lizzie had been wild in the bedroom and liked it rough, but this one, she just lay on her back silently, so he had no idea if she enjoyed it. Not that he was bothered if she did or not. It might not be great sex, but Audrey had her uses and she would do for now.

13

'Come back to bed,' Dennis urged.

It was Monday, the morning after Jenny had been to see Gloria to announce that she was getting married. Gloria was pleased for her sister, but it had made her take stock of her own relationship. Her mind had been mulling it over for most of the night and she'd come to realise that Dennis wasn't the man she thought he was. She'd soon discovered he was boring and had no oomph about him. The initial spark she'd felt had quickly been extinguished. She'd jumped in too quickly but probably out of desperation to get away from home. Now she regretted her haste, though she didn't want to go back to Craig's either.

Her restless night had left her tired, but now she was already dressed and ready to begin her morning shift in Queenie's. 'I can't come back to bed. Unlike you I don't have the luxury of doing bugger-all and have to work for a living.'

'Come on, just ten minutes.'

'No, Dennis, you know what Queenie is like. Last time she docked me an hour and I was only seven minutes late.'

'Sod the old cow! Tell her where to stick her job. The pay is rubbish and there's plenty of other jobs out there.'

'Yeah, maybe, but where would we be without my wage until I find one?'

'We'd get by,' Dennis answered.

Gloria was already fed up but hadn't yet spoken up. Now she felt she couldn't bite her tongue any longer and blurted, 'On what, fresh air? And anyway, getting by ain't good enough. You never take me anywhere and I'm sick of being cooped up in your room all the time. Not only that, I can't even afford to buy some new clothes!'

'Hey, calm down. What's brought this on? Oh, I know, your sister's getting married and you want an outfit.'

'Yes, I do, but that's got nothing to do with this. It's you . . . us . . . I'm bored!' She sat on the edge of the bed and pouted, hoping to get some sympathy from Dennis.

'Gloria, I thought you liked spending time alone with me.'

'Yes, I do, but I'd like us to go out more too.'

'You've never complained before.'

'I am now and it's all very well you telling me to find another job, but what about you, eh? Why don't you get off your arse and go to work? Why should I have to graft when you don't?'

'Oi, drop the bloody attitude! If you don't like it, you know where you can go,' Dennis said petulantly and rolled over in the bed.

Gloria knew that now she'd put him in a bad mood, it would be futile trying to talk to him. Instead, frustrated, she stomped out of the room, slamming the door behind her.

★   ★   ★

Jenny sat in her usual place at work. It was a long bench with seven women on one side of her, four on the other and twelve opposite. Thelma sat two seats down with a cigarette hanging from the side of her mouth and, as usual with her, she looked depressed. Jenny couldn't blame her; after all, Thelma had an uninvited guest in her home — Gloria.

However, not even Thelma's miserable face would dampen Jenny's spirits today. She couldn't stop thinking about Craig. If she hadn't been such an introvert, she would have liked to shout from the rooftops that they were getting married.

'Did you have a nice weekend?' Joan sitting beside her asked. She was a rotund woman who wore thick-lensed National Health glasses. The other women would often joke with Joan, referring to her specs as the bottoms of milk bottles. Joan never seemed to mind and gave back as good as she got. She was a jolly woman and Jenny liked her, but Joan could never be described as quiet.

'Yes, it was lovely, thanks,' Jenny answered.

'Really! What was so lovely?' Joan pried.

Unable to hold her wonderful news in any longer, Jenny blurted, 'My . . . my boyfriend proposed to me and I said yes. We're getting married.'

'Blimey! Did you hear that, girls? Jenny's getting married.'

Jenny cringed. She hated drawing attention to herself and now wished she'd kept her mouth shut. Straightaway she was bombarded with questions, one woman asking who she was marrying and what was he like, another asking when and where they were getting married. There was a cacophony of female voices and all eyes were on her. She felt her cheeks burning and wanted to get up and run away, then to her relief she saw Miss Aston appear on the factory floor.

'Quieten down, ladies,' Miss Aston bellowed above the noise of the women. 'What's all this fuss about?'

'It's Jenny, Miss, she's getting married,' Joan told her.

'Congratulations, Jenny, that's wonderful news, but now all of you get back to work. You can chat about it later when you're on your lunch break.'

A few of them murmured, 'Yes, Miss,' and seemingly satisfied the woman returned to her office, which overlooked the factory floor.

Jenny felt a gentle dig in her side and Joan quietly asked, 'You haven't told us about the bloke you're marrying yet.'

'His name is Craig. He's a carpenter and lives upstairs from my gran.'

Though they had both spoken quietly, Thelma must have heard and leaned their way to hiss, 'Yeah, and he's deaf.'

'Deaf? Well, that's a turn-up for the books. At least he won't be able to hear you nagging him!' Joan said and chortled.

'Never mind about wedding bells, what are you going to do about your bloody sister?' Thelma asked.

'I've tried to persuade her to come home but she won't listen to me,' Jenny replied, acutely aware that most of the women were trying to eavesdrop on the conversation. So far the gossip hadn't reached them, so she hoped Thelma wouldn't mention anything about her living with Craig. They slept separately, but she knew nobody would want to believe that. Most people preferred to think the worst of others and she'd often hear about someone being slagged off, maybe because it took them away from their own unhappy or mundane lives.

'You've got to do something,' Thelma moaned. 'It's bad enough having to listen to them at it, but now they're rowing too. She's a tart, like your mother, and if you can't make her shift I'll resort to my own ways of getting her out.'

'My mother isn't a tart, nor is Gloria,' Jenny said and could feel her heart racing.

'Huh, did you hear that, you lot? Lizzie is a trollop and her daughter's going down the same road. Ain't that right, ladies?'

None of the women answered Thelma, nor did they speak up in defence of Jenny's mother and sister. She felt sick inside, knowing that if they heard that she was living with Craig, they'd turn on her too.

'Huh, nothing to say, Jenny. Well, I'm warning you, it would be better for Gloria if she went of her own accord.'

Jenny wasn't sure what Thelma could do but heard the threat in the woman's words. Gloria had refused to listen to her, but she would have to try again. She said hastily, 'Leave it with me.'

131

'You've got 'til the end of the week. If Gloria ain't gone by Saturday, she'll be sorry.'

Jenny felt protective of her sister and wanted to front Thelma out, but with everyone listening and watching, she just nodded her head. All thoughts of Craig were gone for a while as she worried about her sister instead.

⋆   ⋆   ⋆

After finally giving in to Dwight, Lizzie set off for her mum's flat in the hope that Edith would know where to find Gloria. If she didn't, she'd have to ask Henry, but after the way he'd kicked off the last time she was there it wasn't something she looked forward too. Still, it had been ages since she'd seen the boys, so she could kill two birds with one stone.

It was beyond her why Dwight thought the girl should come and live with them, but he'd kept on and on about it, intimating that she wasn't a good mother. She couldn't allow him to think badly of her, not if she was going to get her hands on his wealth.

Lizzie used a key she'd had for years and flounced into Edith's, calling, 'It's only me, Mum,' as she walked into the lounge, to find her mother in her usual armchair listening to the radio.

'Huh, look what the cat's dragged in,' she said, looking her up and down.

'Hello, Mum, how are you?' Lizzie responded, choosing to ignore her mother's derisive remark.

'I'm fine, not that you'd care. What do you want, Elizabeth?'

132

Her mother rarely called her by her full name. As a child, being called 'Elizabeth' meant she was in trouble.

'I don't want anything, just to see you. Shall I make us a cup of tea?'

'I've just had one and don't try to pull the wool over my eyes. I ain't stupid. You haven't been to see me for months, so I can guess you're only here 'cos you want something.'

Lizzie sighed and said, 'All right, there is something.'

'I knew it!'

'I'm looking for Gloria. Do you know where she is?'

'Of course I do and so should you. You're her mother for Christ's sake. Fancy not knowing where your own kids are. You're a bloody disgrace.'

'And you wonder why I don't come and see you more often. Can you blame me? This is what I get every time and I'm sick of it.'

'Well then, you should never have walked out on your children. I'm embarrassed to call you my daughter.'

Lizzie drew in a long, slow breath to quell her rising temper. If she was to find Gloria's whereabouts she'd have to have to remain calm and not goad her mother. Another alternative would be to wait outside the factory gates where Jenny worked and ask her, but she preferred to keep away from the place and the snide comments from the other women who worked there. 'Mum, please, just tell me where Gloria is.'

'What do you want with her?'

'I've heard she's living with a man and it ain't right.'

'That's rich coming from you.'

'I ain't sixteen, and I intend to take her home to live with me.'

'What's come over you? Are you suddenly developing a conscience?'

'Look, are you going to tell me where she is, or not?'

'I suppose so, considering you're doing the right thing for once. Too little, too late, if you ask me.'

'I didn't ask you, so can you please stop digging at me and just tell me where she is.'

'Digging at you! My God, Lizzie, I ain't even started! Do you have any idea what those poor kids have been through? No, how could you when you've barely seen them.'

'Mum, I don't need this right now. I just want to know where my daughter is.'

'What about the rest of them? You've got five kids, not one.'

'Gloria is my priority at the moment.'

'So it doesn't matter to you that Henry has been knocking six bells out of Jenny and terrifying the life out of Pamela and the boys?'

Lizzie knew she'd have to placate her mother and said, 'Of course it matters, but I ain't got room to take them all in. As it is Gloria will have to sleep on my sofa, but at least she won't be living with a bloke and risking getting knocked up.'

'Yeah, well, no thanks to you but the others ain't living with their father now. Jenny moved them all out and already Pamela's stopped wetting the bed, Timmy's not having nightmares any more and Peter's so much better. Jenny has done the right thing, but she's only twenty-two and shouldn't be forced to look after her brothers and sisters. That's your job! You're their mother!'

Lizzie ground her teeth. She felt the urge to stick two fingers up at her mother and walk out, but she still hadn't discovered where to find Gloria.

'What's this? No reaction. Nothing to say?' her mother asked sarcastically.

'Mum, I don't know what you expect me to do. I've told you I haven't got room for them so just tell me where Gloria is, and I'll go. Me being here clearly upsets you.'

'She's living with a bloke called Dennis above Queenie's fag shop.'

'What, the shop under the railway bridge?'

'Yes, that's the one. She works in there too.'

'Thanks, Mum. I'll go and see her right now. Once I've got Gloria sorted I'll go to see the rest of the kids. Where are they living?

'They're settled, happy, and they don't need you turning up only to bugger off again for months on end.'

'They're my kids. I love 'em and I've a right to see them.'

'Love! You don't know the meaning of the word.'

Lizzie could see her mother was in the mood for a fight, and that it would be pointless to argue with her. At least she knew where to find

Gloria, and that would do for now. She smiled sardonically and said, 'If you say so, Mum, but I'm going now.'

Her mother sniffed and turned her head away, saying nothing as Lizzie marched out. Lizzie didn't care. She had to persuade Gloria to live with her and planned how to achieve that as she hurried to Queenie's shop. One thing was for sure, she wouldn't shout and bawl like her mother. You could catch more flies with honey than spite.

★ ★ ★

Gloria made no secret of her bad mood and had been rude to several customers that morning. Queenie wasn't in the shop to hear her, not that it would have made a difference to Gloria if she had been. She was in half a mind to walk out. If Dennis wasn't prepared to work, then why should she?

As Gloria stacked some shelves behind the counter, she gritted her teeth when the bell above the door rang, signalling another customer. She turned around and was staggered to see her mother walk in.

'Hello, sweetheart,' her mum said cheerily.

'Hello,' Gloria answered, but she couldn't bring herself to smile.

'Your gran told me where to find you. I was wondering if I could have a word.'

'If you want,' Gloria responded, with a shrug of her shoulders.

'What time do you get a break?'

136

'I don't. If you've got something to say, just say it.'

'Oh . . . right . . . ' her mum answered awkwardly as she looked around the shop. 'I hear you're living upstairs with a man.'

'Yeah, what of it?'

'Look, I don't know how to put this, especially coming from me. We both know I'm not exactly an angel, but, well . . . you're too young to be living with a bloke. It'd be different if you were married.'

'Yeah, you're right, that *is* rich coming from you. I ain't being funny, Mum, but it's none of your business.'

'I know, but surely you don't want to ruin your reputation. Believe me, I know what it's like. I've had women looking down at me, calling me a tart, and I don't want that to happen to you. If you come and live with me, you can still see Dennis and . . . and it would be lovely for us to spend some time together. I . . . I miss you.'

It was unlike Gloria to be lost for words, but she stood with her mouth open as she tried to digest her mother's offer. The fact that her mother was missing her was the last thing she expected to hear.

'I realise that me showing up out of the blue and asking you to come and live with me is probably a bit of a shock, but what do you say?'

'Err . . . I don't know,' Gloria answered slowly.

'I've got myself a smashing man, Gloria, rich too. He's always spoiling me rotten with presents and I'm sure he'd do the same for you. He says you should be with us, under our roof, and not

137

shacked up with a bloke.'

'Oh, I see. So this is all your boyfriend's idea, is it?'

'Of course not. We both agree it's for the best. Come on, we can have some proper girlie fun together and Dennis can call in whenever he likes.'

Gloria would never admit it to anyone, but though she'd put a front on and acted like she hated her mother, in truth she'd missed her. She hadn't allowed any of her siblings to see, but she'd often cried in the bathroom, longing for her mum's comfort. Gloria also knew that what Jenny had said about Dennis was correct. He *was* lazy, and he wasn't good enough for her. She'd had enough of him but living with Dennis was better than moving back into Craig's cramped flat. Maybe her mother's offer was the perfect solution. 'Yes, all right. I'll come and live with you,' Gloria answered, and at last smiled at her mum.

'Really? Oh, Gloria, that's wonderful. What time do you finish? I can come back and help you pack your things.'

'I don't need your help. I haven't got a lot to pack.'

'If you're sure, I'll come back and wait outside for you. I'm so excited that you're coming to live with us, and I can't wait for you to meet Dwight.'

Gloria frowned. Dwight? Surely not the American who'd offered her tickets to the dancehall? It had to be: there couldn't be two Dwights in Balham. Gloria recalled the lustful look she'd seen when he'd copped an eyeful of her cleavage and was sure he'd been flirting with her. She shuddered. The man was old enough to be her father. Still, she reasoned, once he realised who she was he'd probably regret his behaviour in the shop. He'd behave himself, at least she hoped so. If he didn't, Dwight would feel her knee sharply in his groin.

14

That evening, Henry came home with a used handbag for Audrey. He'd found it in one of the dustbins and thought it looked in good nick. It was cream leather with a gold clasp. The only flaw Henry could see was a small ink stain inside. He hoped Audrey would like it or at least be appreciative of his efforts. His wife had never been grateful for anything he'd brought home, except his wages. The good stuff that people threw out never ceased to amaze Henry, yet Lizzie would always tell him to get the flea-bitten rubbish out of her house.

' 'Ere, love, I got you this today,' Henry said as he sat at the kitchen table and slid the bag across.

Audrey was busy stirring something on the stove, but when she turned to look, Henry saw her eyes well up. 'What's wrong? Don't you like it?' he asked.

'Yes, it's lovely, thank you,' Audrey said as she ran her hand over the bag. 'I've never had anyone bring me presents.'

'It ain't new, but I'm always finding quality stuff like this. If you like it there'll be plenty more where that came from.'

Audrey smiled at him, but the smile was weak. He noticed a small purple bruise on her left cheek, probably left by one of his fingers when he'd slapped her the night before. He felt bad about it now, but fuelled with beer and brandy she'd narked him when she'd accidentally knocked over his glass. 'Look, I'm sorry I lashed out at you last night,' he offered, talking to her back as she attended to the saucepan. 'Just try and be a bit less clumsy in future.'

'I'll do my best, Henry,' Audrey answered quietly.

'Right, what's for tea?' he asked, satisfied that she didn't seem to be harbouring any ill-feelings towards him.

'Pork chops. I'm just making the gravy for you. Is that all right?'

'Yeah, it's fine,' he said, fishing in his pocket. 'Tell ya what, here's a few bob to put in that handbag. Treat yourself to something tomorrow.'

'Oh, thank you,' Audrey said, then turned to quickly scoop up the coins.

'Get a move on with my grub. Once I've got it down me neck I'm gonna have a quick wash then shoot out again. It's darts night in the Bedford. Fancy coming? Most of the wives will be there.'

'Err . . . yes . . . if you like,' Audrey said as she placed his plate of food in front of him and a smaller one opposite for herself.

Henry didn't mind her tagging along. He used to enjoy having Lizzie on his arm to show off, but he'd always had to keep one eye on the dartboard and another on her. Audrey wasn't a head-turner like his wife, so he didn't have to worry about other blokes chatting her up.

He picked up his knife and fork and looked from Audrey to his plate piled high with the

141

chop, vegetables and boiled potatoes. He smacked his lips together and shoved a forkful of hot food in his mouth. 'You turn out a good meal, Audrey. Once you've had yours, go and tidy yourself up a bit. Wear that cream dress you had on the other day, it'll go nice with your new bag.'

Audrey nodded, and after eating about half of her dinner she scampered out of the kitchen whilst Henry scoffed his. He'd suggested the cream dress as it was the only outfit he knew of that didn't make her look quite as frumpy. He hoped she'd put on a bit of make-up too, but wasn't there a saying, something about not being able to make a silk purse out of a sow's ear? Yeah, he thought, that certainly applied to Audrey.

★   ★   ★

Jenny leaned against the kitchen worktop and out of earshot from the boys she said to Craig, 'My gran said that my mum called in to see her earlier.'

Pamela had gone to a friend's house for tea, and Timmy and Peter were playing in a camp they'd made in the bedroom from two old sheets and a broken broomstick.

'Did Edith mention that we're living up here?' Craig asked quietly.

'No, she refused to tell my mum where we are, but she was more interested in finding Gloria.'

'Gloria, why?'

'She said it isn't right that Gloria's living with

Dennis. She wants her to move in with her and her new man Dwight.'

'Really? She didn't seem bothered when you told her. I wonder why she's changed her tune.'

'Who knows what goes on in my mother's head? I just hope she has more success with Gloria than we did, especially after what Thelma said at work today. She threatened that if Gloria doesn't move out by the end of the week, she'll be sorry.'

'I don't like the sound of that.'

'Nor me.'

'Try not to worry. I can't see Dennis letting his mother chuck her out, and even if she does, Gloria will have your mum's offer.'

'Yes, that's true, and I suppose if Gloria is going to listen to anyone, it's our mum,' Jenny said, finding her smile again. 'Guess what else happened at work today?'

'You got a pay rise?'

'No.'

'You got an extra day's holiday?'

'No.'

'I give up, but judging by that happy face it must have been something good.'

'I told everyone about us getting married.'

Craig chuckled, then said, 'I wish I'd had someone to tell today. I've been bursting with it but seeing as there's only me in my workshop . . . I have to keep pinching myself to make sure this isn't all a dream. Honestly, Jen, you've made me the happiest man in the world.'

Jenny felt the same, but unlike Craig, she wasn't good at putting her feelings into words.

'Me too,' she whispered, and looked up at him shyly from under her lashes.

He gazed at her longingly which made her stomach flip with excitement, then he embraced her and they kissed.

'Yuk, that's disgusting,' Timmy said.

Jenny pulled away from Craig to see the boy standing in the kitchen doorway, and smiling at him she said, 'No, it isn't.'

'Peter, Jenny was snogging Craig,' shouted Timmy over his shoulder.

'What, again?' Peter said as he turned up to stand beside his brother.

'Yes, again. You two are always kissing and holding hands but I don't know why. I kissed Maggie Yates when we was playing kiss chase, but it was 'orrible.'

Jenny stifled a giggle, and Craig was obviously fighting to keep a straight face as he asked, 'What was so horrible about kissing Maggie Yates?'

'Her lips were wet and tasted of milk that had gone off. I ain't never kissing a girl again.'

'You will, Timmy, when you meet the girl you love.'

'No way! But you must really love my sister 'cos you're always kissing her.'

'I do. I love her very much indeed.'

'Can I have a biscuit please, Jenny?' asked Peter, losing interest in what they were talking about.

'After your tea. It won't be long so get that camp in my room tidied up, please.'

'Yeah, all right. Come on, Peter, you can be

the Red Indian now,' Timmy said as the boys went running off again, forgetting all talk of kissing.

Jenny smiled at Craig. 'They're not used to seeing so much affection. I don't recall my mum and dad having a cuddle in front of us, let alone a kiss.'

'Well, they'd better get used to it, because I intend to kiss you as much as I can, Mrs Brice,' he said, leaning over to gently rub his full lips on hers.

'I'm not Mrs Brice yet,' she whispered.

'No, but you will be and the sooner the better.'

'Should we think about finding a bigger place before we arrange our wedding?'

'Yes, probably. Once we're married we'll need our own bedroom, and that's impossible here.'

Jenny was pleased that Craig was being practical. As much as she wanted to be his wife, she knew they needed more space. Their own bedroom, she thought with a shiver of excitement, wondering what it would be like to share a bed with Craig.

*　*　*

Gloria had expected Dennis to beg her to stay — that he'd tell her things would be different and he'd get a job. Instead, as she'd packed her bags he'd sat on the bed reading a comic. She had stormed out, taking great satisfaction in slamming the door so hard behind her that it had rattled on its hinges.

Now, as Gloria walked along Balham High

Road with her mum, she wondered what she'd seen in him. She originally thought that as Dennis was older than her he was a real man, but he'd turned out to be idle and childish, even sulking when he didn't get his own way. He might have dazzled her with his good looks, but he'd soon bored her with his lacklustre personality.

Dennis was a part of her past now, Gloria realised, and she suddenly felt alive again. Maybe she would take Dwight up on his offer and accept tickets for the dance. It was a good place to meet young men and she felt confident that she'd attract plenty of attention.

Her mother interrupted her thoughts, saying, 'I don't think you should leave Queenie's until you've got another job.'

'Maybe not, but I suppose I could ask Jenny to get me into the factory.'

'I don't think you'd enjoy working there, love. The women are a load of catty gossips.'

'That's not what Jen says. She reckons they're a nice bunch.'

'Your sister thinks everyone is lovely but take it from me, they wouldn't be nice to someone like you.'

'What do you mean by that?' Gloria asked indignantly.

'You take after me in looks, and you've got a great figure. Women don't always take to people like us. I think it's jealousy.'

'If you say so, but I've never had a problem and I quite fancy working with Jenny. She'd be able to introduce me to all her mates.'

'Are you having a laugh? Most of the women in that factory are old crones, and outside work Jenny doesn't have any mates. No, I really think you'd be much better off at Queenie's.'

If Gloria was honest, she didn't relish the idea of working in a factory, but if she stayed at Queenie's she was bound to see Dennis and didn't fancy that. 'I dunno, Mum, it's boring in the shop.'

'It'll be even more boring in the factory and longer hours too.'

'Yeah, but I'd earn more,' Gloria answered, beginning to wonder why her mother was so keen to talk her out of working with Jenny.

'Yes, you'd earn more but you'd be working a damn sight harder for it. If I was you, I'd stay put. You've got a cushy little number there.'

'What's so cushy about it?'

'You don't have a boss breathing down your neck all day, and it's good hours. I bet you get plenty of little bonuses too, eh?'

'Bonuses, off Queenie, you've got to be kidding!'

'No, not from Queenie. I mean the sort of bonuses you help yourself to . . . you know, packets of fags and that?'

So that was it. Her mother wanted her to pinch cigarettes. She should have known. There was always a hidden agenda with her mum. 'I don't help myself to anything. That would be stealing,' she lied.

'Huh, if you say so, but I know you, Gloria Lombard. I bet you've got your hands in the till too.'

Gloria had helped herself a few times, but she wasn't going to tell her mother that. 'You said this Dwight bloke is wealthy, so how come you're looking for free fags?'

'He's shrewd with his money, and though generous in other ways, he thinks I'm a bit of a spendthrift so he sometimes keeps me a bit short. We live in his association flat because he doesn't believe in wasting money just to put a roof over our heads. He prefers to spend his dosh on buying me nice things. You wait until you see the earrings he bought me — and look at this.'

Her mum held out her hand and Gloria gasped as the sunlight caught a large stone on her mother's middle finger.

'See, a diamond ring. I've never had diamonds in my life. I had that crappy topaz ring your father palmed me off with as an engagement ring, but Dwight buys me expensive gifts.'

'Let me look at that,' Gloria said and dropped her heavy bag to grab her mum's hand.

She peered at the ring. It was the biggest diamond Gloria had ever seen, which made her doubt it was real. In fact, she was sure she'd seen dress jewellery very similar in Tooting indoor market. She looked at her mother's beaming face and couldn't believe her mum would be deceived by a bit of glass. 'It's smashing, but are you sure it's a real diamond?'

'Of course. Dwight told me it is.'

'And you've known him for how long?'

'Pack it in, Gloria, you're just peeved because Dennis didn't buy you anything nice. Don't worry, you'll find yourself a man soon enough,

148

only this time make sure it's a bloke with plenty of money.'

Gloria picked up her bag and resumed walking with her mother in silence. If the woman wanted to believe Dwight was buying her diamonds, then she wasn't going to be the one to burst her bubble. After all, she didn't want her mum to be leaving him, not now, when she was just about to move in.

When they reached Dwight's flat, her mother showed her around. Much to Gloria's disappointment, she immediately noticed there was only the one bedroom.

'Don't worry, Dwight has bought you this,' her mum said, indicating a funny-looking sort of cabinet. 'It opens up into a bed. Clever, isn't it?'

'Yes, but this must mean I've got to sleep in the front room. Bloody hell, Mum, I moved out of Craig's place because it was so cramped, and this ain't much better.'

'Jenny's boyfriend? You've been living with Jenny's boyfriend?'

'Yes, we all have, in a one-bedroom flat above Gran's. It was why I was so keen to move in with Dennis.'

'Jenny's a sly one. There's me thinking she's a good girl, but all this time she's been shacked up with her fella.'

'It's not like that, Mum. I had to share a room with her and Pam. Craig slept in the front room with the boys.'

'Blimey, that's ridiculous.'

'I know, but Jenny couldn't take another

149

beating from Dad and she was worried it would be one of us next.'

'Come off it, Gloria, your dad ain't *that* bad.'

Gloria looked at her mother in disbelief. She'd been fooled by the ring and now seemed unable to accept the truth about her husband. 'Mum, he nearly killed Jenny,' she said seriously. 'She ended up in hospital.'

'Yeah, well, he used to belt me at times, but he never went that far.'

Gloria looked at her mum in disbelief again. She hadn't asked about Jenny's injuries or shown any sympathy. It made her question if she really knew her own mother at all. They heard the front door close and Gloria noticed her mother's demeanour completely change. She preened and seemed to become very giggly, which gave Gloria the impression that her mum was nervous.

'What a treat for a gentleman to walk into his home and find two mighty pretty ladies before him. I'm Dwight, but I'm sure you already know that, and you must be Gloria. It's a real pleasure to meet you.'

Gloria's suspicions had been correct. Dwight was indeed the man she'd met in Queenie's though he didn't seem to recognise her.

'I'm so happy that your momma has brought you here to live with us in my very humble abode. You are very welcome. Lizzie darlin', have you offered this young lady some iced tea or lemonade?'

'No, not yet. Would you like a drink, Gloria?' her mum asked.

'Yes, lemonade if you've got some, please.'

'You sit yourself down and let your momma spoil you for a bit. Fetch us both a glass, Lizzie.'

Her mum left the room as Gloria sat on the edge of a worn brown sofa and Dwight sat opposite her in a rickety rocking chair.

'I love this old chair,' he mused, running his hands over the smooth wooden arms. 'It reminds me of home, relaxing on my momma and papa's porch. I used to spend many hours rocking back and forward, gazing out at the corn fields and watching the little black girls. Their dark skin would glisten in the blazing Alabama sun, just like black pearls. You ever seen a black pearl, Gloria?'

Gloria tried to smile at him, but his gaze became intense and she didn't like the way he was licking his lips. She felt uneasy and was pleased when her mum came back with two glasses of lemonade.

'I was just telling Gloria about my momma's porch. You know, we were so poor that my momma used to make my clothes from fertiliser sacks, but then my grandpappy struck gold and we were the richest farmers in the state.'

'Gold? I thought you said your granddad found oil on his ranch?'

Gloria saw an instant look of panic on Dwight's face which was quickly replaced with a smile as fake as the diamond he'd bought her mum. 'Yeah, darlin', black gold. That's what we call oil.'

It might sound plausible, but Gloria knew that Dwight wasn't telling the truth, though her mother seemed happy with his answer. She'd only been in his presence for ten minutes but already knew he was a liar and was surprised that her mother hadn't seen it too.

Gloria already deeply regretted agreeing to live with them. She was too proud to go back to Dennis and couldn't stand the thought of living in the cramped conditions at Craig's. This, it seemed, was the best option out of a bad lot — for now.

15

Henry held on to the back of the dustcart as it headed towards the depot. He was almost finished for the day, but he wasn't looking forward to going home. Audrey had been living with him for over two months now, and he'd become very bored with her. She was so predictable, a creature of routine. She did the washing on Monday, ironed on a Tuesday, and every day he knew what to expect for his dinner. After a Sunday roast, Monday would be shepherd's pie, Tuesday a stew, Wednesday chops, Thursday stuffed hearts, Friday fish and Saturday sausages. He was even bored with Audrey's meekness now, and her lack of conversation. She rarely laughed either and just lay there during sex. Henry didn't like to admit it, but he missed Lizzie challenging him and her passion between the sheets.

It was coming up to the end of August and this weekend was a bank holiday. There was a long-standing tradition of all the men on the dustcart taking their families to Margate for the day. Henry tutted at the thought of dragging Audrey along with him, then unexpectedly felt sad as he realised this would be the first year he hadn't taken his children. He remembered the previous year. Early on Sunday morning they had all set off in Dodgy Donnie's old pick-up to meet the rest of the families. His kids always enjoyed riding in the back of the open-top truck. It had been a sunny day and the girls had taken the boys into the sea. He'd bought them all ice-creams and a fish and chips lunch, and the boys had ridden the donkeys on the beach. There'd also been on rides in Dreamland, the funfair, and even Timmy throwing up hadn't ruined the day. It had been a laugh, and after several pints he'd slept for most of the journey home. This year's trip would be very different without his children and Henry realised that at times like this he missed them.

The dustcart came to a stop and Henry jumped off.

'See you Sunday, mate,' Ray, the driver, called.

'I dunno. I might give it a miss this year.'

'Why would you do that?' Ray asked, and now the rest of the dustmen were waiting for his answer too.

'It's a family day, and you all know my situation. It ain't like I've got kids to bring.'

'That don't matter,' Ray said. 'Look at Willie, he comes by himself every year, ain't that right, Will?'

'Yes, it's better than sitting on me tod at home.'

'There's only the wife and me,' one of the other men said.

'I never thought of it like that,' Henry said, thinking that a few beers with the blokes would be better than staring at Audrey's plain face all day.

'Right, we'll see ya Sunday then,' Ray said, and waved as Henry trudged off.

154

'Yeah, see ya,' Henry called. He'd be aware that his children were absent, but that didn't mean he couldn't enjoy himself. Although the only way he'd be able to do that was to leave Audrey at home and go alone.

* * *

'Do you really think we can afford it?' Jenny asked Craig.

They were standing in the back garden of a modern three-bedroomed house that had recently been vacated and was being offered for rent by one of Craig's customers.

'Yes, just about. We've got enough saved for the deposit and rent in advance. As long as we don't go spending like we've won the football pools, I think we can manage the weekly rent.'

Jenny impulsively threw her arms around Craig's neck, then leaned back so he could read her lips. 'It's wonderful,' she gushed. 'The boys can have the small room, I'll share with Pamela and once we're married — ' She stopped mid-sentence, suddenly embarrassed at mentioning the marital bedroom.

'I'd better hurry up and make a decent woman of you,' Craig said, then gently kissed her. With his arms around her waist, he pulled his face back and said, 'I'll tell Mr Cockerill that we'll take the house.'

'Oh, Craig, it's perfect, I can't wait to move in. You don't show it, but you must be fed up with us all being squeezed into your flat.'

'No, not at all, Jenny. It's funny really, but

Pamela and the boys feel like my own family. I missed out on having any brothers and sisters, and my parents have been dead for a long time. When you're deaf, people shy away, so I haven't found it easy to make friends. I work by myself all day, and it can be lonely sometimes, but having you all living with me has made me the happiest I've been in a long time. I love having a full home, and I want ours to be filled with lots of our children too.'

Jenny stood on tiptoes to reach up and kiss him. She didn't like to think of him being lonely and was glad he no longer felt that way. It was a blessing they'd fallen in love, and now she couldn't imagine a life without Craig.

★   ★   ★

Gloria stuffed two packets of cigarettes in her handbag before finishing work for the afternoon. She'd remained working at Queenie's and thankfully had seen very little of Dennis. On the couple of occasions she had bumped into him, he'd barely acknowledged her, not that she was bothered. She'd held her head high and ignored him too.

'See you tomorrow, Queenie,' Gloria said as she left the shop with her stolen goods. Then as the door closed behind her, she muttered, 'You stupid old cow.'

Queenie was really getting past it and had now given over the stocktaking duties to Gloria. It made it so much easier for her to pinch things, and though she didn't pay Dwight any rent, he

156

was happy to accept the cigarettes and cigars she brought him.

When she arrived home, Gloria was pleased to find the flat empty. It was rare to have the place to herself so she planned to have a long soak in the bath. After gathering her nightdress from a small space her mum had made for her in a chest of drawers, she went into the bathroom to turn on the taps. It was only as she closed the door that Gloria noticed a hole had been drilled through it, about halfway down. Frowning, she went to the other side and bent down to peer through. She was shocked to see that she was looking directly at the bath. Bile rose. Dwight must have drilled the hole. How long had it been there? How many times had he spied on her when she was having a bath?'

Gloria's anger mounted. She'd put up with Dwight staring at her whenever he thought she wasn't looking, and knew he sometimes sneaked into the front room at night to gawp at her when he thought she was sleeping. She'd managed to rebuff the unwanted attention that he lavished on her when her mother wasn't around, but this — this was the final straw.

Gloria stomped back into her mother's bedroom and pulled down her large bag from the top of the wardrobe. She had no choice but to ask Jenny if she could move back in with them, but as she hurriedly threw clothes into the bag, her mother arrived home.

'What are you doing, Gloria?' she asked, looking perplexed as she stood in the doorway.

'What does it look like? I'm leaving. I can't live

under the same roof as your boyfriend any longer.'

'Why? What has Dwight done?'

'He's a pervert! He's always looking at me, pestering me, and now he's drilled a hole in the bathroom door so he can watch me when I'm having a bath.'

'Oh, love, don't be daft. Dwight's not like that. I'm sure there's a perfectly reasonable explanation for the hole. This is an old building and it's probably woodworm.'

Gloria wasn't surprised that her mother was defending the man. She was totally smitten with Dwight and refused to see he was anything but perfect. Also, as long as the so-called expensive gifts kept coming, Gloria knew her mother would never accept what she'd told her. She said angrily, 'It's not woodworm. It's man-made, I'm sure of it, and I'm getting out of here.'

'Fine, suit yourself, run off back to Dennis or your sister. After everything Dwight's done for you, this is how you repay him.'

'What! What's he done for me?'

'He's housed you and has never asked for a penny!'

'Yeah, well, I'm pretty sure I know how Dwight wants me to show my gratitude.'

'You dirty cow! You've got a disgusting mind to think something like that! When we found out you were living with Dennis, it was Dwight's idea that you come to stay with us. He hadn't even met you yet he wanted to protect you.'

Gloria fumed and couldn't keep her mouth shut. 'That's rubbish. He *had* met me. He came

158

into the shop before you turned up. He flirted with me and asked my name. When I told him he must have realised that I'm your daughter and hatched a plan to get me to live with you. He was probably looking to replace you for a younger version, the dirty bastard!'

'Shut up, Gloria! Not only is your language disgusting, you're telling lies. Dwight likes a real woman, not a bit of a kid.'

'You're blind, Mum. It's Dwight who tells lies, but you refuse to see it. Why is that, though? Is it that you're more interested in his money than hearing the truth?'

Gloria saw her mother's eyes narrow and then she said, 'Do you know what I think, Gloria — I think you're trying to turn me against Dwight because you want him for yourself.'

'What! Are you listening to yourself? Do you really think I would want your pervert of a boyfriend? Bloody hell, you're off your head! The pair of you deserve each other.'

Gloria didn't care that she hadn't packed all her belongings. She had to get out and pushed past her mother. As she steamed along the small hallway, she heard her mum shout, 'I'll be glad to see the back of you.'

Gloria clenched her teeth. She was sickened that her mother hadn't believed her — that she hadn't see the way Dwight ogled her. At least Craig only had eyes for Jenny, so she'd be safe there, albeit overcrowded.

16

It was a balmy Saturday morning in September, two weeks since Jenny and Craig had viewed and accepted the house. Today was moving-in day.

'Gran's going to have the boys today and give them their dinner. That'll give us a chance to unpack without them causing havoc,' Jenny said to Craig as he wrote 'KITCHEN' on a packed box. 'I was worried it would be too much for her, but she insisted that she can manage.'

'It shouldn't take us long to get sorted, not with all hands on deck.'

'Actually, it's only going to be us. Pam couldn't get the time off from her Saturday job, and Gloria, well, you know what she's like. Don't get me wrong, I'm happy she's back with us, but I wish she'd do more to help.'

'She probably doesn't want to break her nails,' Craig said, though without rancour. 'Never mind. I'm sure we'll manage. Talking of Gloria, where is she?'

'Still in bed. I'll give her a shout.'

Jenny went into the bedroom and pulled the curtains open as she said, 'Time to wake up, sleepy head.'

'Argh,' Gloria moaned, and rolled over to face the wall.

'Come on, Gloria, up you get. We've got a busy day and I need to get the rest of this room packed before the removals van arrives.'

'What's the time?'

'Gone eight and time to get out of bed,' Jenny said firmly.

'The van ain't due yet so bugger off, will ya, and close the curtains. Blimey, can't a girl get a lie-in?'

'Not when we're moving into a new house.'

'What's the big deal? I'm still not going to have my own bedroom.'

'Once I marry Craig, you'll only be sharing with Pam. By the way, we've been talking about that and have decided to set the date for the beginning of November. It's only going to be a small do in a register office, but I'd like you to be a witness.'

Gloria pushed herself up in the bed, smiling with delight now. 'Really? Oh, Jen, I'd love that. Who's going to be the other witness?'

'Craig is going to ask his uncle.'

'Are you going to invite Mum and Dad?'

'Dad, no. Craig wouldn't want him there, not after what he put me through. I'm not sure I want him there either. I haven't made up my mind about Mum.'

'She won't come without Dwight, and he's the last person I want to see. I'm not sure I want to see Mum either. I told her what Dwight was up to, but she wouldn't believe me.'

'I know, you poured it out when you came back to live with us, and I don't know why I even considered inviting her. I'm sorry. I'll strike her off my list, but come on, get up now and I'll make you a cuppa.'

Jenny closed the door behind her, thinking it

was a good job that she and Craig had opted for a register office. At least she wouldn't have the dilemma of who would walk her down the aisle, though a part of her longed for a loving father — one who would stand proudly beside her to give her away. It was a pipe dream of course. Neither of her parents gave a damn about her, or any of their children. All they both seemed to care about was themselves.

★ ★ ★

'Shut the fuck up!' Henry shouted, though he doubted Audrey could hear him downstairs over the noise of the hoover. He now regretted bringing home the carpet that someone had thrown out.

With a sore head and feeling angry, he gave up trying to get any more sleep and climbed out of bed. In just his underpants he stomped downstairs and into the front room to see Audrey vacuuming while humming a tune. She had her back to him and hadn't seen him, so Henry yanked the plug from the wall.

Audrey spun around and when she saw the disgruntled expression on his face, her own paled. 'I'm sorry, Henry, I didn't mean to disturb you.'

'Did you really think I could sleep through that racket? Are you thick or something?'

'I just wanted the place to be nice and clean for when you woke up.'

'You hoover this fucking carpet every day, woman, so it can't be dirty.' Henry took a deep breath in an endeavour to calm down and then hissed, 'Just make me some breakfast.'

He went back upstairs to his room, exasperated with Audrey. He knew she tried her best, but everything she did lately irritated him. Henry sat on the edge of the bed and pulled his trousers on, going over a conversation he'd had in the pub the night before with a mate he hadn't seen for a while, Micky Mallen. The man had said he'd seen Gloria working in Queenie's fag shop and she'd told him that Jenny was getting married. It had floored him and once again he'd realised that at times he missed his children.

When they'd first left, he'd expected that without his money to support them, Jenny would soon come running back, but that hadn't happened. It had been so long that he now realised they weren't going to return. If he wanted to see his kids, he'd have to go to them. He knew where Jenny worked, and now Gloria too, so it wouldn't be hard to find out where they were living.

As Henry stood up, his head pounded. He wasn't up to looking for them today, but he'd get round to it eventually. For now he just wanted an aspirin, and some food in his stomach.

17

Jenny opened her eyes and looked around expecting to see Pamela and Gloria still asleep. To her surprise, their beds were empty. They'd been living in their new home for two weeks now, yet she noticed Gloria's bag remained mostly unpacked.

She stretched her arms and yawned, then remembered today was Saturday, September the 23rd, her birthday. There'd been no mention of it, so she doubted anyone had remembered, but it didn't matter. She was so happy, happier than she'd ever been, and was looking forward to being Craig's wife.

As she walked down the stairs, Jenny could hear her brothers giggling in the kitchen and thought it was unusual for everyone to be up before her. She hoped they weren't up to mischief but trusted Pamela to be keeping an eye on them. She opened the kitchen door and was astounded to be greeted with a united 'SURPRISE'.

Her brothers, sisters and Craig were standing around the kitchen table. In the centre she saw a big iced cake, and balloons were strung to the backs of the chairs.

'Happy birthday, Jen,' Timmy piped.

'Yeah, happy birthday,' Peter repeated.

'We wanted to surprise you with a birthday breakfast,' Craig said, and walked over to kiss her cheek. 'Happy birthday, darling.'

'I helped Pamela make the cake,' Timmy said, then Peter added, 'Me too. I helped an' all, didn't I, Pam?'

'Yes, and I couldn't have done it without you both,' Pamela said, and ruffled Timmy's hair.

'Sit down,' Gloria instructed. 'We've already eaten, there's tea in the pot and I'm the one who is going to cook your breakfast, the full works.'

Jenny wasn't feeling hungry, but as they'd all made such an effort, she didn't like to say no. She took a seat whilst Craig poured her a cup of tea. She wasn't used to so much fuss and attention and it felt quite overwhelming. It was nice, though, as she hadn't realised how much her family appreciated her.

'Can I give Jenny her present now?' Peter asked.

'Yes, of course you can,' Pamela agreed.

Peter and Timmy ran from the kitchen then quickly returned with a gift wrapped in pretty floral paper which they shoved into her hands.

'We made it, didn't we, Peter?' Timmy said.

As she tore the paper away, Jenny saw a hand-painted picture that she recognised as their new house, and standing in front of it the boys had painted all of them including Craig. They were holding hands and every person, though not really recognisable, wore a big smile.

'It's us, and our house,' Timmy said.

'Do you like it, Jen?' Peter asked.

Jenny felt a lump in her throat and found it difficult to speak, but managed to say, 'It's beautiful.'

Timmy came to stand by her side. 'Craig made the frame for it. Where are you going to put it?'

She dashed away a tear and put an arm around her brother's waist. 'This is going to take pride of place above the fireplace. Thank you, I love it.'

Timmy and Peter exchanged smiles and it warmed Jenny's heart to see them looking so joyful. She looked at the painting again, and thought they'd captured their happy family brilliantly.

Pamela whispered, 'Happy birthday,' and handed her a small package in brown paper.

'Thank you,' Jenny said as she opened the gift to reveal a small bottle of Evette perfume. 'Oh, Pamela, you shouldn't have spent so much on me,' she cried, taking off the cap to sniff the contents. 'It smells gorgeous.'

'I saved some of my wage from Woolworth's, and I got a staff discount.'

'I like Pam working there. She always brings home bags of broken biscuits,' Timmy chirped.

'Yes, but as I don't get them for nothing it would be nice if you didn't scoff them so quickly.'

'Here you are, happy birthday, Sis,' Gloria said and handed Jenny an unwrapped lipstick. 'It's a deep red and will look smashing with your colouring. Honest, it'll look so much better than that pale pink you wear.'

Jenny doubted she'd have the nerve to wear anything so bold. 'Thank you, it's lovely,' she fibbed, not wanting to hurt Gloria's feelings.

'And finally, this is from me,' Craig said, handing her an intricately carved wooden box. 'I made it in my workshop. I thought you could use it for jewellery and keepsakes.'

Jenny peered at the lid, noticing the small love hearts and delicate flowers. It was the most stunning piece of woodwork she'd ever seen.

'Open it then,' Craig added.

She lifted the lid to see a small black velvet pouch inside. She undid the white ribbon that fastened it, then gasped when she tipped out an engagement ring.

'Well, are you going to put it on?' Craig asked.

Jenny nodded, unable to speak for fear of bursting into tears.

'Give it here,' Craig said, and slipped the ring onto her finger. 'Now it's official. You are the future Mrs Brice.'

Full of emotion, Jenny was still unable to speak. She jumped up from her seat and threw her arms around Craig.

'I love you, Jenny. Happy birthday, sweetheart.'

'Unhand your man,' Gloria said dramatically as though in a play, 'and let me have a look at that ring.'

Jenny pulled away from Craig and held out her hand.

'Nice,' Gloria said shortly.

Pamela was more forthcoming, 'It's lovely, Jenny, really lovely.'

The ring was a small cluster of diamonds set in gold, but if Craig had carved her a wooden one, she'd have cherished it just as much.

'Thank you, all of you. This is the best birthday I've ever had,' Jenny said as tears slipped from her eyes.

'Why are you crying then?' Timmy asked, sounding concerned.

'These are not sad tears, darling. They're tears of happiness.'

'Girls are weird,' he answered then lightly punched Peter's arm, saying to him, 'Come on, I'll race you upstairs.'

As Jenny sat down, Craig pulled out a chair opposite her. 'Your birthday hasn't finished yet. Pamela is taking the boys to see your gran later for their tea, and I'm going to cook you a slap-up meal while you put your feet up and relax.'

'Another meal being cooked for me. Oh, that's lovely.'

'You'll have the place to yourselves too,' Gloria said as she turned sausages over in the pan. 'I'm going out on a date with Hughie Halbert. He's taking me to the cinema.'

'Hughie Halbert . . . where do I know that name from?' Jenny asked.

'You were in the same class at school as Deirdre, his sister,' Gloria replied.

'Oh yes, I know who you mean. Isn't he Deirdre's older brother?'

'Yes, he's twenty-five, and before you say anything else, unlike Dennis he works, and no, I won't do anything I shouldn't. He's got his own car, you know,' Gloria said, then placed the cooked meal on the table.

'Thanks, this looks smashing,' Jenny said, deciding that though she thought Hughie was too old for her sister, she was better off keeping her thoughts to herself.

'Enjoy,' Gloria said, 'I'm going for a bath.' She flounced towards the door.

Pamela scraped her chair back and said, 'Wait, can I use the bathroom first? I have to get ready for work and I'm already running late.'

'Go on then but hurry up. I suppose I can do my nails while I'm waiting,' Gloria answered and followed Pamela upstairs.

'I feel ever so spoiled,' Jenny said to Craig.

'You deserve to be. The way you've kept this family together and looked after everyone is amazing. It's about time we did something nice for you in return.'

Jenny could feel her emotions rising to the surface again and fought to hold back the tears. This really was the best birthday she'd ever woken up to and so different from the year before when she'd been sporting a cut cheek thanks to her father. Those days of fear and abuse seemed a long way behind her and, as she looked at her ring again, Jenny knew she'd never forget how special this birthday was.

★ ★ ★

Henry hadn't eaten the eggs and bacon that Audrey had prepared for him. One look at her despondent face had put him right off his food. Instead, he'd thrown some clothes on, walked out without a word, and was now sitting reading the paper over a cup of tea and a bacon sandwich in Bernie's Café.

Bernie, the owner, came over to Henry's table and picked up his empty plate. 'Do you want anything else, mate?'

Henry looked over the top of his newspaper. The skinny man had a dirty white apron on. His thin, dark grey hair was greased back and from where Henry was sitting he could see bunches of hair sticking out of his nose. He grimaced, but even the sight of Bernie was more welcoming than having to look at Audrey. 'No thanks, Bernie. That sandwich was spot on.'

'Glad you enjoyed it. How's your lot? I ain't seen them in a while.'

'I dunno, mate. They've all left home.'

'I'm sorry to hear that, Henry. It must be hard for you.'

'Nah, not really. At least I can get some peace and quiet now. What about your missus, she all right?'

'No, she's coughing her bleedin' lungs up day and night, but the stubborn old bat won't go to the doctor's. That's why I'm here by myself, doing the cooking and seeing to the tables too. I could do with a hand so if one of your girls is up for it, tell 'em there's a job going.'

Henry didn't want to admit that he hadn't seen his daughters. 'Yeah, when I see them, I'll let them know.'

'Ta, do you want another cuppa?'

'No, thanks, mate,' Henry said and as he folded his newspaper, his eyes suddenly locked on the date. Jenny would be twenty-three today and an idea struck him. With it being her birthday, it could be the perfect opportunity to

170

make an inroad back into his kids' lives. Firstly, he needed to buy a birthday card, then he'd drop into Queenie's and if Gloria was working he'd wheedle their address out of her. If Gloria wasn't there, it would have to wait until Monday, but one way or the other he'd find out where they were living.

A short while later, Henry walked into Queenie's but was disappointed to see an old woman behind the counter instead of his daughter.

'What can I get you?' she asked.

'I was hoping to have a word with my daughter, Gloria.'

'She doesn't work on Saturdays. She'll be here on Monday morning . . . I hope.'

'Can I leave this for her?' Henry asked and held out the card.

'What do you think I am, a bloody postwoman?' the woman retorted.

'No, but it's a birthday card for my other daughter. I'd like Gloria to pass it on to her.'

'Why don't you give it to her yourself?'

'I would, but I'm not sure where they're living.'

'If you're her father, that's a bit odd, but it's none of my business. You'll find them on Osward Road. I don't know what number, though Gloria did mention that they've got a big red rosebush in the front garden.'

'Thank you. Give me a box of them chocolates and keep the change,' Henry said, handing the woman some coins.

He placed the chocolates and the card inside his folded newspaper and headed for Osward

Road. He didn't know what sort of welcome he'd get, but he was their father and surely they'd at least be a bit pleased to see him.

*   *   *

Dwight had his back to Lizzie in bed, so she rolled over and snuggled up behind him. She began to rub her hand over his chest and nuzzled his neck, but to her disappointment Dwight responded by climbing out of the bed.

She didn't know what was wrong with him lately but felt he was slipping away from her. He'd become distant, their daily lovemaking was now weekly, and the luxury gifts were no longer forthcoming. 'What's wrong, Dwight? Something seems to be bothering you,' Lizzie asked, wanting her man to open up and share whatever was troubling him.

Dwight ran a hand through his hair, then blurted, 'You! It's you that's bothering me.'

'Why? What have I done wrong?'

'Nothing, Lizzie, but I think it's time you moved on.'

'What? Are you kidding me? I thought we had a good thing going on.'

'Yes . . . *had*. It *was* good, but it's run its course. You're a great gal, but it's over. I've got to work tonight, and when I get home I'd like to find you gone.'

'Gone! But where am I supposed to go?'

'I'm sure you'll work something out, you're a bright woman,' Dwight drawled as he walked to the bathroom.

Lizzie rolled over onto her back, staring at the ceiling as her mind reeled. Dwight sounded so cold and detached, but surely she could persuade him to change his mind. She reached over to the bedside table and took a cigarette out of the packet. After lighting it, she took a long drag and considered her options. She wouldn't beg, but she knew how to turn him on. She'd lie low today, but when he returned from work later she'd show him exactly what he'd be missing.

★   ★   ★

Gloria padded down the stairs with a towel wrapped around her as Jenny walked out of the lounge. Her sister gave her a stern look, then told her to get back upstairs and put some clothes on.

'But I need my hairbrush and it's on the sofa.'

'I'll get it for you, and in future please don't walk around the house half-naked.'

Gloria rolled her eyes and tutted. She didn't see what all the fuss was about. She was covered up and it wasn't as if Craig ever took any notice of her in *that* way. Still, she turned around and went back upstairs. Once in her bedroom, she pulled a crumpled skirt from her bag which she thought would look nice with Jenny's pink blouse. She knew her sister wouldn't mind her borrowing her clothes, so after rummaging in Jenny's wardrobe she found the blouse and put in on, whilst looking out of the bedroom window. The room was at the rear of the house and overlooked the small back garden. Timmy and Peter were playing on a seesaw that Craig had made for them and Gloria smiled. Jenny had found herself a decent man and she hoped she'd have the same luck with Hughie.

She gave her skirt a shake, but as it still needed ironing she went through Jenny's wardrobe again. She considered most of her sister's skirts to be too long but found a pair of slacks which she'd never seen Jenny wear. She tried them on and decided they looked elegant on her and showed her shapely figure. As Gloria admired her outfit in the mirror, she heard a knock on the street door, but left one of the others to answer it.

Jenny still hadn't turned up with her hairbrush, so, now dressed, Gloria went back downstairs. She stopped in her tracks midway, staring in disbelief when she saw her father at the front door. Jenny had opened it, but she couldn't see her sister's face and could only guess her reaction.

'So ain't you gonna invite your old man in?' he asked.

Gloria suddenly recovered her wits and dashed down the rest of the stairs to stand by her sister's side.

'Hello, love, you look well,' her dad said cheerily when he saw her.

'What are you doing here?' Gloria asked suspiciously.

'It's Jenny's birthday so I've brought her a card, look, and some chocolates.'

Her father held out the gift to Jenny who seemed reluctant to take it.

'How did you know where to find us?' Gloria asked.

'The old bird in the fag shop told me. It's a bit of a walk up the hill to get here and I'm parched. Any chance of a cuppa?'

Gloria looked at Jenny. Though their dad sounded affable, she could see her sister was nervous, and noticed small beads of sweat glistening on her forehead. She wanted to tell her dad to go away and leave them alone, but it might arouse his temper.

It was Jenny who managed to stutter, 'I . . . er . . . d-don't think it's a good idea. It . . . it would upset the boys to see you.'

'Leave it out, I'm their dad. How's seeing me gonna upset them?'

'They're scared of you, Dad. We all are,' Gloria blurted.

'Don't be daft. Granted, I might have lost me rag at times, but I never laid a hand on them boys.'

'Maybe, but what about Jenny?'

'Look, Gloria, I know I've made mistakes and as I said, I lost me rag now and then, but I never ran off and left you, not like your mother. I've got every right to see my boys, and I'm holding out the olive branch here. How about a bit of give and take?'

To Gloria's surprise, Jenny pulled the door open wider and said, 'All right, come in, but please don't raise your voice or it'll frighten them.'

'Have a bit of respect for your old man. I don't need you telling me how to treat me own sons,' he snapped.

Gloria saw her sister flinch and instantly knew

this was a mistake. They should have slammed the door in his face and been done with it. At least Pamela wasn't around. Her nerves were so much better now, and bedwetting was a thing of the past, but seeing their father again could cause a backward step.

'Sorry, girl, I didn't mean to snap. It won't happen again.'

Jenny pulled the door wider, and when they walked into the front room she invited him to sit on the sofa. 'Gloria, do you mind making a pot of tea?'

'Yeah, all right,' she agreed, but didn't like leaving Jenny alone with their dad. As she left the room, she heard him telling Jenny to open the birthday card.

Craig had come into the kitchen through the back door. 'What's wrong?' he asked. 'You look as white as a sheet.'

'My dad is here. He's in the front room with Jenny.'

'What! Stay here, and keep the boys in the garden,' Craig said urgently, then hurried from the room.

Craig was right: until it was clear they'd be safe, it was best to keep her brothers out of harm's way. She was glad Craig was there to look out for Jenny. She knew how much he loved her and that he wouldn't allow her to be harmed in any way. Gloria opened the back door and called to the boys, 'Stay out there until I tell you to come in.'

'Why?' Timmy asked.

'Because I said so, that's why. If you do as

176

you're told, Craig will give you sixpence each and later on I'll take you to the sweetshop.'

'Yay!' they both cried in unison. 'Come on, Peter, let's get back on the seesaw,' Timmy squealed.

Satisfied that her brothers would be safe, and anxious to know what was going on in the front room, Gloria poured her dad a cup of lukewarm tea from the pot and took it through. However, the moment she walked into the room, she sensed the tension in the atmosphere and prayed her dad wouldn't kick off.

'Thanks,' her dad said as he took the tea.

'Mr Lombard, I appreciate you're here to see Jenny on her birthday, but we have plans for today. In future, rather than make a wasted journey, I suggest you let us know in advance that you're coming,' Craig said.

'What plans?' her dad asked, and then Gloria noticed he looked disgusted as he slurped the almost cold tea.

'I can't say. It's a surprise for Jenny.'

'Don't give me that bullshit, sonny. I know when I'm not welcome.'

'Right then,' Craig said. 'I'll be honest with you. No, you're not welcome. This is my house and I'd like you to leave, please.'

Gloria cringed. She guessed her father wouldn't take kindly to Craig throwing him out and expected the cup and saucer to go flying, but instead her dad placed them calmly down and stood up. He looked deflated, like a pricked balloon, and for a fleeting moment she felt sorry for him.

'I admire you, son. It takes a brave man to stand up to me. You know I could knock you through to next door, but you've stood your ground and been straight with me. I'll go, but I would like to make arrangements to see my boys and Pam. Is that all right?'

'I'm not sure . . . ' Craig said doubtfully.

Jenny cut in. 'You can see the boys, but not right now. I need time to prepare them.'

' 'Prepare them'? What do you mean?'

'Dad, I told you, they're frightened of you, and Pamela is too. When we lived with you her nerves were in a terrible state and she used to wet the bed. She's so much better now and I'm not sure she'll want to see you.'

Once again Gloria held her breath, but her father remained calm as he said, 'If she doesn't, that's fine. We can wait until she's ready, but I'd still like to see my boys. How about I come back next Saturday, say at eleven o' clock.'

Jenny hung her head for a moment, then she nodded and quietly said, 'Yes, all right.'

'Great, happy birthday, Jen, and I'll see you next week.'

Much to their astonishment and relief, he left without any aggravation. Craig saw him out, and once Gloria heard the door close behind him, she turned to Jenny and spat, 'What on earth are you thinking? Why are you letting him come back?'

'I don't have much choice, Gloria. If Dad choses to, he could take Pamela and the boys back to live with him. He's their father, which means he has rights, whereas we have none. At

178

least, this way, if he sees them occasionally, it might be enough.'

Gloria slumped. She hadn't thought of that. Jenny was right, and they'd have to tread carefully. 'At least he's coming back on a Saturday again, so Pamela will be at work,' she mused.

'Yes, and it gives me a week to prepare the boys. Craig, you'll be here, won't you?' Jenny asked.

'Too bloody right! I wouldn't leave you, or them, alone with him, not for a minute.'

Gloria reluctantly realised that Jenny had done the right thing. She was about to go back up to her room when she remembered she'd told her brothers to stay outside. 'Bugger, I forgot. I'll tell the boys they can come in now, and Craig, give 'em both sixpence.'

'All right, but why?' Craig asked.

''Cos I told them you would.'

'Good, isn't it, Jenny? Your sister doesn't pay a penny towards anything and now she's giving away my money too,' Craig said jokingly.

'If you're giving it away, I'll have some,' Gloria said brazenly.

'No chance,' Craig replied, grinning.

'Spoilsport,' Gloria told him, smiling too as she picked up her hairbrush and went upstairs. She had to admit that now they were out of Craig's cramped flat, it was nice living with them in this house. There was always a pleasant atmosphere, with lots of laughter, but now that her dad had turned up she feared it was all going to change.

179

18

'We have the house to ourselves and your dinner awaits,' Craig said as he walked into the room that evening, acting like a posh waiter with a tea-towel draped over his arm.

Jenny giggled. All thoughts of her father's visit earlier had been pushed to the back of her mind. She was determined not to let it ruin what had been a very special birthday. She followed Craig through to the kitchen and beamed with delight. Craig had made such an effort to make it look beautiful. He'd put candles on the table along with flowers in a vase and, as she went to sit down, he rushed to be behind her.

'Allow me,' he said as he pulled out her chair.

She looked over her shoulder, and said softly, 'This is perfect.'

'And so are you, my love. I've never tried it before, but I've got us a bottle of wine. It's French. The chap in the shop said it's good so I'll have to take his word for it.' He poured the liquid into a glass tumbler. 'I apologise for the lack of wine glasses.'

She picked hers up, clinked it with Craig's, and then took a sip of the chilled white wine.

'What do you think?' Craig asked.

'It must be an acquired taste, but I'll persevere.'

'Yes, I know what you mean. I hope you're

hungry 'cos I've made enough to sink a battleship.'

'Yes, I am, but don't give me too much,' Jenny said. Craig was a good cook, the result of once living alone, and he didn't mind doing a share of the chores either.

He took a big pot from the oven and placed it on the table. It smelled delicious and Jenny thought it looked like chicken stew.

As Craig dished up, he said, 'The chap in the shop where I bought the wine said this dish would go perfectly with it. It's French, and called cock a van, or something like that. Tuck in.'

'Cock a van . . . what does that mean?' Jenny asked, bemused.

'I've no idea, but I had right fun and games trying to get hold of some of the ingredients. I ended up having to go up West. I hope you like it?'

'It's . . . different,' Jenny answered. She wasn't sure about the unfamiliar flavours, but she quite liked it, and drank the last of her wine.

Craig refilled her glass, saying teasingly, 'You've got the acquired taste then?'

'It's certainly grown on me. Is this what they eat and drink in those posh restaurants in Chelsea?'

'I don't know, but I would imagine so.'

'As you sell your furniture in Chelsea, I thought you would eat there too.'

'No, I send out my catalogue and get orders for pieces. I rarely have time to venture out. Sometimes I could do with an assistant, and you never know, maybe one of your brothers would like to work for me in a few years.'

'It'll be more than a few years, but as they're keen to spend the day with you, one of them might want to follow in your footsteps. Excuse me a mo,' Jenny said, and stood up to leave the table. It was only then she noticed she felt a little wobbly.

'Are you all right?' Craig asked, jumping to steady her.

'I think the wine has gone to my head. Will you help me upstairs to the bathroom, please?'

'Come on then,' Craig said, and with his arm around her waist he gently edged her along the hallway.

'I quite like this feeling,' Jenny giggled. 'I think it's the first time I've ever been drunk.'

'You're not drunk, darling, just a bit tipsy. Now, slowly up the stairs.'

'I love you, you do know that, don't you?' Jenny gushed.

'Yes, and I love you too.'

'You're amazing . . . and so dishy . . . you're going to be the best husband ever . . . '

'And you're a little more tipsy than I thought,' Craig laughed, then opened the bathroom door and eased her in. 'Are you sure you can manage in there?' he called through the door.

'Yes . . . I'm fine,' Jenny answered and after using the toilet she washed her hands and splashed cold water over her face. 'I feel a bit better now,' she told Craig as she left the bathroom.

'That's good,' Craig said, smiling with amusement.

Jenny ventured along the landing. She felt herself swaying slightly, her head spinning and asked, 'Do you mind if I lie down for ten minutes?'

'No, of course not. I'll clear up the kitchen while you have a little nap.'

Jenny staggered again. 'Oops, I don't think I can make it to the bedroom.'

Craig quickly wrapped his arm around her waist and guided her. He sat her down on the bed, removed her slippers and as she lay back he said softly, 'There, you'll be all right now.'

'Please . . . don't go,' Jenny pleaded, and took his hand to pull him down next to her. She wanted Craig to hold her, to kiss her . . .

'Jenny . . . '

'Take your shoes off,' she husked.

Craig quickly removed them and then rested his head beside hers on the pillow. He turned to look at her, their faces so close that their noses almost touched. She gazed into his eyes and he gently kissed her as he pulled her body closer. Jenny felt excitement stirring, and this time, as Craig's kisses became more passionate, she didn't protest. His hands began to roam over her body and then ventured inside her top. She groaned with pleasure and pushed closer to him, feeling his manhood grind against her inner thigh. As Craig continued to caress her Jenny felt a longing for more. It felt so good, she didn't want it to stop, and then she allowed him to tug down her knickers.

'Oh, Jenny . . . I want you so badly,' Craig said in her ear as he rolled on top of her.

Her legs parted, and after a bit of a fumble he

entered her. She felt an intense burning sensation, but Craig was gentle and moved slowly. Soon the pain subsided and was replaced with overwhelming pleasure. She felt a wave of euphoria rise through her body and writhed her hips against him. He responded to her excitement and thrust harder, then with a groan of ecstasy he collapsed on top of her.

'Oh . . . Jenny,' he gasped.

Jenny lay still, sweating and panting for breath. She wasn't sure what had happened, but she'd enjoyed it.

'Are you all right?' Craig asked as he moved off her.

'Yes, I'm more than all right,' she answered. 'I know we should have waited until our wedding night, but I'm almost your wife.'

'Yes, you are, and once we're married the only thing that will be any different is a bit of paper.'

Jenny snuggled into his arms. She wanted to stay there forever but forced herself up to arrange her dishevelled clothes. 'Pamela will be back any minute with the boys.'

'Crikey,' Craig said, quickly arranging his clothes too.

Jenny smiled softly as she watched him. She'd thought her birthday had been special this morning, and only her father turning up had marred it. Now she had lost her virginity to the man she loved, and he'd soon be her husband. Once again she decided this was her best birthday — ever.

★ ★ ★

Lizzie had stayed out of Dwight's way for most of the day, and when he'd left for work at the dancehall he hadn't said goodbye. Once the door had closed, she'd set about getting everything prepared for when he came home.

She'd tidied and cleaned the flat, putting fresh sheets on the bed. Then she'd bathed and put on her most alluring underwear under a provocative dress. She's applied her make-up with care, styled her hair and sprayed herself with perfume.

The scene was now perfectly set, the lights dimmed and soft music playing as Lizzie draped herself on the sofa, waiting for Dwight. She checked the clock. It was just after midnight and he was due home at any moment. Lizzie adjusted herself for the umpteenth time, and quickly downed the last of the gin in her glass. When she heard a kerfuffle at the door, her ears pricked. He was home, but Lizzie was sure she heard a woman tittering.

Dwight came into the front room with his arm draped around a young woman who almost fell through the door. With the amount of lipstick Dwight had smeared around his mouth, it was obvious that he'd been snogging the woman. No, not a woman: she was more like a teenager. Fuming, Lizzie leaped off the sofa and snarled, 'What the hell's going on?'

'I thought I told you I didn't want you here,' Dwight drawled.

'Well, I'm not going so you can get rid of that tart!'

'No, Paula isn't going anywhere . . . but you're welcome to join us,' he said with a smirk.

Slowly it dawned on Lizzie what he was suggesting, and her stomach lurched. 'You dirty, filthy bastard! Gloria was right about you all along!'

'Ah, Gloria, Gloria . . . such a shapely young lady. I sure do miss the sight of her in her skimpy nightdress, especially at night, when it was hot, and she'd kick off the covers. Her little nightie used to rise, and I'd see those sweet cheeks . . . '

Lizzie felt bile rise in her throat. When Gloria had lived with them, Dwight *had* been hankering after her, yet she'd been too blind to see it. Though Gloria had told her, she hadn't wanted to believe it, but there was no denying it now. She ran from the room with her hand covering her mouth.

Once Lizzie had thrown up, she wiped her mouth and washed it out with water from the tap. She could hear Dwight and the teenager cavorting in the front room. It was too much for her. She wanted to get out, but where could she go at this time of night? As quickly as possible she threw some clothes in a bag and was careful not to leave her precious jewels behind. At least she had them to either sell or pawn. She stomped from the bedroom and briefly paused on the threshold of the front room. Dwight and the girl were on the sofa; he had his hands all over her and was oblivious to her watching him. Lizzie knew it was pointless to say anything and with her teeth clenched she walked out. She'd have liked to smash their heads together, but all she could do was vent her anger on the front door as she slammed it with all her might behind her.

Lizzie stood in the dark street and fought back tears. She'd never felt so humiliated and alone in her life. She was at a loss about where to go. She had no money, just the jewellery in her coat pocket, but that wasn't going to do her any good in the dead of night. She'd lost her mother's key, didn't know where her children were living, and had no friends to call on.

That only left Henry, and as much as she'd prefer to never see her husband again, he was her only option.

19

It was Sunday morning, and as Jenny sliced a loaf of bread she felt like she was walking on air. Even the impending visit from her father in six days' time wasn't enough to diminish her smile. When Gloria breezed into the kitchen, Jenny thought her sister looked just as happy too.

'Your date went well then?' she asked.

'Yep! Hughie's taking me out again later, for a drive in the country.'

'I didn't hear you come home. It must have been very late.'

'Not really, but you was out for the count. Craig waited up for me, made sure I was home safe and sound, bless him. He'll be a good father when you have kids, much better than ours.'

'Yes, he will, but it wouldn't take much to be better than Dad.' Jenny paused for a moment then said, 'Gloria, I've been thinking, and it might be best if we don't tell Pamela. She'll be at work so there's no need for her to know that Dad's coming here.'

'Yes, you're right. We don't want her starting all that bedwetting malarkey again.' Gloria frowned. 'I've only just noticed how quiet it is. Where is everyone?'

'Craig dragged Pamela and the boys out for an early-morning walk. He thought I needed a bit of peace.'

Gloria noticed her sister's eyes flit to the

empty wine bottle next to the bin. 'I see, bit of a sore head, have we?' she teased.

'It isn't too bad, but I won't be drinking that French stuff again. The others will be back for their breakfast soon so I'm doing egg sandwiches. Do you want one?'

'No, thanks, I'm watching my weight. I'll just have an apple and a glass of water.'

Jenny looked at her sister in disbelief. Gloria had never worried about her weight before and for good reason. She had developed early, had a perfect figure and was lucky she could eat whatever she liked without piling on the pounds. 'What's brought this on? You look the same as always so why are you worrying about your size?'

'Hughie commented on my backside. He said it looked big in those trousers I was wearing.'

Jenny's hackles rose. She didn't like the idea of Hughie criticising Gloria, especially as it wasn't true. 'That's rubbish. There's nothing wrong with your figure.'

'It wouldn't hurt to lose a few pounds.'

She hadn't met him yet, but Jenny doubted Hughie was the right man for her sister. If he felt anything for Gloria, he'd be praising her, not slating her.

★　★　★

Lizzie sat at the kitchen table that had once been so familiar to her. 'It was good of you to let me in last night,' she said.

'I could hardly leave you out on the streets at silly o'clock in the morning, but I ain't happy

189

about this. You take fucking liberties, you do,' Henry said belligerently.

'Would you like some breakfast, Lizzie?' Audrey asked quietly.

'No, she fucking wouldn't,' Henry barked. 'If she wants something to eat, she can get it herself. Don't you go waiting on her.'

Audrey's body tensed, her voice barely above a whisper as she said, 'Sorry, Henry.'

Lizzie felt sorry for her and said, 'Thanks, Audrey, but why don't you sit down, and I'll do us all a nice fry-up. It's the least I can do after staying the night.'

Audrey looked at Henry as though waiting for his approval, and when he nodded his head she pulled out a chair and sat down.

'Right then,' Lizzie said as she set to work. She cut some bread and put it under the grill to toast before putting lard into the pan to fry some eggs.

'I saw Jenny yesterday,' Henry said, his tone milder.

'Oh yeah, how is she?'

'She looks happy with this bloke of hers. He was all right, nice lad.'

'And the rest of them?'

'I didn't see Pam and the boys, but Gloria was there, looking all grown-up.'

'She may look grown-up, but she's still only sixteen. Where are they living?'

'In Osward Road. I went round to give Jenny a card.'

'A card. What for?' Lizzie asked, then her eyebrows rose as the penny dropped. 'Of course, it was Jenny's birthday, but with everything that was going on yesterday it slipped my mind.'

'Yeah, about that. Look, Lizzie, I couldn't give a toss that you got chucked out, so don't go thinking you can stay another night. Once you've had your breakfast you can bugger off.'

'But, Henry, I haven't got anywhere to go,' Lizzie begged as she placed the food on the table. 'Please, you've got spare rooms. Can't I stay for a bit, just until I get myself sorted?'

'No, you can't. What do you think this place is, a fucking hotel?'

'Henry, I can pay, look . . . ' Lizzie reached round to where her coat was draped over the back of her chair and pulled the jewellery from the pocket. She slapped it down on the kitchen table. 'That lot's gotta be worth a few bob. I'll take them down to the pawnshop when it opens tomorrow.'

She watched as Henry picked up one of the earrings, then the ring. She saw the corners of his mouth begin to lift and thought she'd won him round, but his smile turned into a chuckle, then a roar of laughter.

'What . . . what's so funny?'

'You stupid cow! This ain't worth nothing . . . it's just paste.'

'No, Henry, you're wrong. What would you know about fine jewellery?'

He held out the ring to Audrey and said, 'Have a butcher's. It's fake, ain't it?'

'I . . . erm . . . I . . . ' Audrey stuttered.

'I said look at it,' Henry snapped. 'You used to work in a jeweller's when you was younger, so you'll be able to say if it's real.'

191

Audrey picked it up and it didn't take her long to say, 'Yes, it . . . it's fake.'

Lizzie's teeth clenched. Dwight had already humiliated her, and now this. 'The lying, conniving, cheating bastard,' she seethed. 'You should sort him out, Henry. Go round there and break his fucking neck. He was after our Gloria, you know.'

'What, your American fancy man was trying to get hold of my girl?'

'Yes, he was, though I had no idea what he was up to and only just found out. He's a sick pervert, Henry, and you ought to show him what for. Give him a good bleedin' hiding.'

'You'd love that, wouldn't you? Me slapping your ex for you. Do I look like I've just got off the last banana boat, eh? Well, do I?' Henry roared, smashing his fist down on the table.

Lizzie jumped. 'No, Henry, you don't, but I swear I'm telling you the truth.'

'You can swear all you like, but I don't believe you. You've only come out with this now because the geezer has conned you and you want payback. Forget it, Liz, I ain't doing your dirty work for you. Now eat your grub then get out!'

'Well, thanks for nothing,' Lizzie said, deflated. It was clear that Henry wasn't going to let her stay, so not only was she homeless, with fake jewels she was penniless too.

20

A week after her birthday, Jenny woke up on Saturday with a feeling of foreboding. She'd spoken to her brothers and though they didn't seem keen on seeing their dad, they hadn't been overly upset either. The same couldn't be said for Pamela. They hadn't wanted to tell her that he was visiting, but as Jenny realised she would probably hear about it from her brothers, she decided it would be better coming from her. Both she and Gloria assured her that she didn't have to see him, yet even so she'd wet the bed twice that week.

Rain hammered against the window. Today was so different from last week. Jenny looked at her ring to remind herself of the good things in her life. Surely her dad would only be here for an hour or so, and hopefully, if she handled it well, they'd all get through it unscathed.

The smell of burnt toast wafted up to her room. Jenny threw the bed covers off to trudge downstairs and through the smoky hallway to the kitchen. 'What's going on in here?' she asked, and saw Craig waving a tea-towel in the air.

'Craig burned my toast,' Peter said, stifling a chortle.

'I can see that. Pam, open the back door.'

The smoke soon cleared, and Craig attempted to toast another couple of slices. 'Do you want some, Jenny?'

'No, thanks. I'll just have a cup of tea,' she said. Her stomach was in knots and she couldn't face breakfast.

'I've got to go,' Pam said as she scraped back her chair.

It was early for her to leave for work, but Jenny guessed she wanted to be out of the house in case their father turned up ahead of time. 'Dad won't be here until eleven o'clock. You don't have to go yet.'

Gloria had been in the bathroom and walked into the kitchen with her hair in rollers, her nose wrinkling. 'Blimey, who's trying to set the house alight?'

'Craig,' the boys answered together.

'Do you want some toast, Gloria?' Craig offered.

'Nope, bread doesn't do my waistline any favours. Hughie says I should steer clear of the stuff, along with chips, chocolate and cakes.'

Jenny bit her tongue. The more she heard about this Hughie, the less she liked him.

'Does that mean I can have your puddings from now on?' Timmy asked.

'We only have pudding on Sunday.'

'Ain't it Sunday tomorrow?' Timmy asked.

'Yes, and you'll be able to have my roast spuds too if you like 'cos Hughie said they ain't no good for me neither.'

'That's not fair, I want them. Roast spuds is my favourite,' Peter whined.

'All right, you can share them,' Gloria said impatiently, then added, 'Anyway, I probably won't be here for dinner tomorrow, so you'll be

194

able to have the lot.'

'Oh, why's that?' Jenny asked but had already guessed it would be something to do with Hughie.

'Hughie hasn't said anything yet, but I think he's going to invite me to meet his parents tomorrow. He's picking me up around three, so I'll find out then.'

'Will you invite him in?' Jenny asked. 'I'd like to meet him.'

'Er . . . no,' Gloria answered bluntly.

'Why not?'

'I couldn't bring him in here! I haven't been inside yet, but you should see where his parents live. In comparison to this, their house is like a bloody mansion and it's on the posh side of Wandsworth Common.'

'Our house is nothing to be ashamed of,' Jenny said defensively. She and Craig had worked hard to provide this family home and she kept it spotless. 'I was at school with Hughie's sister, Deirdre, and she didn't act as though she's better than us.'

'She wanted to fit in so she played it down. Their father wanted them to have a normal education, but really they're nothing like us. He's a barrister or something fancy like that and Hughie told me his mother insists that they dress for dinner. I think they must be rich because they've got staff too, a cook and a maid.'

'Don't let it overwhelm you,' Jenny advised. 'Money or not, we're all the same under the skin.'

'I did wonder if I should curtsy when I meet

them,' Gloria said with a laugh.

'They're not royalty.'

'Maybe not, but I should learn to speak a bit better.'

'Is this Hughie's suggestion?' Jenny asked.

'Yeah, he reckons I sound common and if I want to fit in with his friends and family, I'll need to practise my pro-nun-si-a-shon. Blimey, I can hardly say the word.'

Jenny found herself biting her tongue again. It seemed Hughie wanted to mould Gloria into the type of woman he wanted, but with such different backgrounds she wondered if it was possible. For Gloria's sake, Jenny hoped so, though she'd have preferred her sister to find a man like Craig. He never judged her or tried to change anything about her. In fact, at least once a day, he'd tell her how beautiful he thought she was. Jenny looked across the kitchen at him and thought how lucky she was. Not only had he rescued her, but he was gorgeous too. She'd found her perfect man and now they had their perfect life. She hoped it wasn't about to be disrupted by her father.

★   ★   ★

Henry felt a twinge of nervousness as he approached the house where his children lived. On his last visit he got the impression that his presence wasn't wanted, but they were his children and he'd come to realise he missed them. He hoped the gifts he'd brought would win them over.

He knocked on the door and plastered on a big smile. 'Hello, love,' he said when Jenny opened it, once again struck by her red hair that made her stand out as different from the rest of them. 'I'm glad this rain has stopped. Nice weather for ducks though.'

'Come in,' she answered without returning his smile.

He followed her through to the front room and saw that the boys weren't there. He hoped Jenny hadn't changed her mind about letting him see them. She had no right to do that, and there'd be trouble if she had. He'd demand that they, and Pamela, came home with him, but in truth it would be an idle threat. He didn't really want them, preferring just to visit them now and then. He liked the peaceful life he had now, and the extra money in his pockets, and he didn't want to give Lizzie any excuse to call round. Still, if needs be he'd show his hand and that would show his stuck-up daughter who was in charge.

Craig stood up as he entered the room and offered him a seat on the sofa which Henry accepted before asking, 'Where are the boys and Pamela?'

'Pam's at work. She's got a Saturday job. Gloria will bring Timmy and Peter in from the back garden shortly, but first I want to lay down some ground rules,' Jenny answered.

Henry's temper flared, though he hid it well. The cheeky bitch, he thought, who was she to lay down rules? If Jenny kept this up he'd sort her out, but for now he took a deep breath and

197

managed to say calmly, 'Go on then, let's hear them.'

Craig stepped in to answer. 'If you raise your voice it will frighten the boys, and obviously there must be no violence.'

'I've never laid a hand on my sons and I'm not about to start now,' Henry protested. This was none of Craig's business, and it he'd didn't keep his mouth shut, he'd bloody well flatten him.

'All right, Dad, I'll ask Gloria to fetch the boys in,' Jenny said.

The men stared at each other in silence until Jenny returned. Henry noticed Peter was holding onto Jenny's skirt and peeping at him from behind it. Timmy had a firm grip on Gloria's hand and it looked like he was trembling. It puzzled Henry. He couldn't understand why they seemed so afraid of him. 'Peter, Timmy . . . Look what I've got for you in this bag,' he said, keeping his voice soft as he pulled out a pigskin football that had been kicked into his backyard. Next he pulled out a marionette. He'd found the puppet in a box by a dustbin on his rounds and had mended the strings. It was nearly as good as new.

Timmy was the first to cautiously approach. Henry leaned forward with the puppet and showed him how to make it dance. At last Timmy smiled, then asked if he could have a go. Henry handed him the toy and he soon mastered the skill of manoeuvring it.

'Look, Peter, look at the funny man dancing,' he said gleefully.

Peter let go of Gloria's hand and joined in, but

after a short while asked, 'Can we take the ball in the garden?'

'Yes and perhaps Dad would like to have a kick around with you?'

'Yeah, you go and set up something for a goal and I'll be out in a minute,' Henry said to his sons.

He waited until they were out of earshot, then asked Jenny, 'Why are they so scared of me? What fucking nonsense have you been feeding them?'

Craig stepped in front of Jenny and answered, 'With respect, Mr Lombard, Jenny hasn't told them anything. In fact she never says a bad word about you. Your children are frightened of you because they've witnessed your violent temper. They've seen you beating their sister, so badly that she was carried off in an ambulance, and they've only recently stopped having nightmares about it.'

Some of what Craig said hit home. Yes, Henry thought, he'd been vile to Jenny, yet as he turned it over in his mind, denial set in. He hadn't been that bad. Overall he'd been a good father and provided for them. They'd never gone hungry, or without clothes and shoes as he had as a child. It hadn't been easy, bringing them up without their mother, and all right, he might have taken his frustrations out on them, but he wasn't going to stand for Craig pointing that out. 'With fucking respect, my arse. My family business has got nothing to do with you, so keep your mouth shut,' Henry growled as he got to his feet.

Craig stood his ground and said, 'Before this

gets out of hand, I think you should leave.'

'Yeah, and before I grind your cocky fucking face into the floor.'

Henry saw his daughters, and Craig too, recoil in obvious fear. Good, he thought, that'll fucking teach them. He glared at them before marching out, slamming the front door behind him, then in blind fury he spun around and punched it.

'Shit, that hurt,' Henry ground out as he nursed his hand, sure he'd broken knuckles, but gained some satisfaction in seeing that he'd left a big dent in the wood. It was their fault. They'd wound him up. They'd ruined what was supposed to be a pleasant hour with his kids and he'd never forgive Jenny or Craig for this. Never, and it would be a mess of their own making if he chose to claim back his younger children.

21

Pamela had come home from work and seen the dented front door. She guessed that their father had caused the damage and she'd become withdrawn since, with her nightly accidents resuming. Jenny struggled to keep up with washing her sister's sheets, especially getting them dry now that the weather had taken a turn for the worse.

Over a week had passed since their father's visit, and on this Sunday morning it was raining heavily again. Jenny noticed that her brothers seemed bored and restless. Pamela was sitting in a corner reading a book, seemingly in a world of her own. Gloria was busy making herself look beautiful for her man, and Craig was doing some extra hours at work to get a special order fulfilled.

'Who wants to come and see Gran with me?' Jenny asked.

Timmy and Peter's hands shot into the air and they both excitedly said, 'Me!'

'What about you, Pam, do you want to come?'

'Yes, all right.'

'Get your coats and your wellies on, and boys, no arguing with each other. You know it gets on Gran's nerves when you two start bickering.'

'Will Gran have cakes for us?' Timmy asked.

'I expect so, she normally does.'

It didn't take them long to reach Edith's flat.

The boys ran on ahead and knocked on the door whilst Jenny and Pamela caught them up. When the door opened, Jenny was astonished to see her mother.

'Ain't you going to say hello?' she said.

Peter and Timmy wrapped their arms around her waist, both saying, 'Mummy!', clearly pleased to see her.

'What are you doing here?' Jenny asked.

'Your gran is putting me up for a while. Come on in. She thought you might call in to see her today.'

As they walked in, the boys jabbered at their mother with excitement, talking over each other, but this already seemed to get on her nerves. 'For Gawd's sake, shut up, the pair of you,' she demanded. 'I can hardly hear myself think.'

They both fell silent, and as they entered the front room, their gran said, 'Well now, ain't you a sight for sore eyes.'

'Hello, Gran,' Jenny greeted her, Pamela too, while the boys remained quiet.

'Now Jenny, your gran told me you're getting married. Have you set a date yet?'

'Er . . . yes . . . November.'

'Could be a bit chilly, but I've got that nice white fur stole. It'll be good to give it an airing.'

Jenny knew if she told her mother in front of the boys that she wasn't invited, there'd be an explosion, so kept it to herself for now and asked, 'Why are you staying here?'

''Cos she ain't got nowhere else to go. No other bugger is stupid enough to put up with her,' Edith said, then added, 'Pamela, take the coppers from my dish on my dressing table and take the boys up the newsagent's to get some sweets. Get a move on 'cos he'll be closing soon. He only opens to sell the Sunday papers.'

'Come on, Peter,' urged Timmy. 'We can get some flying saucers!'

'I don't want to go . . . I want to stay here with my mummy.'

'I'll still be here when you get back,' their mother told him.

Once Pamela had left with the boys, Edith said, 'Lizzie, go and make us a cup of tea.'

'Jenny can make it.'

'Don't be so bloody lazy. The girl has only just got here.'

'Yeah, yeah, all right,' she said with obvious reluctance as she went to the kitchen.

Jenny was pleased to have a chance to quiz her gran and asked, 'How long is she staying here for?'

'Who knows? Not long, I hope. She turned up the other week after that Dwight chucked her out. Apparently, she'd stayed at your father's for a night, but he don't want her there, not now he's got himself a new woman.'

'A new woman?' Jenny parroted, shocked.

Lizzie walked back into the room to catch the last part of the conversation and said, 'That's right. Did you know your dad has a woman called Audrey living in my house?'

'No,' Jenny said, amazed that her mother would refer to it as *her* house.

'Quiet little thing, and a bit on the plain side for Henry's tastes. I felt sorry for her. Your dad wasn't very nice to her and she didn't stand up for herself. More fool her. Now then, Jenny. I hear you're living in a nice house with three bedrooms.'

Jenny instantly knew where the conversation would be going next. 'Yes, that's right, though it's still a bit of a squeeze.'

'Surely there's room for one more little one?'

Just as Jenny had expected, her mum was angling to come and stay with them. 'No, there isn't, and even if there was I wouldn't take you in. Gloria told me what Dwight was up to, and that you refused to believe her. She won't want to see you, and you won't be invited to my wedding.'

'You nasty little mare,' her mother screeched.

'Shut up, Lizzie,' Edith ordered. 'After what's gone on, I can't believe you expected an invite.'

'Bloody hell, all right, Dwight had his eye on Gloria, but he didn't touch her. If you ask me she made a big fuss about nothing and anyway, I ain't with him now.'

'Yeah, but only because he chucked you out,' Edith remarked.

'Please,' Jenny said, 'Pamela and the boys will be back soon, and I don't want them to hear us arguing. They've seen and heard enough of rows and violence.'

'Yeah, sorry, love,' her gran said.

'Fine. I'm going to the toilet,' Lizzie said.

As soon as her mother was out of sight, Jenny said, 'Gran, Craig's uncle is going to pick you up for the wedding. If Mum's still here, I hope she doesn't make it difficult for you.'

'Whether she's here or not, I won't miss your special day. Do you need any help with your dress or flowers?'

'There's no need, thanks. I won't be making a big fuss, and Pamela is dying to help.'

'All right, love. I doubt you'll get much help from Gloria. Talking of which, how is she?'

'She's busy with Hughie, her new boyfriend,' Jenny answered.

'You need toilet rolls,' her mother said as she walked back into the room.

Edith rolled her eyes and said, 'I don't see why. There's nothing wrong with cut-up squares of newspaper.'

Jenny laughed, then a knock on the door signalled that Pamela was back with the boys, and she was relieved when the atmosphere in the room lightened. It wasn't going to be easy to drag her brothers away from their mum, and she knew there would be tantrums and questions later. She'd tell them that they might see her again when they came to visit their gran but, knowing her mother, she would soon be off with another man. When that happened, it would probably be months before she turned up again.

★　★　★

'Hughie, it's not really nice weather for a drive in the country,' Gloria complained.

He was taking her to a quiet lovers' lane that they'd frequented on a couple of occasions. She knew what for, but she'd found making love on the back seat of his Ford Popular to be

205

uncomfortable, though they did have a giggle.

'We have an alternative that I was going to suggest to you later, but now you've brought the subject up . . . '

'Oh yes, do tell,' Gloria said, trying to sound well-spoken.

'My father has a flat in Holborn which he keeps for when he's working at the courts, but he very rarely uses it nowadays. If I tell him he needs someone to keep an eye on it, a sort of live-in housekeeper, you could take the job on. That means you could stay there and then I could come and see you whenever I like.'

'I like the sound of that, but I'm not sure about living in Holborn.'

'You wait until you see the place, it's very swanky and you'll love it.'

'I'm sure it is, but I don't know anyone in Holborn and how would I get to work?'

'You won't have to. You'd earn a wage as the housekeeper.'

Gloria gazed out of the passenger-side window as she mulled over the idea. She didn't enjoy working in Queenie's and had always imagined herself living somewhere up town. 'OK, I'll do it, but why can't you move in with me?'

'I'm afraid that would be out of the question. My father would never allow me to live there. He has always made it quite clear that if I want my own place I have to find the funds to pay for it. Don't worry though, I'll be a frequent visitor — very frequent.'

Gloria was a bit disappointed but felt a thrill of excitement at the thought of living in the flat with Hughie probably turning up every evening. It would be their own little love nest in an upmarket area. It was perfect, and she couldn't wait to get home to pack her bags. The only fly in the ointment was her sister, but there was no need for Jenny to know the whole truth. She'd just tell her that she'd got a live-in job in Holborn, a step up from Queenie's, and that might even impress her.

22

Craig looked out of the window as he finished making his and Jenny's sandwiches to take to work. The sky was heavy with dark clouds, and he expected it to rain soon. It had poured for days now, and he hoped the weather would clear before their wedding day. His stomach churned. Every time he thought about their wedding, he felt a rush of excitement and nerves. It was now nearing the end of October, with just over two weeks to wait until he could call Jenny his wife.

The kitchen door flew open as Timmy and Peter rushed in, chattering to each other about school. Pamela followed shortly after them, and then Jenny. Craig looked at her dishevelled hair and loved the thought of soon waking up next to her every morning.

She walked over to him, yawning, and kissed his cheek. 'Good morning,' she said chirpily, but then glanced out of the window. 'Blimey, look at that sky.'

'Yes, it looks like more rain on the way. There's tea in the pot and I've made you Spam sandwiches.'

'Spam again . . . can I have cheese tomorrow?'

'Yes, all right, but I thought it was only Gloria who doesn't like Spam.'

'I used to, but I've gone off it,' Jenny said, then frowned. 'I miss Gloria. I know she's only been gone a few days, but I hope she comes to see us soon and lets us know how she's getting on in Holborn. Fancy her living there, who'd have thought it?'

'You know Gloria. I'm sure she's fine and living the life of Riley,' Craig said reassuringly. He spotted Timmy sticking his finger in the jam jar. 'Oi, I saw that. What have you been told about fingers and jam?'

Timmy hunched his head down. 'Sorry, Craig, but I was only getting a fly out.'

'Oh, yeah, so where's the fly?'

'It flew away, that's why they're called flies. Why ain't birds called flies too?'

Craig tried not to laugh. The boy was wily, quick with an excuse and a question to distract, but finding he didn't really have an answer he just said, 'Birds aren't insects. Now pour out some milk for you and your brother. Your toast is nearly ready.'

'Jenny, can I take the boys to see Gran after school?' Pamela asked.

'I should think so, but why?' Jenny asked.

Craig knew Jenny was thankful that her mother hadn't stayed long at her gran's. She'd gone off with a bloke, taking a couple of pounds from Edith's purse with her. Edith hadn't seemed too worried about the theft. She was just glad to see the back of her, and now things were back to normal.

'My friend Linda has invited me to hers for tea, so I thought I'd ask Gran to keep an eye on the boys until I pick them up again. I can make sure it's only for about an hour,' Pamela answered.

'Don't worry, I'm sure Gran won't mind keeping an eye on those two until I finish work, so you can stay for more than an hour. Tell you what, you can ask Linda if she'd like to come with us on Saturday. I need to go shopping for something to wear for the wedding, and as Gloria isn't likely to show her face, I could do with your opinions.'

'Linda would love that! Where are we going shopping? There's not much around here except that snooty boutique.'

'I thought we could hop on a bus to Clapham Junction. There's that big department store, Arding and Hobbs,' Jenny answered, then said, 'But don't tell Craig, 'cos it's quite expensive in there.'

Craig laughed. 'I may not be able to hear you, but I can see your lips moving.' He was pleased to see that Pamela was coming out of her shell again, and she'd stopped wetting the bed too. When her father turned up, Pam's nerves had caused her to make a few mistakes at Woolworth's and she'd lost her Saturday job. It was a shame because she'd enjoyed working there. He walked over to Jenny and kissed her on the cheek. 'You just make sure you get yourself something really nice to wear.'

'I'll do my best,' Jenny said, beaming at him.

Craig smiled back. It was a typical Tuesday morning, and, like every day since Jenny had come into his life, he enjoyed each minute of it.

★ ★ ★

It was nearly lunchtime and though Jenny was hungry, the thought of Spam sandwiches made her stomach heave. She'd gone right off the tinned meat lately, though Spam used to be one of her favourites.

'I can't believe you're not going to have a party or even a drink down the pub after your wedding. I was looking forward to a bit of a knees-up,' Joan said in her usual loud voice.

'Yeah, me too,' said Nora, who sat opposite Joan.

'Me and all,' Thelma parroted. The woman had been friendly towards Jenny since Gloria had left Dennis.

At that comment, everyone started laughing, with Nora saying, 'Oh, do me a favour, Thelma. An invite for tea with the Queen wouldn't put a smile on your miserable mug, let alone a knees-up in the boozer.'

'Yeah, well, just 'cos I ain't smiling like a bleedin' Cheshire cat don't mean I ain't happy,' Thelma answered as the ash fell from the cigarette in her mouth.

'I've known you all my life, Thelma, and you've been miserable since 1934,' Nora retorted.

The women all laughed again loudly, the sound echoing over the noise of the factory machinery and the heavy hailstones pelting the roof outside.

'What do you expect? That's when I married Wally,' Thelma shouted.

'You weren't any happier when he died,' Joan teased.

'You never saw me dancing on his grave, but believe me, I did. The day that 'orrible bastard kicked the bucket was the happiest of my life.'

This made the women laugh even louder, but then Miss Aston, their boss, appeared, and they quietened down. 'Jenny, could I have a word, please, in my office.'

Jenny could feel herself turning bright red and noticed several of the women nudge each other and whisper under their breaths.

As Jenny stood up, Miss Aston said to Joan, 'And could you come too, please.'

'Aw, Miss, we was only having a laugh. We've been working and ain't slowed down,' Joan protested.

'I have no doubt, but please, come along now, chop chop.'

Jenny and Joan followed Miss Aston. 'I wonder what this is about,' Joan whispered.

Jenny had no idea, but as they reached the top of the stairs, she could see two uniformed policemen in Miss Aston's office. They looked at her gravely when she walked in and her heart began to thump with fear.

'Jenny, take a seat, dear,' Miss Aston instructed. 'Close the door, please, Joan.'

Something had happened, something bad, and Jenny began to shake. When Miss Aston spoke she wanted to put her hands over her ears, or to run out of the office, anything to prevent her from hearing what the policemen were going to say.

'Jenny, I'm very sorry to tell you that these officers have some awful news for you.'

212

'No . . . oh no,' she whispered, and her mind raced with terrifying thoughts.

The older policeman spoke first. 'I'm afraid there's been an accident in the workshop where your fiancé Craig Brice worked.'

Jenny leaped up and asked frantically, 'What sort of an accident? Is he all right?'

'No, Miss, I'm sorry, he isn't. It appears the weight of the hailstones was too much for the roof to take and it caved in, trapping Mr Brice beneath it. The emergency services were dispatched, but there was nothing anyone could do.'

Jenny saw Miss Aston signal to Joan and the chubby woman responded quickly by rushing to Jenny's side and putting an arm around her.

Jenny shook her head, muttering, 'He knew the roof needed replacing . . . it was old, see . . . he was going to get it repaired next summer.'

'Does Mr Brice have any next of kin?' the younger officer asked.

'He's got an uncle . . . why?'

The policeman cleared his throat before saying, 'There needs to be a formal identification.'

'Identification of what?' Jenny asked.

'Of Mr Brice's body,' he answered uncomfortably.

'Craig's body . . . I don't understand.'

Again, the policeman cleared his throat. 'Mr Brice Craig . . . he was killed in the accident.'

Jenny felt her breath catch in her throat, and as reality set in she felt a crushing pain engulf her. It was physical, like someone had squeezed all the air out of her. She gasped for breath, but none came. Her chest began to hurt as it got tighter and tighter.

Miss Aston ran from behind her desk and shoved a brown paper bag in front of her. 'Breathe into this.'

Jenny pushed it away.

'Do it, Jenny . . . like this,' Miss Aston said and held the bag to her lips.

'I . . . can't . . . breathe,' Jenny gasped, and held her hands to her chest.

'It's the shock, but you'll be fine in a minute. You just need take a few breaths into this bag.'

Jenny grabbed it from Miss Aston and found that the woman was right. After a few minutes, her breathing became easier, and she crushed the bag in her hands.

'Is there anyone you'd like us to call for you?' Miss Aston asked gently.

Yes, she'd like them to call Craig. He was the person she'd turn to for comfort in bad situations. He was her best friend and the only person she wanted to be with right now. She shook her head, wanting nobody else.

'Is there anyone at home for you?'

Craig should be there, she thought, waiting there with his arms open to cuddle her and take away her pain. 'No,' she managed to gasp.

'Well, do you have someone in your family you could be with?' Miss Aston probed.

'My gran,' Jenny croaked.

'Tell us where she lives, and we can take you there,' the older policeman offered.

Jenny stumbled to her feet and managed to

give them her gran's address. She craved air, wanted to run, to get out of this office.

'Right, off you go with these policemen, and Jenny, don't worry about coming back to work until you're ready.'

Jenny followed the officers, feeling dazed and unwilling to accept what she'd been told. It couldn't be true. It just couldn't. The rain was heavy, and they dashed to the car, one of the officers solicitously holding the door open for her. As she sat in the back seat, staring at the rain running down the windows, she felt cocooned, and unable to face the enormity of what had happened, Jenny's mind closed down. She felt numb now, distant, void of emotion. She didn't want this feeling to wear off — she wanted to stay like this forever.

★　★　★

Edith saw the police car pull up outside her flat and was flabbergasted when her eldest granddaughter emerged from the back seat. Two policemen got out too. She pulled back the net curtain and noticed the girl's face was white as a sheet. Worried, she hurried as fast as she could on her sore hips to open the door.

'What's happened?' Edith asked, searching Jenny's face for answers.

As soon as Jenny saw her gran, her face crumpled. 'Oh ... Gran ... it's Craig ... they're saying he ... he's dead.'

At that moment, Edith felt her heart break. Her poor, poor granddaughter. Jenny fell into her arms, sobbing uncontrollably, and Edith could feel the girl's body trembling. 'That's it, my girl, you let it out. Come inside,' she said gently.

The policemen nodded at her, walking behind them as Edith led Jenny to the front room. She gently urged her to sit on the sofa, then sat beside her, holding her hand. 'Can you tell me what happened, love?'

Jenny sobbed, tears running down her face unheeded, her nose running as she gasped, 'I . . . I was numb when I was in the police car. It was better when I was numb. Oh . . . Gran . . . I can't bear it. I can't.'

As she hugged her granddaughter, Edith quietly addressed the policemen. 'What happened?'

The older officer repeated what he'd told Jenny, then asked, 'Do you know where we can locate Mr Brice's uncle?'

'I know he lives in Peckham somewhere, but I don't know his address. There's a telephone number for him though, in the sideboard drawer. He was coming to pick me up for — ' Edith stopped speaking. She was going to say, 'For the wedding', but that wouldn't be happening now. Oh dear God, she thought, it was going to be hard enough for Jenny to deal with her grief, let alone live through her wedding day. It was only a couple of weeks away, but instead of a celebration they'd be burying the love of Jenny's life.

'Thank you,' the officer said after rifling in the drawer. 'I've found a number, but only a first name.'

'Yes, John, but that's as much as I know,' Edith replied.

'It's all right, with the number that will be enough. If there's nothing more I can do, we'll see ourselves out.'

'I can't think of anything at the moment,' Edith told him.

Alone again, Jenny continued to cry, but at last she drew in juddering breaths and said, 'I can't believe he's gone, Gran. I can't take it in . . . it doesn't seem real. Part of me believes that when I get home he'll be there and that this is just an awful nightmare.'

'That's a normal reaction, love. Your mind doesn't want to accept it.'

'Gran . . . it's unbearable,' Jenny cried, tears flowing again.

'I know we aren't a family of churchgoers, but I've heard it said that God never gives us more than we can cope with.'

'I don't believe that 'cos I can't cope with this!'

Edith held her granddaughter as the girl continued to sob. She wished she could take away her pain or at least find some words of comfort to offer. After a while, Jenny's tears subsided again, so Edith gently asked, 'Would you like a cup of tea?'

'Ye-yes, please.'

Edith didn't like to leave Jenny alone, not even for a few minutes whilst she boiled the kettle, but the girl seemed calmer. As fast as she could, Edith brewed a pot and poured two cups. With shaking hands, she managed to carry them through on a tray, and after placing it on a side table she handed one to her granddaughter.

The cup rattled in the saucer as Jenny said, 'I . . . I don't know how I'm going to break it to Pamela and the boys. They think the world of Cr-Craig.'

'There's no easy way, love, but I can do it if you like?'

'It should come from me, but . . . but I dread it and they'll be here in a few hours. Pamela is going to drop the boys off here after school. She was going to ask you to look after them while she has tea with her friend.'

'Right then, we can sit them down and tell them together,' Edith said, relieved that Jenny didn't have to go home for a while.

She watched her granddaughter take a sip of tea before returning the cup to the saucer. Tears began to flow again, and Edith's eyes filled too. She had been through two world wars and lost her husband prematurely to tuberculosis, yet this was the first time in her life she'd wished for the power to turn back time.

23

It was a dreary Friday morning in November. Lizzie sat under the dryer at the hairdresser's and chatted away to the woman next to her, her voice loud so the other woman could hear her. 'My chap is taking me out to dinner tonight, so I want to look my best.'

'Shame about the weather and there's no sign of it changing.'

'I know, and it'll play havoc with my set and blow dry.'

'You'll need an umbrella, that's for sure. I just wish it would stop soon. My blinkin' roof is leaking. I've got three buckets in my girls' bedroom and two in my own.'

'Oh dear, that's a bit of an inconvenience,' Lizzie said.

'Yes, it is. Mind you, I shouldn't complain, not after that poor chap was killed at work a couple of weeks ago when his roof came down. Did you hear about it? Tragic, it was.'

'No, I've not heard a thing.'

'It was awful. A lady in the queue at the post office told me that he was screaming for help for half an hour before he passed away. They couldn't get to him, and it turned out he was deaf, so he couldn't even hear that people were there trying to help him. Apparently, he was only young and all.'

Lizzie's mind whirled. Young and deaf? No,

surely not! Surely it wasn't Craig! Jenny was supposed to be getting married tomorrow, and for the first time in years, Lizzie's heart went out to her daughter. She had to find out — had to know. She called to the hairdresser, 'Excuse me, Miss, can you take this off me, I need to go.'

'But you're not done yet.'

'I know, but something's come up . . . I just remembered I need to be somewhere.'

'But what about your hair?'

Lizzie didn't answer, and as the hood was lifted she frantically pulled the rollers out. She'd get soaked walking to her mother's flat, but she had to know where Jenny was so this time she'd demand that her mum gave her Jenny's address.

⋆ ⋆ ⋆

Gloria had to change trains twice to get from Holborn to Balham and thought to herself that it was a pest of a journey. She hadn't seen Jenny or her other siblings since she'd moved to Holborn, but it had been the best two weeks of her life. Now though, as the tube pulled into Balham station, Gloria realised she was looking forward to seeing her family. She felt a bit guilty for not being around to help her sister to arrange the wedding but knowing Jenny she'd have managed without her. Gloria stood up and grabbed her overnight bag. She'd brought enough clothes for the weekend, but it was heavy, and the handles cut into her hand. She now regretted packing so much make-up, and probably one pair of shoes would have sufficed.

As she left the station the wind howled and blew her umbrella inside out. Sod it, she thought, knowing that she was going to look a bedraggled mess by the time she walked up the hill to her sister's house. Her pace quickened, and it was a relief to arrive at Osward Road. She let herself in, knowing that at this time of day the place would be empty. The kids would be at school, and Jenny and Craig at work, but she couldn't wait to see the look on their faces when they arrived home to find her there.

Gloria closed the street door behind her and turned, nearly jumping out of her skin when she saw Jenny standing in the hallway. 'Blimey, Jen, you nearly gave me a heart attack.'

'I heard someone coming in. I didn't mean to startle you.'

Jenny looked awful, her hair a greasy mess. Gloria frowned. Jenny's clothes were scruffy too and looked unwashed. She'd expected to be greeted with open arms and big smiles, but instead her sister looked terrible, miserable, her eyes dark-rimmed. 'You look awful. What's wrong? You're not ill, are you? Not the day before your wedding!'

'There isn't going to be a wedding,' Jenny said disconsolately and then turned to walk into the kitchen.

Gloria followed her, and asked, 'Why not? Surely Craig hasn't dumped you.'

Jenny slumped onto a chair at the table, her eyes pools of pain as she looked up at her. 'He's dead, Gloria. Craig was killed in a terrible accident at work.'

Gloria felt as if someone had punched her in the stomach. This couldn't be right, not Craig, he was such a good man. She pulled out a chair and sat opposite her sister, then reached across the table to take Jenny's hand. 'I'm so sorry. I had no idea.'

'I didn't know how to get in touch with you, so we had to go ahead and make the arrangements.'

'When did this happen?'

'Not last Tuesday, the one before. We buried him on Monday. It was only a small funeral, just a few of us there. To be honest, it's all a bit of a blur.'

'I should have been here for you,' Gloria said, cursing that she hadn't left Jenny her address when she moved to Holborn. 'I'm so sorry.'

'You weren't to know.'

'How have the others been?' Gloria asked, aware how much Pamela and her little brothers adored Craig.

'Hard to say. Timmy and Peter were upset at first, but they seem to be getting over it. Pamela's still very quiet, but we don't really talk about it.'

'Is there anything I can do?'

'No, not really. The wedding service has been cancelled, the kids are at school, and with rent to pay I've got to go back to work on Monday. Oh, Gloria, it seems wrong that life just carries on . . . but . . . but I miss Craig so much.'

Tears began to run down Jenny's face and, judging by the puffiness of her eyes, Gloria could see she'd done a lot of crying. 'I don't know what to say. I wish I could make it better for you.'

'There's nothing anyone can say. It hurts too much, but I'm hoping work will be a distraction. Somehow I doubt it, but we need my wages.'

'I suppose you're fighting to put on a front for Pam and the boys too.'

'Yes, but it's so hard.'

'I can stay for a couple of days, and I'll do what I can to help you,' Gloria said, though in truth she felt helpless in the face of so much grief.

Jenny wiped her cheeks with the back of her hand, then pulled a handkerchief from her sleeve to blow her nose. It was awful to see her sister in this state, especially as Jenny had always been the strong one. Gloria bit her lower lip. She would do what she could, but she had to leave on Monday morning to get back to Holborn.

The thought of leaving her family while they were grieving made Gloria feel a bit guilty, but, she reasoned, Jenny said she was going back to work on Monday, so she wouldn't really be needed. Thank goodness, she thought, because she didn't want their unhappiness to rub off on her.

★   ★   ★

Edith was surprised to see Lizzie and frowned, wondering if yet another man had thrown her out.

'Hello, Mum. It's raining cats and dogs out there. I'm wet through but had to come. I was in

223

the hairdresser's and heard something worrying.'

Edith drew in a breath, dreading having to talk about Craig's death and the circumstances again. Brusquely she said, 'If it's about Craig, yes, he's dead.'

'Oh my God, so it's true! Poor Jenny, how awful for her. She was supposed to be getting married tomorrow too. How is she?'

'As you'd expect, not great.'

'I should be there for her. She'll be needing me.'

'You're a bit bloody late. Craig's been buried since Monday.'

'If I'd known, I'd have been there. Give me her address, Mum, and I'll go to see her now.'

'The last thing that girl needs now is you turning up. She's got enough to deal with without you upsetting her and the kids again.'

'I don't know why you think seeing me upsets them all so much.'

Edith shook her head in disbelief. She thought she'd raised her daughter well, but when she'd abandoned her kids, Edith had realised that Lizzie was a bad apple. 'I don't *think* you seeing your kids upsets them . . . I *know* it does because I've seen it with my own eyes. Granted, the boys especially love you, of course they do, 'cos you're their mother, but when you come and go like you do it confuses them. Every time you turn up they think you're going to stay, but you don't and when you leave they're hurt all over again. They need a full-time mum, not one who keeps disappearing from their lives.'

'Mum, I don't need you nagging me again. I

know I'm not much of a mother, but regardless of what happened in the past I'm here now, and I want to comfort Jenny.'

'She's very fragile at the moment, and if you upset her it could tip her over the edge.'

'I won't, Mum, I just want to be there for my girl.'

Edith wasn't convinced, but Lizzie seemed adamant. She'd have liked to check up on Jenny herself, but her hips were so bad she couldn't manage to get to Osward Road.

'All right, I'll give you her address on one condition . . . don't be there when the kids get home from school, and come back here to let me know how she is.'

'That's two conditions,' Lizzie said with a smile.

'This is serious, and I don't appreciate you being flippant. I mean it, Lizzie, you'll only be able to stay there for two hours and then I'll expect you back here. And go gently with Jenny.'

'What do you take me for? Of course I will.'

Edith scowled. She could have torn strips off Lizzie for pinching money out of her purse when she'd buggered off, the thieving madam, but with all that had happened since, it hardly seemed important now. Lizzie's father had been a thief, and though she'd endeavoured to keep it secret from her daughter, it seemed Lizzie was following in his footsteps.

She prayed she wasn't making a mistake as she scribbled down Jenny's address, hoping that, despite her reservations, Lizzie really could comfort her daughter.

* * *

Henry had been into Bernie's Café and was now headed for the Bedford pub. He didn't really relish the thought of beer after the skinful he'd downed the previous night, but anything was better than going home and looking at Audrey.

'Hello, mate,' Ernie greeted him as he walked into the smoky room.

Ernie had started work on the dustcarts the week before and had fitted in well with the blokes, but Henry hadn't had a proper chance to get to know him yet. 'Do you want another in there?' Henry asked, pointing to the dregs in Ernie's pint.

'Yeah, go on then. I told her indoors I'd only be having the one, but me boy has got a load of his mates round for his birthday. Cor, you wanna hear the racket. I didn't realise a bunch of seven-year-olds could make so much noise.'

'Two pints, please,' Henry said to the barmaid he'd been gaping at.

'Is this your local then?' Ernie asked.

'This and every other pub in Balham.'

'I'd better get moving after this one,' Ernie said after taking a swig of beer. 'My missus is about to drop her fourth kid, so I'd best get back to help her clear up after the party.'

'You're catching me up. I've got five.'

'Yeah, I heard. I think my Linda is friends with your Pamela.'

'Is she? I don't see much of 'em these days, you know how it is.'

Ernie belched before saying, 'Yeah, Ray was

telling me. Sorry about that, mate.'

'Can't be helped, it's one of those things.'

'Shame about your eldest though. It was supposed to be her wedding day tomorrow, but that's not going to happen now.'

Henry had heard about Craig's death — most of Balham had been talking about the tragic accident — but this other bit of information was new to him and he asked, 'What's this about her wedding day?'

'From what I've been told it was all planned. They were all set to be getting married, but then Craig went and got himself killed. My Linda said Pamela is devastated, so I can't imagine how your eldest must be feeling.'

Henry hadn't really wanted the beer in the first place, but now he'd gone right off it. He hadn't had an invite so had no idea that the wedding had been planned so soon. He'd given her a bit of a hiding and she'd taken the kids away, probably to punish him, but until now he hadn't realised that her hatred for him went so deep.

When he'd heard about Craig, he'd considered going to visit to offer his condolences but thought better of it. After all, the last time he'd seen the bloke they hadn't exchanged pleasantries and he suspected that Jenny would slam the door in his face.

Now, though, it was different. It was bad enough that she'd lost Craig, but to have to cancel the wedding was an added blow. They'd had their differences, but he had to admit that Jenny had been like a mother to the kids when

Lizzie had left. Huh, Lizzie — it was unlikely she'd be supporting the girl, and he doubted Edith was well enough to be there.

Henry frowned. He didn't suppose that Jenny was in any fit state to look after the kids now. He drew back his shoulders. It was his responsibility as their father to step up and until Jenny was well enough to take over the reins again, they'd just have to put their differences aside.

24

Jenny woke up late the following morning to find the sun beaming through a crack in the curtains. She was pleased it had finally stopped raining and thought it would be a nice day to take the boys over the common. Then she remembered. Craig was dead, and her body jolted at the realisation. It was the same every morning. Those first few moments of waking seemed normal until her brain caught up and she'd remember the harrowing truth.

To make matters worse, today was supposed to be the happiest day of her life. 'Oh, Craig . . . I miss you so much,' she whispered as she stifled a sob.

It had been a long night for her. She'd laid awake for most of it, crying silent tears, and now felt exhausted. She closed her eyes, escaping into sleep again, and woke much later to see that her sisters' beds were empty.

Jenny knew she should get up, but all she wanted to do was to curl up in a ball under her covers and cry in anguish. There would be no wedding, she would never be Craig's wife and it was more than she could bear.

★   ★   ★

Downstairs and out of Jenny's hearing, Gloria asked, 'Pam, can you believe Mum's audacity?'

229

They were talking in the kitchen, whilst their brothers played in the back garden. 'I'm glad I'd taken the boys out to give Jenny a bit of peace and quiet, so we didn't see her,' Pamela replied, elbow deep in soapy suds in the sink.

'She rabbited on about how sorry she was, and what a tragedy it was, but then started harping on about how upset she'd been at not being invited to the wedding. Honestly, that woman doesn't have a sensitive bone in her body! I got rid of her as soon as I could.'

'It sounds about typical of Mum, and I'm glad you refused to wake Jenny. It's nearly lunchtime now, though, so do you think I should take a cup of tea up to her?'

Gloria thought the longer Jenny stayed in bed today, the better it would be for all of them. 'No, let her sleep. Today is going to be especially tough for her. Tell you what, why don't you take the boys out again, perhaps round to Gran's. I think it'll be difficult for Jenny to put on a brave face today and it's not good for them to see her upset.'

Pamela nodded as she dried her hands on a tea-towel. 'She was trying to hide it, but I heard her crying last night.'

'Well, it's no wonder. She reckons she's going back to work on Monday, but I don't think she's really up to it.'

Pamela didn't comment; she rarely did. In fact, Gloria had been surprised that Pamela had said anything this morning. She watched her sister gather the boys into the kitchen, then waved them off as they left to visit their gran.

She heard the front door close behind them, then turned her thoughts back to Jenny and wondered if she was awake, consumed with sorrow and grief. 'Best leave her be,' she said to herself as she scraped her chair back and began to search for the biscuit tin.

The kitchen door creaked open and Gloria turned to see Jenny walk in. She could tell her sister had been crying but was relieved that she was now dry-eyed. Gloria snatched her hand back from the biscuit tin and said, 'There's tea in the pot, do you want one?'

'Yes, please,' Jenny answered as she pulled a chair out and slumped down. 'Where are Pam and the boys?'

'They've gone to see Gran,' Gloria replied. She refrained from asking how Jenny was feeling in case it started the tears off again and asked instead, 'Would you like a bacon sarnie?'

'No, thanks. I can't face the thought of food.'

Gloria took a seat opposite Jenny and pushed a cup of tea across the table towards her. She felt awkward and didn't know what to say. She wanted to avoid any talk of the wedding but knew it would be inevitable.

Jenny stared into her cup as she spoke, 'I would have been Mrs Brice in an hour.'

'I know. Look, Jen, I realise today is probably one of the most difficult days of your life, but I'm not sure moping around the house and dwelling on it is a good idea.'

'Actually, burying Craig was the worst day of my life,' Jenny said sharply.

'Of course, I'm sorry, I didn't mean it like that.'

231

'No, I'm sorry, you're only trying to help.'

'I really want to, but I don't know how,' Gloria said.

'You can't, but you're right. I shouldn't sit around all day dwelling on what was supposed to be happening, but I don't have the energy or the inclination to do anything else. I just want Craig . . . '

Gloria heard her sister's voice break, then saw tears forming in her eyes. She jumped from her chair and ran to Jenny's side, just as they heard a knock on the front door.

Jenny dropped her head into her folded arms on the table, her voice muffled, 'Please, I don't know who that is, but don't let them in. I know people want to be nice, but I can't face seeing anyone, not today.'

'I'll get rid of 'em,' Gloria assured her sister, then went to answer the door. When she pulled it open, her heart sank to see their dad standing there. 'Oh, great,' she said sarcastically, 'this is all we need! First Mum, and now you.'

'I've come to see how Jenny is.'

'How do you think she is? She should be at the register office saying her vows but instead she's breaking her heart in the kitchen.'

'I know, that's why I'm here.'

'As I told Mum, seeing her isn't going to help, and the same goes for you.'

'Gloria, what's done is done, I can't change the past, but Jenny needs her family around her now.'

'She's got her family around her, *Dad*.'

Her legs were shaking and her heart pounding,

but she bravely went to close the door in his face. Her dad pushed against it, and she saw a flash of anger in his eyes.

'I just want to see my girl and make sure she's all right,' he hissed.

'Jenny doesn't want to see anyone.'

'Look, Gloria, I'm not anyone. I'm her father.'

His voice had softened, but Gloria didn't trust him. 'Dad, please, any day but not today. She's really not up to it.'

'Let him in,' she heard Jenny say and looked behind to see her sister standing in the kitchen doorway.

'But . . . but . . . '

'Just let him in,' Jenny repeated.

Gloria stepped back and pulled the door open wider. She wanted to quietly warn her dad to behave himself, but fear of his temper stopped her speaking up.

'Thank you,' he said humbly as he passed her and walked up to Jenny with his arms open.

To Gloria's amazement Jenny responded by falling into them, then she heard her sister sobbing into their father's chest.

'It's all right, my girl,' Henry soothed as he held Jenny's wracking body.

After a while Jenny pulled away and wiped her wet face on the sleeve of her winceyette dressing gown.

'Gloria, get your sister a tissue,' he said, gently leading Jenny through to the kitchen.

Reluctant to leave them alone for long, Gloria dashed upstairs and grabbed some toilet paper. When she hurried back into the kitchen her dad was sitting opposite Jenny and telling her how sorry he was to hear about Craig's death.

'It was horrible, Dad. Two policemen came to the factory, then they took me to gran's house. Later on I had to tell Pamela and the boys, and they all took it badly too.'

'You've been a brave young woman, Jen, you've done well.'

'I haven't. I fell apart at his funeral. I wanted to hold it together and be strong, but I couldn't.'

'No one would expect you to. Here, it ain't much, but have this — ' their dad pulled out three ten-shilling notes from his jacket pocket and placed them on the table 'towards the cost of the . . . you know . . . funeral.'

'Thanks, Dad, but Craig's uncle paid for everything.'

'Well, keep it anyway, I'm sure it'll come in handy for something.'

'It will. I don't know how I'm going to manage this place without Craig,' Jenny answered.

'You can come home, all of you, if you like?'

Gloria watched the scene in disbelief. She'd heard the adage that blood is thicker than water, but she hadn't expected Jenny to forgive their father so quickly, or to seemingly need him.

Jenny stood up and went to gaze out of the kitchen window, her back to them. 'I don't know, Dad. It's the home me and Craig made together, and I don't think I'm ready to leave the memories behind yet.'

'All right, but when you are, you'll be welcome.'

Gloria couldn't listen to this farce any longer

and blurted, 'Dad, you must be mad if you think we'd come back. Has it slipped your mind how you treated us? How you used to beat Jenny black and blue, once putting her in hospital?'

Jenny spun around, but their dad quickly said, 'Yeah, I know, but I wasn't myself after your mother walked out. It was hard for me, bringing you lot up on my own. We managed and none of you ever wanted for anything.'

Gloria looked at her sister and rolled her eyes. It angered her that there was no sign of an apology from him, just feeble excuses. And as for managing, well, they'd managed far better without him. She saw Jenny compliantly nod at their father and felt the urge to scream at her, but instead she took a deep breath, fighting to calm down. This wasn't the time. Jenny had been through enough. It was as if Craig's death had beaten her down more than their father ever did.

★ ★ ★

Jenny poured herself another cup of tea as Gloria saw their dad out. She'd been surprised at how much comfort she'd felt when he'd opened his arms to her. She'd wanted to stay enfolded, cocooned in his arms, and it made her realise how much she'd missed a father's love. He'd said he found it hard when their mother walked out, and worse, Jenny knew she'd gone off with another man. No wonder he'd become bitter and twisted, and Jenny found herself forgiving his atrocities.

Gloria stormed back into the kitchen with a

scowl on her face. 'How could you let him back into our lives again? I can't believe you would even consider moving back home with him!'

'He wasn't always bad, Gloria. Don't you remember how you all used to ride around on his back with Dad on all fours pretending to be a horse? Or when he used to play hide and seek and jump out from the wardrobe making you jump and giggle?'

'So? He used to play with us, big deal! Have you forgotten how he treated Mum? It was no wonder she walked out.'

'You've seen what Mum's like, how many men she's had, so maybe she carried on when they were together.'

'He still shouldn't have clouted her.'

'Maybe she drove him to it, but think back, Gloria. He was once a good dad . . . and only changed when Mum left. The one thing losing Craig has taught me is that life is too short. If I can forgive him, surely you can too?'

'No . . . never! You're too bloody nice, making excuses for him, but I ain't like you. I ain't forgetting that he used to knock us about, mainly you, and I hate him!'

It shocked Jenny to hear the venom in her sister's voice. 'You've got to let go of the bitterness, Gloria, it will only make you unhappy.'

'I know you're hurting right now, and I think it's marred your judgement, but that man nearly killed you and terrified Pam and the boys. Just because you've forgiven him, taking them back to his house would be selfish and bloody stupid.'

236

Jenny sucked in a deep breath as anger rose. She'd already foreseen that her wages wouldn't come close to covering the rent and bills. If she asked Gloria to come back and contribute, they'd have a chance, but she knew what Gloria's answer would be. 'I don't know what you expect from me. I can't run this place by myself, surely you can see that? Would you rather see us out on the streets?'

'No, of course not, but there must be something other than moving back with Dad?'

'If there is, I don't know what. Gran's flat is too small, and she couldn't cope with us all there. Gawd knows where Mum is, so it seems Dad's is the only option. I'm paid up until the end of the month, but then I have no idea what will happen to us. Anyway, you saw what Dad was like. I think he's sorry for how he treated us, and it would be like having our old dad back.'

'I wouldn't bet on it. All I heard were excuses. He didn't say he was sorry, so I hope you know what you're doing.'

Before her dad's visit, Jenny had dismissed any idea of moving back in with him and wasn't even sure he'd allow it. Now though, despite what Gloria said, she felt bridges had been mended. With his offer, the worry of how she was going to look after Pam and her brothers had lifted. Their dad would take care of them all, and she would be able to grieve in peace.

25

On Monday morning, Jenny had left for work knowing that, when she returned home, Gloria would have returned to Holborn. She'd been grateful for her sister's short visit and felt it had taken some of the pressure of looking after Pamela and boys from her shoulders. She didn't begrudge her sister her new life, but wished things were different. If Gloria moved back in with them and found herself a local job, Jenny wouldn't have to worry about moving back in with their father.

The factory gates loomed ahead, and Jenny could see a flurry of people, some on bicycles, others walking. Then she heard Thelma's voice.

'You're back then,' the woman said as she walked alongside Jenny.

'Yes.'

'Sorry about your fella. Rotten luck that.'

'Yes,' Jenny managed again.

'Looks like rain,' Thelma said as she indicated the dark clouds above.

'Probably,' Jenny answered. The day was as grey as she felt.

They were soon at the clocking-in machine, and as Jenny grabbed her card she began to question if she'd made a mistake in coming back to work so soon. Thelma hadn't said much but she knew Joan and some of the other women would have plenty to say. Jenny just hoped she could hold herself together. If she could get through today, then she'd manage tomorrow too. One day at a time, that's what her gran had told her, just take one day at a time.

★ ★ ★

Gloria was pleased to be home and away from the gloom of her sister's house. Her heart went out to Jenny, but she felt sure her sister would survive without her.

She kicked her shoes off and walked through to the fitted kitchen. The large apartment had high vaulted ceilings and long sash windows draped in luxurious heavy cream curtains. It felt so airy and bright compared to where Jenny was living. She'd had enough tea over the weekend to sink a battleship, so opened the fridge to get herself a bottle of cola. As Gloria reached inside, she noticed an opened bottle of white wine. She was sure that it wasn't there before she'd left. Then she saw two wine glasses in the sink. She walked over and picked one up and immediately saw that it had pink lipstick on the rim. It wasn't hers; she mostly wore red. Hughie had told her that her father rarely used the place, but she wondered if he'd visited whilst she'd been away. She didn't think it would be Hughie as he knew she was going to see her sister.

Feeling flummoxed, Gloria wandered through to the sitting room to find that it all looked in order. Then she went to the bedroom. The covers on the bed had been thrown over but it was clear someone had been in it. If Hughie's father had used his apartment, she was glad she hadn't been around.

Gloria straightened the bed, then ran herself a bath. Hughie would be over later, and she wanted to be fresh for him. Once he arrived, she'd get to the bottom of who the mystery visitor was.

26

It had been nearly a week since Henry had visited Jenny, and as he stood supping his pint in the Bedford, he told Ray what had happened.

'That's good news, mate,' Ray said, 'I'm glad you and Jenny have sorted out your differences.'

'Yeah, me and all. I just wish it could have been under better circumstances.'

'I bet, but life goes on. Did you hear Ernie's missus had a boy last night?'

'Yeah, we've had a whip round for 'em. Loony Lee's holding it 'til Ernie comes back to work. Tell you what, Ray, it ain't the same without you driving the cart. That bloody Lee slows us down.'

'I know, mate, but I ain't fit to drive with this arm. Doctor reckons I'll have to keep it in the sling for another week. Good job it ain't me drinking arm, eh?' Ray said and raised his pint with his good arm.

'Well, the sooner you get back behind the wheel, the better!'

'Tell me about it. I'm bored shitless at home with her indoors chewing me ear off. I can't wait to get back to work, but talking about her indoors, I'd better be off. I promised the old battleaxe that I'd be back by seven 'cos she's going round her sister's. Something to do with her niece getting married, but I've got to be honest, I switch off when she starts going on about dresses and all that.'

'Huh, can't say I blame you,' Henry said and chortled. 'See ya later, Ray.'

Henry swigged the last of his pint and considered whether to order another, but he was hungry and, since it was a Friday, he knew he had a nice bit of fish waiting for him at home.

He pulled open the pub door and was hit by the icy wind outside. He hated this time of year, and even the thought of Christmas in a few weeks did nothing to cheer him up. It was hard, working in the cold. His fingertips were cracked, and his cheeks felt chapped. Still, he knew Audrey would have the fire going and even though she bored him, for once he was looking forward to getting home.

★   ★   ★

Jenny sat on the sofa with her feet tucked under her. She gratefully sipped the cup of hot cocoa Pamela had made her before she had taken her brothers upstairs for a bath. It had been an arduous week, but she was glad she'd gone back to work. After the initial condolences from the women, it felt like some normality had returned to her life, though the nights were still long and painful.

She could hear the boys splashing around, and their laughter brought a small smile to her face. Life carried on regardless, but she knew hers would never be the same again. After the way she'd felt about Craig, she couldn't imagine ever falling in love with another man. She doubted

242

she'd ever get married or have children of her own, but it didn't matter. She had Timmy and Peter, and she'd always have her memories.

* * *

Edith pulled her cardigan closer around her as she looked out at the dark street through her net curtains. She saw her new upstairs neighbours hurrying towards home with their heads bowed against the wind and packages under their arms. She wondered if they'd been doing some early Christmas shopping or getting some things in for the baby. They seemed like a nice couple and were expecting their first child.

Edith hadn't mentioned them to Jenny. She thought it might be upsetting for the girl and just hoped Jenny didn't bump into them when she called in tomorrow. Edith was eager to see her granddaughter and keen to know how she'd fared back at work. It couldn't be easy for Jenny, but Edith thought it was for the best. After all, sitting around all day and wallowing wouldn't be good for her.

The smell of freshly baked scones wafted through from Edith's kitchen. She'd made a dozen and a fruit cake. Peter and Timmy always appreciated her cooking and Pamela looked like she could do with a bit of feeding up. As she bent down to take the scones from the oven, she sighed heavily when she heard her daughter's voice.

'It's me, Mum.'

Edith wanted to shout, 'Bugger off,' but

instead she placed the scones down and walked through to the front room to see Lizzie unbuttoning her coat. It looked new and a bit flash, but Edith had no doubt Lizzie's latest fancy man had bought it for her.

'It's freezing out there. Why have you only got one bar on the fire?'

'What do you want, Lizzie?'

'Nothing . . . I was passing so thought I'd pop in to say hello. Something smells nice. Are you baking for the kids again?'

'Don't pretend to be interested. What are you *really* doing here?'

'Oh, Mum, why do you always think I've got an ulterior motive?'

''Cos I know you, Lizzie Lombard, so come on, out with it,' Edith answered through pursed lips.

Lizzie slung her coat over the back of an armchair and then plonked herself in it. 'My chap has gone to see his mum today so I thought I'd pop in to see you.'

'A likely story. More like you've come to rob off me again!'

'I won't ever do that again, Mum. I'm sorry, but I was desperate. I'm all right for money now, though . . . look,' Lizzie said and reached into her handbag and pulled out a handful of notes. 'I can pay you back.'

'Huh, I can guess where you got that money from. No doubt you pinched it from your new *chap*.'

'No, actually, I didn't have to. Owen is very generous.'

'Yeah, I bet he is and I can guess why!'

'Oh, Mum, don't be like that. It's nice to be looked after for a change.'

'How about looking after your children? Or are you gonna leave that up to Jenny?'

'Give it a rest, Mum. Now I'm settled with Owen, I intend on seeing a lot more of my kids.'

'Oh, I'm sure they'll be thrilled about that,' Edith said sarcastically.

'If you're gonna be like this, I may as well leave.'

'Don't let me stop you,' Edith replied. She didn't believe for one minute that her daughter would have more to do with her children, and until she did, Edith couldn't bring herself to be nice to her.

Once the door closed behind Lizzie, Edith shook her head and sighed heavily. Trouble always seemed to follow the woman wherever she went and she left a trail of devastation behind her. Edith blamed herself for her daughter's behaviour. She'd done her best to raise the girl well but somewhere along the line she must have done something wrong. The only good thing to come out of her daughter's life was the kids, especially Jenny.

Edith heaved herself up from her chair and walked through to her bedroom. She sat on the edge of her bed and reached across to her dressing table. On a glass plate she had a matching trinket box, brush and hand-held mirror. Cecil had bought her the set as an anniversary gift, or more likely pinched it, but inside the trinket box was her mother's wedding ring. She took it out and held the thin band of gold. She'd always worn it after her mother's death but now it was too small to go over her swollen arthritic finger joints. She treasured the item dearly and thought back to the day when her mother had taken it from her finger and slipped it onto hers. In her last breaths, her mother had whispered, 'I'm going now, but wear this and I'll always be with you.' She'd died then, and as Edith had held Lizzie, a crying baby in her arms, she'd shed her own heartbroken tears too.

She didn't have her own wedding ring. That had been lost at the wash baths years ago, but her mother's was even more precious to her. She took a pad and pencil from her bedside drawer and wrote a well-thought-out note. Edith didn't have much to pass on, but she wanted to ensure her mother's wedding ring went to Jenny. Lizzie would probably sell it, not that it was worth much, but she knew Jenny would cherish it as she did.

27

Gloria rolled over onto her back in the large double bed and lay spreadeagled across it. She was fed up and didn't know what to do with herself. Hughie had only called in once during the week and had told her he was busy all this weekend. She'd thrown a little sulky tantrum, but Hughie said he was committed and couldn't get out of it. Instead, he'd given her some money to treat herself. This had appeased her at the time, but now she felt frustrated. There was only so much shopping a girl could do.

She sat up, threw her legs off the bed and went to look out of the window. All seemed quiet below, but Gloria could see the Saturday-morning hustle and bustle on the main road at the top of her street. She pursed her lips in thought. Shopping or death through boredom? She didn't feel she had much of a choice, other than to pay her family a visit, but with Jenny and her grief that seemed even less appealing.

Gloria wandered through to the kitchen and threw open the fridge door. The half-finished bottle of wine was still there. Hughie had explained that his sister and her friend had used the apartment in the knowledge that she'd be away, and though she hadn't been happy about it, Gloria knew she had no choice in the matter.

She reached for the wine bottle, pulled out the cork, then took three large gulps. The taste made her shudder, but she persevered and quickly swigged down more. 'Cheers,' she said aloud, then finished the rest.

She left the empty bottle on the side and, feeling a little heady, sashayed into the sitting room, straight to the drinks cabinet. Hughie would tell her that it wasn't good form to drink at this time of the morning, but Hughie wasn't here. 'Sod him,' she slurred, and filled a large cut-crystal glass with brandy.

She knocked back several mouthfuls, and for a moment thought she was going to be sick. The feeling passed, so she took a few more sips. The room was beginning to spin, and her vision became blurred. She'd never been drunk before and, having seen her father over-indulge over the years, the idea had never appealed to her. Now, though, she found she liked the feeling and poured herself another. 'Whoopsie,' she giggled as she spilt brandy on the highly polished mahogany cabinet.

She swayed across the room with her glass in hand and switched on the gramophone. After a quick flick through the records, she selected Cliff Richard and the Drifters. It took several attempts, but she eventually managed to place the needle on the vinyl correctly and began dancing to the tune of 'Living Doll'.

'Sod you, Hughie,' Gloria shouted over the music. 'That's what you think I am . . . your living bloody doll!'

As the record came to an end, Gloria downed her drink and poured herself another. She slumped onto the sofa and held the expensive glass to her lips. 'I bloody loves you, Hughie, but I don't fink you feel the shame way,' she slurred, and drank some more. Her eyelids felt heavy and once again she felt the urge to vomit. The glass slid from her hand as she tried to stand up. Her legs wouldn't do what she wanted them to, and she fell back onto the sofa. Then the world turned into darkness and she faded into oblivion.

★　★　★

'Are we going to see Gran today?' Timmy asked as he ran into the kitchen, with Peter close behind.

'Yes, but before we get ready to go, I want to talk to you,' Jenny replied with her stomach in knots. She'd been feeling nauseous since she'd first woken and dreaded the conversation she was about to have.

'Are we in trouble 'cos Peter broke the lampshade?' Timmy asked.

'No, nothing to do with that. Sit down, boys, and you too, please, Pam.'

Jenny saw Peter give Timmy a sly punch on his arm and mouth the word 'Grass'. Timmy responded by poking his tongue out at his brother.

'I know you all really like living here, and I do too, but unfortunately we can't afford to stay. My wages alone won't pay the rent and bills,' Jenny said, and took a deep breath. 'So, I . . . I've sent a letter to Dad and told him we're going to move back home, and before you get upset, I

249

promise you it won't be like it was before.'

'But . . . but,' Timmy began to say, his bottom lip quivering.

Jenny interrupted, 'Like I said, I promise you it won't be like it was before. Dad really wants us to come home, and I honestly believe he won't be as angry as he used to be. I realise none of you like the idea of moving back, but we have to.'

Peter was pale, and Jenny saw that her sister was close to tears as she fled the room.

'Pamela . . . ' Timmy shouted after her.

'It's all right, leave her be,' Jenny said quietly.

'But Dad might hit you again,' Peter said.

'He won't,' Jenny assured him.

'When are we going?' Timmy asked.

'Next weekend.'

'Can we take the seesaw Craig made us?' Timmy asked.

'I expect so.'

'Can we go outside and play on it now?' Peter asked.

'Yes, darling, but put your coats and hats on,' Jenny answered, pleased that they didn't appear overly upset by the news. It hadn't been easy to tell them, and she'd expected much more protesting than they'd displayed. That just left Pamela, and she knew her sister was going to take a lot more convincing.

★　★　★

Later that day, Jenny arrived at her gran's flat and was both surprised and disappointed to find her mother there. Timmy was the first to run in,

250

closely followed by Peter. They looked pleased to see her and squealed with delight as Lizzie hugged them. Jenny on the other hand didn't share in her brothers' joy, and Pamela even less so.

'What are you doing here again?' Jenny asked.

'I popped in hoping to see you all,' Lizzie answered, then turned her attention to her boys. 'Hey, look at you two, I think you've grown a couple of feet! Oh my, you're so handsome,' she cooed as she cupped each of their faces in turn and kissed their cheeks. 'Your gran's been baking, and she's got some delicious scones for you.'

Lizzie walked through to the lounge with a child on each hand and Edith beamed at the sight of her grandchildren. Jenny thought it was sad that her gran never looked at her mum in that way, but Edith didn't make any secret of her disapproval of her mum walking out on them.

'Lizzie, make a pot of tea,' Edith ordered, 'and you boys, come and give your gran a kiss.'

Timmy and Peter both planted a quick peck on their gran's face, then followed their mum as she ambled through to the kitchen. Jenny could see that their noisy chatter went over their mother's head and thought it a shame that she didn't take much interest in them.

With the room now quiet, she whispered to her gran, 'How come she's here again?'

'Gawd knows. She turned up the other day and all. I reckon she just wants to show off how rich her new bloke is. She's been throwing a bit of money around and even paid back what she robbed off me.'

'Oh, right. While the boys can't hear, I wanted to tell you that we're moving back to Dad's next weekend.'

Her mum came back into the lounge and smiling, said, 'Really? That's nice, love.'

'It isn't what any of us want, but with Craig gone I can't afford the rent on the house. I don't like saying this, Mum, but when we're back at Dad's, please don't come to see us.'

'Leave it out, Jenny. I know you're all grown-up now, and Pamela isn't a kid any more, but I want to see my boys.'

'I can bring them to see you, or meet you on the common, but please, don't come to Dad's house.'

'Why should I stay away? It was my house too and my name's still on the rent book.'

'I know, but Dad gets funny whenever you turn up and he used to take it out on us. I don't want to risk that happening again.'

'He's got that Audrey living with him now, so I don't see why my visits should upset the apple cart.'

'I'd rather not take the chance. Please, just stay away, for a while at least.'

'Yeah, all right, but don't you go bad-mouthing me to the kids. In fact, if they ask why I haven't been to see them, you can tell them it's because *you* told me not to,' her mother answered is a hissed whisper.

Jenny nodded, relieved that her mum hadn't argued too much and said quietly, 'Thanks.'

Her brothers walked in, Timmy carrying a fruit cake on a plate.

'Can we stay with you, Mummy?' Peter asked.

'Yeah, can we?' Timmy repeated.

'Jenny said we're going back to Dad's house and I don't want to!' Peter added with his bottom lip stuck out.

'Are you sure about this, Jenny?' her gran asked, sounding worried.

'Yes, but it's going to be all right this time,' Jenny assured her.

'Can we stay with you, Mummy?' Timmy asked again.

Jenny wished her mother hadn't been here, today of all days. It was only going to upset the boys and now she regretted visiting.

Her mother appeared nonchalant as she answered her children, saying, 'No, darling, I'm sorry but you can't. It just isn't convenient at the moment.'

Convenient! Her own children were an inconvenience! Jenny shot a look at her gran who looked equally irate. She hoped her gran wouldn't say anything though as it would only upset the boys.

'Can we live with Gran then? We all used to live upstairs in Craig's flat and that's the same size as Gran's,' Timmy pleaded.

'I know, but you can't expect your gran to share her bedroom with all of us,' Jenny answered.

'But me and Peter could sleep in here,' Timmy said.

This time, her mother answered. 'There really

isn't room for your gran, Pam and Jenny in that one small bedroom. It wouldn't be fair on your gran either. She's old and frail and needs her peace and quiet.'

Edith leaned forward in her armchair. 'Bleedin' cheek!' she protested. 'I may be getting on a bit, but I ain't frail! One small fall and you're writing me off to the knacker's yard.'

'Sorry, Mum, but you know what I mean. You couldn't cope with them all and anyway, they're better off in their own home with their father.'

Her gran lowered her head for a moment, and then it was clear that she wanted a private word when she said, 'Jenny, I've got a pot of jam in one of the cupboards to have with that cake, come and help me look for it.'

Once in the kitchen, her gran lowered her voice and said, 'You don't have to move back in with him. You can come here. You all managed upstairs so I'm sure we could down here.'

'Thanks, Gran, but Mum's right. It would be too much and honestly, things will be different this time at home, I'm sure of it.'

'I think you're making a grave mistake, but it's up to you. I just want you to know you're always welcome here so if you change your mind, the offer is there.'

Jenny gave her gran a gentle hug. 'Thanks, but this is for the best.'

As they walked back into the front room, her mum announced, 'I nearly forgot, I've got something for you all,' and opened her handbag. She handed Peter, Timmy and Pamela a five-pound note each, then said, 'And before you ask, yes, you'll still be getting Christmas presents.'

Pamela accepted the money with a small smile but didn't say anything. The boys looked at each other, then back at the money. 'Thanks, Mum,' Timmy exclaimed. 'We're rich, Peter!'

'This is for you, Jenny,' Lizzie said, and gave her two ten-pound notes.

'Twenty pounds!' Jenny exclaimed. 'How on earth can you afford to give me this much?'

'Off her fancy man no doubt! Just make sure you spend it on yourself, for a change,' Edith answered.

'I . . . erm . . . ' Jenny said.

'Just put it in your bag and be done with it,' her mum urged.

'All right, and thank you,' Jenny answered, surprised.

Timmy and Peter were busy discussing what they were going to spend their money on. Whilst they were distracted, Jenny watched her sister's face fall as their mum approached the small table where Pamela was sitting. She pulled out a chair and asked, 'Are you all right?'

Pamela nodded.

'You're very quiet . . . are you sure you're OK?'

'Yes.'

'Are you looking for another Saturday job?'

'Yes.'

Her mother looked frustrated at Pamela's unresponsive conversation, then asked, 'How's school?'

'Fine.'

'Are you doing anything nice this weekend?'

'Yes, me and my friend Linda are going to Streatham ice rink.'

'Blimey, you wouldn't get me balancing on a thin bit of metal, but it sounds fun. Be careful, you don't want to be falling over and bruising that pretty face.'

Pamela nodded, and Lizzie turned to Jenny.

'How's Gloria?' she asked.

'She's a housekeeper in a fancy apartment in Holborn.'

'Good for her! She was wasted in that Queenie's shop. How did she come to be living up town?'

'She's got herself a fella from a wealthy family and he set it up. She seems happy, though I don't like the idea of her — ' Jenny lowered her voice ' — you know . . . sometimes being alone with him in the house.'

'Oh, Jenny, stop being such an old mother hen. People don't worry about that sort of thing any more.'

'Yes, they do,' Edith said firmly.

'Maybe your generation do, but youngsters nowadays have much more freedom.'

'Don't kid yourself, Lizzie. If Gloria gets herself in the family way and she's not married, she'll be ostracised around here.'

Jenny didn't think this was an appropriate conversation to have in front of her brothers and jumped in to change the subject. 'You've met her, Mum. What's Audrey like?'

'Quiet, like a little mouse. She does as your father tells her and, don't say I said anything, but she's got dodgy eyes. I was sitting at the kitchen table and I didn't know if she was looking at me or watching the kettle boil.'

Her mother laughed but Jenny noticed her gran throw her a stern look and her mum quickly added, 'She seems nice enough though.'

After an hour, their bellies full of cake, Jenny said they should go. Peter ran across the room and jumped onto their mum's lap to wrap his arms tightly around her neck. 'Can't we stay longer?' he whined.

'No, darling, but I'm going as well now,' she told him.

'I wanna stay,' Peter wailed.

'Now then, there's no need for that racket,' Edith told him.

Peter sniffed and quietened down. He never back-chatted their gran and thankfully Jenny managed to get them to leave without any further objections.

It saddened her to return home knowing that Craig wouldn't be there, but she had packing to do. It wasn't going to be an easy task and she dreaded the thought of going through Craig's things, but it had to be done. She was still finding it difficult to accept, but she knew he was never coming back and her life would never be happy without him.

★   ★   ★

Henry's morning had been relaxing. He'd had a lie-in, was full from a hearty breakfast Audrey had prepared, and had finished reading the newspaper from cover to cover. He thought about going to the pub, but it was bitterly cold outside, and he felt comfortable next to the roaring fire. He glanced up at the mantel clock and noticed an envelope lying against it. He stood up to retrieve it, and as he tore the envelope open, he shouted, 'Audrey . . . how long has this letter been sat up here?'

Audrey came rushing into the room to tell him, but by then Henry was too engrossed in what Jenny had written to listen. He smiled happily. They were coming home, all his children except Gloria who was living up town in Holborn.

He looked across at Audrey, who was nervously wringing her hands as though expecting to be told off for not telling him about the letter. Christ, she got on his nerves, but with his girls back, he had no need of her any more. 'Get your bags packed, you're leaving,' Henry coldly told her.

'But . . . I . . . I was going to tell you about the letter. I . . . I just forgot.'

Henry spoke slowly. 'Ain't I speaking English? I said, get your bags packed. My kids are coming home, and I want you out of here by Friday.'

'But, Henry, if you let me stay, I can look after them. Please, please let me stay.'

'No, and don't beg, woman, it won't change my mind.'

'But where will I go?'

'I dunno, back to your aunt's house where you came from. It ain't my problem, just get your stuff and go, the sooner the better.'

Audrey began to cry and started to speak again, but as Henry couldn't be bothered to repeat himself he quickly marched past her. He grabbed his coat off the newel post and went out, heading for Osward Road. In her letter, Jenny had asked his permission to return. He had never been one for writing so thought he'd tell her face to face.

28

Gloria pulled on her dressing gown and went to join Hughie in the sitting room. It was early on a Sunday afternoon in December and they'd just finished making love. He'd turned up a couple of hours earlier and had taken her straight to bed.

'Would you like a drink?' Hughie asked as he poured himself a straight vermouth.

'No, thank you,' Gloria answered and tried to hide her feeling of disgust at the thought. After waking up a couple of weeks earlier smothered in her own vomit and with a pounding headache, she'd vowed never to touch alcohol again.

She sat on the sofa whilst Hughie took a window seat and lit a long cigar. There was only a week to go until Christmas Eve, yet he hadn't mentioned the coming festivities. She smiled at him and asked, 'Have you bought me something nice?'

'I left some money on the dressing table for you,' he answered as swathes of smoke drifted towards the high ceiling.

'No, silly, I mean for Christmas.'

'Oh . . . I see. Erm . . . maybe.'

'You haven't, have you? Well, you've got all of next week to go shopping, and you know what Marilyn Monroe sings . . . '

'I'm afraid I don't.'

'Stop teasing, Hughie!' Gloria said, then sang the line, '*Diamonds are a girl's best friend.*'

'You're just as sexy as Marilyn, until you start to sing,' Hughie said cheekily.

Gloria stretched her legs out on the sofa, allowing her dressing gown to fall open and reveal her slender thighs as she purred, 'As you know, I may not be able to belt out a tune, but my skills lie elsewhere.'

'They certainly do.'

'About Christmas . . . '

'What about it?' Hughie asked.

'I assume we're going to your parents for lunch?'

'We? What do you mean, we?'

'Me and you, obviously,' Gloria said and rolled her eyes.

'Don't be ridiculous, darling, you're the hired help.'

Gloria looked at him incredulously. She wasn't sure if he was joking. 'I beg your pardon! On paper, maybe, but I'm your girlfriend.'

'Oh, Gloria . . . beautiful, sexy, Gloria. I think you've misunderstood our arrangement.'

'What bloody arrangement?'

'I pay you to be the housekeeper and for your other special services. Nothing more.'

'What?' Gloria sputtered. Her mind raced. Yes, Hughie always left money for her, but she'd thought he was being generous, not giving her payment for sex!

'Oh, darling, don't look so hurt. You can't possibly believe that I would take a girl like you to meet my parents? I'm engaged to be married to Lord Braithwaite's daughter. I thought you knew.'

Gloria's head spun and her stomach flipped. Hughie thought she was nothing more than his common bit on the side. How could she have been so stupid?

'Be a good girl and fetch me a sandwich, the sliced steak in the fridge would be perfect with a smidgeon of mustard.'

Gloria walked through to the kitchen in turmoil and absently took the steak from the fridge. As Hughie's words replayed in her mind she felt humiliated, and anger began to fester. She'd had no idea that he was engaged, he'd never mentioned it. If he had, she would never have slept with him. She slammed the plate of steak down and stomped back into the sitting room, hands on hips as she screeched, 'You bastard. I don't talk posh like you and I don't have a rich family, but you're no better than me. In fact, you're nothing but a two-timing, lying, conniving wanker and I feel sorry for Lord Braithwaite's daughter!'

She flicked her hair back and marched to the bedroom, slamming the door behind her. She'd have liked to slap the smug expression off Hughie's face, to kick him in the groin and ruin his crown jewels. 'Argh,' she screamed in frustration, then hurriedly threw on some clothes. She grabbed the bag she'd arrived with and stuffed it with her clothes. She had so many new outfits, it was soon full, so she'd have to leave the rest behind. In her heart, she was hoping Hughie would tap on the door and tell her he was sorry. She wanted him to say that he'd made a dreadful mistake and that he didn't

262

want to marry his bit of posh totty.

Gloria knew that would never happen and stifled a sob as she finished packing. She then picked up the money Hughie had left on the dresser. It felt tainted, but Gloria swallowed her pride and stuffed in into her handbag, deciding that as she'd kept the place spotless, it was her housekeeping wages. With one final glance around the opulent bedroom, she braced herself and opened the door. Her head was held high as she walked through to the hall, aware of Hughie looking up at her, but he didn't speak. She forced herself not to meet his eyes as she moved past him, her head still high as she opened the front door. Without a backward glance she stepped outside and, holding on to her dignity, she somehow managed not to slam the door behind her.

Her life in Holborn was over, and with a saddened heart Gloria headed to Balham. She knew that Jenny and the others were there now but dreaded the thought of living with her dad again.

★　★　★

Pamela and her friend Linda had taken Timmy and Peter to see the Nativity scene at the local church. Jenny was pleased as it gave her the chance to wrap some Christmas presents. A week had quickly passed since they'd moved back to their dad's and, to Jenny's relief, they'd settled in well. A chicken and potatoes were roasting in the oven whilst her dad had an afternoon doze in his armchair.

Jenny sat on the floor with gifts and wrapping paper around her. As her father slept and gently snored, she looked up at him and studied his face. He was beginning to show his age and his dark hair now had flecks of grey. She had pushed the memories of his violence to the back of her mind. Since losing Craig, what had happened in the past didn't matter to her any more. She and Craig had been robbed of their future, and though it was going to be hard, Jenny knew she had to make a new one. Thankfully, her dad hadn't so much as raised his voice, and her initial reservations were beginning to subside. Moving back under his roof hadn't been what Jenny had wanted for her family, but it was the only way she could see of keeping them all together. She now felt assured she'd made the right decision, and it was surprisingly comforting to be back in familiar surroundings.

Her dad had even given her some cash to buy presents for Pam and the boys. She'd added the money her mother had given her, and, looking at the stack of gifts, Jenny realised she'd probably spoiled her family. However, after what they'd endured this past year, she thought they deserved it and looked forward to seeing their faces when she piled the presents under the tree.

Another wave of nausea washed over her. She'd been feeling tired and sick all week and had put it down to nerves, but fear of her father had turned out so far to be unfounded. Bile rose in her throat. Leaping to her feet, Jenny held her hand over her mouth and dashed upstairs where she only just made it to the bathroom. After being sick she pulled the chain to flush it away, and then splashed cold water on her face. She looked in the mirror over the sink to see pale skin and dark circles under her eyes. It was then that the penny dropped. She wasn't feeling poorly through nerves. She didn't have a tummy bug. She was pregnant.

★　★　★

'What's that bleedin' racket?' Henry bellowed as he was rudely awoken by the sound of hammering on the front door.

'It's all right, Dad, I'll get it,' Jenny called as she ran downstairs.

'It'd better not be another lot of bloody carol singers,' Henry mumbled to himself, then heard Gloria's voice. He thought she sounded distressed and pushed himself up from his armchair. As he walked into the hallway, Jenny was ushering Gloria through the door. He could see his daughter looked upset, and then noticed the large bag she was carrying. It didn't take much working out. Jenny had told him about Gloria's housekeeping job in Holborn, and about the fella she was seeing. She'd probably lost the job, and looking at the state she was in, maybe her fella too. 'Are you all right, love?' he gently asked.

'Yes, but . . . '

'If you've lost your job, you can move back in, and as for your bloke, has he knocked you about? 'Cos if he has, I'll kill him.'

'No, Dad, but he . . . he . . . '

'If he ain't clouted you, I don't need to hear the details. You can talk to your sister about it while I go down the road for a pint.'

His daughters stood in silence as he grabbed his coat and walked past them. 'See ya later,' he called, and for once he was pleased that Jenny didn't flinch as he passed her.

★   ★   ★

Gloria sat at the kitchen table with a sweet cup of tea, but the look of sympathy on her sister's face made her want to cry again.

'Did you tell Dad the truth?' Jenny asked her.

'Yes . . . Hughie never laid a hand on me, but he's been seeing another woman and they're engaged.' She couldn't bring herself to tell Jenny the whole story, it was far too embarrassing.

'Oh, Gloria, I'm so sorry. You had no idea?'

'None. It all came out when I pushed him about going to his parents' house for Christmas. He was appalled at the idea. Apparently, I'm not good enough for them. This girl he's marrying is the daughter of some Lord or something. Hugh's a stuck-up bastard and I'm fuming as much as I'm upset.'

'Oh, Gloria, that's terrible, and for you to find out a week before Christmas!'

'I know. Turns out he was using me . . . he never loved me . . . ' Gloria could feel tears pricking her eyes and quickly sipped her tea. She didn't want Jenny to see how hurt she really felt.

'If you ask me, it was the other way around.

You're too good for him! I bet his fiancée doesn't know he was seeing you.'

'Maybe I should tell her, let her know what she's letting herself in for.'

'I'm not sure that's a good idea. It's her lookout and you'd be better off staying out of it.'

'I'll think about it, but the way I feel right now, I've a good mind to find her and tell her exactly what her precious bleedin' boyfriend has been up to. He wouldn't like that, would he?'

'No, I'm sure he wouldn't but it won't achieve anything.'

'Yes, it will . . . it'll make me feel better! Anyway, how's Dad been and where's this Audrey woman?'

'Audrey was gone before we got here. I don't know if he threw her out or if she left of her own accord. As for Dad, he's been as good as gold. Even Pam is coming out of her shell a bit.'

'Yeah, but it's early days yet and I've got a horrible feeling it won't last.'

'I think you're wrong, Gloria. I'm sure he regrets what he did. Honestly, I know he's not perfect but he's just like he was before Mum left.'

'He used to give her a few backhanders and I don't think leopards change their spots. He's a bully, and you of all people know exactly what he's capable of.'

'I do know, but like I said, I think he regrets it. I'm willing to give him another chance, can't you do the same?'

Gloria drummed her fingers on the table. With nowhere else to go she didn't have much choice.

Hughie had seen to that. The thought of that man left her with a feeling of bitterness. He had no right to treat her like a tart, and now he was living the life of Riley whilst she was back stuck living with her family. Gloria's lips set in a grim line. She'd only stay as long as necessary. Her mother had found an escape by using men and she could do the same.

29

Edith woke up early on Christmas morning, her favourite day of the year. She'd always enjoyed the festivities, especially when her husband had been alive and Lizzie had been young. Cecil had been a rogue but, thanks to his rich pickings, Lizzie had always had an abundant stocking and there'd been plenty of food on the table. Perhaps that's why her daughter was the way she was. Spoiled. She'd been an only child and had never wanted for anything. Edith thought maybe she and Cecil had made their daughter selfish, and wished she had brought her up differently. Still, it was too late now, but at least Lizzie hadn't shown her face for a while and wouldn't be around today to upset the children.

Edith threw the bed covers off, then shoved her feet into her worn slippers. She'd slept in her dressing gown to ward off the cold and now shivered as she walked through to the front room. She flicked on one bar of the electric fire, knowing that by the time her grandchildren arrived the room would have warmed up.

Next, she went into the kitchen and filled the kettle. As it warmed on the stove, Edith checked the Christmas cake. She was pleased. It had been maturing for over a month and it looked moist and rich. She was sure Jenny and the kids would appreciate it.

With a cup of tea in hand, she walked back

into the front room and looked at the small pile of gifts on the sideboard. The nice couple upstairs had done the shopping for her and she'd wrapped them in bright paper. She didn't have a tree but the colourful paper chains that Timmy and Peter had made gave the flat a Christmassy feel.

It would be a few hours until they arrived, so Edith sat in her armchair and pulled a blanket over her legs. In the quietness, her mind drifted back to Christmases past, and she sighed, thinking about how much she missed Cecil.

★　★　★

'Come on, Jen, wake up . . . Father Christmas has been!' Timmy squealed with excitement.

Jenny could feel her brothers jumping on her and opened her eyes to see their eager faces. They must have already been downstairs and seen all the presents she'd placed under the tree last night.

'I think Father Christmas made a mistake 'cos he only leaves gifts for good boys,' Jenny teased.

'But we've been good, haven't we, Peter?' Timmy protested.

'Yes, and he's brought us loads of presents!'

'Right then, you'll have to get off me if you want me to get up,' Jenny said.

The boys climbed down, and Jenny threw the bed covers off. She always found this time of year magical, with her brothers believing in Father Christmas, but now she had a secret reason for it feeling so special. She smiled and took a quiet few seconds to think of the life growing inside her. Then, as she gathered her thoughts and pulled on her dressing gown, she said, 'Come on, let's go and see what Santa has brought.'

Timmy grabbed one of her hands, Peter the other, and they pulled her from her room to the top of the stairs. At the same time, their father came out of his room, fully dressed in his best outfit and with his hair greased back. Jenny was surprised to see him looking so smart at this time of the morning and looked him up and down.

'It's Christmas so I thought I'd make the effort,' he said, seeming self-conscious and a little uncomfortable.

'You look nice, Dad,' Jenny told him, then added, 'Merry Christmas.'

'Yeah, and you.'

'Come on!' Timmy urged impatiently and dashed downstairs with Peter close behind.

Jenny followed with less haste and she walked into the front room. Gloria and Pamela were sitting on the sofa, and the boys were standing in front of the tree.

'Gloria said we had to wait for you . . . so can we open them now?' Timmy asked eagerly.

Jenny turned to see their dad standing awkwardly in the doorway. She smiled at him and then said, 'Go on then, Timmy, but check the names on the labels. They're not all for you.'

The boys dropped to their knees and began ripping at paper. Jenny enjoyed seeing them so happy, but it didn't take away the pain of missing

Craig. She should have been at home, with her husband, and they should be looking forward to having a baby together. Her hand inadvertently went to her stomach as she thought about the new life nestled in her belly. It was a time of mixed emotions for her, but at least she still had a part of the man she'd loved.

'Look, Timmy, I've got a Scalextric!' Peter exclaimed.

'I've got a space hopper!' Timmy said with equal enthusiasm.

As more presents were opened, Pamela began to pick up the discarded wrapping paper, then their dad moved closer and offered to help Peter set up the racing track for his new electric cars.

Gloria opened her gifts but didn't appear enthralled. Jenny thought the gifts were probably quite trivial compared to what her sister had been used to receiving from Hughie. Within ten minutes, all the presents had been opened, and apart from Gloria everyone seemed extremely pleased. Even their father liked his flat cap and braces.

Jenny left her family in the front room and went through to the kitchen. Pamela had offered to peel the potatoes today and Gloria said she'd get the Brussels sprouts and carrots ready. That only left the turkey to cook. Their dad had brought it home last night and Jenny had gasped when she'd seen the size of it. She wasn't sure it would fit in the oven. There was enough to feed a small army and she thought it a shame that their gran wouldn't come for Christmas lunch. Their

dad had offered to collect her, but Edith had told
Jenny that she'd rather stick pins in her eyes than
sit around the same table as him. Instead, Jenny
promised to bring the children to see her this
morning.

'Erm . . . ' Jenny heard her dad behind her and
turned to face him. He looked unusually
sheepish.

'I've got you this . . . ' he said and pulled a
small gift box from his trouser pocket.

Jenny took the box but didn't know what to
say.

'Open it then,' her dad urged.

She lifted the lid and gasped when she saw a
heart-shaped pendent decorated with small pink
stones, on a fine gold chain.

'Merry Christmas, sweetheart,' her dad said
quietly.

'It's beautiful, thank you,' she said softly. Her
dad had never given her a gift before. He'd
always left it to their mum, and she wondered
now if this was his way of saying sorry for what
he'd done to her.

'Ain't you gonna put it on?'

Jenny's hands shook as she fiddled with the
small clasp.

'Give it here,' her dad said.

She handed him the necklace, turned around
and lifted her fuzzy red hair. With the chain
secured, she turned back to face him.

'Looks nice on you. Right, you gonna put the
kettle on? I'm bleedin' gasping.'

Jenny smiled at her father. It had been a
tender moment, and she was pleased she'd

forgiven him, but her mind was troubled. He was yet to discover that she was carrying Craig's child.

30

It was unusual that Timmy and Peter wanted to stay at home rather than visit their gran, but it was Boxing Day and they wanted to play with their new toys.

'But we saw Gran yesterday,' Timmy whined.

'You can leave them here. I ain't going anywhere and I'll keep an eye on them,' Gloria offered.

'OK, thanks,' Jenny answered, 'but I think Gran will be disappointed.'

She knew their dad was dozing in the living room, and as it was drizzling outside, she told the boys to go upstairs to play. Once they were out of sight, she looked at her sisters, wondering how they were going to react to her news.

'Spit it out, Jenny. I can see you want to talk to us about something,' Gloria said.

'Yes, you're right, I do.'

'Go on then, what is it?' Gloria coaxed.

Jenny lowered her head and looked down at her tummy. The small bump was beginning to show so there'd be no hiding it soon. She had so many fears and worries about bringing a child into the world, especially one without a father, but was also overjoyed to have a small part of Craig living on. 'The thing is . . . I hope you'll be happy for me 'cos I'm over the moon . . . I'm pregnant.' There, she'd said it and now a smile spread across her face.

'No way! And is ... is it ... ' Gloria cautiously began to ask.

'Yes, of course it's Craig's. I can't believe you'd think there was anyone else.'

'Yeah, sorry.'

'Obviously I'm worried about what people are going to say, but I couldn't be happier.'

'That's lovely, Jenny,' said Pamela.

'Lovely — do you really think so?' Gloria asked scathingly. 'Have you any idea how people round here will treat Jenny? No, of course you ain't 'cos you're just a kid.'

'How — how will they treat her?' Pam asked.

'Like a slut, that's how. Bloody hell, Jenny, I'm surprised at you. I thought you of all people would've known better.'

'I don't care what you say, Gloria. This baby is like a gift from heaven to me. If Craig hadn't have been killed, I wouldn't be an unmarried mother. I would have a husband and this child would have a father.'

'But he *was* killed, Jenny, so you never got to marry him. Your child is a bastard, plain and simple.'

Pamela gasped as Jenny scraped her chair back, her face suffused with colour. 'How dare you refer to my baby like that!'

'I'm sorry but I'm only speaking as I find. You'll hear a lot worse once you really start to show.'

Jenny was about to retaliate again, but then realised that she'd been shouting at her sister. 'Oh God,' she said worriedly, 'I hope Dad hasn't heard any of this.'

'What if he has? He's going to have to find out sooner or later.'

Jenny walked over to the kitchen sink. She felt sick and didn't know if it was the pregnancy or Gloria's cruel words that had upset her. She turned on the tap and poured herself a glass of water.

'I'm sorry, Jenny, I don't mean to sound mean, but after the lectures I've had from you about *my* morality, I'm shocked that you let this happen. Still, at the end of the day we're all family and if you're happy, then I'll be happy for you.'

Jenny spun around and faced her sister, glad that her attitude had softened. 'Really? Thanks, Gloria, it means a lot to have your support.'

'Of course you have, and I'll tell you what, if I hear anyone bad-mouthing you or being nasty, they'll have me to deal with.'

Jenny looked down at her stomach and said, 'Did you hear that, baby? Aunty Gloria will look after you.'

The girls laughed, but it ended abruptly when Pamela asked, 'When are you going to tell Dad?'

'I'm not sure. It's not something I'm looking forward to.'

'If I was you,' Gloria said, 'I'd make sure he knows about it before he finds out from someone else. Once they get wind of this where you work, it'll fly around Balham.'

'Yes, you're right.'

'Talking of work, when it comes out that you're pregnant, won't that Miss Aston sack you?

'Yes, probably. I can't see her letting me stay.'

'When that happens, how will you afford to look after the baby?'

Jenny sat back down at the table and sighed. 'I haven't worked that out, but . . . but maybe I can find key-holder cleaning jobs, ones where I could take the baby with me. I just hope Dad doesn't throw me out.'

'I can't believe he'd do that. After all, you're carrying his grandchild,' said Gloria.

'Let's hope he sees it like that.'

'Have you thought of any names for the baby?' Pamela asked.

'Yes, as a matter of fact I have,' Jenny replied. 'Craig for a boy, obviously, and maybe Claire for a girl. It's the only name I can think of that's similar to Craig.'

'They're really nice, Jenny. I hope you have a girl . . . I can't wait to be an aunt,' Pamela said.

'Yeah, she's right, Jen, they are nice names. If Craig's up there watching over you, he'd be chuffed to bits.'

'Yes, he would, and I think you'll be an amazing mum,' Pamela added.

Jenny was touched and struggled to hold back tears. She didn't think her heart would ever fully mend, but at least she had Craig's baby to cherish. She would have more than just memories, and for the first time since his death she believed in a happier future.

★   ★   ★

Lizzie was looking forward to seeing the looks on her children's faces when she turned up in a flash car and handed out their Christmas presents. She was in the passenger seat next to Owen and on her way to Henry's house. It was Boxing Day, and she hoped they wouldn't be too disappointed that she hadn't visited them yesterday. She'd been stuck with Owen and his overbearing mother. It had been miserable, but she'd pasted on a fake smile, delighting them with a pleasant Christmas lunch. She reckoned the old girl would surely pop her clogs soon, leaving Owen as her sole inheritor. She had a fancy house near Wimbledon Common, hinted at savings and wore expensive jewellery.

Despite being bored stiff with Owen, Lizzie thought it would be worth sticking around to reap the benefits. She liked the idea of living in Wimbledon, though she was very comfortable in his three-bedroom flat in Du Cane Court. She sometimes had to pinch herself to make sure she was awake and wasn't dreaming. It didn't seem like that long ago that she was stuck in a loveless marriage living on the poverty line with five children. Now, she lived in luxury in Balham's most exclusive residence.

★ ★ ★

When they pulled up outside Henry's house, Lizzie told Owen as she climbed out of the car, 'You wait here. I'll bring the kids out.'

She knocked on the front door, and when Gloria opened it, she shouted, 'Surprise! It's your mum!'

Gloria looked over her shoulder, then stepped

outside, pulling the door closed behind her. 'What are you doing here?' she whispered angrily.

'It's Christmas, Gloria, what do you think I'm doing here?'

'Christmas was yesterday, and anyway I thought you told Jenny that you wouldn't come here?'

'Yeah, well, I couldn't let Christmas pass without seeing you all. Go and get the others, I've got a surprise for you.'

'Mum, please, just go before Dad knows you're here.'

'No, Gloria, I won't. I'm sick to the back teeth of everyone trying to keep me away from my children. Now go and get the others and stop making a scene in front of Owen,' Lizzie hissed.

'I can't believe you've brought your boyfriend here too!'

'Oh, Gloria, stop harping on, will you?'

The door opened again and, seeing her, Timmy yelled, 'Mummy.'

'Merry Christmas, darling,' Lizzie said, and when Peter came running out, she added, 'You too, darling.'

The boys threw their arms around her, but as Lizzie looked up she saw a horrible expression on her daughter's face. It reminded her of the way her mother would look at her. 'Timmy, go fetch Pamela and Jenny. I've got gifts for you all in the boot of that car,' Lizzie said, and pointed to the dark blue Volvo where Owen was now standing next to the driver's door.

'Is that *your* car?' Peter asked as Timmy ran indoors.

'No, it belongs to Owen. You can say hello in a minute.'

Timmy dashed back out, with Pamela and Jenny behind. Pamela's face was blank, but Jenny looked livid as she spat, 'What the hell are you doing here?'

'Don't be like that. You can't expect me to stay away over Christmas, but don't worry, I'm not stopping.'

'You promised, Mum,' Jenny said.

'I never made any promises, but I don't expect to be invited in. I just want to give you your presents, so come over and say hello to Owen while I get them from the boot.'

The boys were already examining the car and bombarding Owen with questions about how fast it could drive, and could they have a ride. 'Give him a bit of peace, boys,' Lizzie said, then making the introductions. 'Girls, this is Owen, my good friend.'

The man smiled but said nothing as Lizzie opened the boot, saying, 'Owen drives across Europe in a rally race. He went to Monte Carlo in January and said he's going to take me next time.'

'Good for you,' Gloria said snidely.

'Can we come?' Timmy asked excitedly.

'No, darling, children aren't allowed, but maybe one day, when you're a big boy, you could race your own car.'

'Where's Mondycar?' Peter asked.

'Monte Carlo . . . it's a long way away,' Lizzie answered. 'Right, who wants a Christmas present?'

'Meeeeeeeeee,' the boys yelled in unison and ran to the back of the car.

Lizzie pulled out their presents, and as she handed them out she glanced up to see that Henry had pulled back the net curtain to glare at her through the downstairs window. She smiled weakly at him but got a menacing grimace in return.

Jenny saw her father and began to shake, but Lizzie put it down to the girl being cold. It was December, after all, and she was only wearing a thin blouse. When she looked back at the window, Henry was gone, but then Lizzie's heart sank when she saw him storm out of the house.

His arms were flailing in the air and he was screeching obscenities. 'What the fuck do you think you're playing at?'

'I brought the kids their Christmas presents,' Lizzie answered.

'They don't fucking need your presents, so you can shove them up your fucking arse. Kids, give 'em back to your mother . . . NOW!'

Lizzie could see Peter was beginning to cry and his face had turned white. Timmy clung to Pamela's skirt and was quick to hand back the large wrapped box he'd been given.

'Now, now, my man, there's no need for this,' Owen said as he walked towards Henry.

Lizzie quickly jumped in between them. She knew Henry wouldn't take kindly to Owen trying to calm him down and feared he would wallop him. Owen wasn't a big man, and she didn't reckon his chances up against her husband. 'Please, Henry, it's Christmas . . . let's not upset the kids, eh?'

'If you don't want the kids upset, you shouldn't have come round. Now take your fucking fancy man in his poncy car and piss off!'

'OK, OK . . . we're going . . . I'll see you soon, kids,' Lizzie said as she steered Owen back towards the car.

'No, you fucking won't,' Henry barked, then turned to his children and shouted, 'Get inside, the lot of ya.'

Lizzie climbed into the passenger seat and watched as her children fled indoors. It was tragic to see her boys crying and Pamela looking so fearful. Gloria was snarling at her and Jenny had her head down.

'That didn't go very well,' Owen said.

'Just get me away from here,' Lizzie answered.

As they drove down the road, Lizzie looked behind out of the rear window and watched Henry fade into the distance. She never wanted to see him again, but that would mean she'd never see her children either.

★　★　★

'The fucking cheek of it, turning up here with a bloke!' Henry growled as he paced the front room floor.

Jenny stood in the doorway. She could feel herself trembling as she watched and listened to her father furiously ranting. Then he stopped and turned to look directly at her.

'Who was he? He looked like a right fucking relic she'd dug up from the cemetery!'

Jenny was too afraid to answer.

'I said, who the fuck is he?'

Her dad shouted the question at her, causing her to flinch and tense, but still she couldn't answer. He marched towards her and Jenny quickly stepped to one side.

'Where's the boys? I hope they gave back them presents . . .'

Jenny's steps were small and fast as she followed her father up the hallway and into the kitchen. She could see through the window that Peter was huddled in the corner of the garden desperately holding his Christmas box tightly to his chest, and it looked like Gloria was trying to coax it from him.

Her father pulled open the back door and stomped into the small garden. 'Did your mother give you that?' he screeched at Peter.

Gloria spun around, looking petrified.

Peter nodded his head, his face pale.

'Give it to me,' their father said through gritted teeth.

'No . . . my mummy gave it to me . . . it's mine . . .'

Gloria tried pleading with the boy, 'Please, Peter, give it to Dad. You've got lots of new toys from Santa, you don't need this one.'

'But I want this one . . . it's from my mummy . . .' Peter snivelled.

'You spoilt fucking brat. Give me that box or I'll knock you into next year!'

As soon as Jenny heard her father's threat, she ran across the patchy grass, trying not to slip on the mud. She stood defiantly in front of Peter and stared at her dad.

'Get out of my way. The boy needs to learn that what I say goes . . . MOVE!'

Jenny stood her ground, though she was shaking with fear and hoped her legs wouldn't give way. She had seen the force of her father's temper before and closed her eyes momentarily against what she knew was coming. Jenny braced herself, but instead of a punch he roughly shoved her, and she tumbled sideways, fighting to regain her balance as he advanced to tower over Peter.

Her father's voice was slow and deliberate as he glowered at his son and growled, 'I'm warning you, boy, you've got one last chance to give that present to me.'

Peter's face looked frozen with fright, but he hunched down low, still gripping the box. Jenny saw her father clench his fist and without thinking she instinctively grabbed his arm, pulling him towards her.

'Gerroff me,' he shouted and violently shrugged her away.

Undeterred, Jenny grabbed at him again. 'Please, Dad . . . No . . . '

Once again, her dad managed to throw her off, only this time it was followed by a sharp blow to the side of her head. He'd punched her, but she hadn't seen it coming. She still fought desperately to keep him away from Peter, but he jabbed his elbow into her midriff, so hard it left her winded. Before she could recover, his large hands pushed aggressively against her chest, and the force of his strength sent her stumbling backwards in the slippery mud. She lost her footing and fell, hitting the ground hard. It was all happening so quickly that Jenny didn't have time to think, she could only react. When she saw her father's booted foot coming towards her she instinctively tried to protect her baby by rolling over, but it was too late. He stamped on her violently, the boot landing on her stomach.

'No, Dad,' she heard Gloria scream as he lifted his foot again, 'Don't. She's pregnant!'

Jenny rolled to her side, clutching her belly as pain ripped through her. She heard Peter sobbing somewhere behind her and tried to move, but the pain held her in its grip. She hoped her father hadn't hurt him too and was then aware of Gloria crouching beside her, a hand gently brushing her hair. 'Dad . . . ' she managed to gasp.

'It's all right, he's gone.'

Another cramp ripped through her stomach, taking Jenny's breath away. When she opened her eyes, in the mud, she saw the chain with the heart pendant her dad had put around her neck the morning before. It was broken, just like her, and Jenny knew she'd never mend.

'I . . . I think I'm bleeding,' she cried.

'I'll call an ambulance.'

'My baby . . . ' she groaned, and as tears slipped from her eyes she silently prayed for the precious life of her child.

31

Gloria sat beside Jenny's hospital bed. She thought her sister looked peaceful in sleep, contented even, but she knew Jenny would be facing unbearable heartache when she woke. She wished now that she'd listened to her instincts. She'd had a terrible feeling about her father, but never imagined it would lead to this. Poor Jenny, she thought, first losing Craig, and now his baby. She'd never say so to Jenny, but in the long run, maybe this was for the best. Jenny struggled to look after their brothers and could do without another child. After all, Gloria didn't want to be lumbered with them.

'What . . . where . . . ' Jenny whispered, sounding confused as her eyes flickered open.

Gloria jumped up and leaned over her sister. 'It's all right, you're in hospital, Jen. It's me, Gloria.'

'My baby . . . Is my baby OK?'

Gloria ignored the question and poured some water from a jug on the small cabinet next to the bed. 'Here, drink this. I bet your mouth is as dry as a camel's.'

Jenny slowly pushed herself up, wincing. She took the glass, but then asked again, 'Is my baby all right?'

Gloria bit on her lower lip. She detested her father for causing her to say the words she knew would break Jenny's heart. 'No, I'm so sorry.

You've lost the baby and had to have a small operation.'

Jenny's face crumbled, and then tears flowed, her body wracked with sobs. It was gut-wrenching to see, and Gloria felt totally ineffective as she tried to comfort her sister.

After what felt like an eternity, Jenny drew in juddering breaths and said, 'The baby was all I had left of Craig. I've lost them both now and there's nothing I can do to bring them back. I don't think I can bear it.'

'I'm so sorry, Jen,' Gloria muttered feebly. She didn't know what to say but knew spitting venom about their father wouldn't help. 'The nurse told me that there wasn't any serious damage done and you can still have children in the future.'

'I only wanted Craig's baby. There'll never be another one.'

Gloria wanted to tell her that she might feel differently in years to come but doubted Jenny would want to hear that now. Instead, she handed her sister a handkerchief and sympathetically nodded her head.

'Do they know how I lost the baby? Do they know Dad did this to me?'

'I don't think so, but you need to tell them what happened.'

'No, and you keep quiet too.'

'What! Jenny, for the life of me, I cannot understand why you would protect that man!'

'I don't want to protect Dad, but I have to think about Pam and the boys.'

'They'd be better off without him . . . we all

would,' Gloria snapped.

'Where are they? You haven't left them at home with him, have you?'

'No, of course not. Dad buggered off after he attacked you, but Pam took them to Gran's. If he's back home now, he'll probably be drunk.'

'You'll all have to stay with Gran until I get out of here.'

'Yeah, we will, and to be honest, I'm not sure you'll be able to get Peter to go back to that house, not while Dad is there. I've never seen him like that before . . . he was as stiff as a board when I tried to pick him up . . . rigid with fear.'

'I don't know what to do, Gloria. We won't be able to stay at Gran's for long. I can't afford to rent a flat with bills, food, and clothes to buy for them too. It was why we moved in with Dad again, but there's no way we can go back there now.'

'If you only had to keep yourself you'd manage. Once you're back at work you could find a little bedsit, and I could do the same. At the end of the day Pam and the boys aren't your responsibility, or mine. I think the best thing to do is put them in a children's home. They'd be fine, clothed, fed, and, best of all, they'd be out of Dad's way.'

'No, no,' Jenny protested, dashing the tears from her eyes. 'I won't hear of it. I refuse to allow this family to be split up. We've only got each other, and we need to stick together.'

'All right, calm down. It was only a suggestion,' Gloria soothed, kicking herself for adding to Jenny's distress. She had just lost her

289

baby, but now had to worry about Pam and the boys too. 'Look, if I get a job in the factory with you, we could pool our wages. We won't be able to afford much, but we'd manage.'

'Possibly,' Jenny answered, 'but it isn't great pay, especially for women. If we can stretch to rent something, it'd be a right dump.'

'Who cares? Anything's got to be better than living with *him*,' Gloria said. She didn't fancy having to spend her wages on her siblings, but with Jenny in this state, and nowhere else to live, there was little choice.

The ward sister rang a bell, which signalled that visiting time was over. Gloria found it hard to cope with Jenny and her tears, felt useless, and was pleased to hear the sound. She couldn't wait to leave the hospital. 'I've got to go, but I'll be back tomorrow. Try and get some rest,' she said, and kissed her sister on the cheek.

As she turned to walk away, Gloria saw Jenny's eyes well up again. It was horrible to see her sister in such distress, but she wasn't clever enough to find the words to comfort her. Anyway, Gloria told herself, maybe Jenny was best left to cry out her pain and grief alone.

★　★　★

'She was going to tell you today, Gran,' Pamela whispered, 'but I don't think she's having a baby now.'

Edith could see how upset her granddaughter was, but worse, how was poor Jenny feeling? She'd lost several babies herself over the years,

290

but never in such violent circumstances. Edith wished now that she'd insisted they moved in with her instead of allowing them to go back to that evil bastard. She took a deep breath and put on a brave face. She had to be strong for the sake of her grandchildren but wanted to cry for Jenny.

'Let's hope she and the baby are fine. Gloria will be here soon, and she'll be able to tell us more. Now try not to worry, and go and check on your brothers. They're far too quiet in my bedroom which means they're probably up to no good.'

Once Pamela had left the lounge, Edith sat back in her armchair and looked upwards, talking to her dead husband as though he could hear her. 'If you're watching all this, Cecil, I hope you make sure Henry gets his comeuppance!'

* * *

Henry rolled through his front door to be confronted with silence. His mind was fuddled with beer, but he knew his kids had left again. 'Fuck 'em,' he drawled, and staggered through to the front room.

The Christmas tree was up, and toys littered the floor. The box from Lizzie that Peter had been protecting was abandoned next to the sofa. Henry kicked it, sending it flying across the room. Then, in his mind's eye, he saw the image of Jenny lying in the mud as he booted her stomach. The thought made him cringe with self-loathing and he slumped onto the sofa. He was sure Gloria had said that Jenny was pregnant.

He replayed the scene over and over until he couldn't bear to think about it any longer and stumbled through to the kitchen. There, he found his bottle of whiskey. He swigged down several gulps, then looked at the bottle in his hand. Whiskey, he thought, his new best friend. At least it would stop him from remembering what he'd done . . . for now.

32

The seeing-in of 1962 bypassed Jenny. Her body had healed but her mind was tormented by images of her lost child. Would the baby have been a boy or a girl? She wondered if it would have had Craig's sandy hair, or her red unruly frizz. She longed to hold the child in her arms and look into its eyes to see Craig looking back at her. Gloria's voice interrupted her thoughts.

'Hello, Gran, where are the boys?'

'Pamela's taken them to the swings over the road,' Edith answered.

'That's good, and Jenny, Miss Aston wants to know when you're coming back to work.'

Jenny looked up from where she was sitting on the sofa. It was Monday, the second week of the new year. Gloria had stuck to her promise and was now working at the factory, and Pamela and her brothers were back at school.

'Did you hear me, Jen?' Gloria asked.

'Erm . . . yes. I don't know . . . soon.'

'I think she wants something a bit more concrete than 'soon'.'

'Maybe it would do you good, love, you know, take your mind off things,' her gran said with her voice full of sympathy.

'I suppose,' Jenny answered, but she felt she didn't have the energy to face returning to work.

'Shall I tell her you'll be back next week?'

'No, I'll come in with you tomorrow,' Jenny

replied, though she dreaded the thought. Her gran was probably right, it would do her good, and they needed the money. Her gran tried to pretend that she didn't mind them all being there, but she'd noticed the woman's patience was wearing thin and she'd snapped at the boys a few times. It was time they started saving and looking for a place of their own. Her sisters were sharing a single bed and she was sleeping in with her gran, but it wasn't comfortable for any of them, least of all her brothers, who were sharing a sofa. Despite the cramped sleeping arrangements, Jenny wasn't sure if she wanted to leave. She'd always felt safe at her gran's flat and had spent many hours hiding there, away from her dad or her parents arguing, but now it felt different. Everything reminded her of living upstairs with Craig. There was no escape from her memories or anguish, but a part of her wanted to stay and be close to Craig.

⋆　⋆　⋆

Henry hadn't been back to work since Christmas, even though it was their busiest time of year. He'd blamed it on a bad back, but there was nothing wrong with him. He'd found solace in whiskey and had been drunk for nearly two weeks. All his Christmas tips had been spent on alcohol, and now his pockets were empty.

He looked at the alarm clock by the side of his bed. It was six-thirty, but he didn't know if it was morning or evening. He wasn't even sure what day it was. He crawled out of his filthy sheets and into the bathroom. His guts hurt, and his head was pounding. As he leaned against the sink, he looked at his reflection in the mirror with repulsion. In the mornings, when he was sober, he had to face the consequences of what he'd done to Jenny. He still blamed Lizzie, but there was no excuse for possibly damaging or even killing his unborn grandchild. The thought of it turned his stomach and he hung his head over the toilet. He knew he'd gone too far this time, and she'd never forgive him.

* * *

Owen reached over and lit Lizzie's long pink cigarette.

'I do like these cocktail cigarettes, they look ever so sophisticated,' she said as her eyes flitted around the bar. It was an exclusive members club near Harrods in Knightsbridge and Lizzie was busy trying to spot celebrities.

'So, what do you think?' Owen asked.

'Sorry, darling, I wasn't paying attention. What do I think about what?'

'A winter holiday, somewhere with blue skies and golden sands. Anywhere away from this miserable weather.'

Lizzie had never been abroad before and was thrilled at the idea. 'Yes, that would be wonderful,' she answered, 'but I'd need a new wardrobe. None of my clothes are suited to somewhere exotic.'

As she'd expected, Owen pulled out his cheque book and, using his gold pen, signed a blank check. 'Take this into Harrods in the morning and get what you need.'

Lizzie accepted the cheque with a wry grin, then folded it in half and slipped it into her bra. She leaned across the small, round bistro table and kissed Owen's cheek. His aged skin felt papery on her lips. He'd never told her his age, but she guessed he must be in his late sixties. 'Thank you,' she said sweetly. 'So, where are you going to whisk me away to?'

'I'm not sure, maybe Spain or Malta.'

Lizzie didn't know anything about either country and wasn't sure where they were. She didn't care, she was just excited about travelling abroad. 'How long will we be away?'

'As the weather seems stuck in a rut, I thought we may as well make the most of it and come back in the spring.'

'Really? Goodness, I thought you was going to say a week or two.'

'Is it a problem for you?'

'No, but I should go to see my kids, let them know that I won't be around for a few months.'

'Wouldn't it be better to write to them? Surely you don't want to be confronted by your ex-husband again?'

'No, I'll be fine. They always visit my mum on Sundays, so I'll see them there. Perhaps you'd like to drive me?'

'Certainly, I'd like to meet your mother. I'm sure she'll be more amenable than mine.'

Lizzie sipped her gin and tonic. She couldn't wait to tell her family about the holiday. They'd be so excited for her! It'd be good to show her mum that she'd done well for herself and had met an honest man. One who could afford to look after her. She just hoped her mother wouldn't see through her charade. Lizzie was good at putting on a front, but her mum always seemed to know what she was up to. In truth, she didn't love Owen, but she loved his money, and once he'd inherited from his decrepit mother, she didn't think it would be too long before she'd be getting an inheritance too. However, before she could bring that about by marrying Owen, she had to divorce Henry.

33

'Jenny . . . Jenny . . . '

Jenny could hear Gloria's voice calling her name and could feel her sister gently shaking her, but she didn't want to wake up and open her eyes. She'd been dreaming about Craig, and it had felt so real that she hadn't wanted it to end.

'Come on, you've got to get up if you're coming back to work today.'

Jenny opened one eye and saw her sister was already dressed and wearing a full face of make-up. Gloria looked more like she was going to a dance than to work. She opened her other eye and pushed herself up in bed. 'That's a bit much for the factory, isn't it?'

'What's wrong with bringing in a bit of glamour to the place?'

Jenny didn't answer but she suspected there was more to it. Knowing her sister, she thought Gloria probably had her eye on one of the blokes now that Hughie was out of the picture.

Pamela walked in carrying a cup of tea. 'Gran made you this,' she said as she handed it to Jenny.

'Thanks. Am I the last one up?'

'Yep, so get a move on,' Gloria told her.

Jenny sipped the hot tea. It wasn't like Gloria to be conscientious about being on time for work, and it confirmed her suspicions. 'So who is he?' she asked.

'What?' Gloria answered, and flounced towards the bedroom door.

'Don't pretend you don't know what I'm talking about. Who have you got your eye on at work?'

'Blimey, can't a girl make an effort without getting interrogated? Anyway, it's not like I've got loads of outfits to choose from. Pam only managed to pack a few things for us.'

Gloria walked away before Jenny could question her further but hoped to get the truth out of her as they walked to work. She was right about their clothes though. Pamela had been in a state of panic waiting for the ambulance to arrive, and sick with fear that their dad would come back. Somehow she'd managed to throw some clothes in bags for them all, but Jenny knew they needed the rest of their things. She'd been putting off thinking about how to retrieve them, but it really was time to work out a plan.

Jenny pushed the thought aside for now, and taking a deep breath, she forced herself out of bed. The room felt cold. She shivered as she pulled on a cardigan and dashed to the bathroom. She found toothpaste splattered over the sink and strands of Gloria's long blonde hair in the plughole. The bath had been left with a scum-line, and a wet towel had been thrown in the corner. Their gran was a stickler for cleanliness — no wonder she was becoming irritated. Jenny quickly tidied up before getting herself ready.

When she was finally able to brush her hair, Jenny gave up any hope of trying to tame it, but she didn't care how she looked. It was going to be difficult enough walking through the factory gates, let alone worrying about her appearance.

★　★　★

'It's bloody freezing,' Gloria moaned as she walked alongside her sister on the way to work. Miss Aston had given her a job a week ago, and though she found the work boring, she liked the banter with the women. There was one fella who had caught her eye too, and she'd seen him looking at her in the staff canteen. The women sat on one side of the room, and the men on the other, but she'd bumped into him in the corridor and he'd told her his name was Brian. Since then they'd met in secret a couple of times, and though it was only in dark corners of the factory, they'd struck up a bit of a romance.

As they reached the gates, Gloria grabbed her sister's hand. 'There's something I need to tell you,' she said, and paused, swallowing hard before she continued. 'The women, they know what happened.'

'What do you mean?' Jenny asked.

'They know you lost a baby.'

Jenny's eyes flared with panic, 'How do they know . . . did . . . did you tell them?'

'Of course I didn't. Joan's daughter works at the hospital and recognised you. She shouldn't have, but she told Joan.'

'Oh no, what are they going to say? They know I wasn't married . . . Oh, Gloria, this is terrible . . . I don't think I can go in there.'

'Don't be daft. They're all really upset for you. None of them think badly of you. They know you was going to marry Craig and honest, Jen, you'll get nothing but sympathy.'

'I can't do this . . . I don't want their sympathy . . . ' Jenny said as she turned to walk in the opposite direction.

'Wait . . . Jen . . . ' Gloria called, and caught up with her sister. 'Please, Jenny, I swear it'll be all right. You've been through so much . . . you can do this.'

Jenny slowed, nodded her head and turned towards the factory again. 'Do they know that Dad caused my miscarriage?'

'No, love. As far as they're concerned, you fell down the stairs . . . *again*.'

★ ★ ★

Once Gloria and Jenny had clocked in, they walked onto the factory floor. The room fell silent, but Gloria didn't notice. She was too busy trying to spot Brian. He appeared from behind some ducting and flashed her a flirty smile. She quickly glanced around before smiling back at him and then sat down two seats along from Jenny.

'Good to have you back, Jenny, and we're all really sorry for your loss,' Joan said.

The other women offered quiet condolences, and then Miss Aston summoned Jenny to her office. In her sister's absence, Gloria listened as the women speculated about what was going on. Some thought Jenny could be getting the sack, others suggested Miss Aston was giving Jenny a warning. After ten minutes, Jenny returned, and Gloria noticed her sister's face was bright red.

'All right?' she mouthed.

Jenny nodded and sat next to Joan.

'What was all that about?' the large woman asked.

'Nothing . . . she just wanted to make sure I was all right,' Jenny answered, her cheeks flaming again.

'She's a good egg, that woman. We could've had worse. The supervisor at Mackson's was a right bleedin' witch. You couldn't even spend a penny without her timing you,' Joan told them.

As the hours dragged, Gloria kept glancing across at her sister and was pleased to see that she seemed to be getting on all right. A new woman, Tina, sat between them. She'd started the day before Gloria. She was talkative, and told them that she was married with three teenage girls and her husband worked on the railways. Gloria thought she seemed nice enough — not really her cup of tea, but she noticed Jenny seemed to be getting on well with her.

Brian walked across the factory floor and Gloria's eyes followed him. She admired his broad shoulders and long legs, and the way he swaggered. His black hair had a teddy-boy quiff at the front, and she wondered how he dressed when he wasn't wearing overalls.

'Oi, Brian, sing us a bit of Elvis,' Joan shouted.

'Not today, ladies, but if you come down the Grove on Friday, I'm doing a turn.'

'Ooaa, I'll see if my old man fancies that,' Joan

answered, then said to Tina, 'He does a great Elvis impression, swings his hips like him and everything. Smashing voice, you should come.'

'Thanks, Joan, but my husband ain't really a fan of Elvis.'

'How about you, Gloria? Fancy a night out on Friday?'

Gloria jumped at the chance. She liked Elvis Presley but the thought of seeing Brian outside the factory gates was even more appealing.

$$\star \quad \star \quad \star$$

Henry felt exhausted, but he'd forced himself out of the door and was just walking into the depot as his colleagues filed out of the works building, ready to jump on the dustcarts.

'Ray, me old mucker,' Henry called, and all heads turned.

As he ambled towards the men, he noticed a strange look on their faces. A few of the blokes shook their heads and ignored him before they sloped off. Big Al's face was like thunder and he looked as if he was ready to take a swing at him, but Ernie pulled him back.

'What's going on?' Henry asked.

Willie looked Henry up and down, then spat on the floor. 'If I was a younger man, I'd put you on your arse,' he growled.

'I'll fucking do it . . . ' Big Al shouted, but again Ernie grabbed the man.

'Does someone wanna tell me what I'm supposed to have done?' Henry asked, directing his question at Ray.

Ray stepped forwards and led Henry to the rear of the dustcart. 'We've heard what you done to your daughter. It don't sit well with any of us, Henry. We're all family men and what you did . . . well, it's disgusting.'

'Is that right? And what is it you've heard?' Henry demanded, his bravado covering the fact that his heart was hammering in his chest, and he prayed they didn't know the full story.

'Your Pamela is friends with Ernie's girl. Pamela was in a state and told Linda everything. How could you, Henry? After what Jenny's been through, how could you beat her up like that? She's your daughter, man, you're supposed to protect her, not half kill her.'

Henry hung his head in shame. He felt awful about it and didn't need Ray reminding him, but what the man said next left him reeling.

'You need to clear your locker and leave. The blokes refuse to work with you, and I can't say I blame them.'

'I'm sorry, Ray . . . '

'It's not me you should be apologising to. We've known each other a long time, and I never expected you to stoop so low. I've watched Jenny grow up and if she was mine, I'd be proud of her. I certainly would never have kicked a kid out of her,' Ray said, shaking his head in disgust.

Ray's words struck Henry like physical blows. He turned to walk away, sick with shame, and Ray called, 'A word of warning, Henry. Keep your head down and watch your back.'

34

'I wish you wouldn't do that in here, it stinks,' Edith said to Gloria as she painted her nails.

'Sorry, Gran, but I need to be sitting at a table.'

'Why don't you go out with your sister tonight? I'm happy to watch the boys,' said Edith, addressing Jenny.

'No, thanks, Gran,' she answered. She'd got through the week at work but the last thing she felt like doing was watching Brian Cuddy prance around on stage imitating Elvis.

'It'd do you good. Most of the women are going, even Tina, and you get on well with her,' Gloria urged.

Jenny did like Tina, but she still didn't feel like going out.

'Go on, girl, get your glad rags on,' her gran said.

Jenny was beginning to feel ganged up on. 'What glad rags?' she said, once again reminded that she needed to collect their belongings from their father's house, but the thought of it terrified her.

'You can wear my blue jacket and long dress. It's too small for me now and it's real silk,' her gran offered.

'Leave it out, Gran, she can't wear that! Blimey, that fashion went down with the *Titanic*,' Gloria said with a laugh.

'All right, well what about your mother's red skirt with the jacket and black trim? It's brand new. I think Lizzie got it from a charity shop, but I don't think she ever wore it. She left it in my wardrobe. Try it on, it'd look lovely on you, Jenny.'

'Gran, how can it be brand new if it came from the charity shop?' Gloria asked, laughing again.

'Oh, shut up, you know what I mean. At least it's fashionable, all the girls are wearing it, like that Kennedy woman.'

'She's got a point,' Gloria said.

'It'd be a bit dressy for the pub,' Jenny protested, still not convinced she wanted to go.

Gloria blew on her nails. 'It's better than your drab work clothes!'

'Go and try it on,' her gran urged.

Jenny knew they wouldn't shut up until she did as she was asked and heaved herself up from the sofa. She went into the bedroom, flicked through her gran's wardrobe and then pulled out the suit to hold it against her. It would probably fit, but it wasn't something she'd have chosen to wear.

Gloria came into the bedroom and looked at the outfit. 'Perfect. It'll look lovely on you.'

Jenny reluctantly slipped into the skirt and jacket, then Gloria told her to do a twirl. She felt silly, and uncomfortable in the smart jacket.

'You look ever so classy. Go on, say you'll come with me tonight?'

Jenny knew that her sister would keep pushing and reluctantly answered, 'All right, but I'm not going out until Pamela comes back with the boys. I'll need to put them to bed.'

Her gran limped into the room and said, 'Don't be daft, love. Pamela's old enough to see to them now. She can settle them down, so borrow your sister's lippy and get yourself orf out.'

★ ★ ★

Forty-five minutes later, Jenny and Gloria walked into the smoky pub, where she spotted the crowd of women from work, sitting around tables in front of the small makeshift stage. It sounded like spirits were high and even Thelma looked to be enjoying herself.

'Here they are,' Joan shouted above the noise. 'Grab a seat, girls. Brian will be on in a minute.'

'We'll get a couple of drinks first,' Gloria called as she pulled Jenny towards the bar.

Jenny nodded, but already she was regretting coming. With a glass of lemonade, they threaded their way back through the small crowd, and sat at tables the women had pushed together.

'Good to see you, Jenny,' said Tina, as Jenny took a seat next to her. 'I left my husband at home with the girls. I didn't think he'd let me come, but he told me to enjoy meself. Brian's already been out and told a few jokes. He's ever so funny, but I can't wait to see him doing Elvis. Is he good?'

'I don't know, I've never seen him, but I've heard he is,' Jenny answered.

'You look smart. Look at me in me only going-out dress. I've had it for at least five years.

I tell you, you need deep pockets with three kids. I can't remember the last time I had a new outfit.'

'You look lovely,' Jenny said, feeling self-conscious.

'Your sister's done up nice too, but then she always is. I couldn't be bothered to put me face on to go to work. She must get up at the crack of dawn.'

'That's Gloria for you.'

'You two seem very different,' Tina said, but before Jenny could say anything, Brian jumped on stage and the women cheered.

He began to coo 'Love Me Tender' and Jenny thought he really did sound like Elvis. She noticed that he seemed to be looking at her sister a lot, and Gloria appeared to be enjoying the attention. Surely Brian couldn't be the man her sister had her eye on?

Tina must have seen it too and said pointedly, 'Isn't Brian married?'

'Yes, to Sarah. I heard she used to work at the factory but left a while back to have a baby. They've got another one on the way now.'

'It ain't my place to say, but I think you ought to have a word with Gloria, 'cos there's clearly something going on with them two.'

Jenny sipped her drink and watched the way Gloria and Brian were looking at each other. If Tina could see what was going on, then so would the other women, and it wouldn't go down well with them.

★　★　★

Gloria came out of the toilet to see her sister waiting for her with a stern look on her face.

'What are you playing at?' Jenny asked.

'I don't know what you mean.'

'Don't give me that. What's going on between you and Brian?'

'Nothing . . . just a bit of fun.'

'You know he's a married man?'

'So?' Gloria answered with a shrug.

'Back off, Gloria. His wife used to work in the factory and is friends with most of the women. She's having their second child and they won't take kindly to you flirting with him.'

'Don't start telling me what to do again, Jenny. You don't know the full story so keep your nose out,' Gloria hissed.

'I don't need to know the full story, all I need to know is that Brian has a wife. You're playing with fire so just stay away from him.'

'No, I won't,' Gloria answered, 'I like him, and he likes me.'

'Have you been seeing him?'

'So what if I have? He ain't happy with his wife and wants to leave her.'

'For Christ's sake, Gloria, you've only been working at the factory for two weeks and already you're starting trouble! Joan and the rest of them will rip shreds off you if they get wind of this.'

'Yeah, well, I don't care what they think.'

'You should! Do you really want to be that woman who breaks up a family?'

'I knew you'd be like this . . . but just remember, you ain't Little Miss Perfect!' Gloria snapped.

'What's that supposed to mean?'

'Work it out,' she answered briskly and stomped off, pulling open the door to march from the room.

Gloria was fuming. Jenny was quick to spout off about her behaviour, but her sister had been the one who'd been pregnant without a husband. It infuriated her that Jenny continued to act as if she was untarnished and had never done anything wrong. Not that she thought seeing Brian was wrong. He'd told her he'd married Sarah when he was seventeen and hadn't really loved her. Now, at twenty-five, he was miserable because Sarah had grown into a fat old nag. He'd said he'd leave her, but not until after she'd had the baby. Gloria had told him she'd wait for him, and in the meantime, she planned on finding a bedsit. A love nest where she could be alone with Brian and where he could join her once he'd left his wife.

Jenny wouldn't like it, Gloria knew that, and it would scupper their plans of pooling their wages to rent a flat once they'd saved a deposit. Gloria scowled. She didn't see why she should be responsible for her siblings, and despite agreeing to it, she now didn't want to pool her wages. The sooner she found a bedsit the better, and Jenny could like it or lump it.

35

The atmosphere between Gloria and Jenny was tense, and Edith had picked up on it. As Jenny peeled potatoes for Sunday lunch, Edith cornered her granddaughter.

'What's going on with you and Gloria? You've hardly spoken since you came home on Friday night and I've seen the way you've been looking at each other.'

'Gran, you don't want to know, trust me.'

'If I didn't want to know, I wouldn't be asking, so come on, out with it.'

Jenny placed the knife on the kitchen side, took a deep breath and turned to look at her. 'She's seeing a bloke from work . . . he's married.'

Edith rolled her eyes and shook her head. The apple hasn't fallen far from the tree, she thought, and Gloria was just like her mother, with the morals of an alley cat. 'I take it you've had a word with her?'

'I did, but it didn't go down well and now I don't know what to do. His wife used to work at the factory, so everyone knows her, and to make matters worse she's got a baby on the way.'

'This is going from bad to worse,' Edith said as she rubbed her hip.

'See, I told you that you wouldn't want to know.'

'I'm glad you told me. I'll have a word with her.'

'I don't think she'll listen, Gran, you know what she's like.'

'Yes, as I was thinking, she's just like her mother.'

Their conversation was interrupted when they heard Peter's high-pitched voice shout excitedly, 'Mummy's here!'

'Talk of the devil,' Edith said. 'I wonder what she wants this time.'

Edith walked through to the front room and was surprised to find Lizzie standing next to a man. He was very smart in his expensive-looking suit but appeared to be old enough to be her father.

'Mum, this is Owen, my very good friend. Kids, say hello to your uncle Owen,' Lizzie told them.

While the boys just stared at the man, Edith thought, uncle, my arse. She couldn't bring herself to greet a man who was seeing a woman young enough to be his daughter.

'Put the kettle on, Jen, there's a good girl,' Lizzie urged.

Edith raised her eyebrows at Jenny as she walked back into the kitchen. Pamela hadn't said a word and Gloria was standing with her hands on her hips looking Owen up and down.

'Can we go for a ride in your car, Uncle Owen?' Timmy asked.

'Well . . . er . . . '

'Maybe later,' Lizzie said, interrupting him.

'Are you living with him?' Gloria asked.

'Yes, dear. We live in Du Cane Court, on the third floor. You know, when I was your age I always wanted to see inside those flats. The grand art deco style sticks out like a sore thumb on Balham High Road ... well, I wasn't disappointed. Owen has three bedrooms and there's even a radio built into the wall. When we get back from our holiday, perhaps you'd like to come and visit?'

Peter and Timmy jumped up and down, both yelping, 'Us too. Can we come?'

'Of course, my darlings.'

'Huh, three bedrooms,' Gloria said with a huff, 'and there's us lot crammed in here.'

'What do you mean? I thought you were back with your father?'

Edith noticed the boys suddenly become very subdued and Pamela was staring out of the window. She was about to explain, but Gloria beat her to it.

'Yeah, we were, until you showed up with a boot full of presents and ruined everything,' Gloria snapped.

'How did that ruin everything?'

'You have no idea what that man did to — '

Jenny walked back into the room carrying a tray and said hurriedly, 'Leave it, Gloria.'

'No, I won't! Why should I?'

Edith quickly stepped in and said, 'Because you're upsetting the boys.'

'Did I hear you say that you're going on holiday?' Jenny asked.

Edith thought it was clever of her granddaughter to change the subject so smoothly.

'Yes,' Lizzie answered, 'that's why I'm here. Owen is taking me away until the spring, so I wanted to say I won't be around for a while. I'll send postcards though and bring you back some wonderful presents.'

'Huh, we hardly see you anyway, so going away won't affect us,' Gloria said scathingly.

'There's no need for that,' Lizzie snapped, 'and you still haven't told me why you're all living here.'

'Never mind that. You said you'll be away. Where are you going?' Jenny asked as she handed around cups of tea.

'Spain, a small fishing village called Benidorm. Owen showed me some pictures . . . miles of golden sand and clear blue sea.'

'Can we come?' Peter begged.

'I'm afraid not, darling.'

'Mummy, I've only been to Margate. Where's Spain?' Timmy piped.

'It's a long way away and we'll be travelling on an aeroplane! I'm a bit scared. I don't understand how those big tubes of metal stay up in the sky. But, no, before you ask the same question as Peter, you won't be able to come as you'd miss too much school.'

'But school is boring,' Timmy whined.

'So, you said you're going to be away for a few months?' Gloria mused.

Edith could see the cogs of her granddaughter's brain turning and knew where this line of questioning was going. She smiled wryly, thinking this could put Lizzie in an awkward situation.

'Yes, Gloria, that's right. Owen has booked us into a fabulous hotel. We fly out on Saturday and won't be home until the end of March. I'm sorry I'm going to miss Peter's and Pamela's birthdays, but I'll make it up to them when I get back.'

'So Owen's three-bedroom flat . . . is it going to be empty?'

'Well . . . yes . . . apart from the cleaner who comes in twice a week.'

'Seeing as it's your fault we're living here, just while you're away, couldn't we stay in Owen's flat?'

As much as Edith was mortified by Gloria's behaviour with a married man, she had to admire her audacity now. It would be interesting to see how Lizzie reacted.

Lizzie looked uncomfortable and squirmed in her seat. 'I . . . I . . . I erm . . . don't know about that.'

Owen cleared his throat before saying, 'I don't see any reason why not.'

Lizzie's eyes widened, she blinked and said, 'Are you sure, sweetie?'

'It seems ludicrous that your children are living here when there's an empty flat available. That's as long as you don't mind, Mrs Austin?'

Owen had gone right up in Edith's estimation and she smiled at the man. 'I think it's a lovely idea, and please call me Edith.'

'If you pack your things, I'll pick you up on Saturday before we fly out.'

'We don't have much, most of our stuff is still at Dad's house,' Gloria said.

'Oh, I see,' Owen said, now looking as uncomfortable as Lizzie had.

'That's very kind of you, and thank you, Owen. I'm afraid we can't afford to offer much in the way of rent,' Jenny said.

'I wouldn't hear of it,' Owen replied.

Now that the man was showing some decency, Edith decided she'd like to know a bit more about him and fired questions at him about his occupation, his family and, finally, his age. She learned he was a retired accountant who had sold his successful accountancy firm. His mother was widowed, he had no living brothers or sisters and had never been married. When he told her he was seventy-two, Edith tried not to splutter her mouthful of tea across the room. She wasn't a genius and it didn't take one to guess that Lizzie was slyly waiting to get her grubby hands on Owen's wealth.

'Jenny, perhaps Owen would like a slice of my fruit cake?' Edith said, warming to the old gentleman but thinking he was a fool.

'No, thank you, we'd better be off. My mother will be expecting us for lunch. Edith, it has been a pleasure to meet you.'

'Likewise,' Edith replied.

'Please don't go, Mummy,' Peter began to cry.

'You heard your Uncle Owen, they've got to be somewhere else for now, but you'll see Mummy next week,' Edith soothed, and pulled the boy onto her lap.

Jenny saw them out, and as soon as she had closed the front door and walked back into the front room, Gloria and Edith broke out into giggles.

'What's so funny?' Pamela asked, the first time

she'd spoken since they'd arrived.

'Your *Uncle* Owen . . . ' Edith said as tears of laughter streaked her face.

'What about him?'

'Oh . . . oh . . . ' Edith said, and tried to catch her breath. 'It doesn't matter, sweetheart, but . . . but take the boys into the bedroom and sort out a game for them to play.'

Pamela tutted as she walked off with the boys, and as soon as they were out of sight, Edith spluttered, 'Can you believe he ain't got a clue about your mother's game?'

'I know, and did you notice how she was trying to talk all posh?' Gloria said.

'What game?' Jenny asked.

'Well, love, if your mother sticks this one out, she could end up a wealthy woman!'

'I doubt that. They never last,' Jenny said.

'Oh dear, there's us laughing but you look down in the dumps,' Edith said. 'Are you all right, love?'

'Yes . . . it's just that this move will only be a temporary measure. When they come back, Owen will want us to move out.'

'You don't know that, love. He seems a nice bloke, and with three bedrooms he might let you stay.'

'Two noisy boys and three girls. Huh, pigs might fly,' said Gloria.

'Maybe we should just stay here and save up the deposit to rent our own place as planned,' Jenny said.

'No, even if it's temporary we should still move in and it'll give Gran a break. We can still save. Owen said he doesn't want any rent money from us,' Gloria answered.

Edith eyed Gloria suspiciously. The girl had never shown concern for her before, so why now? Still, she had to admit having them staying had been disruptive. She was accustomed to peace and quiet, but now she was used to them, she'd probably miss them. She said, 'If he wants you to move out when they return, you can always come back here.'

'Thanks, Gran, but hopefully by then we'll have enough saved to look for a place of our own.'

Edith saw Gloria flush, but had no idea why. At least Lizzie's visit had eased the tension between the girls, and that was something, but she had a sinking feeling that Gloria was up to no good. She just didn't know what.

★　★　★

Henry staggered outside with an empty whiskey bottle and squinted against the late-morning sun. His dirty shirt was unbuttoned, his feet bare and his face unshaven. He lifted the lid of his dustbin to discover it was full and hadn't been emptied again. He was sure the rest of the street had empty bins and guessed his ex-colleagues were boycotting his house. 'Wankers,' he shouted, and threw the lid to one side. The sound of it clattering to the ground attracted the attention of his neighbour.

The elderly woman was sweeping her doorstep but stopped to call out, 'The rent man has been around again, looking for you.'

'He can fuck off!'

'There's no need for that, Henry. If you ain't careful, you'll find yourself on the streets.'

'Fuck 'em . . . Fuck the lot of ya,' Henry answered, and stumbled back indoors.

He threw himself onto the sofa and reached down the edge of the cushion in search of lost change. He found an old sweet, but no money. Not even enough for a bottle of beer. He looked around his front room in despair. The place was no longer a home, just a burden choking him. He couldn't pay the rent or the bills and even if he did have money, he knew he'd spend it in the off-licence. Everything surrounding him was a cruel reminder of the terrible thing he'd done to Jenny, and now there was no whiskey left to blur the memory. He'd been ostracised by his friends from work and pushed out of a job he loved. His children had left and were never coming back. There was nothing for him here.

Henry stood up and swayed as he buttoned his shirt. It took him a while, but he managed, albeit unevenly. He found his boots and pulled them on but couldn't be bothered to lace them. Then he grabbed his coat, stuck two fingers up to the house, and walked out.

36

It was mid-week, and though Jenny and Gloria walked to work together, they'd done so in silence. Gloria refused to discuss anything to do with Brian, and Jenny had given up trying. It was Gloria who broke the silence. 'We really need to think about picking our things up from Dad's.'

'I know, but to be honest I've avoided it because the thought of seeing him scares the life out of me.'

'Maybe me and Pamela could go?' Gloria offered.

'No, I won't have either of you put in that situation. I'll do it.'

'I don't want you going there alone. I'll come with you.'

Jenny thought about it for a while, then agreed. 'Right then, let's get it over with. We'll go tonight on our way home from work.'

They carried on without any further conversation, but as they approached the factory gates, Jenny noticed that Thelma and Nora were outside. They were glaring at Gloria which made Jenny's heart sink.

'Here she is, the tart,' Thelma said, her cigarette hanging from the corner of her mouth as usual. Then she threw the cigarette on the ground in front of Gloria and stepped out to tread on it. 'You're the spit of your mother. She's an old slag too,' she sneered.

Gloria went to sidestep the woman, but Nora quickly moved in front of her.

'Nothing to say for yourself?' she asked snidely.

'Not to the likes of you, no, I haven't,' Gloria answered calmly.

'The likes of me? Did you hear the cheeky bitch, Thelma? We all know what you've been up to with Brian and it ain't on.'

'It's none of your business.'

'That's where you're wrong, see. His wife Sarah is my cousin so that makes it my business. And the women here, they all have a lot of time for Sarah. The same can't be said for you.'

'I couldn't give two hoots about what you lot of gossiping old cows think. Move out of my way, or else.'

'Or else what?' Nora said, leaning towards Gloria.

Jenny could see the situation escalating, and quickly intervened. 'Come on, that's enough. You're acting like kids fighting in the school playground. Nora, let Gloria pass before we're all late for work.'

'I'd stay out of it if I was you,' Thelma warned.

'Yeah, that's right, Jenny, 'cos you might act all sweet and innocent but we all know you was up the duff and you weren't married. They say it's the quiet ones you've got to watch. If you ask me, you're no better than your sister,' Nora goaded.

Jenny felt as if the woman had shoved a knife into her heart but refused to allow her distress to show. Before she could say anything, she heard a loud crack, and gasped as Gloria slapped Nora across the face.

'Don't you *ever* talk about my sister like that,' Gloria shouted, then roughly shoved Nora out of her way. 'Jenny, come on,' she ordered.

Jenny was shocked but quickly followed her sister.

'Bloody interfering witches. Who do they think they are?' Gloria said, clearly fuming.

'I did warn you this would happen. I wonder how they found out?'

'I dunno. Me and Brian have been careful not to be seen together. They've probably noticed him looking at me and are just jealous.'

Jenny didn't think jealousy had anything to do with Nora and Thelma's animosity and worried what was going to come next. If Nora and Thelma knew about Gloria, then she had no doubt that the whole factory knew too. As she took her clocking-on card, her hand was shaking, unlike Gloria, who acted blasé.

Gloria must have picked up on Jenny's nerves and said, 'Don't worry about them. I won't have them saying anything about you.'

Jenny wasn't concerned for herself. She was anxious for Gloria and knew how the women could be. Walking onto the factory floor would be like entering the lion's den.

★ ★ ★

Lizzie looked at the open suitcase on the bed. If she wanted to get the lid closed, she'd have to forgo taking so many outfits. She hadn't realised

322

how difficult it would be to pack for such a long holiday, and re-read her checklist.

Owen walked into the room and chuckled at the sight of the overflowing case.

'It's not funny,' she told him. 'I've got to leave some of these things behind, but I don't know how I'll manage without it all.'

'How many pairs of shoes have you packed?'

'Only seven. I've already taken out one pair of slippers.'

'Seven? How can you possibly need fourteen shoes when you only have two feet?'

'I need different styles for different outfits. You wouldn't understand,' Lizzie said and pouted.

'I certainly don't, and I'll leave you to ponder your dilemma whilst I go to the bank to collect the pesetas. By the way, your passport arrived this morning. I've put it with mine in the bureau.'

'How exciting! I've never had a passport before. I hope my picture has done me justice.'

'It's not a fashion shoot, Lizzie, it's a legal document. Anyway, I'll see you later.'

Lizzie waited until she heard the front door close then dashed through to the large lounge. Thankfully, Owen had left the key to the bureau in the lock. She eagerly opened the pull-down lid and soon found her passport on top of a pile of official-looking papers. She was pleased with the image of herself, especially as it made her look ten years younger.

Before she locked it away again, Lizzie had a quick nose at the rest of the documents. She found their flight tickets, some legal jargon about ownership of the property and Owen's birth certificate. It was all very boring, but then her interest was piqued when she came across a long, white envelope with the words Last Will and Testament in fancy writing on it.

Lizzie pulled the will from the envelope. She knew she shouldn't be looking but couldn't resist. She quickly scanned the words, most of which she didn't understand, then saw the sole beneficiary of Owen's estate — Caroline Hancock.

'Who the hell is Caroline Hancock?' Lizzie said out loud and read the name again. She couldn't recall Owen ever mentioning her, and as he'd never been married, she wondered if the woman was an ex-girlfriend. Lizzie's lips were tight as she put the will back in the envelope. Whoever this woman turned out to be, Lizzie was determined that it would be *her* name on Owen's will, not Caroline Hancock's.

★ ★ ★

'What did Miss Aston want?' Jenny asked Gloria as they headed to their father's house after a long day.

'She told me not to bother to come to work tomorrow.'

'Oh no, Gloria, that's all we need! I told you seeing Brian would cause problems.'

'Actually, it was nothing to do with Brian. It was Nora, she told Miss Aston about me slapping her.'

'That's still to do with Brian,' Jenny said

through pursed lips. 'To tell you the truth, after today's events I can't say I'm looking forward to going back in tomorrow.' There'd been snide comments all day from the women, though mostly directed at Gloria. Tina had confided in Jenny that the cat was out of the bag because Brian had been boasting about how easy Gloria was. Jenny had cringed when she'd heard and wondered if she should tell Gloria. Surely it would stop her seeing him?

'Anyway, you don't have to worry about me and Brian. It's over,' said Gloria.

'Good, I'm glad you finally came to your senses. Better late than never, I suppose,' Jenny answered with relief.

'I didn't come to my senses — he dumped me,' Gloria said, though she didn't appear too upset.

'Oh, well, I hope you've learned your lesson and you'll stay away from married men in the future.'

The look on Gloria's face told Jenny that she was about to say something sarcastic, but both women stopped in their tracks and stared open-mouthed at their dad's house.

'What on earth . . . ?' Gloria muttered.

They quickened their pace and, as they drew closer, they saw their belongings stacked up on the pavement against the small garden wall.

'He's thrown all our stuff out! It'll be ruined,' Gloria said, aghast.

Jenny opened a bag to see her father's clothes too, not just their things, and she looked at them, bewildered.

'Your father did a bunk owing a load of rent

money,' a woman's voice called out.

Jenny turned to see her neighbour. 'I'm sorry, Mrs Boghurst. I don't understand. Do you mean my dad's moved out?'

'Yes, like I said, he done a bunk. He walked out on Sunday, leaving the door wide open. He'd been hiding from the rent man for weeks and when they saw he'd left, they chucked out all your stuff. I've got a few bits indoors I saved for you, stuff I thought might be worth a few bob, but 'alf your things have already been pinched and the rest will be soaked through from the rain we had last night.'

Jenny couldn't understand why her dad hadn't paid the rent. He'd always made sure he was up to date. It didn't sound like him. 'Do you know where he is?' she asked.

'No, but he was stinking drunk again. From what I've seen he ain't been sober since Christmas, and as he ain't been going to work it's no wonder he couldn't cough up the rent money. The locks have been changed and I've heard there's a new family moving in.'

'Great!' Gloria moaned as she continued to rummage. 'So we can't get in to get my perfume or nothing.'

'Or the boys' seesaw that Craig made for them, and the picture they painted for my birthday,' Jenny whispered sadly.

'Do you want to come in and pick up your bits?' Mrs Boghurst asked.

'Yes, thank you,' Jenny replied. 'I'll just help Gloria to sort through the rest of this stuff, then we'll be round.'

Together they sifted through the damp piles of clothes and broken toys. Whoever had put their belongings outside hadn't taken any care. Jenny managed to find a few outfits for them that looked salvageable and stuffed them into a large bag they had borrowed from Tina. It was disappointing to find so many of their things ruined, but what they'd saved would have to do. Gloria grabbed the bag and said, 'Let's go and see what Mrs Boghurst has got.'

There wasn't much, but Gloria was pleased to find her perfume and some make-up, along with her manicure set. There were a few toys too, in one piece, and, fortunately, Jenny's birthday picture. She thanked the woman for saving them. They didn't stay long, and between them they struggled home with the heavy bag of damp clothes, and the things Mrs Boghurst had rescued.

Jenny walked beside her sister, thinking about her dad. At one time, she might have made excuses for him, but that was in the past. He had killed her baby, and as far as she was concerned he could drink himself to death.

37

Lizzie sat on the beach with her knees tucked up to her chest. She sank her toes into the warm sand and adjusted her large-brimmed hat. As she looked out at the blue Mediterranean, she hugged her legs and sighed.

'Are you all right, my dear?' asked Owen. He'd made it clear that he wasn't a fan of sunbathing on the beach but would tolerate an hour or so if it kept Lizzie happy.

'Yes, it's so nice here, I don't want to leave,' Lizzie answered, thinking about a damp and grey London.

'I thought you'd be bored by now, but we still have a week of our holiday left.'

'Bored? Are you joking? This is idyllic, Owen. I'm even getting used to Spanish food, though I'm still not sure about that octopus stuff,' she said and wrinkled her nose.

'We can come back again later on in the year, but I have to return to take care of some business.'

Lizzie wasn't interested in whatever business Owen needed to attend to, but she did wonder if it had anything to do with Caroline Hancock. She still hadn't broached the subject of his will and hadn't worked out a way of asking about the woman without letting on that she'd been snooping. 'What business is more important than soaking up this wonderful sunshine?' she asked, hoping he'd shed some light on the mystery woman.

'I have financial matters to attend to that can't wait, papers that need signing and such.'

'I thought your financial dealings were handled by your old accountancy firm?'

'Mostly, but this is a personal matter I have to attend to.'

'Is it your mother? Is she OK?' Lizzie asked, pushing further for information.

'As far as I know, she's fine, although I think she's terrorising that new young nurse she hired. No, this is about my niece.'

'Your niece? But I thought you didn't have any family?'

'I don't . . . well, apart from my niece. Her mother, my sister, was killed during the war. She was in an underground station when a bomb ruptured the water and gas mains. She and her husband didn't survive, but their young daughter Caroline did, though she was left with devastating injuries.'

'Oh, my goodness, Owen, why have you never mentioned this before?' Lizzie asked. It was tragic, but she was pleased she'd finally discovered who the name on the will belonged to.

'I find it hard to talk about. My sister and I were very close and dear Caroline is . . . well, she's not very well.'

'What's wrong with her?'

'Her injuries left her in a wheelchair and with brain damage. She's unable to look after herself and needs constant care. The home she's in have informed me that they can no longer provide the specialist attention she requires, so she's moving to a new home, in Devon. Hence the need for me to return to London.'

'Oh, the poor girl! I assume you'll be going to see her?'

'Yes, but it's more to sign papers really. She doesn't know who I am. I'm not even sure if she knows who she is. It's awful, she was such a bright little thing and now she can't so much as feed herself.'

Lizzie thought it would be a waste for Owen to leave everything to a girl who wasn't able to appreciate it. Then it occurred to her that Owen was paying for her care and the money he was bequeathing would be for her continued expenses. It left Lizzie in a bit of a dilemma. She couldn't see how she'd get Owen to change his will, but there had to be a way.

⋆　⋆　⋆

Gloria had stopped for a coffee in the ABC Café with Jack, a man she worked with in her new job as a sales assistant in Sainsbury's. She arrived home later than usual and saw Pamela in the entrance. Her sister was laughing and enjoying the company of the old chap who worked in the lobby. It was nice to see the girl with a smile on her face, but Gloria was surprised to see her chatting away. Once she got indoors, she found Jenny in the kitchen tidying away the washing-up from dinner.

'Hello, you're late. I've saved you some dinner, it's in the oven.'

'Thanks, Jen, I'm starved. I went for a coffee with Jack. He's a nice bloke, you'd like him.'

'Is there romance in the air?' Jenny asked.

'No, not with Jack. He's not my cup of tea but I do have a laugh with him.'

'Please tell me he doesn't have a wife.'

'No, and even if he did, we're just friends. He works on the butcher's counter. He'd make someone a good husband but not me.'

'Just watch you're not leading him on. If you're going out for coffees with him, he might get the wrong impression.'

'Bloody hell, Jenny, give it a rest. I told you, we're just friends. By the way, I saw Pamela on the way in. Blimey, she gets on great with the chap in the lobby. I've never known her to talk to anyone like she does with him,' Gloria said with a little chuckle.

'I know. She told me the other day that he said these blocks of flats were earmarked by Hitler to use as his headquarters. Good job the Germans didn't win the war, or we'd be homeless.'

'We will be in a week. Have you thought about what we're gonna do when Mum and Owen are back?'

'We can't stay here, that's for sure. Shame though, the boys love sharing their own room and, like you say, Pamela seems like a different girl.'

'Back to Gran's?' Gloria asked.

Jenny pulled out a chair from the table and sat down as Gloria tucked into a warm plate of sausages and mash. 'We might not have to go back to Gran's. I've been saving as much as I can, and I hope you have too. I've seen a little house for rent off Bedford Hill. It's only a two-bedroom and it hasn't been modernised, but it's cheap.'

'What do you mean, not modernised? Don't tell me it's got an outside lavvy?' Gloria asked, dismayed.

'Yes, but that's not the end of the world and I think between us we could easily afford it.'

'I dunno about this, Jenny. I'm earning good wages at Sainsbury's and I fancy finding myself a bedsit.'

'But, Gloria, I couldn't afford the rent by myself. Please, I thought we were doing this together,' Jenny implored.

'Yeah, well, I might have given you that impression, but I've changed my mind and I want my own place. Why don't you ask Owen to help out?'

'The kids aren't Owen's responsibility.'

'Maybe not, but they aren't mine either, or yours come to that.'

'But we're a family, we have to stick together . . . I can't believe you would be so selfish!' Jenny snapped.

'You're the one who's being selfish by expecting me to put a roof over their heads!'

'But if you don't help me, you'll force us back to Gran's and that's not fair on her. Please, have a think about it.'

'Sorry, Jen, but there's nothing for me to think about. Gran said she liked having you all there, and I reckon she'll be happy as Larry if you all move back in.'

Gloria couldn't fail to see the look of disgust that Jenny threw at her before she scraped her chair back and stormed out of the kitchen. Uncaring, Gloria shrugged her shoulders. If Jenny wanted to be lumbered with looking after Pam and the boys, then that was her lookout.

38

Henry felt a sharp jab in his ribs and rolled over on the concrete step. He was vaguely aware of a man leaning over him, then he heard a gruff voice say, 'Oi, get up, you can't sleep 'ere!'

'Piss off,' Henry groaned with his eyes tightly closed.

'Move on or I'll get the Old Bill onto you,' the man said.

Henry opened his eyes and looked over his shoulder. A short, stocky man was jabbing him in the side and scowling at him.

'Did you hear me? I said sling your hook,' the man shouted.

Henry squinted at the sun setting behind the man and wondered where he was. He felt cold and shivered as he sat upright. That's when he noticed the three steps in front of him and glanced behind to see a door.

'That's right, I live here, and I don't want to be stepping over you to get to my front door. Bugger off, you dirty tramp.'

Henry felt unsteady as he stood up. 'Sorry, mate,' he said meekly and stumbled down the steps. He didn't know how long he'd been sleeping or where he was, but he felt the strong desire for a drink. His mouth felt furry and dry, his stomach ached, and his hands were trembling. He felt in his trouser pocket but all he found was an old butt, a roll-up which he assumed he'd picked up off the street some-where. He noticed he was wearing a black coat that was too short in the arms. He wasn't sure where it had come from as he couldn't remember the last few days. In fact, he could hardly recall the last few weeks.

He needed a drink. As he wandered aimlessly down the unfamiliar street, he tried not to think about the moment he'd kicked his pregnant daughter in the stomach.

★ ★ ★

'We're home,' Lizzie called as she opened the front door to Owen's flat. Two excited young boys ran towards her and Jenny appeared at the end of the hallway.

'Hi, Mum,' Jenny said, and Lizzie noticed that, for a change, her daughter looked genuinely pleased to see her.

'Hello, darling. Would you make us a cup of tea, please? We're parched, and Owen is coming up with our bags. I can't wait to show you all the presents I've brought back and tell you about Spain!'

Lizzie walked into the lounge to see Gloria looking as unwelcoming as ever. 'Hello, love. Where's Pamela?'

'She's got a Saturday job in Harper's.'

'Oh, the haberdashery shop?'

'Yes, that's the one.'

'Oh well, I'm sure I'll see her soon. What do you think of my sun tan?' Lizzie said and twirled around showing off her brown legs.

Gloria answered with a curt 'Nice'.

'Mummy, can we have our presents please?' Timmy asked.

'Yes, in a minute. Give Owen a chance to bring up the suitcases.'

Lizzie noticed there were two bags on the floor next to where Gloria was standing. That was a good sign. It meant her children had packed and were ready to leave, though she still expected her sons to ask if they could stay.

Jenny came into the room and Lizzie asked, 'Did Peter and Pamela have good birthdays?'

'Yes, Peter had a couple of friends over from school and Pam made him a lovely cake. Pamela's birthday was on the first Saturday she started work in Harper's, but she went to Linda's house afterwards for tea.'

'Good. And has everything been all right here?'

'Yes, it's been smashing. Pamela has made friends with the fella in the lobby and the boys have really enjoyed having a room to themselves.'

'Can we stay, Mum?' Timmy asked.

'Please, Mummy, we will be really, really, really good,' Peter pleaded.

'Huh, I can't wait to hear what excuses you're going to come up with this time,' Gloria muttered.

'Gloria, this is Owen's home and I'm just staying as a guest. I can hardly ask all and sundry to stay here too, now, can I?'

'All and sundry ... that's a nice way to describe your children!'

'Come on, Gloria — Mum's just walked

336

through the door. Why don't you go and finish making the tea? It'll give you a chance to calm down.'

Thankfully, Gloria stomped off and Lizzie immediately felt the atmosphere lighten. Then she heard Owen coming through the front door, huffing and moaning.

'Christ, woman, I'm surprised the aeroplane could take off with the weight of your cases,' he called.

Lizzie chuckled and even Jenny grinned.

Soon after, he walked into the room gasping for breath, his face glowing and perspiration running down his cheeks. Once he put the cases down, he drew a deep breath, and then said, 'Hello, Jenny, Peter and Timmy.'

'Can we have our presents now, please?' Peter asked.

'Don't be rude, say hello to your Uncle Owen first,' Lizzie told him.

'Hello,' the boys said quickly in unison.

'That's better,' Lizzie said. 'Owen, be a sweetie and put the cases on our bed.'

Gloria came in carrying a tray of tea in fine bone-china cups, and placed it on the long mahogany table that stretched the length of the windows.

'Smashing, thanks, Gloria. I love Spain, but I've missed a good old-fashioned cup of English tea,' Lizzie said and picked up a cup before sitting on the velvet-covered chaise longue. She pulled her skirt above her knees, once again showing off her tan. 'If you give Owen a bit of time to recover from lugging my cases around, he'll be happy to run you all back to your gran's. I take it that's where you'll be going?'

'We are, but Gloria's found herself a room in a flat at the end of the High Road. She'll be sharing with a girl she works with in Sainsbury's,' Jenny answered.

'I want to stay here with you,' Peter cried.

'And me, please, Mummy?' Timmy said.

'I've already explained why you can't, but now I'm settled here I'll be able to come and see you more often. Stop snivelling, Peter, there's a good boy,' Lizzie said impatiently, then turned to Gloria and asked, 'Sainsbury's? I thought you were working with Jenny.'

'I was, but now I'm not,' Gloria answered flatly.

'So, do you want to hear about Spain?' Lizzie asked.

'No, not really, and it's a shame they can't stay here with you,' Gloria said. 'Jenny was going to move us all to a little house, but I let her down and she can't afford it. I think she's mad. After all, Pam and the boys aren't her responsibility, they're yours.'

Lizzie, fearing Owen would hear, wished Gloria would shut her mouth. 'As I said, I am only a guest here. If I had my own home, things might be different, but I'm sure your gran will be pleased to have you back.'

'Is that it, Mother? That's all you have?' Gloria demanded.

'Gloria, I don't know what you expect from me.'

'I expect you to house your own children, but

338

you don't seem to give a shit about them.'

Owen came back into the room, and barked, 'I'll thank you not to use that language, young lady, or to take that tone with your mother.'

'Stay out of it, *Uncle* Owen. This has got nothing to do with you and I'll speak to my *mother* how I see fit.'

'That's enough, Gloria,' Jenny said, 'Owen was good enough to let us stay.'

'Come off it, it was no skin off his nose. They can't wait to get rid of us now though, eh?'

'You are a very petulant young woman, Gloria, and if you continue to upset your mother with your outbursts, I will ask you to leave . . . immediately.'

Gloria picked up her bags and shouted, 'Don't worry, I'm going. I can't stand to be around this fiasco any longer.'

'Wait . . . ' Jenny called.

Gloria ignored her and marched across the lounge. As she passed Owen, she sneered and said, 'My mother only wants you for your money, but you're too bloody stupid to see it.'

'That's enough,' Owen said. 'Get out!'

They heard the front door slam and then Peter burst into tears. 'It's all right, darling,' Lizzie said placatingly, 'take no notice of your sister, you know how moody she can be. Tell you what, shall we have a look in my cases for your presents?'

It worked. Peter stopped crying and she led him through to her bedroom. The gifts were a good distraction and put a smile back on her sons' faces. She played with them for a while, and then when she returned to the lounge, Lizzie saw that Jenny had their bags.

It was such a relief. She loved her children, but they could ruin everything for her. As it was, Gloria had blatantly pointed out the obvious to Owen. She could only hope he hadn't believed what her daughter had said.

39

Jenny yawned and shook her head, trying to wake herself up. She'd been back at her gran's for nearly a week and, with Pamela fidgeting in bed beside her, she hadn't been sleeping well. She was just grateful it was Friday and she had the weekend off to look forward to.

'Are we keeping you up?' Tina asked.

'Sorry, I'm shattered. I can't wait for six o'clock and to get out of here.'

'It can't be easy for you, all living in a one-bedroom flat. Mind you, I've only got two bedrooms, so my three girls have to share. They're always bickering, it drives me mad.'

'Luckily, my lot don't argue too much, but I think the boys are struggling with school because they're not getting a good night's kip on the sofa. I'm going to have to get on to the council and see if they'll give us somewhere, but I'm worried they'll want to take the boys into care.'

'You're old enough to be their legal guardian,' Tina said.

'Yes, but I don't know how you go about sorting all that sort of stuff out. It's not ideal at Gran's, but maybe it's better the devil you know. I dunno, I'll see how it goes.'

'Tell you what — why don't you come over to mine tomorrow night? I'm having a little birthday bash, nothing fancy, just a few people,

341

some drinks and nibbles. It'll take your mind off things for a while.'

'I didn't know it was your birthday,' Jenny answered, dodging the invitation.

'Yes, on Sunday. I'll be forty, so Terry said we should celebrate it. You'll come, won't you?'

Jenny didn't want to, but she was so tired she couldn't quickly think of a good excuse to get out of it. 'I . . . erm . . . I . . . '

'No excuses, Jenny Lombard! I shall expect to see you at seven and I'll be ever so disappointed if you don't turn up. You wouldn't want to ruin my birthday?'

Jenny didn't want to upset her friend and said, 'Thanks, Tina, I'll be there.'

★ ★ ★

'What you doing this weekend?' Jack asked as he walked along the High Road with Gloria.

They'd finished work and Gloria was looking forward to getting home. Her feet were killing her, and she needed a nice long soak in the bath. 'Not much. Me and Gail might go to the pictures tomorrow night. Wanna join us?'

'Nah, it's all right, thanks. I've already got plans.'

'Suit yourself. I'll see you on Monday,' Gloria said as Jack turned off at his road.

'Yeah, see ya,' he called back.

She didn't have much further to walk and was glad she and Gail had found a flat close to work. The furniture was a bit tatty and only one gas ring worked on the hob, but they both liked the place. Gail was a few years older than Gloria and had moved out of her parents' house because her mum was having their seventh child. The house was already overcrowded and she was embarrassed her mother was still having children at the age of forty-six. Gail had said she was going straight from work to see her mum, so Gloria had the place to herself. As she turned the corner, she heard a familiar voice that made her stomach turn.

'Hello there, pretty lady, what a pleasure to bump into you.'

There was no mistaking Dwight's American accent, and she ignored him as she picked up her pace.

He must have run because he appeared at her side and said, 'Didn't you hear me calling? Where are you off to in such a hurry?'

'Yes, I heard you, but I don't want to talk to you,' Gloria answered and hoped that would be an end to it.

'Don't be like that, Gloria, you'll break my heart into a thousand pieces. You're looking mighty fine and I'm proud to be walking with you.'

'Just go away,' she said brusquely.

'Gloria, so glorious. She stabs me in my heart, over and over, but I can't help myself and keep coming back for more. It's a pain that feels so, so, so good,' Dwight said and licked his lips as he mockingly held his hands to his chest.

Gloria thought he sounded pathetic and hoped that if she didn't respond, he'd get the message and leave her alone.

'Are you on your way home?'

Gloria continued walking and remained silent.

'I'll escort you and ensure you get safely to wherever it is you're going. It's such a beautiful evening and how better can a man spend his time but with such a beautiful woman?'

Gloria realised she wasn't going to shake him off so easily and spun on her heel to face him. 'You're a dirty creep, Dwight. I don't like you, and I never will, so just bugger off and leave me alone.'

He held up both hands, and thankfully he didn't pursue her as she marched off again. He made her feel uncomfortable, and she shuddered at the memory of him ogling her with lust in his eyes. When she reached her front door, and placed the key in the lock, Gloria glanced over her shoulder, relieved that he hadn't seen where she lived.

As soon as she stepped through the door, she kicked her shoes off, then turned to close it, but to her horror Dwight appeared as though from nowhere. He pushed against the door and before she could stop him he was in the hall.

'Aren't you going to ask me in, pretty lady?'

'Go away,' Gloria shouted, 'or I'll scream.'

'I like it when a lady screams because then I know I'm giving her pleasure. Your momma was a screamer, she loved it hard. Are you a screamer, Gloria? Are you like your momma? Do you like it hard?'

Gloria was really scared now. She wanted to run, but Dwight was blocking the doorway. She couldn't get past him and daren't run to her room. There was only one thing she could do and could only hope it would work. 'I'm a screamer all right,' she said, and taking a deep breath she let out an ear-piercing screech.

Dwight looked shocked but didn't budge. She took another deep breath and screamed again as loudly as she could.

'I'm only playing with you,' Dwight drawled. 'Now hush up, and I'll be on my way.'

At last he walked out, and Gloria frantically shut the door. She was trembling and her heart was thumping. She leaned back against the door and rested her head on the wood as she took a few long, slow breaths.

She began to calm down, but then her eyes widened in disbelief when Dwight spoke again.

'I'll be seeing you, pretty lady,' she heard him say through the letterbox.

He was on the other side of the door. There were only a few inches of wood separating them and Gloria stood motionless, hardly daring to breathe, listening for every sound. Had he gone, or was he outside, waiting to come in and get her? Her body flinched, and she stifled a yelp when she heard a knock.

'Please . . . please go away,' she whispered.

'Hello? Is everything all right in there?' a voice said.

It sounded like a woman and relief flooded through her. Someone must have heard her screaming. Slowly and with trepidation, Gloria opened the door a fraction and peeked out. A small, rotund, middle-aged woman was on the doorstep with a thickset, burly man by her side.

'I'm Rose, and this is Charlie, my husband. We live next door and thought we heard someone screaming. Are you all right, love? You look like you've seen a ghost.'

Gloria pulled the door open wider and looked past the couple to make sure there was no sign of Dwight. 'Yes, I'm . . . I'm fine now. Thanks. I was so scared . . . '

'What happened, love, do you want to tell me?' Rose asked softly.

'A man . . . he, erm . . . oh, God, a man followed me home and tried to get in. I didn't know what to do . . . I screamed . . . ' Gloria suddenly found herself in floods of tears and felt Rose's plump arms around her.

'It's all right, love, you're safe now. Get your shoes on. You're coming back to mine.'

Gloria wiped her wet face with the back of her hand and slipped her feet into her shoes. She didn't know the strangers on her step, but never had she been so grateful.

'Would you like my Charlie to go and fetch a policeman?'

'I . . . I don't know.'

'It's all right. Let's get you a cup of tea and then you can decide.'

Gloria nodded and allowed Rose to lead her next door. She sat on their comfortable sofa and drank sweet tea. She couldn't get the leering look in Dwight's eyes out of her mind, and she was still trembling. 'Do you mind if I stay here until my flatmate Gail comes home?'

'You stay as long as you need. I've got a big stew in the oven, so you won't go hungry. Now, what about that policeman?'

Gloria was still undecided. She could name Dwight and tell the police where he lived but as he hadn't harmed her, she doubted they'd do much. 'I know the man. He was my mum's ex-boyfriend. He didn't hurt me, just frightened me. If I report him to the police, do you think they'll arrest him?'

'I'm sure they will, and if not, they'll probably give him a warning and tell him not to come near you again. Them screams we heard were blood-curdling. I said to my Charlie, I thought there was a murder going on. You must have been very scared, so I think you should do something.'

'Right then,' Gloria said, feeling stronger, 'can we ask Charlie to get the police?'

40

'I've packed some sandwiches for the journey,' Lizzie said, trying to hide her thrill about a trip to Devon.

'Are you sure you want to come?' Owen asked. 'I'm worried you'll find Caroline's condition rather shocking.'

Lizzie wasn't in the least bit concerned for Owen's niece, she was simply looking forward to what she saw as another holiday. 'I wouldn't like to think of you doing this alone,' she lied.

Owen stepped closer to her and kissed her gently on the cheek. 'Thank you, Lizzie, you're a good woman.'

Lizzie smiled sweetly at the old man, convinced she'd soon have her name on his will. When she was sitting in a car with him for hours it would give her the opportunity to talk some sense into him. After all, what good would all his and his mother's money be to Caroline?

'We'd better get off if we want to miss the Saturday-morning shoppers. There's a nice inn about halfway between here and Devon. I've stayed there before, they do a very nice game pie. If we stop there overnight, we'll arrive in good time to visit Caroline tomorrow.'

'OK, I'm *game* if you are. Let's go. Devon, here we come!' Lizzie said and realised she sounded a bit too upbeat. 'I'm sorry, Owen, I'm just trying to keep your spirits up.'

'No, it's fine, Lizzie. I've no doubt moving to a new care home will be distressing for Caroline, but I'm sure she'll soon settle in. She's been at Askwith House for most of her life, so maybe a change of scenery will do her good. You're right, let's make this an enjoyable trip.'

Before long they had left London and Lizzie was watching green fields pass by. Her tummy rumbled. 'Would you like a sandwich?' she asked.

'No, thank you. I don't eat while I'm driving and I'd rather you didn't eat in the car when we're on the move. I'll pull over shortly.'

Lizzie wished now that she hadn't skipped breakfast. She began to realise how boring the journey would be and had forgotten how odd Owen could be at times. He had funny little ways that really grated on her, though she did a good job of hiding her irritation. When they'd been in Spain, he'd insisted that she didn't swim in the sea and only use the hotel pool. She hadn't understood his reasoning about fish using the oceans as lavatories but had done as he'd asked. He'd also annoyed her with his pointless rule about setting his stupid alarm clock for seven in the morning. They were on holiday, but Owen said he didn't want to waste the day. He'd also stuck to his rigid ten o'clock bedtime. That had really got on her nerves as, from what she'd seen, Spain didn't liven up until ten.

About half an hour later, Owen pulled over into a small farm track. 'We'll have a ten-minute break here,' he said, and turned off the engine. 'You should stretch your legs.'

Lizzie didn't need telling twice and climbed out of the car. She arched her back as she breathed in the country air. 'There's nothing fresh about this,' she said, wrinkling her nose at the smell of fertiliser.

'Indeed. They must have been muck-spreading. Apparently, it's good for you. My father would tell me it puts hairs on your chest.'

'I don't want a hairy chest, thank you very much,' Lizzie answered and got back in the car. The awful smell had killed her appetite and she couldn't wait to get away from this spot. She tapped her foot impatiently as she watched Owen leisurely strolling back and forth with his hands behind his back.

'Come on,' she muttered to herself, then wound down the window. 'Can we go now, please?'

'I thought you wanted a sandwich?'

'No, not in this stench.'

Owen climbed back behind the wheel and Lizzie noticed he was smiling. 'What's so funny?' she asked.

'You. You're a town girl through and through. I find it astonishing that you can't tolerate the smell of the countryside, yet the pollution in London doesn't bother you.'

'Granted, London is mucky, but it doesn't smell as rotten as this.'

Owen started the car and they reversed onto the road. 'I'll stop again shortly, and I'll try to find somewhere more to your liking,' Owen said with amusement.

He seemed in a good mood, and as they drove

along Lizzie hoped she wasn't about to ruin it. 'Your niece, Caroline . . . you pay for all her care?'

'Yes, it's what my sister would have wanted.'

'It's lovely that you care for her, but what will happen to Caroline if anything happens to you?'

'You mean, when I die?'

'Yes.'

'I've made provision for that in my will. Du Cane Court and my shares will be sold, then all monies, including what I may inherit, will be left in trust. There will be sufficient to look after Caroline for the rest of her life.'

'What's a trust?' Lizzie asked.

'It's a group of people, in this case my solicitor and my accountant, who will look after my assets on behalf of Caroline.'

'Is that wise?' Lizzie asked, feigning concern.

'Very. Neither party can release money without the other's signature.'

Lizzie thought for a moment, and then said, 'But surely they could be working in cahoots and swindle your money for themselves?'

'I suppose that *could* happen, but I think it most unlikely. I've known my accountant since he was a very young man. He started his career in my business and I trust him implicitly.'

'I hope you're not being a bit naïve, Owen. I don't think you should trust anyone when it comes to money.'

'I agree with your sentiment. In my lifetime I've seen some very unscrupulous activities. Money can bring out the worst in people: greed, lies and mistrust. However, once I've passed on, there isn't much I can do.'

'Couldn't you leave your money to a loved one? I honestly think you'd be better off putting your trust in family.'

'I don't have any family, Lizzie, you know that.'

'You have me . . . '

'Huh, I see, but you're not family.'

'I could be . . . if you married me . . . '

Owen fell quiet and Lizzie saw his knuckles turn white as he gripped hard on the steering wheel. Then he suddenly swerved to the side of the road, stopped the car and put the handbrake on. He turned in his seat to look her directly in the eyes. She smiled at him and fluttered her eyelashes. This is it, she thought, he's going to ask me to marry him.

'Lizzie, I enjoy your company very much. You make me feel alive and forget that I'm an old man. But we both know we're not in love. I'm happy to have you living with me, and to take you out and about, on holidays abroad and such. In exchange, I benefit from a beautiful woman's company. However, there will be no marriage, and I want to make it clear that you will never be a beneficiary of my will, though I have left some provision for you. Now, with that said, are you happy with this arrangement?'

Lizzie's face dropped as all hopes of becoming a wealthy woman were suddenly dashed. 'I thought you loved me,' she said and forced tears to fill her eyes.

'No, Lizzie, and you don't love me. It's no use pretending, though I do think you could have a good career on the stage,' Owen said with a cynical chuckle.

Lizzie looked at the old man with contempt. She thought about all the nights she'd allowed his gnarled hands to grope her and the times she'd pleasured his wrinkled and sagging body. She'd tolerated his slobbering kisses and put up with him being stuck in his stupid old man's ways. For what? It hadn't got her anywhere. 'How much provision have you left me?' she asked.

'Three hundred pounds.'

'Is that it? Surely I deserve more than a lousy few hundred quid?'

Owen started the car again and said coldly, 'Lizzie, if you don't like it, you know what you can do.'

★ ★ ★

It was early Saturday evening and Pamela was helping Jenny prepare to go to Tina's birthday party.

'Ouch, that hurts,' Jenny said, wincing as Pamela pulled her hair into a high ponytail.

'Stop being such a baby.'

'Hark at you, sounding just like me and all grown-up. When did that happen?' Jenny said.

'I'm fourteen and I'll be leaving school next year.'

'Yes, you will,' Jenny mused. 'I hadn't really thought about it. What will you do? Work full-time in Harper's?'

'I hope not. I like making clothes, but I don't

reckon I'll ever be good enough to be a fashion designer. Instead, I was thinking of hairdressing.'

'That's a wonderful idea. You're great at doing hair and the only person I know who can do anything with my mop.'

'Do you really think so?'

'Yes, definitely,' Jenny answered with gusto. She felt proud of Pamela, especially considering what the girl had been through.

'Right, you can look in the mirror now.'

Jenny went to look in the one on her gran's dressing table and admired her reflection. 'Wow, Pam, it looks smashing. You definitely should take up hairdressing.'

Once she'd dressed, Jenny walked into the front room. She was happy with her appearance but still felt self-conscious.

'Jenny, you look a million dollars,' her gran gushed.

'Yeah, you look really pretty,' Timmy said, but soon went back to the Lego model he was building with Peter.

Jenny could feel herself blushing. 'Thanks, Gran. Are you sure you don't mind me going out tonight?'

'Don't be daft. Go on, bugger off, and make sure you have a good time.'

★ ★ ★

When Jenny knocked on Tina's door, twenty minutes later, her friend opened it with a glass in her hand.

'Jenny! You look fantastic. Come in, I'll

354

introduce you to everyone.'

Jenny followed Tina along the narrow hallway and then into a surprisingly large lounge. As soon as she walked in, she wished she could have walked back out again. There were at least a dozen people looking at her as Tina announced, 'Hey, everyone, this is Jenny, my friend from work.'

Jenny was met with an array of people saying hello to her, and once again she felt herself turning red. 'Erm, this is for you,' she said quietly to Tina and handed her a gift with a birthday card.

'Ah, thanks, Jenny, you shouldn't have. Come through to the kitchen and I'll get you a drink.'

Tina danced her way along the hall and into the well-appointed kitchen, saying with a smile as they entered, 'What can I get you?'

'Just a lemonade, please.'

'We can do better than that! How about I add a wee bit of Martini?'

'Oh . . . I . . . erm . . . don't know . . . '

'Go on, it's a party!' Tina urged.

'OK then, but only a few drops.'

Tina poured Jenny her drink then opened the gift she'd given her. Jenny was pleased that her friend seemed delighted with the fancy bubble bath. It had been Pamela's idea; she'd told Jenny that it was Gloria's favourite.

'Thanks, Jenny. I'll have to hide this away to make sure my girls don't get their hands on it.'

Jenny hadn't noticed but a young man had walked into the kitchen behind her. Tina looked past her and said, 'Jack, this is my friend Jenny.

Jenny, meet the baby of the family. This is Jack, my youngest brother.'

Jenny turned around to be greeted by a good-looking man with hair even redder than hers.

'Hi, nice to meet you,' Jack said.

'Er, you too,' Jenny answered awkwardly.

'So, you work with my sister. You have my sympathies.'

Jenny smiled. Jack seemed pleasant enough.

'I see we have matching hair. Do you have Irish roots too?'

'No . . . well, I don't think so.'

'There must be a bit of Celt in there somewhere, wouldn't you say so, Tina?'

'Yes, someone in your family line was a Scot or a Paddy,' Tina answered.

Jenny had always wondered where she'd got her red hair from. Then she had a vague recollection of her gran once telling her that one of her ancestors had come across to England during the Irish potato famine.

'Actually, in the past, I think there was someone from Ireland in my family,' she said.

'See, I knew it, you've got a bit of Irish in you,' said Jack, adding, 'All the best-looking women come from the Emerald Isle.'

Jenny was already blushing, but now she could feel her face burning.

'Stop trying to chat up my mate and take this plate of sausage rolls through to the lounge,' Tina ordered. 'Honestly, Jenny, he's terrible.'

Jenny didn't answer but she thought Jack was very nice.

'We can have a chat later when Big Sis isn't listening,' Jack said and winked at Jenny as he walked off with the plate.

'Sorry about my brother. He thinks he's a bit of a ladies' man, but truth be known he's all talk. He's a lovely lad, but could do with a good woman to sort him out.'

'What do you mean?'

'Well, he's got a heart of gold but needs to grow up a bit, that's all. A sensible woman would see him straight.'

Jenny wasn't sure if Tina was hinting at something. She thought Jack funny and very easy on the eye, but her heart still belonged to Craig and always would.

$$\star \quad \star \quad \star$$

Later that evening, at ten o'clock on the dot, Owen demanded they retire to their room. They'd arrived at the inn in time for dinner, but since their frank chat earlier Lizzie had sulked and spent the rest of the journey mostly in silence, and there had been little conversation at the dinner table.

Lizzie huffed as she followed Owen up the creaky stairs and into the cosy room. She undressed and slipped into the large four-poster bed but kept her back to Owen. He turned off the bedside light, and almost immediately she felt his hand cupping her bottom.

'I don't think so, Owen,' Lizzie snapped at him in the dark. 'If you want our *relationship* to continue, then you'll have to rethink the provision you're leaving me.'

'I'm sure we can negotiate and come to an arrangement that we're both comfortable with,' Owen said huskily as he pushed his groin into her rear.

'How much are you prepared to increase your offer?' Lizzie asked and ground her bottom against his engorged manhood.

'Five hundred,' Owen said quickly and tried to thrust himself into her.

Lizzie pulled away and reached behind to hold his penis. 'Five thousand,' she replied, knowing she was pushing her luck.

'One thousand,' Owen offered and groaned as Lizzie began to pull his foreskin up and down.

'Three,' from Lizzie.

'Two,' Owen answered.

Lizzie was happy with that and eased Owen into her. She writhed in fake delight. Two thousand pounds! It wasn't the fortune she'd hoped to inherit but prostituting herself to him had earned her a guaranteed nest-egg.

★   ★   ★

It was after midnight when Jenny arrived home. She quietly opened the door to find the place in darkness. She tiptoed down the hallway and into the front room, hoping not to disturb the boys.

She got a fright when she heard her gran say, 'You're home.' She adjusted her eyes in the gloom to see her sitting in her armchair.

'Turn the light on, love,' her gran whispered.

Jenny switched on the ceiling light and asked,

'What are you doing sitting in the darkness?'

'Call me nosy, but I wanted to know if you had a good time.'

Jenny dropped onto the sofa. 'I did and I'm so glad I went now. It was fun.'

'Good, it's about time you started letting your hair down.'

'I met a nice chap called Jack. Turns out he works with Gloria. Small world.'

'It certainly is, but I wouldn't like to paint it. You got on well with Jack then?'

'Yes, but I think it was a bit of a set-up on Tina's part.'

'Will you be seeing him again?' her gran asked with a glint in her eye.

'I don't think so. He did ask me out on a date, but I turned him down.'

'Why? You said he's nice and you got on well with him.'

'I know, but I don't feel I'm ready, Gran. It's too soon.'

'Sweetheart, it's been six months since Craig died. I know it feels too soon for you, but it always will. I was the same after your grandfather died. It still feels like yesterday, but it's been years. It doesn't matter whether it's six days, six weeks, months or years, it'll always hurt. You just learn to live with it.'

'I don't think I'll ever date anyone again. Craig was the love of my life and nobody can replace him,' Jenny said as a tear slipped from her eye.

'I know you can't replace Craig but you can still find happiness with someone else. I wish I'd taken the bull by the horns when I was still young enough. You don't want to end up alone like me. Craig would want you to be happy, wouldn't he?'

'Yes, of course he would.'

'Would he want you to be lonely for the rest of your life?'

'Well, no, I suppose not.'

'Right then, you should go on a date with Jack.'

'I don't know, Gran. How can I see another man when I'm still in love with Craig?'

'Does Jack know about Craig?'

'Yes, I told him. He's so easy to talk to and it felt like I'd known him all my life.'

'Jack sounds like an understanding young man and you'd be silly to let him slip you by.'

'I do like him, but he doesn't give me butterflies in my stomach like Craig did.'

'It's not all about passion. Friendship is just as important in a relationship. Go on, give Jack a chance . . . '

'It's too late, I've already turned him down and I'll probably never see him again.'

'You said he works with Gloria. She could have a word with him or you could pop into Sainsbury's and tell him you've changed your mind.'

'I couldn't possibly do that! But yes, I suppose Gloria could say something, though she's not normally very subtle,' Jenny said with a small laugh.

'I'm pleased you're taking my advice, but it's getting late and if you're going on a date, you'll need your beauty sleep. Go and carry the boys through, I'll make up their bed.'

Jenny was tired, but she felt a flutter of excitement at the thought of seeing Jack again. She knew she wouldn't sleep well and would be wrestling with her conscience all night. She just couldn't shake off feeling guilty at the thought of betraying Craig's memory.

41

'That was a busy day,' Jack said on Thursday as he and Gloria left the building. 'I'll be glad to get home.'

'Yeah, me too, but I'm going round to see my sister.'

'Say hello to her from me. I'll see ya tomorrow.'

'Yeah, see ya, Jack,' Gloria replied and waved as she walked in the opposite direction. The High Road was bustling with late shoppers on their way home and workers filing from the array of shops as they closed. As she drew closer to Balham underground station, she could hear the old beggar man playing his flute. He was usually only there on Saturdays, but Gloria thought he might have realised how busy weekdays could be. She began to rummage in her bag for some coppers to put in his hat. She loved the sound of his flute and didn't mind giving him a few pence in appreciation of his music.

A train must have pulled in on the platform below and a steady flow of people began to emerge from the various exits at street level. Gloria dodged them to get to the flute player and dropped some coins into his flat cap. She was about to walk away when she noticed another beggar sitting hunched up against the wall. She did a double take; there was something about him that looked familiar. She walked towards

362

him, peering at the dishevelled figure, and could hardly believe her eyes. 'Dad?'

Her father looked up with red-rimmed eyes. She barely recognised him. His dark hair was dirty and straggly, and he had an unkempt beard.

'Hello, Gloria!'

Her brow furrowed as she studied the state of him. 'Dad, what on earth has happened to you?'

'I, er . . . I had a bit of bad luck. Will you buy your old man a drink, love?'

'You've got to be kidding me! The last thing you need is a drink. I'll take you home and you can have a bath and a hot meal, but there's no way I'm getting you any alcohol.'

'Please, love, just a drop?'

'No, Dad, look at you — you're a mess,' she said, and grabbed his arm to help him to his feet. He appeared to be unsteady, so she wrapped her arm around his waist. The stench from him was vile and made her want to vomit, but somehow she held on. 'Come on, let's get you home.'

They'd only taken a few steps when another tramp staggered towards them and offered her father a toothless smile. He was carrying a bottle wrapped in newspaper, which she guessed contained some form of alcohol.

'Henry, I got us some . . . ' the vagrant said, holding up the bottle.

'Good on ya, Bill,' her dad answered and pulled away from her.

'Who's this beauty?'

'Gloria, my daughter.'

'Hello, darling, you gonna give your dad's best

mate a kiss?' Bill said as he lurched towards her.

Gloria jumped backwards, and yelled, 'Get off me, you filthy old git! Come on, Dad, we're going.'

'I — I think I might stay with Bill, but thanks, love.'

Gloria watched, astonished and mortified, as he stumbled along the street with his friend. He was beyond help and she pitied him, but he'd made his choice.

★ ★ ★

Jenny was pleasantly surprised when Gloria walked in. It wasn't like her sister to visit, especially during the week.

'And to what do we owe this honour?' her gran asked jokingly.

'I miss Jenny's cooking,' Gloria said, smiling.

'Your timing is spot-on, I'm just about to dish up,' Jenny told her. 'You can give Pamela a hand laying the table.'

'Actually, there's something I want to tell you. Where's Peter and Timmy? I don't want them hearing this,' Gloria said in a low voice.

'They're doing some colouring in Gran's room. What is it? Are you all right?' Jenny asked, suddenly concerned.

'Yes, I'm fine, but I had a bit of a run-in with Dwight. Mum's ex.'

'What happened?' their gran asked with a scowl on her face.

'He followed me home and forced his way in. Nothing happened. I screamed so loud that the neighbours came round. Anyway, to cut a long story short, he's been arrested. Turns out that when I complained to the police about him, they matched him up with complaints from other women.'

'Bloody hell, Gloria. When did this happen?' Jenny asked.

'Friday, after work. I'm all right, honest. Gail hasn't left my side and Charlie next door keeps checking on us, but I must admit I feel better now I know he's behind bars.'

'Will you have to give evidence in court?' Edith asked.

'Not if he pleads guilty. He's being done for assault on one poor girl. They said he'd been hanging about outside the secondary school too. What a creep!'

'Sounds like you had a lucky escape,' Jenny said as Timmy came running into the room.

'Escape from what?' he asked.

'Hello, you,' Gloria answered. 'Escape from the zoo . . . you . . . you're a monkey.'

'No, I'm not, I'm a lion,' Timmy said and roared loudly.

'Go and wash your hands and make sure Peter does too. Dinner's ready,' Jenny told him, and indicated to Gloria to follow her into the kitchen.

'Are you sure you're all right?' she asked.

'Yes, really, I am. You won't believe what else has happened.'

'Go on.'

Gloria stepped closer to her sister and whispered, 'I saw Dad on my way here. Oh, Jen, you should have seen the state of him. He was begging outside the tube station and looked like a proper tramp. He was as drunk as a skunk too.'

Jenny raised her eyebrows, but she wasn't sure how she felt about hearing her dad was in a bad way. He'd brought it on himself and he didn't deserve her sympathy, but part of her felt sorry for him.

'I offered to take him home and give him a bath and some food, but he was more interested in drinking with his alky mate.'

'Has it bothered you, seeing him like that?'

'I don't know ... not really, but it wasn't nice,' Gloria answered. 'He made his bed and after what he did to you, he deserves to bloody well rot in it.'

Jenny nodded in agreement, belying how she really felt. She'd spent months hating her father for causing her to lose Craig's baby, and she'd never forgive him that. She had thought that she wouldn't care if he drank himself to death, but now that he probably was doing just that, it saddened her.

'Come on, Jenny, don't let hearing about Dad upset you. I wish I hadn't told you now.'

'I'm fine,' she said, busying herself dishing up portions of shepherd's pie. When the plates were full, Gloria helped her to carry them through to the dining room table, where Jenny forced herself to say cheerfully, 'Sit down, you lot, and I hope you're hungry.'

'By the way, Jenny, what did you do to my friend Jack?' Gloria asked. 'He's been in the doldrums since he met you on Saturday.'

Jenny could feel herself blushing again, and answered, 'He asked me out, but I turned him down.'

'You've broken his heart,' Gloria said with a laugh.

'Actually, Jenny's changed her mind, haven't you, love?' Edith said from her armchair.

'Oh, I — I don't know about that.'

'You should go out with him, Jenny. He's a really nice bloke, and you've already got something in common.'

'What's that?' asked Edith.

'Their hair. Both gingers, the pair of them.'

'There you go, it's meant to be,' Edith said and smiled.

'Do you want me to tell him that you've changed your mind?' Gloria asked.

'I'm not sure.'

'Yeah, you are . . . I'll tell him to meet you at seven-thirty outside the cinema tomorrow night.'

'No,' Jenny answered quickly, 'not there. That's where me and Craig had our first date.'

'OK then, how about the ABC Café?'

Jenny thought about it before answering. The café could work. They could talk, and she knew she'd enjoy his company. 'Yes, fine,' she said, and once again felt nervous excitement knot her stomach.

★   ★   ★

Lizzie was pleased to be back from Devon. It hadn't turned out to be quite the mini-holiday she'd been expecting. She'd found it disturbing

367

to see how upset Owen's niece was, and how poorly the young woman had been.

As she unpacked her bag, Lizzie tried to clear her mind. Owen had promised her the sum of two thousand pounds, but it had only been a verbal agreement. Now she had to ensure she got it in writing.

'I'm going to call in to see mother. Would you like to come?' Owen asked.

Lizzie couldn't think of anything she'd rather do less. 'Sorry, no, I've got a headache and think I'll have a lie-down,' she fibbed.

'Would you like me to bring you an aspirin?'

'Yes, thanks, Owen.'

Lizzie took her shoes off and slipped under the bed covers, then Owen returned with a pill and a glass of water. He looked at her and curled his bottom lip before saying, 'Would you undress before you get in the bed? Your clothes will be dirty after such a long day and we don't want the dirt transferred to our sheets.'

Lizzie huffed as she climbed back out of the bed and peeled her clothes off.

'And please don't leave them piled on the floor,' he moaned.

She gathered her garments and threw them onto a chair in the corner of the room, saying sharply, 'There, happy now?'

'Yes, thank you.'

'Good. And before you go, can you call your solicitor?'

'What for?'

'To make an appointment to have our arrangement made legal.'

'There's no rush. I'm not planning on dropping dead, unless you have a murderous intention in mind?'

'Don't be silly. It's just that I'd feel better if our agreement is put in writing.'

'Very well, I'll get on to it tomorrow, but I've been thinking and I believe two thousand pounds is rather extravagant. I'll have Ronald draw up the papers for one thousand.'

'No way! You agreed to two thousand. You can't change your mind now.'

'I can, Lizzie, and I have. If you find the offer unsatisfactory, then please feel free to leave.'

Owen turned and walked away, leaving Lizzie fuming. The scheming old sod, she thought. It wasn't fair. Owen could live for another ten years and it didn't seem worth her while to endure him for a measly grand. Then a thought occurred to her. Perhaps she could work on his mother.

42

'I've got a message for you,' Gloria said to Jack as they walked home on Friday evening.

'Is it from your sister?' Jack asked, perking up.

'Yep!'

'Tell me then,' Jack urged.

'What's it worth?'

'Stop mucking about and just tell me what she said.'

'Spoilsport. Jenny said she'll meet you at the ABC Café tonight at seven-thirty.'

'Really? You're not winding me up? She really said that?'

'Yes, so you'd better be there.'

'I will, don't you worry. Blimey, I'd better get a move on. Thanks, Gloria, have a good weekend . . . I know I will!'

'Yeah, see you on Monday, and make sure you take good care of my sister or you'll have me to answer to,' Gloria called as she waved goodbye.

Once alone in the street, though Gloria knew Dwight was locked up, she still checked around her. He'd unnerved her more than she cared to admit and she hurried the rest of the way home. Gail had said she was going to be late, so that meant she'd be alone in the flat for the first time since the incident. She shuddered at the thought, and decided she'd call in to see Rose and Charlie. They always made her feel welcome, and Rose normally had a tasty pot of something stewing. She wished her mum could have been more like Rose and realised she missed the security of a family home.

★ ★ ★

Tina had been pleased when Jenny told her she was meeting Jack that night, and she finally admitted that she'd tried to orchestrate them getting together. Now, as Jenny approached the café, she could see Jack's red hair and once again her stomach fluttered with nerves.

'Hello, Jenny,' he greeted her, 'fancy seeing you here. Are you meeting someone?'

'I . . . I . . . erm . . . ' Jenny said, confused and embarrassed.

'I'm only larking about. I'm so glad you changed your mind about seeing me. You look knock-out.'

'Thanks,' Jenny replied. His humour was similar to Craig's. She thought Craig would approve of Jack and she felt a little more relaxed, though she knew her face probably matched her hair.

Once inside and seated, Jack ordered them coffee. 'I'm gonna own up,' he said, looking a little uncomfortable. 'This is my first date. I've never actually been out with a woman before and my hands are sweating. Look.' He held his palms towards her.

'Goodness, they really are,' she said, surprised. 'I wouldn't have guessed you're nervous. You come over as confident.'

'I normally am, but there's something about

you that has a funny effect on me. Anyway, if I find meself tongue-tied or me hands shake when I'm drinking me coffee, you'll know why.'

Jenny giggled and instantly warmed more towards him. He was so open and honest and there didn't seem to be any hidden agenda with him. 'I'm nervous too,' she admitted.

'Blimey, what a pair,' Jack said, grinning.

They talked for hours, until Jenny noticed the café floor was being mopped, ready for closing time. She realised it was gone ten.

'I'll walk you home,' Jack offered.

Once they stepped outside, she felt his hand slip into hers. It didn't feel wet any more, and Jenny smiled. Like her, he was more relaxed now.

'Can I see you again?' he asked.

'I'd like that,' Jenny answered. She'd had a wonderful evening. But suddenly she fell quiet.

'Are you OK?'

'Yes, I think so,' Jenny answered. 'I feel a bit guilty because I've just realised that I've hardly thought about Craig all night.'

'From what you've told me, I think he'd understand and wouldn't want you to feel bad. He sounds like he was a really nice bloke, someone I'd have wanted as a mate.'

'Yes, I think you'd have got on well with him.'

'Listen, Jenny, I don't know what happens to us when we die, but if Craig is around, or if he can hear me, I'd like him to know that I'm going to take very good care of you. I reckon he'd like that.'

'Yes, he would,' Jenny croaked, fighting tears,

and for the first time she felt she could let a little bit of Craig go.

43

Six months had passed since Owen had signed the papers by which, in the event of his death, one thousand pounds would be left to Lizzie. She was still far from happy with the arrangement and determined to get her hands on more money. For some time now she had been worming her way into favour with Owen's mother. She'd run errands for her, kept her company for hours at a time and now, every Friday afternoon, she fixed Patricia's hair.

In the woman's home now, Lizzie wound Patricia's thin white locks around a roller and piped, 'I'd love to see any photos of Owen as a baby. Do you have any?'

'Yes, a few, but he was an ugly child, fat with piggy eyes. He did blossom as a young man, but I'm afraid he now looks much like he did as a baby.'

'Oh, Patricia, you are so wicked,' Lizzie said, and laughed.

'One must speak as one finds. His father was never blessed with a fair face either.'

'I've been thinking . . . it seems a waste of money to be paying your nurse to look after you on a full-time basis considering how much time I spend with you. If you want you could cut her hours to part-time.'

'No, I don't want to,' Patricia answered abruptly.

'It was just a suggestion. I don't like to see you throwing your money away, that's all.'

'Why would you be concerned about *my* money?' Patricia asked.

Lizzie knew she'd have to tread carefully. The woman was old, but she still had her wits about her.

'I'm not,' Lizzie lied, 'I'm just frugal and don't like to see money being wasted.'

'You don't seem to be very frugal with my son's money.'

Lizzie thought quickly and defended herself by saying, 'Owen likes me to buy nice things for myself.'

'I'm sure he does and I'm sure he is handsomely rewarded for his generosity. That's the problem with Owen — he's always had a liking for sluts.'

Lizzie stared down at the top of the old woman's head, shocked at what she'd heard. She was tempted to respond by jabbing the sharp end of the comb into her scalp. Instead, she swallowed hard and said, 'I hope I've misunderstood you, Patricia, and you're not implying that *I'm* a slut?'

'No, Lizzie, I never imply. I'm sorry, I should have made myself clearer. You're a slut. There, no misunderstanding now.'

'Patricia, why are you being so horrid? I've spent hour upon hour keeping you company, and I thought we were friends.'

'No, Lizzie, we will never be friends. You're no

different from the many other gold-diggers my son has taken to his bed over the years. You are just one in a long line of sluts after his money. You are far from the first and you won't be the last.'

'I'm not a gold-digger,' Lizzie protested.

'Don't take me for a fool, girl. I know my son and he's probably told you you're not in his will so now you're after my money. Do you really assume I am so ignorant that I wouldn't know what you're up to? I've been here before and I must say, I rather enjoy playing the game. However, I'm tired of you now and look forward to my next opponent.'

'You evil bitch,' Lizzie sneered, 'if it wasn't for me, you'd be a lonely old woman cooped up all by yourself in this big house. I call in to see you twice a week out of the goodness of my heart, and this is the thanks I get!'

'The goodness of your heart? Come now, Lizzie, we know there is nothing good about your heart.'

Lizzie stood in stunned silence as Patricia rang a bell to summon the nurse. When the young woman appeared, Patricia instructed, 'Please see Mrs Lombard out and ensure she doesn't help herself to any of my belongings as she leaves.'

'How — how dare you?' Lizzie stammered.

'Oh, I dare, and do give my regards to Owen.'

Speechless, Lizzie grabbed her coat and marched past the nurse. She didn't look back as she stomped out of the large house and into the chilly October winds. The cold hit her immediately, and she pulled her coat on, fuming that the old cow had been playing her. She'd invested so much time into getting around the woman, but it had turned out to be for nothing.

Lizzie was no better off than she was six months ago, and now knew she never would be.

★　★　★

'Are you seeing Jack again this weekend?' Gloria asked.

'Yes, he's taking me out to dinner later,' Jenny answered and couldn't hide the big smile that broke out across her face whenever she spoke about him.

'Somewhere posh?'

'I doubt it. Knowing him, it'll be to a Wimpy Bar.'

They were sitting in their gran's lounge and talking quietly as Edith had dozed off in her armchair. Jenny's relationship with Jack had blossomed over the past six months, though she'd had her reservations about him. Whenever she'd voiced her fears, her gran was always there to listen and tell her she was being silly. Eventually, she'd given in and allowed herself to love him.

'What time have you got to pick the boys up from the party? I was hoping to see them,' Gloria asked.

'Pamela is going to get them on her way home from work. She's really enjoying her new job at Sally's Salon.'

'It's right up her street. When she leaves

school, I bet she ends up working there full-time.'

'Yes, probably. By the way, I forgot to tell you. Mum and Owen took the boys to London Zoo last week.'

'Blimey, what's got into her?' Gloria asked.

'I don't know, but that's several weeks in a row now that she's made the effort to see them. I hope she keeps it up.'

'You know what she's like, so don't hold your breath on that one. Anyway, tell me more about Jack. Is there any particular reason that he's taking you for dinner?'

'Like what?' Jenny asked, but she knew what Gloria was getting at.

'Any hints of an engagement ring?'

'He hasn't said anything to me — has he to you?' Jenny asked excitedly.

'He did mention how well you got on with his mum and that she'd asked him if she needed to buy a new hat . . . '

'And what did he answer?'

'He told her to go shopping!'

'No way! Oh, my God, Gloria! He's going to ask me to marry him!'

'Shush, you'll wake Gran, but yes, I think so. Just don't tell him I said anything.'

'I won't say a word. It's funny, if you'd asked me six months ago, I'd have told you that I was never going to get married, that nobody could ever replace Craig. Somehow, though, and I don't know how it happened, I fell in love with Jack. I realise he has his faults, and sometimes his irresponsibility drives me crazy, but I suppose he's never had to worry about his family like I have mine. You know I think the world of him. I'll never stop loving Craig, but there's room in my heart for them both.'

'I'm happy for you, Sis, you deserve this more than anyone, and it's great to see Jack so happy too. Oh, and you're welcome, just call me Cupid.'

'Yes, thank you. Along with Tina, you played a big role in getting us together.'

'Shame I can't find myself a decent man.'

'You will,' Edith said and opened her eyes.

'Sorry, Gran, did we wake you?' Jenny asked.

'No, love, I wasn't sleeping. I was listening to you two soppy buggers.'

'Good job we weren't talking about you then,' Gloria said and laughed.

'You wouldn't dare.' Edith smiled, then said, 'So, Jenny, it sounds like you'll soon be getting a ring on your finger.'

'I hope so, Gran,' Jenny answered, beaming.

'He's a nice lad, even if he is a cheeky so-and-so.'

Yes, he was definitely that, thought Jenny, and blushed at the memory of him having a cheeky grope of her breasts. He'd laughed at the time and called her a tease, but she was remaining strong on not having sex with him before they were married. She'd once almost been left as an unmarried mother and she wasn't prepared to take that risk again.

It niggled her that Jack didn't seem to take anything seriously and she worried about him sometimes being immature. When she'd discussed her concerns with her gran, Edith had told her he just had a good sense of humour, and that was important in a relationship. Jenny appreciated her gran's advice so she had dismissed her worries, but she'd noticed lately that Jack was a flirt. He was always larking around with other women and it made her feel uncomfortable. She hoped he'd stop once they were married. Her gran had pointed out that no man was perfect, and if that was Jack's only flaw, then she had nothing to worry about. Jenny wasn't sure, though, because in her eyes Craig *had* been perfect. But her gran was probably right: though Jack wasn't faultless, he'd won her heart.

★ ★ ★

Later that evening, Jenny sat across the dining table in the fancy French restaurant Jack had booked. It wasn't the sort of place he normally took her to, and she sneaked a look over the top of her menu to see that Jack was sweating. He had his best shirt on and was fidgeting nervously. Her heart hammered in her chest. He was going to propose at some point during their meal, she was sure of it, and she hoped it would be sooner rather than later, to put Jack out of his misery.

'Are you ready to order?' the waiter asked.

Jenny gulped. She didn't understand a word of the menu and couldn't pronounce half the things. She pointed to something but had no idea what it was. It was food, she was in a nice restaurant, so she thought it would be delicious, whatever it turned out to be.

Jack said he'd have whatever she was having and asked the waiter to bring two glasses of champagne. This was it. There could be only one reason he'd order champagne.

The waiter soon returned with the fizz and as Jenny held her glass, she could feel herself blushing, waiting for Jack to get down on one knee. She would have preferred him not to make a scene but knew that wouldn't be Jack's style.

'Cheers,' Jack said, and clinked his glass to hers.

'Cheers,' she replied, and was surprised when he began to drink his champagne without a proposal.

Perhaps he'd changed his mind? Maybe he wasn't going to ask her after all?

The bubbles of her champagne had settled and as she went to drink, Jenny noticed something in the bottom of her glass. 'What the . . . ' she muttered and peered closer.

'Is there something in your drink?' Jack asked.

'Yes . . . it looks like . . . ' Jenny answered and hooked it out with a fork. Then she gasped, 'It's a ring.'

'It's for you, darling. Will you marry me?' Jack asked, his eyes glistening in the candlelight.

'Oh, yes . . . yes, I will.' It wasn't the proposal she'd been expecting but it was very sweet and amusing.

Jack pushed his seat back and walked around to her. He took the ring and placed it on her finger amid rapturous applause and cheers from the waiters and diners.

'Congratulations,' their waiter said, and

popped the cork from a champagne bottle. 'Compliments of the house.'

Jack returned to his seat and thanked the waiter, then whispered to Jenny, 'I don't really like this champagne stuff. I'd prefer a beer.'

'I don't mind it,' Jenny said as she pointed her nose in the air and pretended to be upper-class.

'I'm so glad you said yes. I've been worrying all day that you'd turn me down.'

'Why would you think that? I love you, Jack, and can't wait to be your wife.'

The waiter appeared again and placed a plate in front of each of them. Jenny looked down at hers and almost screamed. She glanced across to Jack. He looked as horrified as she felt.

'Bleedin' hell, Jen, it's snails!' he said with disgust.

'I can't eat them.'

'Nah, me neither,' Jack replied, then leaned in towards her. 'Shall we get out of here?'

'Yes, please,' Jenny answered and noticed the naughty glint in Jack's eyes.

'Come on then, stand up, and when I say, 'Go', run for it.'

Jenny was appalled at first, but then she grinned. She had never done anything like this in her life before, and it would certainly make the evening a memorable one. With her heart racing, she waited for the signal.

'Go,' Jack hissed, and they ran through the restaurant and out onto the street.

Jenny could hear the waiter calling them, but Jack had hold of her hand and was pulling her along. They turned a corner, then another, before they stopped and fell about in laughter.

'What terrible behaviour from an almost married woman,' Jack said.

'I know, but there was no way I could have eaten them snails. I bet they were right slimy!'

'Fancy a sausage and chips?'

'Yes, that would be perfect,' Jenny answered, and held her fiancé's hand as they headed for the chip shop.

'When do you want to do it?' Jack asked.

'Do what?'

'Get married!'

'I don't know, after Christmas. How about February the fourteenth?'

'Valentine's Day? If that's what you want, but it might be a bit cold.'

'Probably, but I think it'll be romantic,' Jenny told him.

'It means I can't get my hands on you for another four months yet,' Jack said, pretending to moan. 'We'd better start looking for somewhere to live, unless you want to move in with me and my mum once we're married?'

'I don't think your mum would want all us lot invading her house.'

'What do you mean? She'd be more than happy for us to live there, but I figured you'd want us to have our own place.'

'Yes, I would, and it'd be nice if we could afford somewhere big enough for the boys to have their own room.'

'The boys? You mean Timmy and Peter?'

'Yes. They loved it when we stayed at Du Cane Court and they didn't have to share with

Pamela,' Jenny replied, not telling him about when they'd lived with Craig in the house they'd rented.

'They'll be welcome to come and stay some weekends, but I don't think we need to worry about making sure they've got their own room, not just for visits.'

'I don't understand, Jack . . . they'll be living with us, and Pamela.'

'No, I don't think so, Jen. I'm marrying you, not your brothers and sisters.'

'Where do you expect them to go?' Jenny asked, perplexed.

'They can stay at your gran's or your mother can look after them like she's supposed to.'

'No, sorry, Jack, they stay with me. My mother isn't fit to look after them — she's unreliable and drifts in and out of their lives. As for my gran, she isn't well enough to take them on. If you want to marry me, then you need to understand that my family come as part of the package.'

Jack pulled his hand away from Jenny and walked in silence. This had been the last thing that she'd expected. Jack knew what had happened to them — surely he didn't expect her to leave her family behind?

'Are you telling me that if I want you to be my wife, I have to take on a ready-made family that ain't mine?'

'Yes,' Jenny answered simply. It had never occurred to her that he'd think anything different.

'I don't think I can do that, Jenny. I love you, but that's a big ask.'

'I'm sorry, Jack, but that's how it is. I can't compromise.'

'I don't want to lose you, but I don't want your brothers and sisters too. I thought that one day we'd start our own family and I don't see how we will manage that if I've got to support your lot too. Anyway, I ain't ready for kids yet.'

Jenny stopped walking and so did Jack. They turned to look at each other as a light drizzle began to fall. Tears slipped from Jenny's eyes as she pulled the ring off her finger and held it out towards him. 'In that case, I can't marry you.'

'I'm sorry,' Jack said and took the ring.

She never thought for a moment that he'd accept the ring back. She was sure he'd change his mind, and she watched in disbelief as he walked away in the rain. Jenny caught a sob in her throat. He'd gone, leaving her in unimaginable sorrow and pain. Her heart, which he'd helped to mend, was once again broken, only this time she felt it was beyond repair.

44

The moment Gloria walked into her gran's flat, she could feel something wasn't right. She expected to hear her brothers playing and smell the aroma of a Sunday dinner roasting in the oven. Instead, she walked into a silent lounge.

'Hello, love,' her gran said quietly.

'Where is everyone?'

'Pam has taken the boys to the swings and your sister is in the bedroom. She's broken up with Jack and is ever so upset.'

'Broken up with him? I don't understand. I thought he was going to propose to her on Friday.'

'He did, and she said yes, but then he said he wasn't prepared to take on Pam and the boys.'

'Surely he knew what he was getting into when he asked her to marry him?'

'It seems not. She's breaking her heart in there so go and talk to her.'

'I will. Don't worry, Gran, she's got through worse than this,' Gloria said and gave her gran's shoulder a gentle squeeze as she passed.

Gloria tapped lightly on the bedroom door. 'Jenny, it's me — can I come in?'

She didn't hear an answer, so slowly pushed the door open and saw Jenny face-down on the bed she shared with Pamela. Her shoulders were shaking but she wasn't making a sound. Gloria walked across and sat on the edge of the bed.

She gently rubbed Jenny's back. 'Are you all right, Sis?'

Jenny's muffled answer came, 'Yes . . . no . . . I love him . . . '

'I know you do, but if he doesn't know you well enough to know how important your family is to you, then he ain't the bloke I thought he was.'

Jenny rolled to her side. Strands of her red hair were streaked across her pale face and stuck to her skin with tears. Her eyes were swollen and red and her nose looked sore. She looked as if she'd been crying for a long time.

'Pamela asked me what's wrong, but I couldn't tell her I'd split with Jack because he didn't want them.'

'There's no need to tell them the truth, but you can't stay in here crying your eyes out. You've got work tomorrow and you don't want to be going in with puffy eyes, do you?'

'I suppose not. I don't want them to ask me what's wrong, though Tina will have heard by now.'

'Yes, but Tina is your friend and she won't be gossiping. I realise you're upset, and I understand how much it hurts, but you've got to pull yourself together,' Gloria said firmly.

Jenny swung her legs around so that she was sitting on the bed. 'I know you're right. I'm no good to anyone like this and need to put on a brave face. Sod him . . . I'm not going to waste any more tears over Jack, he's not worth it.'

Gloria smiled at her sister and held her hand. 'That's the spirit, Jen, well done. Now, can you get dinner on? I'm starved.'

Jenny smiled weakly back and Gloria knew her sister would be OK. Unbeknown to Jenny, Gloria had an ulterior motive for trying to put a smile back on her sister's face. If Jenny was out of action she might be lumbered with looking after her brothers, and she didn't want that.

★   ★   ★

Owen was off to visit his mother, but after their altercation on Friday, Lizzie didn't want to sit and eat Sunday lunch with the woman.

'I won't be late,' Owen said as he left.

Be as late as you like, Lizzie thought to herself. In fact, the later the better. She couldn't stand to be around him now and had reached the point where she found him absolutely repulsive. She'd made up some feeble excuses to avoid making love, but knew she'd have to give in soon. The thought of it made her shudder.

Now that Lizzie knew she wouldn't be coming into any large sums of money, Owen had lost his appeal and she longed to be away from him. The trouble was, she had nowhere to go. She felt trapped, just like she had when she'd been married to Henry.

She drummed her fingers as she sat on the leather Chesterfield sofa and her eyes roamed the room. An idea began to form in her head. A way to make some money. Owen had many items of value, but she'd have to select wisely. She'd need to take something that he wouldn't notice missing. She knew what he was like and had no doubt that he'd have the police on to her.

Her eyes fell on one of Owen's paintings. She didn't know anything about fine art, but he'd told her they were originals and insured. She couldn't even remember who the artist was and wouldn't have a clue where to sell them. Anyway, Owen was bound to notice an empty space on the wall.

She stood up and began to wander around. The silver tray, the large bronze hunting figurine, the ornate Chinese vase, all of them would be worth money, but not to the likes of Ten-Bob-Terry. He was the man everyone took their wares to. He didn't care if he bought knocked-off goods, and never asked questions. Trouble was, Lizzie knew Ten-Bob-Terry wouldn't be interested in upmarket gear like Owen's that he wouldn't be able to shift.

She ambled through to the bedroom, mentally clocking up the value of everything she saw, but quickly dismissed most things as unsuitable. Then it occurred to her. Owen's late father's watch. She knew he kept it in a secret drawer in the dresser, and quickly found the hidden compartment. 'Silly old sod,' she said aloud when she saw the gold watch, 'you should have put it in the safe.'

Lizzie grabbed the watch and placed it in the bottom of her handbag. Ten-Bob-Terry was always interested in a bit of gold and she knew he'd pay her handsomely for something so valuable. It'd be enough to see her through for a while. She hastily packed her things, anxious to be gone before Owen returned. She doubted he'd immediately notice that the watch was missing, and by the time he did, she'd have sold it. He'd have no proof that she'd stolen it, so she didn't have to worry about the police. She'd be in the clear and with a good few bob in her pocket.

45

On Monday morning Jenny trudged to work, but she would rather have stayed in bed. She couldn't pretend to smile and be happy. She just hoped that if she kept her head down and got on with her work, nobody would notice how miserable she was feeling.

'Jack told me what happened,' Tina whispered. 'I'm sorry it didn't work out between you two.'

'Yes, me too,' Jenny answered.

'He was ever so upset.'

'It was his choice, Tina.'

'Well, not really. In my opinion, it was *your* choice. He thinks you don't love him enough and have chosen your brothers and Pam over him.'

'He shouldn't have made me choose,' Jenny snapped. Her pain was slowly turning to anger as she realised how selfish Jack was being, and she couldn't believe he was putting the blame on her.

'You didn't really expect him to take on your lot, did you?'

'I never made any secret about how things are. Craig never had a problem with it.'

'Jack isn't Craig, and it's unfair of you to compare them, especially as in your eyes Jack would never stand a chance against the perfect Craig.'

'What's that supposed to mean?'

'You put Craig so high on a pedestal that no man is ever going to be good enough. How do you think that makes Jack feel? He can't compete with a dead man.'

Jenny's heart pounded in her chest as anger coursed through her veins. 'How dare you. You didn't know Craig, and as a matter of fact, he was ten times the man Jack will ever be. I can see that now, and in fact I don't know what I ever saw in your brother . . . he's spoiled, childish and self-centred. I'm better off without him!'

'Tina, love,' Joan said, chipping in, 'I know Jack is your brother, but Craig was bloody good to Jenny and her family. I don't know what's going on, but I think you should leave it.'

Jenny hadn't realised how loud she'd been, but she saw now that a lot of the women were looking at her. She lowered her eyes, embarrassed at her outburst. 'Are you all right, Jenny?' one of them asked.

Jenny nodded, her face burning. She clenched her jaw and fought back tears as she continued with her work. Just hearing Craig's name spoken cut her deeply. She missed him, and though she loved Jack, she was angry with him and knew she'd never miss him in the same way she did Craig.

★   ★   ★

Gloria had finished work for the day and as she walked along the road in the same direction as Jack, she kept her eyes fixed firmly ahead and ignored him.

'Are you sending me to Coventry because of your sister?' Jack asked.

Gloria remained tight-lipped.

'You can't put the blame on me. I ain't done nothing wrong!'

'How can you say that?' Gloria asked sharply, 'She's really upset.'

'So am I, but you can't expect me to let your sister make a mug out of me.'

'How was she doing that?'

'Come off it, Gloria, how many blokes of my age do you know who'd want to take on a whole bloody family? It ain't on that she thought I would. I reckon she was asking too much.'

Gloria was ready to jump in and defend her sister, but she thought Jack did have a point. After all, she'd walked away and left Jenny to get on with it. She shrugged her shoulders.

'Does that mean I'm forgiven?' Jack asked with his usual cheeky grin.

'Yeah, I suppose, but you should have known how protective Jenny is over Pam and the boys.'

'I get it, but I don't see why they can't stay at your gran's or go back to your mum. I suggested that to her, but she was having none of it and gave me back the ring. What's a bloke to do, eh?'

'I don't know, Jack. Would you reconsider?'

'I've thought about it all weekend, and as much as I think the world of her, I can't take on your brothers and sister too. Maybe I'm cutting off me nose to spite me face, but I'm only human, and not a bloody angel like that Craig.'

'He really was a good bloke, but I think Craig's memory is always going to be the

393

problem,' Gloria said.

'I'm just glad me and you ain't fallen out over it. Fancy a coffee? I'm buying.'

'Come to mine and I'll make us one. Gail is gonna be late again and I still don't like being there by myself.'

'You're on, and thanks for not giving me too hard a time.'

Gloria glanced sideways at Jack. He was a good-looking bloke with a great sense of humour. He could be a bit irresponsible at times, and sometimes his jokes were irritating, but she'd always thought highly of him and reckoned her sister had lost out. Jenny was a fool to let Jack go, and Gloria had no doubt that some other lucky woman would soon snap him up.

★   ★   ★

Edith pulled her shawl around her as a draught of cold air whirled around her ankles. She'd heard the front door open and looked at the clock on the mantel to see if it was time for Jenny to come home. Her eyes were a blur and she tutted. 'Damn blinkin' mince pies,' she moaned as she squinted, straining her eyes harder.

'Hello, Gran, what's the matter?' Jenny asked as she came through the door.

'Nothing, love, just being a silly old woman and talking to myself. How was your day?'

'Not great. I had a bit of a fall-out with Tina.'

'Over Jack?'

'Yes, but it made me realise something. In comparison to how I felt about Craig, I don't think I loved Jack enough.'

'Maybe it was too soon, and you were on the rebound. I'm sorry I pushed you into going out with him, but I'm pleased to see you've pulled yourself together.'

'I have, and I've been thinking . . . I don't know where to start, but I'm going to see if I can be the kids' legal guardian. If I can get that sorted, I can ask the council to house us. We've put on you for a long time now, and I bet you'll be pleased to have your peace and quiet back.'

'Not really. I enjoy you being here. I know it's too much of a squeeze for you all, but I'll be sorry to see you go.'

'Really?'

'Yes, really. I hadn't realised how lonely I was until you moved in.'

'Come with us then, Gran. We might be able to get a place that's big enough for all of us.'

Edith didn't need to think too hard about the offer and quickly answered, 'Yes, I'd like that.'

'Good. Well then, the sooner I get the legalities sorted out, the better.'

Edith sat back in her chair. She felt better knowing she wasn't going to be alone, especially as her eyes were rapidly deteriorating. She wouldn't tell anyone about them for now, but once they were all settled, she'd get her granddaughter to take her to an optician. A pair of glasses would sort her out, Edith mused, and she smiled, contemplating a happier future.

46

October had rolled into November and brought a big drop in temperature. Lizzie was glad to be inside the warmth of her mother's flat. She'd timed her visit well, ensuring that the children would be at school and Jenny at work.

'Shall I put the kettle on, Mum?' Lizzie asked, as she threw her expensive wool coat over the back of the chair.

'Yes, and get us a piece of treacle tart while you're out there.'

'Oh, Mum, I can't eat treacle tart. I've got to watch my figure, especially now that I'm a single young woman again.'

'Don't kid yourself, Lizzie, you're far from young. What happened to Owen? See through you, did he?'

'As a matter of fact, I left him,' Lizzie answered, ignoring the remark about her age.

'What's the matter, did he write you out of his will?'

'He never wrote me into it.'

'Where are you staying now then?'

'That's the thing. I was with Brian, nice chap, but he's gone back to his wife, so I'm sort of up the creek without a paddle.'

'You needn't think you can move in here. There's barely room enough to swing a cat as it is.'

'No, Mum, when Brian went back to his wife I

took over his bedsit, but I'm a bit short on the rent money.'

'I see . . . You want me to help you out?'

'If you could, Mum, that'd be great. I'll payyou back, promise.'

'Yeah, of course you will, Lizzie, just like you always do,' her mother answered cynically.

'Please, Mum, I wouldn't ask if I wasn't desperate.'

'Go and make that tea and bring me the old tin in the top drawer of my dresser.'

Lizzie put the kettle on the stove and then rummaged in the drawer. She soon found the tin and carefully opened it to sneak a peek inside. She was pleased when she saw there was a fair amount of money. She quietly sealed it again and took it to her mother.

Edith fumbled with the lid, and then asked Lizzie to open it. Lizzie obliged but was surprised when she saw her mother hold the notes close to her eyes. 'Can you see what you're doing, Mum?' she asked.

'Yes, of course I can,' Edith answered, but Lizzie wasn't convinced.

''Ere, but I want the money back,' her mum said and handed Lizzie three one-pound notes.

'Thanks, Mum,' Lizzie said. 'Shall I put the tin away?'

Her mum gave her back the tin and Lizzie took it through to the bedroom. Before she slipped in into the drawer, she quickly swapped the one-pound notes for fivers. She smiled to herself, thinking how clever she was. Her mum would never know, and if it ever came to light,

Lizzie could blame the 'mistake' on her mother's bad eyesight.

★ ★ ★

Jenny tried to concentrate and keep her mind on her work. It wasn't easy, but she was just about managing to hold herself together.

'Are you all right, Jenny? You don't seem to be yourself today,' Tina asked.

After the argument about Jack, their friendship had felt strained for a few days, but to Jenny's pleasure they'd soon made up. 'Yes, I'm fine, thanks. Take no notice of me, I'm just being maudlin. It's coming up to the time when it would have been my and Craig's first wedding anniversary.'

'Times like that are always difficult to get through — birthdays, anniversaries and Christmas.'

'Yes, but I'm trying not to focus on it too much,' Jenny answered, hoping Tina would take the hint and change the subject.

'Good for you. There's a bit of a do on in the Bedford tomorrow night, and a comedian is doing a turn. Why don't you come along with me and my old man? It'll do you good to get out.'

'No, but thanks for asking. Pamela has got plans for this weekend and I don't think my gran is up to looking after the boys by herself. To be honest, I'm not really in the mood for laughing, and I wouldn't want to bump into Jack.'

'I thought you was well and truly over my brother?'

'I am, sort of. I know we'll never be together, but now I'm not so angry and I've found myself missing his company.'

'It's a shame, but if it's not meant to be . . . ' Tina said.

Jenny nodded, but her mind was already drifting back to images of Craig. She told herself to get a grip and tried to think about Christmas instead. She thought about what gifts she could buy for Timmy and Peter, and she wanted to get her gran something special. It was only six weeks away and she was grateful to have something other than Craig to focus on.

★   ★   ★

Gloria had finished work and walked quickly towards home with Jack by her side. 'It's bloody freezing,' she moaned.

'It ain't too bad. I suppose I'm used to it 'cos the butcher's counter is always cold. Are you doing anything nice this weekend?'

'Nothing special and Gail is away until Sunday night. I don't know why she bothers renting that flat with me, lately she's hardly ever in and away a lot of weekends.'

'I thought you didn't like being there alone.'

'I don't, but it's not like there's any room for me at my gran's.'

'Do you want me to come home with you? I ain't got anything planned, so I don't mind.'

'Oh, Jack, that would be nice. Thanks,' Gloria answered.

A short while later, as Gloria opened her front

door, Rose popped her head around the corner and asked, 'Hello, who's this then?'

'Hi, Rose. It's all right. This is Jack, a mate from work. Jack, meet Rose, my neighbour.'

'Nice to meet you,' Jack said.

'Are you hungry?' Rose asked.

'I am, but I doubt Gloria will feed me.'

'You don't know that, you cheeky bugger,' Gloria quipped. 'Mind you, as it happens, I ain't got anything in.'

'You're in luck then 'cos my Charlie's got the trots and has turned his nose up at my hot pot. We're away to his brother's tomorrow and won't be back 'til Tuesday. It won't keep, so hang on a mo and I'll pass it over.'

Rose disappeared indoors leaving Gloria and Jack stifling giggles.

'Here it is,' Rose said and passed a large pan over the small wall between them. 'Mind out, it's very warm.'

Jack grabbed the saucepan and Gloria thanked Rose.

'You're welcome, hope you enjoy it,' the woman said, then at Charlie's urgent call, she grimaced and dashed back indoors.

As Jack followed Gloria inside, he lifted the lid of the pan. 'This smells bloody lovely,' he said, and smacked his lips.

'She makes a smashing stew, but I think it's the only meal she can cook.'

'Let's get stuck in. Have you got any beer?' Jack asked.

Gloria kicked her shoes off and hung her coat on a hook in the hallway. 'As it happens, I have.

Gail bought it, but we've never got around to drinking it — probably 'cos she's never here.'

Once they'd eaten, Gloria sat next to Jack on the sofa and they shared the last bottle of beer.

'This has been nice,' Jack said.

Gloria noticed his face looked unusually serious. 'Yes, it has,' she answered, and locked eyes with him.

Jack slowly leaned in towards her and Gloria's heart began to race as she realised he was about to kiss her. She knew she should resist, but instead closed her eyes and felt his soft lips on hers. As his tongue explored her mouth, Gloria felt his hands in her hair and then he pulled her closer. Lust stirred. It had been a long time since she'd slept with a man and it felt so natural — so good. Jack was her friend, her sister's ex, and she felt a passing feeling of guilt as his hand slipped along her thigh. But she knew then, with tingling excitement, that Jack was going to turn from her friend into her lover.

47

It was two weeks before Christmas. Pamela was at her Saturday job in the hairdresser's, and Timmy and Peter were playing skittles in the hallway.

'Are you doing any Christmas shopping today?' Edith asked Jenny.

'Yes, Gran, I am. Pamela's friend Linda said she'll have the boys for a few hours, so that means I can get round the shops in peace.'

'Do me a favour, get my tin from out of my drawer. I've been putting a bit of money away and a few weeks ago I got the coalman to change up all my coins into notes. You'll be surprised at how much I've squirrelled away. Anyway, it's for you, love. There should be plenty for a good Christmas and some left over to treat yourself.'

'Oh, Gran, that's lovely, thank you.'

'Go on then, go and get it.'

Jenny went into the bedroom and returned with the tin. 'Open it and count it,' Edith instructed.

Jenny flicked through the money, then said, 'Ah, Gran, thank you.'

'I didn't do too badly, did I? Twenty pounds in all.'

Jenny didn't answer but Edith thought her granddaughter was counting the money again. 'Is something wrong?' she asked.

'Erm . . . I'm not sure, Gran, but there isn't

twenty pounds here.'

'Yes, there is, I'm sure of it. There was twenty-three, but I lent your mother three quid.'

'Sorry, Gran, but there's only eight pounds.'

'Are you sure?' Edith asked, confused.

'Yes, look, here's a fiver and here's three one-pound notes. There's nothing else in here.'

Edith couldn't clearly see the notes that Jenny was showing her, but she trusted her granddaughter. 'The thieving bitch,' she cried. 'She's gone and robbed me again.'

'Who? Mum?'

'Yes, who else? Of course it was your mother. It's my own fault, I should have known better.' That was it, Lizzie's last chance as far as Edith was concerned. From now on she didn't have a daughter, and she'd never allow her under her roof again.

★ ★ ★

Jenny felt exhausted after the Christmas shopping and wanted nothing more than to put her feet up and relax.

'Shall I do your hair for you now?' Pamela asked.

'No, I don't think I'll bother going, but thanks.'

'Going where?' Edith asked.

'To the works do. All the women are having a night out. Even Miss Aston is going.'

'So why ain't you?'

'I can't be bothered, Gran, I'm too tired.'

'Nonsense. Go and have a bath, it'll perk you

up, and then you can get dressed to go out.'

'But, Gran . . . '

'No buts, just do it.'

Jenny knew she was fighting a losing battle against her gran and heaved herself up from the sofa. Twenty minutes later, she was sitting on a chair in her dressing gown while Pamela worked wonders with her hair.

'Where are you all going for this works do?' Edith asked.

'To an Indian restaurant on the way to Tooting.'

'Oh, my Lord, you'd never get me eating that sort of muck. You don't know what meat they're using. It'll be so spiced up it could be anything, or it could be off!'

'Tina said she's tried it loads of times and it's really nice.'

'Good for Tina, but she's married to a foreigner, she's used to that sort of stuff.'

'Gran, Tina's husband is from Greece and that's nowhere near India.'

'It's all bleedin' foreign! I don't know . . . you youngsters nowadays . . . you've got some funny ideas.'

Jenny chose to refrain from getting any further into the conversation and could see Pamela was trying not to laugh as she said, 'There, Jenny, all done.'

'Thanks,' Jenny answered and went through to the bedroom to get dressed. It was only then that she noticed what a wonderful job her sister had done on her hair. The girl certainly had talent. She hooked up her stockings and slipped on a smart dress, yet she still wasn't in the mood for going out and wasn't bothered about how she looked. She pushed her feet into her shoes and clipped on a pair of earrings.

'You look nice,' Pamela said when Jenny returned to the front room.

'Don't you think you should have something to eat before you go?' her gran asked.

'Erm, no . . . I told you. We're going to a restaurant.'

'All right, but I don't want to hear you moaning when you get a dodgy tummy.'

Jenny and Pamela exchanged a wry smile. 'I won't, thanks, Gran. See you later.'

It took Jenny nearly half an hour to walk to the restaurant and by the time she arrived, her eyes were streaming from the cold.

'Look at you, Jenny, you look frozen through!' Tina said when she walked in. 'I told you my old man would have picked you up.'

'I'm fine,' Jenny said, though her teeth chattered.

'No, you're not, but one of these spicy curries will soon warm you up.'

Jenny sat next to Tina but didn't take her coat off.

'Your hair looks fabulous. Did your Pamela do it for you?'

'Yes, she's got a real flair for it.'

'Are you talking about Pamela?' Joan asked.

'Yes, just saying how good she is with hair.'

'She's bloody marvellous. I was down at Sally's Salon last week and your sister was doing a practice run on a bride-to-be. Well, she knocked everyone's socks off.'

'Ah, that's nice,' Jenny said and smiled warmly. 'She's a good girl.'

'Yes, she is — not like your other sister!' Joan said and looked directly at Tina. 'Have you told her?'

Jenny saw Tina looked daggers at Joan and then shake her head.

'Told me what?' she asked.

'Go on, Tina, tell her what you told me. The girl has a right to know.'

Jenny looked at Tina for an explanation.

'I'm sorry, I didn't want you to find out this way,' Tina said and glared at Joan again. 'It's Gloria . . . and Jack. They're seeing each other.'

Jenny swallowed hard as she took in the information, but she wasn't sure how she should react. So Gloria and Jack had been dating behind her back. She wondered how long it had been going on. It felt like a betrayal, but as it was over between her and Jack, Gloria hadn't really done anything wrong.

'Are you all right, Jen?' Tina asked.

'Yes, I think so,' she finally replied.

'It's not nice, is it?' Tina said.

'No, it isn't. Part of me feels let down by Gloria, but then I have to ask myself why anything she does would surprise me. I understand she's desperate for someone to love her, but she could have her pick of men. Why choose my ex?'

'I told them what I thought, and I don't think they liked it. They came round last night, and I gave Gloria a piece of my mind. Mind you, I think it was water off a duck's back.'

'It wouldn't have worried her. She's too thick-skinned, but thanks for speaking up.'

'Well, you're my mate and it ain't on. Family should stick together, not stab each other in the back.'

Yes, they should stick together, thought Jenny, but Gloria was her mother's daughter. There were the odd occasions when Gloria could be kind and show sympathy, as she had when Jenny had lost both Craig and her baby. She'd been sympathetic when Jenny had broken up with Jack too, but it seemed it hadn't stopped her dating him. 'Sorry, Tina, but I've lost my appetite. I'll see you at work on Monday,' Jenny whispered. She managed to smile grimly at Joan, but then hurried out of the restaurant, too angry to cry as she made her way home again.

48

Edith had a large tray on her lap covered in small pieces of jigsaw. She couldn't see what pieces went together, but hoped she'd be able to feel her way to solving the puzzle. Timmy had squashed himself beside her on the armchair and was sorting the straight-edge pieces. 'Find the four corners, that'll be a start,' Edith told him.

Pamela was at the table in the window reading a magazine, Peter played on the floor with a toy fire engine and Jenny was eating a slice of apple pie. The loud claps of thunder outside were the only disturbance of an otherwise peaceful late Sunday afternoon.

'When you've finished that, can you get me a piece of pie, please?' Edith asked Jenny.

'It was only half an hour ago when you said you were stuffed!' Jenny said with a laugh.

'I know, but it's my favourite and I can smell it from here. Any chance you'll make one for Christmas?'

'I wasn't planning to as I thought we'd be having Christmas pudding as always,' Jenny answered.

'I'm not keen on pudding. I've tolerated it every year for the past seventy-odd, but I'd much prefer an apple pie.'

'Me too,' Timmy joined in.

'And me . . . Christmas pudding is yuk,' Peter said and pulled a disgusted face.

'What about you, Pamela?' Jenny asked.

'I don't mind, but I know Gloria will be looking for a piece of Christmas pudding. She always finds the sixpence!'

'Oh, Gawd, I hope she doesn't turn up here for Christmas with *him*,' Jenny said quietly to her gran.

'She wouldn't do that . . . would she?'

'Who knows? But if she does it'll make it very uncomfortable for me.'

'I could go and see her at work and ask her not to,' Pamela offered.

'No, but thanks, Pam.'

Pamela peered through the net curtains and said, 'I thought I heard a car and it looks like Mum getting out of it. There's a big, tall fella with her.'

'I hope she's come to pay me back,' Edith said. 'If she ain't, she can bugger off again.'

'What's she got to pay you back for?' Timmy asked.

'Never you mind,' Edith told him.

A moment later, the door opened, and Lizzie flounced in followed by the tall man and said as she brushed rain water off of her coat, 'Hello, you lot, it's raining cats and dogs out there!'

'Mummy,' Peter shouted, and Timmy wriggled down from the armchair.

'That's our peace and quiet ruined,' Edith hissed to Jenny as she eyed the man standing next to her daughter. 'I hope you've come with the money you *borrowed* from me. You know, the cash in my tin.'

'Oh, that, yes,' Lizzie said and opened her

handbag to pull out three pounds. 'Here you are, Mum.'

Edith took the money and held it close to her eyes, then said, 'And the rest.'

'What rest? You lent me three quid, don't you remember?'

'Yes, of course I do, but I know you helped yourself to a bit more.'

'I didn't. Oh, Mum, I think you're confused, but at your age it isn't surprising.'

'You cheeky mare, I'm not bloody senile! There was twenty-three quid in that tin, then after I lent you three pounds, there was only eight quid left. You swapped the one-pound notes for fivers.'

'I didn't, I swear! It's your eyes, Mum, you're as blind as a bat.'

'You're a liar, Lizzie, and a bloody thief!'

Peter began to cry and wrapped himself around his mum's leg. Timmy's face paled, and he looked wide-eyed from his mum to Edith. She realised her grandsons were getting upset, so she dropped the subject of the stolen money. 'For the kids' sake we'll leave it for now, but I ain't finished with you, my girl. Now who's this?' She pointed at the man, who towered over everyone in the room.

'This is Brian, and, boys, he's very good friends with Father Christmas. He has it on good authority that Santa will be personally visiting here at teatime on Christmas Eve.'

Peter stopped crying and peered up at the giant of a man. 'Really? Father Christmas is coming here to see us?'

'Yes, that's what he told me,' Brian answered in a deep, booming voice.

'Is he going to bring us presents?' Timmy asked.

'I expect so, but only if you're very good.'

'Wow, wait 'til I tell all my friends at school!' Peter said.

'If I was you, I'd keep it a secret,' Brian whispered, ''cos otherwise, all your friends will want Santa to visit them too, and then he won't have much time to spend with you.'

'Boys, why don't you go into the bedroom and write Santa a letter,' Lizzie urged. 'Tell him what you'd like for Christmas and then Brian will pass it to Santa.'

'Come on, I'll help you write them,' Pamela offered.

Once they'd left the room, Edith asked, 'What are you up to?'

'Nothing. Brian dresses as Santa for Smith Brothers in Tooting, so we thought it would be fun for the boys if he wears his costume and calls in on them.'

'Bloody stupid if you ask me,' Edith commented in a huff.

'Well, no one's asking you, Mother.'

'You won't let them down, will you?' Jenny asked.

'No, we won't. I said we'd be here, and we will. You just make sure you've got Santa some mince pies. Brian enjoys his treats as Father Christmas, don't you, love?'

'Yeah, one of the benefits of the job,' Brian said and patted his large stomach.

'Brian's got a room over Alfie the grocer's, but there's not a lot of space, so how about we join you for lunch on Christmas Day?'

Edith wasn't keen on the idea, but Jenny, kind as always, answered, 'Yes, Peter and Timmy would like that.'

'Great, right, they should have finished writing their letters by now. I'll go and collect them and then we'll be off,' Lizzie said.

Ten minutes later, once Peter had stopped crying for his mum, Edith was pleased when her peace and quiet resumed. She was still seething with Lizzie for implying that she was losing her marbles and had made a mistake about the missing money. There was no doubt in Edith's mind where that cash had gone, but unfortunately she couldn't prove it. From now on, though, she'd make sure to keep an eye on Lizzie, and, come to think of it, Gloria too.

★ ★ ★

Jenny felt restless and fidgeted on the sofa. Her gran had dozed off in her armchair and was gently snoring. Pamela had taken her brothers for a bath before bedtime.

In the stillness of the room, Jenny's mind turned. She couldn't shake the thought of Gloria turning up on Christmas Day with Jack. She didn't think she'd be able to face it and decided to confront the problem head on.

She popped her head around the bathroom door and said to Pamela, 'I'm going out, but won't be long.'

'Where are you going?'

'To have a word with Gloria. Wish me luck.'

'Good luck,' Pamela said with raised eyebrows. 'I think you might need it.'

Jenny grabbed her coat and an umbrella, then stepped out into the pouring rain. She thought herself mad to venture out in this weather but knew she wouldn't sleep tonight unless she'd spoken with her sister.

It was quite a trek to Gloria's flat, and by the time she arrived, Jenny's lower half was soaked through. Her feet squelched in her shoes, and she could feel cold rain water dripping down her back. She knew she probably looked a sight, but knocked firmly on Gloria's front door, hoping that Jack wasn't there.

Moments later, Gloria came to the door and looked surprised to see her. 'Blimey, Jenny, you're drenched. Come in, what's wrong?'

'Nothing, I just want to have a word with you,' Jenny answered through chattering teeth.

'I'll make you a hot drink. There's towels in the bathroom, get yourself dried off and put my dressing gown on.'

'It's OK, I'm not stopping,' Jenny said and shivered.

'Yes, you are! You can't go back out in that, you'll catch your death.'

'No, really, I'm fine. I just need to ask you something . . . '

'Fire away.'

'You and Jack . . . is it serious?'

'You've heard then. The answer is, I don't know, I haven't given it much thought, but it could be. Why, it's not a problem for you, is it?'

'Actually, it is.'

'I don't see why. You're not with him any more.'

'That doesn't mean I don't still have feelings for him.'

'Well, you'll have to get over them, Jen. You had your chance and you blew it,' Gloria remarked coldly.

'How did I blow it? I loved him, but he obviously didn't feel the same about me.'

'Come off it, you put Pam and the boys before him, and to top that, no man wants to play second fiddle to your dead lover.'

'I thought Jack understood how I feel about Craig, and as for Pam and the boys, they have to be my priority. It's not like they've got anyone else looking out for them!'

'I'm just saying that you should have given a little more thought to how Jack felt. You always make everything all about you.'

'That's not fair,' Jenny said, astounded.

'Jack is just like any other man I know — they like to feel important . . . special. You didn't make him feel that way.'

'And you do, I suppose?'

'Yes, actually, I do. I make him feel *very* special, if you know what I mean.'

Jenny knew exactly what her sister meant and felt that the knife Gloria had stabbed her in the back with was now being twisted and plunged deeper. The thought of her sister sleeping with Jack left her reeling and she felt a pang of jealousy. She didn't want Gloria to see her feelings and tried to remain stony-faced, hoping to sound dignified when she said, 'I hope you'll be very happy together, but please respect my wishes and don't bring him to Gran's.'

'If I can't bring my boyfriend, then don't expect to see me either,' Gloria answered insolently.

Jenny wasn't going to plead with her sister. It was Gloria's decision, and Jenny knew that once her mind was made up, it could rarely be changed. She didn't care that there'd be one fewer for Christmas dinner this year, especially as she was going to have to put up with her mother and Brian. She would put on a front and be nice to them for the sake of the boys, but really she would be glad when the festivities were over.

49

It hadn't been a surprise when Father Christmas didn't turn up on Christmas Eve, least of all to Edith. After lots of tears from Timmy and Peter and many questions about whether they'd been well behaved or not, Jenny had managed to calm them and settle them down to sleep. Of course, when they awoke on Christmas morning to discover Santa had secretly visited in the night, they were thrilled, and the rest of the day passed uneventfully.

Christmas had fallen on a Tuesday, which felt odd to Edith, but as Boxing Day was mid-week, Jenny had an extended holiday. The factory had closed, and she didn't have to return to work until the New Year. Edith was pleased to have her home and thought the break would do her good. She'd looked exhausted lately, as though she was carrying the worries of the world on her small shoulders. Edith wished there was more she could do to alleviate Jenny's burdens, but she could barely get herself out of her armchair lately, and when she did it was a struggle to see where she was going.

Jenny brought her a cup of tea and perched on the arm of her chair. 'Pamela is going out with Linda for New Year. They're off to a dance in the church hall tomorrow night.'

'That's nice. And what about you? How are you going to see in 1963?' Edith asked, though she doubted Jenny had any plans.

'I'll probably sleep through it, but I've decided the New Year is going to be a new start for me.'

'Oh, how's that?'

'I've got to move on, Gran, and leave the past behind. Craig will always have a special place in my heart, but I can't spend the rest of my life mourning for him. As for Jack, he's happy with Gloria now and I should be pleased that she's settled with a decent man who will look after her. I shouldn't blame Gloria for falling for him . . . Jack's a good man and she could do a lot worse.'

'That's very generous of you, love, but are you kidding yourself? I know you didn't fall for him as deeply as Craig, but you still loved the man. No matter what you say, it must hurt to know that he's with your sister.'

'I think I was lonelier than I realised, and, as you once said, on the rebound. I think I thought myself in love with Jack, but it didn't go that deep or it would be him that always fills my mind instead of Craig. Anyway, I'm not going to dwell on it any more. I have decided that 1963 is going to be *my* year!'

'Good on you,' Edith said, and patted her granddaughter's knee. It was nice to hear the girl sounding more positive. She always wore a brave face, but Edith could tell she'd been moping. It was about time Jenny had some good luck, and Edith hoped her positive attitude would bring it to her.

★　★　★

'It's only me,' Jenny heard her mum call as she let herself into the flat. Timmy and Peter ran to greet her, and Pamela sighed heavily.

'Great, let's hear what fairy-tales she comes up with this time for letting the boys down,' Edith grumbled.

Lizzie breezed into the room and Jenny noticed she didn't have Brian with her.

'Hello, sweetheart, is there tea in the pot?' her mum asked as she plonked herself down on the sofa.

'I'll get it,' Pamela said and jumped up. 'Boys, will you give me a hand to carry the cakes in?'

Jenny thought it was an excuse for her sister not to sit with their mum. Pam had been as disappointed as the boys when Brian had let them down on Christmas Eve and Jenny doubted she'd forgiven her mother yet.

'Where's your bloke who lives on top of the beanstalk?' Edith asked sarcastically, though her description of Brian as a giant did put a smile on Jenny's face.

'He's, erm . . . busy. Sorry about Christmas, something came up.'

'It always does with you, Lizzie,' Edith said snidely.

'Yes, well, it couldn't be helped. Anyway, I called in to see if you kids all fancy coming to the funfair at the weekend? There's one set up on Streatham Common and seeing as I missed you over Christmas, I thought it would be a nice way to spend some time together.'

'I'm sure Pam and the boys would enjoy that, Mum, but I'll give it a miss.'

'Come on, Jen, it'll be a laugh.'

'Funfairs aren't really my cup of tea.'

'Suit yourself, but you'll be missing out. Brian said he'll run us up there, so I'll pick the others up at about eleven.'

'What's about eleven?' Timmy asked as he came back into the room carrying two small plates with pastries.

'It's the time I'll be picking you up on Saturday . . . we're going to the funfair!'

Timmy looked elated as he squealed, 'Mummy's taking us the funfair, Peter!'

'I don't want my cake,' Peter said as he ran to the hallway and started to put his shoes on.

'Not today, Peter. I'm taking you on Saturday.'

'Oh, can't we go now?'

'No, Brian is busy today. You won't have long to wait, just today and Friday, then when you wake up the next morning it'll be Saturday.'

'But that's ages.'

'No, it's not, you silly sausage,' Lizzie said with a chuckle.

Given her mother's habit of not turning up, Jenny wished she hadn't told the boys about the fair and feared she'd let them down again.

'I won't be able to come, I'm working on Saturday,' Pamela said.

'Can't you take the day off?'

'No, it'll be really busy in the salon with everyone wanting their hair set for the New Year.'

'You could have a sick day.'

'No, she can't!' Jenny interrupted and threw her mother a scornful look. She didn't think it was right for her mum to encourage the girl to be deceitful or to skive from work.

'Anyway,' Pamela said, unusually speaking her mind, 'there's no guarantee you'll turn up.'

'Of course I will but never mind, it looks like it'll just be us then, boys,' Lizzie said.

Her mother stayed for about an hour and when she left Jenny was grateful that this time her brothers didn't make a fuss. She hoped they'd have fun on Saturday and not be left looking out the window and crying if their mum let them down again.

★ ★ ★

'Tina's having a New Year party on Monday night and she's invited us,' Jack said as he walked beside Gloria on their way to her flat from work.

'I dunno, Jack. The last time I saw Tina, she wasn't very nice to me. She's Jenny's friend and what if my sister is at the party?'

'Tina has got used to us being together now, and if she didn't want you at the party, she wouldn't have invited you. I asked if Jenny's going and apparently she isn't, so how about it?'

'All right, I suppose so, but if your sister starts on me again, you'd better say something this time.'

'Don't worry, she won't, but if she does I'll tell her to mind her own business.'

Once they were indoors, Gloria made them both a sandwich and sat next to Jack on the sofa. 'There's something I've been meaning to ask you,' she said when she finished eating. 'Gail is moving out. She's going back home to help her mum and I can't afford to rent this place on my own. I don't really like the idea of sharing with someone who's likely to be here all the time, and it would mean we'd have less privacy.'

'I think I can see where this is going,' Jack said with a smile.

'Well? Do you want to move in with me?'

'Yeah, I may as well. I'm here more than I'm at home.'

'Really? Oh, Jack, that's great!'

Gloria placed her plate on the floor beside her and leaned over to kiss Jack. 'Our own little love nest,' she whispered, and ran her hand up the inside of his thigh. As she brushed over his manhood, she could feel it bulging against the material of his trousers.

'Yes, you're right,' Jack said, his voice husky, and slipped his hand under her blouse. 'We don't want anyone disturbing our privacy.'

'Have you got a johnnie?' Gloria asked as she eased Jack away, then stood up and yanked down her knickers. 'We don't want any unwanted babies either.'

'Shit, no, I forgot to buy some today. Can't you get yourself on that pill that stops you getting pregnant?'

'No, Jack, only married women can have the pill,' she said, standing in front of him as she undid the buttons on her blouse suggestively, watching as his eyes darkened with lust.

He reached out to grab her hips then pulled her towards him. 'Well, in that case, I'd better marry you.'

50

It was mid-January and though they'd just finished making love, Lizzie was still sulking about Brian having left her to spend New Year alone. She was naked, sitting on the edge of the bed and blowing smoke rings into the air.

'Give it a rest, will ya?' Brian moaned from the other side of the bed. 'How many times have I got to say I'm sorry?'

'You promised me, Brian. It was bad enough that you was with *her* at Christmas, but New Year too!'

'I had to be there for Christmas, for my kids, you know that.'

'You didn't have to be with them for New Year, and I know you went down the pub with *her* . . . with no thought about me stuck in this shithole.'

'Lizzie, we've been over this a thousand bloody times — me mother was staying with us. She said she'd babysit and told us to go out. What was I supposed to do?'

'Leave her . . . for good . . . like you said you would!'

'I will . . . I am . . . but I've got to find the right time.'

'When? Tomorrow? Next week? Next bleedin' year?'

'Soon,' Brian shouted, sounding exasperated. 'Soon, I promise.'

'Your promises mean jack-shit, Brian. I'm giving you 'til the end of the month to get this sorted. If you ain't left your wife by then, well, that'll be it. You can kiss my pretty arse goodbye.'

Lizzie stood up and stepped into her dress, leaving her underclothes in the pile by the side of the bed. She ran her fingers through her hair, then spun around to glare at Brian. 'And another thing,' she ranted, 'you can rent us somewhere half decent to live. I'm sick of the sight of these four walls. I want a proper flat or house, not a poxy room and a shared bathroom.'

'OK, OK, calm down, woman. Take that dress off and come back into bed . . . it's cold in here without you to warm me up.'

'I don't think so. In fact I've a good mind to take all hanky-panky off the menu until you leave your wife. Maybe that'll spur you on to actually do something about it!'

'Fine, if that's how you're going to be, I may as well go back to work,' Brian said and threw off the bedclothes.

Lizzie worried she might have pushed him too far. She didn't want to lose him, but she wasn't happy with him sharing his time between her and his family. 'I'll come back to bed, but I meant what I said about giving you 'til the end of the month.'

'All right, I get it . . . now get your sexy body between these sheets.'

Lizzie let her dress slip to the floor and smiled as she saw Brian's eyes roaming over her naked body. She was sure she could win her man. She'd seen Brian's wife and didn't think she had any competition. The woman was a middle-aged frump who had let herself go. It wasn't any wonder that Brian had been so easily seduced and now she'd laid down her ultimatum, Lizzie felt confident she'd soon have him solely to herself.

★ ★ ★

'Are you going hop picking again this year?' Joan asked Tina.

'Yes, it's the only chance I get of any sort of holiday, but September seems a long way off.'

'I always fancied it, sounds like a right jolly,' Joan said.

'You should come. You too, Jenny.'

Jenny had heard Tina's funny tales of their adventures in Kent, staying in hoppers' huts and enjoying long evenings around a campfire, but the days sounded like hard work. She didn't think her brothers would see it as much of a holiday. 'Thanks, but I couldn't leave my gran for that long,' she said, glad that she'd quickly thought of a plausible excuse.

'Couldn't Gloria keep an eye on her for once?' Tina asked.

'I don't think so. I haven't seen my sister since before Christmas and I doubt I'll be seeing her any time soon.'

'Oh, you haven't heard then . . . ?'

'Heard what?' Jenny asked.

'Bloody hell, there's me putting me big foot in it again. I'm sorry, love, I hadn't realised you and Gloria had fallen out.'

'It wasn't so much a falling-out, but I asked her not to bring Jack to Gran's over Christmas and she didn't like it. Anyway, what haven't I heard?'

'About her and Jack . . . they're getting married.'

'What?' Joan exclaimed. 'But they've not been seeing each other long. Blimey, it was only a few months ago that he asked Jenny to marry him!'

'I know, and I said I thought they were rushing into things, but they're living together now and apparently saving up for their big day. My mum ain't too happy about it. Between us, I don't think she's keen on your sister, Jenny. She reckons the girl is a bit brassy and Jack could do better.'

Jenny was speechless and stared at her friend in shock.

'Are you all right, love?' Tina asked.

'Erm . . . yeah,' Jenny replied, but she wasn't sure how she felt. She hadn't expected their relationship to last for very long, but now, hearing this . . . 'Oh, God,' she said.

'What is it?' Tina asked.

'Jack is going to be my brother-in-law!'

'Yes, he will be. Are you OK with it?'

'To be honest, Tina, I don't think I am. I'm happy that my sister is settling down with a good man, I just wish it wasn't Jack.'

'I know, it must be very weird for you. One minute he's your fiancé, and now he's your sister's. You're over him though, ain't you?'

'I thought I was, but now I'm not so sure. I suppose I'll have to be,' Jenny answered.

For the rest of the day, Jenny worked in silence and tried to stop thinking about Gloria and Jack, but it wasn't easy. She was glad when it was finally time to clock off, and couldn't wait to get home to tell her gran. It was daft to feel like this really, but what she needed right now was a cup of tea and sympathy and her gran was just the person to offer it.

51

The bitter cold weather of January and February passed, spring broke and Easter arrived. Brian had promised Lizzie that this bank holiday Monday would be the last day he'd spend at home with his wife and three children, but once again she doubted he'd keep his word. She'd given up threatening to leave him and concluded that he'd never be able to afford to run two homes. Unless she could find a man with better prospects, she was going to be stuck in this bedsit for the foreseeable. She needed someone who had a few bob, a man who earned a darn sight more than Brian did as a delivery man.

Lizzie placed four chocolate eggs in her shopping bag and set off to her mother's house. It had been a while since she'd seen her children and, as Brian was with his wife and kids for the day, she thought she might as well be with hers. The sun shone, highlighting her blonde hair, as she strode along the street. She knew heads were turning and returned a coquettish smile to a man who cycled past her. He was probably young enough to be her son, but Lizzie was keeping her options open and her preying eyes peeled for a new man to take care of her. She liked Brian, he was kind and gentle, but she was sick of being his mistress and feeling second best to his wife.

'Hello, it's only me,' she called as she let

herself into her mum's. Before she'd even closed the front door, Timmy and Peter had charged up the hallway with great big smiles on their small faces. She was always delighted by the way they greeted her, but the same couldn't be said about her mother and Jenny. 'Let me get through the door,' she said to her sons. 'I've got something for you in my bag.'

'What is it?' Peter asked, jumping up and down on the spot with excitement.

'You'll see in a minute but let me sit down first.'

Lizzie walked into the front room and wasn't surprised to see her mother's disapproving look or Jenny's disenchanted frown. Pamela mostly seemed indifferent as she sat gazing out of the window, and she wondered if the girl lived in a world of her own.

'Nice of you to show your face,' Edith said sardonically.

'Seeing as it's a holiday today, I guessed you'd all be home and I've brought you these,' Lizzie answered and pulled the eggs from her bag.

'Cor, thanks, Mum, it's ginormous,' Timmy said with delight.

'Don't be stuffing yourselves with them now or you'll spoil your tea. Put them in the kitchen 'til after dinner,' Edith instructed the boys.

'But dinner is lots of time away,' Peter argued.

'It's not, it's only a couple of hours, and don't answer me back, young man.'

'Give it to me, Peter, I'll put it away until later,' Pamela said.

'Here's one for you, Pammie,' Lizzie said.

'My name is Pamela,' she said, but took the egg along with the others to the kitchen.

'Put the kettle on whilst you're out there,' Lizzie yelled.

'You've not got Goliath with you today?'

'No, Mum, and his name is Brian.'

'Why isn't he with you?'

'He's with his family.'

'Oh, what family is that then?' her mother probed.

'His children. He's got three girls.'

'I see, and are they with their mother?'

'Yes.'

'So, he's with his ex-wife and kids?'

Lizzie wanted to tell her mother to mind her own business but impatiently answered, 'Yes, that's right, Mum, except she's not his ex-wife.'

'He's married then?'

'Yes, you know he is. Now can we drop it, please?'

'It's no wonder Gloria is the way she is,' Edith said and rolled her eyes.

'How is she? I haven't seen her for Gawd knows how long.'

Lizzie saw her mother and Jenny exchange a look and wondered what was going on. They clearly knew something she didn't.

'She's getting married . . . to Jack,' Jenny answered.

'Jack? But isn't he the bloke you were seeing?'

'Yep.'

'Blimey, that's a bit of a turnaround. When's the big day?' she asked.

'I'm told it's going to be in September, but

Gloria hasn't invited us.'

'Why not?'

'We fell out.'

'Why?'

Jenny sighed. 'Because I told her not to bring Jack here.'

'Why not?'

'Oh, for Christ's sake, Lizzie,' Edith said. 'Ain't it bleedin' obvious? Jack was once going to marry Jenny, but they broke up and now he's going to marry Gloria.'

'Well, if you ask me, it ain't the end of the world.'

'Yeah, well, you're as insensitive as Gloria, so you would say that,' Edith admonished.

Lizzie was beginning to wish she hadn't come now, but then Peter held out his arms and she pulled him onto her lap. 'How are you getting on, Pam?' she asked her daughter when she came back into the room, though she didn't expect much more than a one-word answer.

'Fine. I've been offered a full-time trainee hairdressing job at Sally's Salon when I leave school.'

'Ah, that's smashing. I'll be down once a week to get me hair done on the cheap.' Lizzie smiled and patted her curls. 'Actually, I've got a bit of news too. Well, not news but gossip. Do you remember Mrs Golding? She lived down the end of our street.'

'Huh, how could I forget her?' said Edith. 'She was a right one when we were younger. She tried it on with your father once, scared the bleedin' life out of him.'

'You mean the tiny old woman with the really, really long white hair?' Jenny asked.

'Yes, that's the one,' Lizzie answered.

'What about her?' Edith asked.

'Boys, do me a favour and go and draw me something pretty to put on my wall. My place could do with brightening up and you're so good at doing pictures,' she said, urging Peter from her lap. She waited for her sons to run off then continued, 'I bumped into her the other day and she said her eldest son is doing time in Wandsworth prison. He told her that Henry is in there! Apparently, he got himself nicked for breaking into a pub, that one up near the Common. She said he wasn't after the takings, but the police found him passed out behind the bar with a bottle of whiskey in his hand.'

'From what Gloria told me about the last time she saw him, I can't say I'm surprised,' Jenny said sadly.

'Shocking, isn't it? He always liked a drink, but he's really hit rock bottom now,' Lizzie replied.

Edith shrugged her shoulders and said, 'I don't have any sympathy for the man. He's got what was coming to him.'

'Mum, I know you never liked him,' Lizzie said, 'but he doesn't deserve this. Maybe a stint in Wandsworth will do him good though, sober him up.'

'Prison is too good for him,' Edith said, 'Now no more talk of *him*. Pamela, go and make a fresh pot of tea.'

As soon as the girl was out of sight, Edith

turned to Jenny and said, 'Are you all right, love?'

'Whenever I hear talk of my dad, I'm reminded of the baby I lost.'

'I know, sweetheart, he's a wicked man, but at least you know that you're safe now. From what Lizzie has told us, he's banged up behind bars and can never hurt you again.'

Lizzie frowned, and said, 'Hold on. What's this about you losing a baby, Jenny? Who was the father and what did Henry have to do with you losing it?'

Jenny just shook her head and called, 'Boys, have you finished the pictures?'

A little voice yelled back, 'Nearly.'

'So, you ain't going to answer my questions?' Lizzie said.

'I don't want to talk about it, least of all to you,' Jenny snapped.

Lizzie reeled in shock. Jenny had never spoken to her like that before. Her daughter's face was set, and her mother was looking at her with disdain as usual. Lizzie stood up. She just wanted to get out of the flat and away from the repressive atmosphere. Whatever had happened to Jenny, they clearly didn't want her to know about it, and that was fine with her.

⋆ ⋆ ⋆

Jenny couldn't sleep and worried her fidgeting would wake Pamela. She quietly climbed out of the bed and padded through to the front room. A street lamp threw some light into part of the

432

room, highlighting the picture on the wall that her brothers had painted for her on her birthday. She walked across and stared at the happy scene. Living in that house with Craig had been the best time of her life. The memories came flooding back and though they were filled with love and laughter, the pain of losing the man she'd cherished, and his unborn child, stabbed her like a knife in the heart.

She began to sob and tried to stifle the sound. The news of her father today had brought everything back. Emotions she'd buried — feelings she'd ignored — sadness she'd hidden and even the hate she'd denied. Everything had once been perfect, and Jenny knew she'd never have that again.

★   ★   ★

The next morning, Jenny woke up tired, but better for allowing herself a good cry. She'd needed that, but today was another day and she was determined to put on a bright face.

The rest of the household were already up and buzzing around when she walked into the front room. Her brothers were eating their breakfast, her grandmother was sitting in her armchair with a bowl on her lap and peeling potatoes, and Pamela was tweaking her hair in the mirror.

'Morning, love,' Edith said.

'Good morning. Gran, why are you peeling spuds at this time of the morning?'

'Pamela said she's going to take the boys out for the day, you've got to go to work, so I thought I'd help out by making a start on the dinner.'

'Gran, it's seven in the morning!'

'Yes, well, there's nothing wrong with getting a head start.'

Jenny smiled warmly at her gran, then said to Pamela, 'Where are you all off to?'

'Me and Linda are going to take the boys on a bus to Clapham Common. There's a bit of an Easter fete still going on around the bandstand.'

'That's nice. Take some change from my purse for the bus fares. Timmy, Peter, you be good for your sister.'

'We will,' Timmy answered through a mouthful of bread and jam.

Jenny quickly drank a cup of tea and then set off for the factory. The schools were still on Easter break so the streets were much quieter than usual. As she clocked on, Tina came in behind her.

'All right, Jenny. Did you have a nice bank holiday?'

'Yes, thanks. You?'

'Not really, I was up to my eyes in laundry and me old man's got a stinking cold. Blimey, the way he was carrying on anyone would think he was dying. Still, I suppose anything's better than coming into this place.'

Jenny looked around to check that nobody else could hear her and said, 'My mum came round and told us my dad is in Wandsworth prison.'

'Blimey, that's a turn-up for the books. After what he did, I bet you're happy about that.'

'Sort of.'

'Have you been crying? Your eyes look a bit puffy,' Tina asked with concern.

'I had a bit of a weep last night, but it's done me the world of good.'

'Better out than in. You shouldn't bottle stuff up. I'm glad you're feeling better. Mind you, the thought of coming back into work is enough to make anyone cry,' Tina said and laughed. Jenny forced herself to join in.

''Ere, you'll never guess what happened on Friday.'

'No, Tina, I never will. It's always a madhouse at yours.'

'My eldest decided she wanted to cook some hard-boiled eggs and decorate them for Easter. I said I didn't mind 'cos I would make some sandwiches with them. So I leave her to it and I'm upstairs changing the beds, when all of a sudden I hear this almighty bang. I jumped out of my skin and ran downstairs, and on the way heard another bang, then another. Well, when I walked into the kitchen, you've never seen anything like it! There was egg all over the place, up the walls, all over the cooker, even on the ceiling! Exploding eggs, who'd have thought it? She'd gone out and forgotten about leaving them on the boil and the pan had gone dry. I'm telling you, Jen, the bloody state of my kitchen, she's lucky I didn't crack *her* head open.'

'I'm sorry, Tina, I shouldn't laugh, but . . . '

'Yeah, well, wait 'til we get seated and I'll tell you what happened on Sunday night. The bloody antics in my house, I could write a book about them.'

Jenny looked forward to hearing Tina's stories of her hectic home life. They always made the day pass quicker, and before she realised, it was only two hours to go until home time.

Percy, the oldest man in the factory, slowly walked past the women's bench pushing a trolley laden with components. He rarely spoke, so when Jenny heard him say her name, she looked up surprised.

'Oi, Jenny, Bob said he saw your little sister hanging about outside the gates. She had the little 'uns with her too.'

Jenny quickly said to Tina, 'Cover for me while I go and see what Pamela wants.'

Tina nodded as Jenny dashed across the factory, hoping that Miss Aston didn't spot her slipping out of the building. As she ran across the yard she could see Pamela looking agitated and her heart began to pound.

'Oh, Jenny, I didn't know what to do . . . ' Pamela cried.

'What on earth's the matter?'

'Please, you have to come home . . . now . . . please, Jenny, come home . . . '

Pamela was beginning to cry hysterically, and Jenny began to fear the worst. 'Pam, calm down and tell me what's wrong.'

'It's Gran . . . we came home, and I thought she was asleep, but . . . but . . . I think she's dead.'

Pamela began to wail and that set the boys off. It must have been such a traumatic shock for them, but Jenny found herself numb, unable to feel anything. She had to take control and be strong, but, most importantly, she had to get home, fast. 'Wait here, I'll be two minutes,' Jenny said and hurried back into the factory. She collected her bag and ran up the stairs to Miss Aston's office. She tapped on the door but didn't wait to be told to enter. Instead she burst in and said quickly, 'I'm sorry, Miss Aston, I have to go home. My gran has died.'

Jenny didn't wait for the woman's approval. She flew back down the stairs and out of the factory without clocking off. 'Come on, let's go,' she said, picking up Peter while Pam held Timmy's hand.

They were soon outside their gran's flat. Jenny paused and stared at the front door, praying that Pamela had got it wrong. 'Wait here,' she said to her siblings. Her hand shook as she placed the key in the lock. 'Please, don't be dead,' she whispered.

Once indoors, she walked slowly up the hallway and called, 'Gran . . . '

No answer.

'Just be sleeping,' she said. 'Please, just be asleep.'

She stepped into the front room and stared in horror at her gran in her armchair. The old woman's face was deathly white, and her lips looked blue.

'Oh, no,' Jenny gasped. She ran to her gran's side and gently grabbed her hand, but it felt so cold. 'Wake up, Gran, please wake up . . . '

A dark cloud seemed to descend as she realised the woman she loved so dearly was gone. 'Oh, Gran,' she whispered, 'tell Craig and my baby how much I love them . . . I wish I could come with you . . . '

52

'Where is she?' Lizzie asked Jenny as she burst into the front room of her mother's flat. Pamela had come to get her from Brian's bedsit, but now her youngest daughter said she'd wait outside because she couldn't face going back into the flat.

'I called the doctor and he sent for an ambulance. They've taken her away, Mum.'

'Is she . . . is she?'

'Yes, the doctor said he thought her heart failed.'

Lizzie was surprised that Jenny wasn't crying. She'd always been so close to her gran, but now she seemed to be holding herself together. 'Where are the boys?' she asked as she looked around the room.

'With Linda, Pamela's friend. She dropped them there on her way to get you. I didn't want them seeing Gran being taken away in the ambulance.'

'No, good thinking,' Lizzie said, then turned to look at Pamela, who walked slowly into the room. The girl seemed traumatised. She had hardly spoken as they'd dashed here, and she didn't look any better now. 'You've both had a terrible shock. I'll make you a strong cup of tea,' she volunteered, feeling ineffectual.

'I made Gran a cup of tea . . . ' Pamela said and looked at the cold cup on the side. 'The

boys were playing on the floor in front of her
. . . We didn't know she was . . . dead.' She began
to weep again and ran to the bedroom. Lizzie
went to follow her.

'Leave her, Mum,' said Jenny. 'Let her be. We
need to tell Gloria.'

'All right, Jenny. I'll stay here with Pam while
you go round to Gloria's. She'll have finished
work by now.'

'Can't you go, Mum?'

'Leave it out, Jenny. I've only just found out
my mother is dead and I'm hardly in any state to
go traipsing to Gloria's place. Pam can't go,
you've seen the state of her and I'm sorry, but
that only leaves you.'

Lizzie saw Jenny take a deep breath as though
she was about to argue, but instead she picked
up her bag and walked towards the door.

'Make sure you stay with Pamela until I get
back.'

'Yes, of course I will. Honestly, I don't know
what you take me for,' Lizzie snapped.

She heard the door close, slumped onto the
sofa and looked at her mother's chair. The
imprint of her head could be seen in the back
cushion, and the upholstery on the right arm was
worn where her mum used to rub it when she
was angry. Lizzie regretted she hadn't been nicer
to her mother and that she hadn't been to see
her more frequently, but they'd always had a
strained relationship. As a child, her mother had
often called her a daddy's girl, and it was true,
she was close to her father. Now she had lost
both parents, and though her mother had been

440

hard on her, she'd always been there when Lizzie had needed her.

She dabbed a tear from her cheek and turned her thoughts to what her mother might own of any value. Lizzie would be the sole inheritor, and though her mum had lived frugally, she did have a few nice pieces of jewellery which would rightfully belong to her now.

★ ★ ★

Jenny braced herself before knocking on Gloria's door. She knew there was a good chance that Jack would be there but given the circumstances any animosity needed to be put aside.

The door opened, and Jenny was relieved to see her sister.

'Jenny, what a surprise!'

'I'm really sorry, but I'm afraid I've got some bad news.'

'You'd best come in,' Gloria said and pulled the door open wider as she stepped to one side.

As Jenny walked over the threshold, she noticed Gloria had put on weight. She looked different and the extra pounds were all on her stomach. She stared at her sister's bulging belly. 'Gloria, are you pregnant?'

'Yes, about four months gone, but I'm already as big as a barrage balloon. Jack's not happy about it, but as I told him, it takes two to make a baby.'

Jenny had previously considered the idea of Gloria having Jack's child, and had expected it to hurt, but now she felt nothing, her feelings frozen. 'Is he home?'

'No, he rarely is these days. Come through and then you'd better tell me what this bad news is.'

Jenny followed her sister into the lounge. She was surprised at how old-fashioned and tatty the furniture was. She'd expected Gloria's place to be more modern.

'Sit down. Do you want a drink of anything?'

'No, I can't stay. It's Gran . . . she died earlier today.'

'What? Blimey, that's a bit sudden. It's a bit of a shock.'

'Yes, I realise that, especially in your condition.'

'It must be harder for you. You were always closer to her than me. How . . . how . . . '

Jenny knew what Gloria was going to ask and said, 'Her heart failed, but it was worse for Pam and the boys because they found her. Pam is still in a state. Mum's with her, but I must get back.'

'Do you want me to come with you? I may as well — Jack won't be home for hours, that's if he even bothers to come home at all. I doubt Mum will hang around for long, and I can help with Pam and the boys.'

Jenny thought about it and wasn't convinced that it was what she wanted. It would mean she'd be forced to look at Gloria's stomach and at this moment it was something she'd rather not deal with. 'No, there's nothing you can do, and the boys are at Linda's.'

'We can pick them up on the way. We should be together at a time like this.'

Gloria had a point, and Jenny reluctantly agreed. As they walked along the High Road, Jenny desperately tried to push thoughts of her gran away by probing Gloria about her relationship with Jack. From her sister's few remarks, it didn't sound like things were going well. 'Why doesn't Jack come home until late?' she asked.

'I don't think he can stand to look at this,' Gloria answered, and rubbed her stomach.

'Oh, I see, so he really isn't happy about the baby?'

'Nope. He said it's the last thing he wants to be lumbered with and reckons I've trapped him.'

'But he had already asked you to marry him, so how have you trapped him?'

'I don't know, Jenny, I can't work him out. I don't think he really wants to marry me, but he doesn't have a lot of choice now that I'm up the duff.'

'I hope he comes to his senses soon and it works out for you,' Jenny said, and meant it. Despite everything, Gloria was still her sister and Jenny didn't like to think that she was unhappy, though she wasn't surprised by Jack's behaviour. The night they'd split up, he'd made it quite clear he didn't want a family and wasn't ready for a child.

Gloria's smile looked forced as she said, 'As Gran used to say, it'll all come out in the wash.'

Jenny didn't think the saying covered her sister's situation, but now Gloria had mentioned their gran, she was concerned that she still couldn't feel anything. What was wrong with her?

Her beloved gran was dead. She'd cried at first but now felt nothing, and it wasn't until she thought about never seeing her again, never talking to her, that Jenny felt the surge of pain. When they arrived home, she finally broke, and for once she was glad to have her mother and Gloria around to take care of things while she lay alone in the bedroom to cry out her agony.

53

Two weeks had passed since Lizzie had buried her mother next to her father, yet still Jenny had refused to sort through her gran's belongings. 'You can't make this place a shrine to your gran,' Lizzie said, trying to reason with her daughter.

'I'm not, Mum, I just don't feel ready to do it.'

'I've told you, I'll do it.'

'No,' Jenny snapped, 'Gran would have wanted me to.'

'All right, keep your hair on, but it's not fair on Pam and the boys to have to live like she's still here,' Lizzie said and lit a cigarette. She didn't really think any of her children minded that their gran's things had remained untouched, but she wanted to get her hands on her mother's jewellery.

'I wish you wouldn't smoke in here, you know Gran didn't like it.'

'Well, she ain't here now to voice her opinion,' Lizzie answered sarcastically and instantly regretted it when she saw the angry expression on Jenny's face.

'All right, Mum,' Jenny said, 'let's clear her things away before Pam comes back from swimming with the boys, but I'm only doing this to get rid of you!'

Lizzie brushed off her daughter's scathing remark. 'Fine, and I'll be glad to go, but trust me, you'll feel much better once it's done.'

Jenny bit on her lower lip, 'I know, you're right. Sorry, Mum.'

'It's OK, come on, let's get this over and done with.'

They walked through to Edith's bedroom where her bed had remained untouched. Lizzie placed her arm across her daughter's shoulders and gave her a little squeeze. 'You know, your gran would want you to sleep in her bed. There's no need for you and Pam to be squashed up together now.'

'It wouldn't feel right.'

'Think about it. If she knew that her bed was lying empty, your gran would call you a silly mare.'

'Yes, either a silly mare or a dozy cow,' Jenny said, her voice breaking with emotion.

'Right then, let's get these sheets and covers washed.'

Once the bed was stripped, Lizzie was keen to get to the dressing table, but as she didn't want her motives to be obvious, she went to the wardrobe instead, acting as though she was finding it difficult as she said, 'This will probably be the hardest part, darling. I think we should bag up her clothes and give them to the rag-and-bone man. She always got on well with old Cyril, I'm sure she'd want him to have them.'

Jenny agreed, and, steely-faced, she began to pull her gran's dresses from the hangers. 'I never saw her wear half of this stuff,' she said, holding a dark brown dress in the air.

'No, and a good job too, that dress is blinkin'

awful,' Lizzie said, trying to make light of what they were doing.

Thankfully Jenny saw the funny side and cracked a small smile, but as if she felt guilty, her face immediately straightened again.

'Jenny, your gran wouldn't want you to be sad. You were the apple of her eye, so for the sake of her memory, try to cheer up.'

'It's too soon, Mum.'

'Yeah, maybe,' Lizzie said.

They carried on until the wardrobe was almost empty but stuffed at the back Lizzie found three old handbags that she'd never seen before. She looked inside. One contained a tatty handkerchief, another a blunt pencil, and the last one was empty. Then, as she was about to close the door, she spotted something else, a small box in the far corner. She reached in and picked it up, and when she looked inside, she gasped.

'What is it?' Jenny asked.

'I don't believe it,' Lizzie said, and emptied the contents onto her palm. About a dozen cut diamonds sparkled in the sunlight. 'Where on earth did my mother get these from?'

'I've never seen them before,' Jenny said as she stared at the stones. 'I wonder why they were hidden in the back of her wardrobe.'

'I know my dad was a bit of a thief,' Lizzie said. 'Maybe he stole them, but they were too hot to handle so he hid them. They must have been in there for donkeys' years.'

'But Gran didn't move into this flat until after Grandad died.'

'I know, but a few of his mates helped her to

move,' Lizzie said, searching her memory. 'I remember she wanted to pack her clothes, but they were in a hurry, so they just tied the doors of the wardrobe up and put it on the back of the cart with all her stuff inside.'

'That could explain it, but as they're stolen we should hand them in at the police station.'

'I said *maybe* my dad stole them, I don't know for sure. Even if they were, they must have been missing since before the war. After all this time, I doubt the police would be able to trace the rightful owners. They'd just end up in an evidence room somewhere, and anyway, with no idea if they were stolen or not, I can't see the point of handing them in.'

'Yes, I see that, but what are we going to do with them?'

'Sell them. I reckon they'll be worth a small fortune, and I know just the bloke who'd buy them if he's got the money, or point me in the direction of another fence,' Lizzie said, thinking of Ten-Bob-Terry.

'Fence! So that means you do think they're stolen.'

'Probably, but I still don't think we should hand them in,' Lizzie said, thinking quickly. 'If we do, the police will have lots of questions, and I doubt they'd believe your gran didn't know they were there. If the local rag gets hold of the story, it would taint her name and memory. Surely you don't want that?'

'No, of course not.'

'Right, back to selling them then, and I should get enough from the sale to find my own place and then I can get rid of Brian.'

'But they're not yours,' Jenny said.

'Yes, they are. As far as I'm concerned, this is my mother's wardrobe, and seeing as I was her only child, it makes it mine now.'

'I think Gran would have handed them in.'

'Leave it out! Your gran used to make out she was whiter than white, but she lived a good life on the back of my dad's thieving. The man never worked an honest day in his life, and my mum knew all about it.'

'She obviously didn't know about those.'

'Maybe not, but she didn't make a will leaving anything to you and the kids, so like it or not, these diamonds are mine now. I'll leave you to sort out the rest of her stuff, and you're welcome to it, but I'm off.'

'I don't care about me, but I do care about Pam, Gloria and the boys. If Gran knew about those stones, she would have wanted to look after all of us, not just you. You, on the other hand, have never cared about anyone but yourself.'

Lizzie was almost through the bedroom door but stopped and turned back to look at her daughter. Jenny rarely spoke out to anyone and Lizzie thought the girl was beginning to sound like her gran. She felt a tiny twinge of guilt and opened her bag to take out one of the diamonds. 'Here, have this, it'll help you all out,' she said, then left in a hurry with a clear conscience as she went to find Ten-Bob-Terry.

★ ★ ★

449

The following day, Jenny sat on the edge of her gran's bed and peered at the diamond. 'Oh, Gran,' she said quietly, 'if only you'd known.' Her mind turned over imagined scenarios of how her grandad had come by the precious stones. She wondered if he'd robbed a jeweller's or maybe removed the stones from pieces of jewellery he'd stolen. However he'd acquired them, she knew it hadn't been legitimate.

As she thought about what to do with it, she wrapped the diamond in a tissue and slipped it into her bag. Her mum had mentioned someone she knew who would buy the diamonds, but Jenny didn't know anyone like that and she was too nervous to take it to the pawnshop.

Feeling anxious, she set off for work, tightly clutching her bag and eager to speak to Tina. The woman was worldly-wise, and Jenny hoped she'd give her some advice.

It wasn't until lunchtime that she managed to get Tina by herself. 'Can you nip to the loos with me? I've something I want to show you,' Jenny whispered.

Tina nodded and followed her. Once the toilet door had closed, Jenny quickly checked the cubicles were empty, then pulled the tissue from her bag, unwrapped it and revealed the sparkling stone.

'Christ alive, Jen, where did you get that?'

'It was found in my gran's wardrobe. Do you think it's worth a lot of money?'

'If it's real, yeah, I'd say so! What was your gran doing with something like that in her wardrobe?'

'I don't know, but I'm worried that many years ago my grandad stole it.'

'Bloody hell. What ya gonna to do with it?'

'I'd like to sell it, but I don't know how. If it's stolen I can't take it to a jeweller or the pawnshop, so I'm hoping you can steer me in the right direction.'

'I know a bloke who buys knocked-off gear, but not something like that! I think it'd be a bit out of his price league.'

Jenny remembered that her mother had said something similar and slumped. 'What do I do with it then?'

'I dunno. I can have a word with my old man tonight, see what he thinks.'

'Would you? That would be great. Thanks, Tina. I feel a bit guilty about it, like I should hand it in, but I don't know for sure if the diamonds were stolen or not. Not only that, the council will want to take my gran's flat back, which will leave me and the kids homeless. I desperately need the money to find us somewhere to live.'

'Yeah, well, this should give you enough, but did you say diamonds, plural? Does that mean there's more than one of those?'

'Yes, about a dozen, in all different shapes and sizes. Mum's got the rest of them, but she gave me this.'

'Quick, Jenny, put it away before someone comes in, and keep shtum. Your gran was a right dark horse, bless her.'

'I will. You're the only person who knows about this.'

'Good, keep it that way.'

The women went back to work but Jenny was nervous. She kept thinking about the diamond hidden in her bag. She still suspected it was nicked, and guilt about selling it on niggled at her.

Tina gently nudged her. 'I know you, so I can guess what you're thinking, but don't worry, with no proof they were stolen, you ain't doing anything wrong.'

Jenny's mouth felt dry, and though she nodded, she wasn't convinced. She couldn't hand in the diamond as it would tarnish her grandparents' name. Also, if the diamonds were from a theft, it could still be on record, and handing just one in could land her mother in trouble. She licked her dry lips then clenched her jaw. She didn't like the thought of breaking the law, but at last her mind was made up. Whether it was wrong or not, the proceeds of selling the diamond could secure a home for her brothers and sister. Now she had to hope that Tina's husband would know what to do.

54

Gloria turned off the alarm clock and heaved herself out of bed. Jack hadn't come home again, and when he showed his face, once again he'd probably tell her that he'd stayed at his mum's. With the baby on the way, she reluctantly accepted his excuses, but they were wearing a bit thin.

Once ready, Gloria went out, and as she trudged along the High Road, she pulled her cardigan around her, trying to hide her expanding stomach. It would be impossible to keep her pregnancy a secret for much longer, and she knew she'd have to convince Jack to put a ring on her finger sooner than they'd planned. She'd mentioned it the last time he'd been home, but he'd shouted that he wasn't ready to be a father and had walked out. She wasn't ready to be a mother either, but they'd got into this together and she was going to make sure he faced up to his responsibilities.

She walked through the shop but once again there was no sign of Jack on the butcher's counter. This wasn't the first time he'd skived off work and it was clear that he was defiantly avoiding her. Anger coursed through her. He'd been happy to make love to her without using any protection, even though she'd warned him that pulling out wasn't safe. He'd insisted that it would be, but the baby in her belly proved it wasn't.

'Good morning, Gloria,' the store manager greeted her stiffly. 'Will Jack be joining us today?'

'I don't know, sir,' Gloria answered.

'Is he ill?'

'I haven't seen him.'

'I see. Well, when I do, I'll be telling him that he's fired.'

Gloria stood on the spot as the store manager spun on his heel and walked away. Great, she thought, with another mouth to feed, that was all they needed. Unable to contain her annoyance any longer she turned in the opposite direction, marched from the shop and headed for Jack's mother's house. Enough was enough. She wouldn't allow him to dodge his responsibilities any longer.

★   ★   ★

Jenny waited apprehensively outside the factory gates for Tina to arrive and was pleased when she spotted her friend's bright pink coat.

'Bloody hell, Jen, have you been stood out here all night?'

'No, but I couldn't sleep and was up at the crack of dawn.'

'I told you not to worry, didn't I? I had a word with my old man, and he says he can sell it for you. Mind, he'll expect a drink out of it.'

'Of course, and that's such a relief. Who is he going to sell it to?'

'You don't need to know, but if you're happy about it, give me the stone and he'll shift it tonight.'

Jenny pulled the tissue from her bag and couldn't pass it to Tina fast enough. It was like a heavy weight lifting from her shoulders. She'd felt uncomfortable carrying the diamond around with her, and though she'd just passed on a potential small fortune, she trusted her friend.

Tina glanced around her and stuffed the tissue into her bra. 'There's no chance of anyone getting their hands on it in there,' she said with a laugh. 'Now relax, and tomorrow you'll be a lot richer than you are today.'

The money would make such a difference to them, and for Jenny tomorrow couldn't come quickly enough.

★　★　★

Jack's mother opened the front door and eyed Gloria up and down. She'd made no secret that she'd didn't like her, and since Jack had probably moaned to her about being trapped, Gloria guessed the woman liked her even less. 'Is Jack there?'

'Yes, but he doesn't want to see you. He needs time to think.'

'There isn't time for him to *think*. This baby is coming whether he likes it or not and I won't be able to hide it for much longer.'

'Keep your voice down and get inside. I won't have my family's dirty washing being aired in public.'

Gloria walked in and saw Jack looking at her sheepishly from behind the kitchen door.

'Go on then, speak to him, but don't expect

me to back you up. You should have kept your legs shut and not been such a dirty tart!'

Gloria gave Jack's mother a filthy look as she passed her and quickly closed the kitchen door behind her. She had no doubt that the woman would be standing on the other side with her ear to the wood, listening to every word.

'All right, Gloria,' Jack said. He spoke casually, but this was belied by the way he shifted uncomfortably from one leg to another.

'No, Jack, I'm not all right. You've been avoiding me, and because you haven't bothered going to work, you've lost your job.'

'I didn't like it there anyway,' Jack said with a shrug.

'That's not the bloody point, is it? We have a child on the way and need your wages. I was so upset when the manager told me that I walked out, which probably means I've lost my job too. Not that it really matters because soon I'll be showing, and I doubt they'd keep me on.'

'Yeah, well, I've been thinking, and I'm not sure I can handle all this. I'll support you and the baby, you know, pay for things and that, but I can't marry you,' Jack said and lowered his head.

Gloria had a feeling he'd try and worm his way out of the marriage, but she wasn't having any of it. 'Look at me, Jack,' she demanded.

Jack scuffed the kitchen linoleum with his shoe and kept his head down.

'I said, *look at me!*'

He did, and as their eyes locked, Gloria stabbed her finger into his chest. 'You got me into this situation, and you know it. I am not giving birth to a bastard, so, like it or not, you've got to marry me.'

'You can't make me, Gloria,' Jack told her harshly as he stepped back from her jabbing finger.

Gloria quickly realised that being aggressive wasn't going to work. She managed to squeeze a tear from her eye, and snivelled. 'No, I can't force you, but I know you are a decent man and will do the right thing. I get it, you're scared, and so am I, but we can do this together. I love you, Jack, and so will your baby. Please, don't abandon us.'

Jack's eyes softened, and he said, 'Look, Gloria, I don't want to do that, but well, we once had fun and . . . and this isn't fun any more.'

'It can be. Just because we're having a baby doesn't mean the fun has to stop,' Gloria purred as she ran her hand up his chest and over his shoulder.

Jack smiled and gazed down at her. 'Your tits have got bigger,' he said with a laugh.

'Trust you to notice,' Gloria said, and smiled as she stood on tiptoes to reach his lips. Their kiss was long, and left Gloria feeling breathless as she husked, 'Are you coming home?'

'Yes, but let's stop at the jeweller's on the way and look at getting you a ring.'

55

The next day, Jenny took her bag into the bathroom and locked the door behind her. It was the one place she could have any privacy. She took out the wad of notes and sat on the edge of the bathtub to count the money again. 'Unbelievable,' she muttered, still unable to comprehend that one small diamond could fetch two hundred pounds. Tina's husband had taken his cut which left her with twenty-five quid less, but it still felt like a fortune.

Tina said the diamond had been worth a lot more, but it was all her husband could get for it on the black market. Jenny put the money back in her bag, and though she still felt incredibly guilty, she was pleased she didn't have to worry about the council demanding her gran's tenancy back.

She sneaked through to the bedroom and pulled open the drawer in her gran's bedside table. The money would be safe in there; no one ever went in that drawer. As she was about to stuff the money to the back, she saw a piece of paper, folded in half with her name on it. She took it out and instantly recognised her gran's handwriting. Jenny was curious to know what her gran had written to her, but she sat staring at her name, unable to open the folded piece of paper.

'Jenny, Timmy's got my fire engine and won't

give it back,' Peter shouted from the front room.

Jenny was momentarily distracted, but walked over to the bedroom door and quietly pushed it shut. She sat back on her gran's bed and again looked at the piece of paper. If her gran had wanted her to have the letter, surely she would have given it to her? Maybe she shouldn't read it? No, it was addressed to her, her gran had left it for her to find.

With her hands shaking, Jenny slowly opened the paper and began to read. The writing was unclear, probably because her gran's eyes had been bad, but Jenny was able to understand it. As she read the first line, '*To my dearest Jenny,*' a tear fell from her eye and landed on the end of the letter. It went on to explain about Edith's mother's wedding ring on the dressing table and how much sentimental value the ring held. The words spoke from the page almost as if Jenny could hear her gran's voice. The letter went on to say how proud her gran was of her, and as Jenny read the last line, '*with all my love forever,*' she felt her throat tighten as she tried to stifle her sobs.

Through eyes blurred with tears, she read the letter again, savouring every word. Then she placed it carefully beside her and pulled a handkerchief from her bag and blew her nose. She went to her gran's dressing table, took the glass lid off the trinket box, found the precious ring and slipped it on. It fitted perfectly. Her gran had once worn this ring and her great-grandmother before her. Somehow, it made her feel closer to her gran and she knew she'd never remove it.

The bedroom door opened and Pamela popped her head around.

'Are you OK?' she asked.

Jenny smiled warmly and answered, 'Yes, I am. Look at this,' and held out her hand and the piece of paper.

Pamela sat next to her on the bed and read the letter. She had tears in her eyes when she spoke. 'Oh, Jenny, that's lovely.'

'It is, isn't it? This ring meant the world to Gran so I'm going to treasure it as she did. It's worth more than all the diamonds in the world.'

Jenny took a deep breath and looked lovingly at the ring on her hand, then joined her brothers in the front room. Timmy was squabbling with Peter about something, and Pamela had walked back to the table and was looking out of the window, probably day-dreaming again.

'What are you thinking about?' Jenny asked her sister as she pulled a chair out to sit opposite her.

'Faraway places,' Pamela said and sighed. 'Linda is going on holiday to Cornwall next month. They go every year to a caravan park. She said it's beautiful down there.'

'That's nice,' Jenny answered. 'I feel like I could do with a holiday and I bet you do too.'

'Yes, I'd love one. The last time we went anywhere nice was to Owen's flat in Du Cane Court but that was hardly a holiday.'

'If you could have a holiday, where would you like to go?' Jenny asked.

'I don't really know. One of my ladies in the

salon was talking about Butlin's Holiday Camp in Bognor. She said it was the best holiday she'd ever had.'

'I've read about the place. It looks good fun and something Timmy and Peter would enjoy.'

'What about you, Jenny? Where would go, if you could?'

'I quite like the sound of Bognor too,' Jenny answered, and smiled.

She went into the kitchen to prepare their dinner, wondering if a holiday to Butlin's was possible. She had the proceeds from the sale of the diamond but they needed it to secure a home. There could be enough for a holiday too, but then she'd have no savings, no security. Her gran had told her in the letter to be happy. To live life to the full and only ever regret the things she *didn't* do. It would be reckless to spend the money at Butlin's, frivolous even, but it was only money and money couldn't buy happiness. Jenny glanced again at the wedding ring. It held so many happy memories for the women who had worn it. Perhaps that's what Jenny and her family needed — happy memories — but in that case, new memories had to be made.

⋆   ⋆   ⋆

Gloria was pleased that she'd made amends with her sister, even though it was in devastating circumstances. She still owned a key to her gran's flat but hadn't been there since the funeral. 'Helloooooo,' she called as she let herself in.

Peter came running up to her first, and when she saw the gravy around her brother's mouth, she quickly stretched her arms out and grabbed his shoulders. 'You, young man, can't have a cuddle until you've washed your face, you mucky pup. I don't want your dinner on my nice white blouse.'

'Don't want one, so there,' Peter said, running ahead of her into the front room.

'Hi, Gloria. I'm afraid you're too late for dinner,' Jenny said as she cleared away the dinner plates.

'I wasn't expecting any. I came round because I've got something to tell all of you.'

'Go on then, spit it out,' Jenny urged.

'You are all invited to my wedding.'

'I've never been to a wedding,' Timmy said.

'Nor me.' This from Peter.

'Congratulations,' Pamela said though she sounded flat.

'When is the happy day?' Jenny asked.

'Next month, May the twenty-fifth. It's only going to be in a register office, but we gave notice today and managed to book a cancellation. I'm so excited, I'm fit to burst!'

'Is that . . . *my* ring you're wearing?' Jenny asked, frowning.

'Oh, this,' Gloria answered flippantly as she held out her hand, 'yes, it is. We haven't got a lot of money to spare, so it seemed silly to buy another one when we need to save every penny we can for our coming baby. In the circumstances, I didn't think you'd mind, especially as you only wore the ring for half an hour.'

'That's not the point and it would have been nice to be asked, before you just went ahead and wore it.'

'Not this again. I thought you were over the whole Jack and me thing.'

'I'm happy for you, but I don't want my face rubbed in it, and as for my ring . . . you're welcome to my hand-me-downs!' Jenny stopped talking as her voice began to break and she dashed from the room.

'Yeah, well, I'm used to them,' Gloria called. 'I've had your hand-me-downs all my life, so this is nothing new.'

'Why have you made Jenny cry?' Peter asked, his eyes filling up too.

'I didn't mean to. She's just a bit soft. Anyway, I've got something else to tell you. You're both going to be uncles.'

'Why?' Timmy asked.

'Because I'm having a baby and you'll be its uncle. Both of you will!'

Pamela stood up abruptly and said, 'I'm going to see if Jenny is all right.'

'Don't worry about her, she'll be fine. How do you feel about being an auntie?'

'How am I supposed to feel?'

'Well, at least happy about it.'

Pam shrugged, and sounding very grown-up she said, 'I'm more concerned that you've upset Jenny, and that, worse, you don't even seem to care. I think it might be for the best if you leave.'

'Fine, if that's how you feel I'll go,' Gloria snapped. She'd called round expecting them all to be happy about her news, but instead Jenny had got the hump, and, as far as she was concerned, over nothing.

Gloria stormed off down the road, fuming that her sister had spoiled her good news. She didn't understand what all the fuss was about. Yes, Jenny had momentarily worn the ring, but it was hers now and so was Jack, so Jenny had better get used to it.

56

'Have you changed your mind about going to your sister's wedding?' Tina asked quietly.

'Nope. I've booked us a holiday instead. A week at Butlin's in Bognor.'

'Good for you,' Tina said. 'The kids will love it there. When are you off?'

'Saturday, five days to go. The rest of the week is going to drag.'

'How are you getting there?'

'By train. Pamela knows about it, but I haven't told the boys yet. It'll be a nice surprise for them when they find out they won't be going to school next week.'

'You kept that quiet. When I talked to you on Friday about what I should wear for the register office, you never said anything about a holiday.'

'I know. To be honest, I wasn't sure if I was doing the right thing, but then I finally made up my mind and booked it on Saturday. I know I should be there for Gloria's wedding, but I just can't face it.'

'Nobody can blame you, love. I ain't keen on going myself, but Jack's my little brother. Our mum has been walking about with a face like a smacked arse, so I don't think she's happy about it either, but I think she'll come round once the baby is born.'

Jenny thought she probably would. After all, the baby would be her grandchild. Try as she

465

might, she couldn't see Gloria as a mother. Her sister had such a selfish streak, but maybe having a baby would change her. She hoped it would, for the child's sake, but though Jack was irresponsible, at least he'd never hurt his child, like her father had her.

★ ★ ★

Selling the diamonds hadn't been as easy as Lizzie had expected. Ten-Bob-Terry had laughed in her face, and the pawnshop had eyed her suspiciously. She'd walked out quickly in case they called the police, so she was still stuck with the stones and, unfortunately, with Brian too. She could understand now why the diamonds had been hidden away — her father probably couldn't shift them either. He'd only been a petty thief and she was still dumbfounded that he'd acquired such a haul.

Lizzie sat on the edge of the bed in Brian's grubby bedsit and drummed her fingers on her thigh as she smoked her last cigarette. She hated that she'd come down to this standard of living and now wished she hadn't been so quick to leave Owen. Granted, he was boring and finicky, but at least she could have anything she wanted and not have to worry about where she'd find the money for another packet of cigarettes. Brian gave her what he could afford, but with the rent on his house and his wife and kids to look after, it wasn't much. She drew a long last drag on the cigarette then stubbed it out in the ashtray before rising to her feet.

The diamonds were concealed in the back of her underwear drawer, and after a quick rummage she held them in her hand to gaze at them. They had so much potential to change her life, but, like a pot of gold at the end of a rainbow, the wealth was just out of her grasp.

Lizzie hid the stones away again. She felt so frustrated and gritted her teeth as she paced the small room. If only she could sell them! She racked her brains but quickly dismissed any ideas that sprang to mind. Then she had a thought and stopped pacing. Had Jenny sold her diamond? Her eldest daughter had always been resourceful, and Lizzie wondered if she could hold the key to unlocking her small fortune.

★   ★   ★

Gloria stood in front of the mirror in her bedroom, wearing the outfit she had bought for her wedding, and looked at her reflection. It was a smart cream two-piece suit with a matching pillbox hat and when she'd tried it on, it had fitted her well. Now though, because she couldn't fully zip up the skirt, it hung wrong. Not only that, but the jacket emphasised her expanding waistline.

'Gloria,' she heard Jack shout from the kitchen.

She glanced at the alarm clock on the table next to their bed. It was three-thirty. Jack shouldn't be home from work this early.

'Hang on, don't come in, I'll be out in a tick,' she called back and speedily changed her outfit.

467

'What are you doing home so early?' she asked Jack as she walked into the kitchen.

'It didn't work out for me at Rowland's.'

'What, has he sacked you?'

'No, I walked out.'

'Well, you can bloody well walk back in,' Gloria snapped. It was less than a week to their wedding and they were expecting a child, yet here Jack was without a job — again.

'I can't. I told him where he could stick his job, but don't worry. You know me, I ain't work-shy and I'll soon find another job for a talented butcher like me.'

'It's a shame you ain't talented at holding on to jobs when you get them. We're getting married on Saturday, and you seem to forget we've got to pay for the buffet that you ordered at the pub.'

'We'll manage and I'm sure my mum will help out.'

'I don't want to be beholden to her, thank you very much, and I told you not to go splashing your cash on a buffet that's just a waste of money.'

'For fuck's sake, woman, give it a rest, will ya!'

'Give it a rest? I ain't bloody started yet!' Gloria snarled.

'That's it. I've had it to the back teeth with you nagging me and you ain't even me wife yet!' Jack shouted as he marched towards the front door.

Gloria was close on his heels but missed his arm as she reached out to grab him. 'Where do you think you're going?'

'Out! Anywhere to get away from you. Christ,

I wish you was more like your sister!' Jack shouted over his shoulder, then slammed the door behind him as he left.

Gloria stared at the front door and felt too angry to cry. It wasn't the first time he'd compared her to Jenny and she wondered if he was still in love with her. They seemed to be constantly arguing lately. In fact, the only time they didn't was when they were making love. Jenny had never given herself to him, and now, as she looked down at her swollen stomach, Gloria wished she hadn't either. Jack had talked about feeling trapped, but she felt the same and wondered if there was any chance of them ever being happy.

57

Lizzie let herself into her mother's flat and was surprised to see a suitcase in the middle of the front room.

'Hello, are you off to somewhere nice?' she asked as her sons jumped up to greet her

'Yes, a week away at Butlin's,' Jenny answered.

This was good news to Lizzie. She knew Jenny couldn't have afforded Butlin's on her salary, so the girl must have sold the diamond. 'You'll all enjoy that,' she said to Timmy and ruffled his hair before drawing Jenny to one side. 'Can I have a quick word, please, in private?'

Jenny nodded, and Lizzie followed her through to the bedroom, saying as soon as the door closed, 'I take it you sold the diamond?'

'Yes.'

'How much did you get for it?'

'One hundred and seventy-five quid.'

'Is that all? You were robbed!'

'Maybe, but it's better than nothing, and I just wanted rid of it.'

'You should have held out for more. Who did you sell it to?'

'A friend's husband sold it for me.'

'I bet he got a lot more than that. They must have seen you coming.'

'No, Mum, I don't think they did. They're not like that and he only took a cut of twenty-five pounds.'

'You're too bloody trusting, that's your problem.'

'Not everyone's like you,' Jenny said under her breath but loud enough for Lizzie to hear.

'At least I ain't a pushover. Anyway, this friend, do you think her husband could sell mine?'

'But you just said he ripped me off.'

'Yeah, but at the end of the day, a couple of hundred quid each is better than none.'

'I don't know if he can or not, but I'm not asking for you.'

'Why not?'

'Because I don't want anything more to do with the diamonds.'

'Oh, I see, you're all right, so bugger the rest of us!'

'No, Mum, it isn't like that. I was a nervous wreck carrying that one diamond around and I don't want to carry even more.'

'Well then, introduce me to your friend and I'll ask her myself.'

'I should never have asked her to help me. It put her husband at risk, so I don't want him involved with selling yours.'

'That should be his decision, not yours.'

'It doesn't matter what you say, I'm not going to put you in touch with him. You wanted all those diamonds for yourself, so you can work out how to sell them.'

Jenny left the room, and when Lizzie called out to her to come back she was ignored. It was clear her daughter wasn't going to change her mind, so, annoyed, Lizzie just went to the threshold of the lounge and said through gritted teeth before she left, 'Right then. Have a nice holiday and I'll see you when you come back.'

'Don't go, Mummy,' Peter cried.

'Please don't start, Peter. I told you, I'll see you soon,' Lizzie answered impatiently and left before her son became hysterical. Just before she closed the front door behind her, she heard Jenny shout, 'By the way, Gloria is getting married tomorrow.'

Huh, good luck to her, Lizzie thought, uncaring and too angry to think about it. Just when she needed her, Jenny had refused to help. The girl had turned out to be as selfish as Gloria. Well, from now on, the pair of them could go to hell.

★   ★   ★

The next morning, as the train trundled towards Bognor, Jenny looked at her brothers' elated faces. Their joy had confirmed that she'd made the right decision to boycott Gloria's wedding in favour of a holiday. She looked at her watch. They'd be gathering at the register office about now. She attempted to push all images of the happy couple from her mind. This trip to Bognor was supposed to be a distraction, yet she was finding it difficult to enjoy herself when she knew her sister was about to become Jack's wife. Why did it bother her so much? She didn't love him. She had never truly loved him. Or had she?

'We'll be there soon,' Pamela said.

'Yes, and once we're settled in I'll challenge you to beat me on the dodgem cars,' Jenny chirped, trying to sound jolly.

'Can I come in the car with you, Pam?' Peter asked.

'Yes, all right.'

'I'll be with Jenny and we're gonna smash your car up, ain't we, Jenny?' said Timmy.

'I think the idea is to *not* crash into each other, hence the name *dodgem* cars,' Pamela said, laughing.

They soon pulled into the station and Jenny retrieved their cases from the racks above the seats. 'Blimey, Pam, this one weighs a ton. I reckon you've packed enough to last a month, not a week,' she joked.

After a short bus ride, Jenny was relieved to finally be checking in and making their way to their accommodation. As they walked past rows and rows of identical wooden chalets, Pamela whispered, 'Do you think it looks like a prison camp?'

'No, of course not. It's so clean and tidy, I can't wait to get inside our one.'

'Can we go in the pool?' Timmy asked.

'I want to go to the funfair first,' Peter protested.

'All in good time,' Jenny told them. 'We can do both and more, but first let's get unpacked and then we can explore. Remember, we're here for a whole week, so we haven't got to do everything in one day.'

Over half an hour later, and thrilled with their chalet, Jenny found herself trying to keep up with her brothers as they ran from one attraction to another. 'Wait for me,' she called, 'you'll get lost.'

'Don't worry, we've never lost a child yet,' Jenny heard a voice say from behind and turned to see a pretty woman about the same age as herself wearing a red jacket.

'It's such a big place, they're so excited and I don't want them running off,' Jenny answered and quickened her pace to catch up with her brothers.

'Have you just arrived?'

'Yes, a short while ago.'

'I'm Nancy, one of the children's entertainers. We've got a really good kids' club here and I'm sure your sons will have a wonderful time.'

'I'm Jenny and this is my sister Pamela. Those two little monsters are my brothers, Timmy the eldest and Peter.'

'Oh, I'm sorry, I just assumed — '

'It's fine, it happens a lot.'

'Why don't you let me take them to meet the other younger guests in the club? It'll give you two a chance to find your way around and see what Butlin's has to offer.'

'Oh, I don't know, thank you, but — '

'It's my job, I'd be happy to,' Nancy replied, flashing a big smile that showed her perfectly white teeth.

'If you're sure?'

'Of course I am. The club is being held in the playground area today. You'll find us just behind the dining room. Come and pick them up in an hour or so.'

'All right,' Jenny agreed then called to her brothers.

Thankfully, when Nancy told them about the club, Timmy and Peter were happy to go off with her. Jenny watched them for a while, but they didn't look back; instead they were looking up at Nancy as she chatted to them.

'This is nice, we can relax for a while now,' she said to Pamela. 'Where to first?'

'This way,' Pamela answered, 'I'm sure I spotted a sign for a hair salon.'

Jenny rolled her eyes and followed Pamela. Oh well, she thought, whatever makes the girl happy, though she'd have rather explored the swimming pool.

★　★　★

Gloria sat in the pub with half a pint of Guinness in her hand. Tina had told her it was good for pregnant women, but after one sip she decided she didn't like it.

'Congratulations, or should I say condolences?' Jack's mate Trev said as he plonked himself down on a chair beside her. 'Only larking, you've got yourself a good man there.'

'Thanks,' Gloria answered as she watched Jack down his fifth pint of beer, 'but I think I'll have an unconscious man soon.'

'He's all right. Jack can handle his beer, and if a bloke can't have a good drink on his wedding day, when can he?'

'What are you two having a chat about?' Jack asked as he approached them.

Gloria noticed he was leaning slightly to one side. So much for him being able to handle his beer, she thought.

'Nothing, mate, I was just telling Gloria what a good bloke you are,' Trev answered, then stood up and added, with a wink at Jack before he sloped off, 'I'll leave you newly-weds to it.'

Jack took the seat his friend had vacated and said, 'It's a shame your lot didn't turn up. It would have been nice to see Jenny.'

'Disappointed, are you?' Gloria asked with a sarcastic tone.

'For you, yes.'

'For yourself more like,' she sneered.

'What's that supposed to mean?'

'You're obviously still holding a torch for her!'

'Fucking hell, Gloria, can't you be happy for once? It's our wedding day. I married you, not your sister, though I'm beginning to wonder if I made the right choice!'

With that Jack got up and stormed to the bar. She saw him order a short which he quickly knocked back and then he glanced across at her with a look of disgust on his face. So much for it being the happiest day of my life, she thought, especially as her new husband clearly found her revolting.

58

Friday had come around too soon. Their week's stay at the holiday camp would be over tomorrow, but as Jenny finished her dinner in the large dining hall, she realised she'd hardly thought about Gloria and Jack.

Pamela interrupted her thoughts as she said softly, 'They offered me a job in the hair salon today.'

'I'm not surprised, you've spent most of your holiday in there and when they gave you a chance, I'm sure they were impressed with what you can do with hair.'

'They were. I wasn't allowed to do any cuts or colours, but I was allowed to put a few women's hair up, and they said they were the best styles they've seen.'

'I don't doubt that.'

'I was speaking to Nancy earlier and she said that if I take the job at the salon, I'll get staff accommodation.'

Jenny pushed her plate to one side. 'So you're going to live as well as work here?'

'I'd love to, Jenny, but I'm worried about leaving you to look after Timmy and Peter on your own.'

Jenny checked behind to see that her brothers were still busy filling up their bowls with ice-cream. She'd been left at a young age to care for her siblings, and she didn't want Pamela to have to sacrifice her life too. 'If this is what you really want, then do it. I'll cope. I'm sure I could arrange for someone to have them after school. We'll miss you, but you'll only be an hour away from London.'

'Oh, Jenny, are you sure?'

'Yes, I can see how happy you are, and I don't want to stand in your way. If I was given the opportunity, I'd grab it with both hands.'

'Thank you . . . thank you so much! There's Mrs Dean, the salon manageress. I'll go and tell her that I'd love the job. If she wants me to start straightaway, I'll have to wait for my day off to come and collect the rest of my clothes.'

While Pamela ran off happily, Jenny was left to contemplate the thought of returning to Balham without her. She didn't like the idea of it but staying here was the right thing for her sister.

'Where's Pam?' Timmy asked as he sat back down with his second bowl of ice-cream.

'She's talking to her new boss. Pamela is going to stay here and work in the hair salon. Isn't that exciting?'

'Are we staying here too?' Timmy asked.

'No, darling, I'm afraid we have to go home.'

'I don't want to,' Peter said as he joined them.

'I know how you feel, but we can't stay on holiday forever.'

'My friend in the kids' club said that he lives by the seaside and it's really, really good,' Peter said, then stuck his bottom lip out and added, 'I wish we did too.'

Jenny was about to reply when a rather tall redcoat came to their table and said cheerily,

'There's an end-of-week party in the main hall tonight. I hope you're coming, Jenny?'

Jenny looked up at the man and instantly felt her cheeks turn as red as his jacket. His eyes were just like Craig's and took her breath away. She'd seen him from a distance over the week and knew that he was an instructor at the dance classes. She wished now that she'd had the courage to attend. He'd spoken to her using her name but she had no idea how he knew it, and was too shocked to ask.

'Can we go?' Timmy begged.

'I'm afraid it'll be past your bedtime, young man.'

'But you'll still be coming, won't you?' the redcoat asked.

'I don't think so, I . . . erm . . . I . . . '

'It'll be fun, and I need a dance partner. Please, say you'll come?'

'I'm sure there'll be plenty of women there to dance with.' Jenny blushed.

'Yes, but none as pretty as you,' the redcoat said cheekily.

Jenny couldn't help but smile back at him and felt her stomach flip. She'd have liked to agree but her shyness held her back.

'I'll see you there, Jenny, at half past seven,' he said, 'and if you can't find me, just ask for Nick.'

Pamela came back to the table just as Nick disappeared into the crowds. 'You'll never guess what just happened,' Jenny whispered to her sister.

'Nick came over and asked you to the dance tonight.'

'How do you know that?'

'He's had his eye on you all week but hasn't had the nerve to speak to you. His sister works in the salon and we were having lunch when Nick joined us. He told her about this redhead that he liked, and we soon worked out it was you. It took a bit of doing 'cos he was ever so nervous, but we managed to talk him into asking you out.'

'So that's how he knew my name! He's a redcoat, I wouldn't have thought he'd be the nervous type.'

'He's not normally. I guess that's the effect you have on men,' Pamela said, smiling.

'Leave off, you daft mare.'

'Can you believe this, Jenny, I'm going to be working here and now you're going on a date with a redcoat!'

'It's not a date, just a dance, and it's probably just his job to go round to tell everyone about the party,' Jenny protested. She hadn't come to Bognor looking for romance, she'd come to get away from the anguish of home. A new man in her life was the last thing she needed!

'Well, I think you should go. It's your last night here and you should enjoy yourself.'

'I'll think about it,' Jenny said, but as the tune of 'Poetry in Motion' began to play through the speakers, her thoughts took her to Balham. It had been one of Craig's favourites. He couldn't hear the music, but he could feel the beat and he used to say the words of the song to her. Memories of him filled her mind, along with the pain of losing him and his baby.

There'd been so much misery, but then she'd

found shortlived happiness with Jack, until he'd rejected her family only to move on and start one of his own with her sister. Then her dear old gran passed away. She still hadn't come to terms with that, and living in the flat was a daily reminder — and of Craig when they'd lived upstairs. The more she thought about it, the more she realised she had nothing to go home for.

As the song came to an end, Jenny glanced at the ring on her finger and remembered her gran's written words. She could almost hear the woman whispering in her ear, '*You only ever regret the things you didn't do.*'

With her gran's encouragement, her mind was made up. She was being unusually impulsive, but she felt sure it was the right decision. The boys wanted to live on the coast, and Pamela already had a job here. There was nothing to stop her finding them a home too. She'd be away from the agonising memories of the people she'd loved and lost, and away from any further hurt her mother, father or Gloria could cause.

Jenny felt a surge of renewed energy. She'd told her gran that 1963 was going to be her year, and she'd make it just that. This would be a new start, and Jenny couldn't think of a better way to begin afresh. With a beaming smile and feeling lighter than she had in ages, she announced, 'Pamela, boys . . . we're all moving to Bognor!'

Acknowledgements

Special thanks to my agent, Judith Murdoch, and the fabulous team at Avon Books UK.

Phoebe Morgan, you've been a fantastic editor to work with. I wish you every success in your new role — I shall miss you!

I'd also like to thank Christine Eccles and the contributors in the Facebook group, Battersea Memories. You've helped fill in the gaps of my memories of Battersea on many occasions.

We do hope that you have enjoyed reading this large print book.

Did you know that all of our titles are available for purchase?

We publish a wide range of high quality large print books including:
Romances, Mysteries, Classics
General Fiction
Non Fiction and Westerns

Special interest titles available in large print are:
The Little Oxford Dictionary
Music Book
Song Book
Hymn Book
Service Book

Also available from us courtesy of Oxford University Press:
Young Readers' Dictionary
(large print edition)
Young Readers' Thesaurus
(large print edition)

For further information or a free brochure, please contact us at:
Ulverscroft Large Print Books Ltd.,
The Green, Bradgate Road, Anstey,
Leicester, LE7 7FU, England.
Tel: (00 44) 0116 236 4325
Fax: (00 44) 0116 234 0205

Other titles published by Ulverscroft:

A SISTER'S SORROW

Kitty Neale

When Sarah Jepson's mother Annie dies, Sarah is left with her little brother Tommy to care for. Alone in the world, the two of them must make a life for themselves in the wake of the terrible upbringing they have endured. But when Tommy is struck down by illness, Sarah's new life collapses. Lost in grief, she turns to the handsome Roger to save her — only to find that he is not who he seems . . . Waiting in the wings is George — kind, but brutally scarred, Sarah's never seen him as anything more than a friend. But could all that be about to change?